Rona Jaffe

AFTER THE REUNION

AFTER THE REUNION

Rona Jaffe

A DELL BOOK

Published by
Dell Publishing Co., Inc.
1 Dag Hammarskjold Plaza
New York, N.Y. 10017

Dell ® TM 681510, Dell Publishing Co., Inc.

ISBN: 0-440-10047-X

Reprinted by arrangement with Delacorte Press

Printed in the United States of America

September 1986

10 9 8 7 6 5 4 3 2 1

WFH

For Tom

1) *What were your hopes, dreams, and expectations when you graduated from college, in terms of work, love, and family life?*

2) *Did you achieve them?*

3) *Was there a point in your life where your values, dreams, and/or expectations changed? Please explain.*

—From a questionnaire sent to the Radcliffe class of 1957 twenty-five years later

Prologue

PEOPLE WHO STILL believe in good surprises are always young; the ones who have come to believe surprises can only be bad, or that there will no longer be any surprises at all, are old—no matter what their real age is. The phone rings late at night and the old ones think immediately of disaster: an accident, illness, death. The young ones simply think "I hope it's for me." Of course there are bad surprises; this is life after all, a grab bag. But there are also the other kind. They exist. They do. . . .

Emily Applebaum Buchman had always been afraid of everything, and now that she had come to a point in her life where she thought nothing much, either good or bad, would ever change, she was somewhere between resigned and content. She knew she had a life many other people would envy. She was a rich Beverly Hills housewife, still married to her college sweetheart Ken, who had become a very successful dermatologist, purveyor to the stars; they had two children, Peter and Kate, and her life was filled with charitable good works, healthy outdoor sports, friends, shopping, her family, her appearance, culture, reading . . . the life she had been intended for.

She was forty-six years old now, small and slim, with dark hair and large gray eyes, and her friends told her she was very attractive. This coming June would be her twenty-fifth reunion at Radcliffe, and Emily had decided not to go. She'd been to her twentieth, and had made good resolutions to have a more productive life, even a career, and had left happy and uplifted. The career had turned into part-time volunteer work at Children's Hospital.

It was all right. Life was compromise. You gave up your job to make a home and have children, and then you found there was no room for you to come back. She'd never really been a career-oriented person anyway. She'd had the dream, but not the carry-through. All right.

But it was not all right. . . .

Her children had their own apartments and their own lives. They were no longer a family, if a family meant people who always came home to each other at night and shared their warmth against the cold world outside.

No, it was not all right. . . .

She supposed what had started her thinking in this discontented way again was that letter which had arrived in her mailbox this morning. It was from a woman who had gone to college with her, who was now a writer. Emily had never known her; it had been a big class. Besides, she'd spent almost all her college years going steady with Ken, not paying much attention to anybody. The writer enclosed a questionnaire which was research for an article she'd been assigned to do for *The Ladies' Home Journal*—a sort of profile of what had happened to all the women she had gone to school with. Emily had sat in her dream kitchen in her dream house on top of the mountain, with the view of lush California foliage on one side and Los Angeles on the other, her swimming pool and tennis court just below her, and that questionnaire in her hand was like a small explosion.

"What were your hopes, dreams, and expectations when you graduated from college, in terms of work, love, and family life?"

Better she should have asked her what her dreams were when she first came to college. Bright, pretty, terrified little Emily, entering Radcliffe in 1953 under the Jewish quota, an outsider, with dreams of becoming a pediatrician. Popular, well-to-do Emily, who had more cashmere sweaters than any other girl in the dorm. A good girl who always tried to please, who did what she was told. Told by her freshman advisor that very first week, Orientation Week, that she could never become a doctor, that she was improperly prepared. No one had planned for Emily to have a career in medicine, or anything else for that matter. If Emily wanted so badly to be a doctor, her advisor said, then she should marry one instead. *A good girl who always did what she was told.* So Emily went right off and fell in love with Ken Buchman and captured him.

"What were your hopes and dreams when you graduated from college . . . ?" Ken was her hopes and dreams. Marriage was, and a romantic, harmonious life.

Question Two: "Did you achieve them?" Of course. Oh, yes. *I was given the wrong dream to want and I got it.*

Emily folded the questionnaire neatly and hid it in her handbag. She would probably answer it. But she wouldn't tell the truth. She would avoid the bad parts, the terrible things that had happened. They were nobody's business but her own.

Christine Spark English sat in the den of her beautiful Fifth Avenue apartment overlooking Central Park. The sky was that tentative rose and gray color of twilight in the season between the end of winter and the beginning of spring in New York. She fingered the questionnaire which had arrived that morning in the mail and smiled wryly. She had been different from all her friends at college, and she was sure she was different from all her friends and colleagues now. She had been the only girl of their group in Briggs Hall who did not have money, and did not want to have fun or catch a husband at Harvard. She wanted to be a frumpy bookworm and disguised herself as one, but in spite of this her kindness, intelligence, and lethally accurate wit made her popular with the other girls, even though she didn't want to have anything to do with their frivolous life. And then she saw Alexander.

Alexander English, whose dark beauty made her heart stop every time she looked at him. Moody, mysterious Alexander, whose own private grief and guilt spilled over into the lives of everyone who loved him. How she had pursued him, thinking he was hers at last, never seeing what strangers they really were to each other . . . filling in all his secret, hidden spaces with her own fantasies. . . .

"What were your hopes, dreams, and expectations when you graduated from college?" Alexander, of course. There had never been anything else. Chris's entire life and being and raison d'être had always been Alexander and her magnificent obsession with him. And when she discovered he was homosexual and had been hiding it at school, she still stayed on her quest, hoping to win him, to change him, to make him want her. They became best friends. She became chic and sophisticated, no longer the mousy little schoolgirl. She waited. . . .

He did love her, finally. He married her. She supposed the girls back at school, who only remembered her pursuit of him and now saw the result, would have thought it a perfect happy ending. Chris and Alexander, together at last. Alexander, the handsome, successful New York banker, rising quickly in his father's bank, and clever, attractive Chris, who had always worked in publishing in addition to raising their son, Nicholas. They went on exciting vacations all over the world, the three of them: Chris, Alexander, and their child. They entertained well. Their home life was so pleasant. What a good example she was of an interesting, multifaceted woman! *What a good front she kept up.*

"Was there a point in your life where your values, dreams, and/or expectations changed? Please explain." When was there not? And how could she possibly explain, even if she were willing to? Alexander would cheat. And she would hope not to know.

Chris carefully tore the questionnaire into tiny strips. She couldn't tell the truth, and she had no wish to lie. Let all the normal people answer it. She wouldn't.

Annabel Jones made a paper airplane of the questionnaire and let it sail across the room into her wastebasket. Her aim was off and it landed on the floor. She wondered if that was an omen that she really couldn't dispose of it—and the memories it brought back—so lightly. Annabel believed in omens. Sometimes they'd been right and sometimes wrong, but that didn't stop her from thinking there was something to them. She'd always been a person who went by her instincts and desires, right or wrong, and because she was warmhearted and trusting she had sometimes been hurt. But she had never been stupid. She had only been too romantic. Not in the way her best friend Chris had been, with her obsession for Alexander, but romantic about everything in life, looking at it as if it were a big present. If she had to describe herself she would say that she had always been a rebel —with style.

At forty-six she was even more beautiful than she had been at college. She definitely believed that after forty you had the face you deserved, and to make sure of it she'd had a facelift, even though Radcliffe girls never had facelifts. She still had her tall, lithe figure, although she loathed every moment of the exercises she forced herself to do in her few spare moments from work. She still had her southern accent, even though she'd been living in New York for years. The half-floor-through in the East Side brownstone she'd found when she first came here and got her first job had become almost a national monument, and she never intended to give it up. She owned her own Madison Avenue boutique now, Annabel's, she had a wonderful relationship with her twenty-two year old daughter Emma (although Emma was so busy with her own career that they hardly ever saw enough of each other) and she still slept with attractive much younger men whenever she had a mind to. Her adored new cat, Sweet Pea, a fluffy white Persian with one blue eye and one copper eye, went over to the questionnaire and tried to eat it. Sweet Pea would eat anything that was inedible. Annabel rescued the paper and held it in her hand, thinking.

It might be nice to be in a magazine. She could say: "I had no dreams and expectations and lived dramatically and happily." Wouldn't that serve them right, those priggish, hypocritical girls who had ostracized and hated her because she went all the way with men. What strange values they'd had then! Chris had been the only girl who had been her friend.

But no, it would take too long to tell them what her life had been, and besides, the past was history. She intended to live for the future. This time when she tossed the paper airplane away her aim was true.

Daphne Leeds Caldwell, the Golden Girl of Radcliffe's class of 1957, married to Richard Caldwell, Harvard's Golden Boy, looked at the questionnaire that had arrived that morning to ruin her day, and knew what was expected of her. People made you a star, and then you discovered you liked it, and you tried to keep on being what they wanted. She'd had a charmed life based on secrets and deception. There were many different ways of being special, and she had made sure everyone knew only the good ones. The Connecticut night was cold, with the heavy feeling of snow coming; a cozy sort of night, the kind she liked. She lit the fire in the living room so that when Richard came home from the city he would be greeted by its cheer, and put ice cubes into the bucket on the bar for his evening drink. The large house was very quiet and neat with all the boys away at school. Daphne poured herself a glass of wine and went to sit by the fire with the questionnaire, wondering what she would write.

At college all the girls—except Chris and Annabel—had admired her and wanted to be like her. She was a tall, beautiful blonde with slightly slanted cornflower-blue eyes; a color so intense they were the first thing you saw when she came toward you. She was a rich debutante, bright, athletic, feminine, cool, and very popular. While most girls were happy to have only one date, often Daphne had two young men bearing her off between them like a treasure. It was inevitable that she and Richard should have ended up together. Dating in the Fifties was a genetic auction: girls were to be mothers, and the best sought the best. But what a lonely lie she had lived! She had been an epileptic ever since she was a child, and she knew no one would marry her if he found out. He wouldn't want his children to have it; he wouldn't even want *her.* People knew so little about epilepsy in those days —they thought you would fall to the floor in a convulsive fit while they stood by in helpless horror and disgust—and in fact that had happened to her as a child. But they didn't know that there were medications to control such things, and that not all epileptics were alike, or that it was possible to outgrow the worst of it and seem so exactly like everyone else that nobody would ever know. No one *had* known about Daphne's epilepsy, even Richard, not in all their years together, until she told him. He had reacted as if she had betrayed him: not because she wasn't perfect, but because she had kept an important secret from him all these years, hadn't trusted him . . . and now he suspected she might have kept others.

And she had.

But she had only done it to keep their marriage happy, without tumultuous crises and arguments that would wound them both and never be resolved. When you lived with someone you learned when to keep quiet about some things. Her one revelation had made a crack in their marriage somehow, and it had never really mended, only been covered by the fragile veneer of the happy years that followed.

"My hopes, dreams, and expectations when I graduated from college were to spend the rest of my life with Richard Caldwell, and I have." Did that sound smug? She decided it sounded romantic and went on. "I worked for a while in an art gallery before we were married, but what I really wanted was a home in the country and a lot of children, and that's just what we've got! We have four wonderful boys."

I have five children. Not four; five.

Lies and secrets.

Daphne lit a cigarette and blew one of the perfect smoke rings she had been famous for at college. Funny, she hadn't made a dumb smoke ring in years. When you started thinking about the past you went right back there with it. She would fill out the questionnaire the way everyone in her class who had known her expected her to, indicating her life was perfect, the way it always had been, always would be. She would mention Richard's great success in real estate, the peaceful pastoral beauty of their home and grounds and garden in Greenwich, the latest scholastic and athletic achievements of their four handsome sons. She would not mention her daughter.

She really wanted to write: "Even if you get what you want, life has its own way of laughing at you."

But she wouldn't. She would write a Golden Girl's answer. Life never laughed at a Golden Girl.

Chapter One

THE BRIGHT SUNLIGHT of another California morning woke Emily at eight o'clock. She moved around and stretched in the large bed and felt the familiar little pinch of desolation, as if she'd been deserted, that she felt every morning. Ken was gone again, off to his interesting day, without even saying good-bye. He would have called it consideration. He was the phantom of the house, and she should be used to it after all these years. But still, like a child, she ran to the hall window to look down at the driveway, to see if his little sports car was still there. It wasn't. There was nothing but her own two-seater Mercedes, all alone. She hoped no one would drive by with robbery or worse on his mind and know there was only one person in the house. That's why she hadn't wanted to sell the station wagon, but Ken said it was silly to keep it now that the kids were living on their own, and besides, he had to buy *them* cars, and neither of them would be caught dead driving around in something as square as a station wagon.

Somewhere out of sight she could hear the voices of the men who worked on the grounds of other people's houses—Mexicans, Japanese—and the sound of someone clipping a hedge. Otherwise all was stillness. A bird squawked. A car drove by, very fast; someone on the way to work. Far away, soft in the morning smog, she could see Los Angeles, where all those other people were starting their day. She might as well start hers, before Adeline came, or she wouldn't have a moment's peace.

It was too late. Engine growling, exhaust smoking, there was Adeline's enormous, ancient convertible, low to the ground like a boat. She got only nine miles to the gallon on it, as she never tired of complaining to Emily, even though Ken paid for her gas. They should have given her the station wagon. But Ken, who adored Adeline, said Emily was crazy to think of it. Why not, Emily asked, since other people bought cars for their housekeepers, and the station wagon was old and not worth very much? He'd just blown up at her. Ken, who had been the most generous of men, had started to act stingy about the strangest things. He'd go out and order cases and cases of the best, most expensive wine, because someone had recommended it, and then he'd glare if Emily bought a dress, which she hardly ever did anyway as she wasn't much of a shopper. She didn't like it when Ken called her crazy—it reminded her of when she had been, and she wished he would think of anything else to call her but that when he got annoyed. He knew how she felt about it, and she had the terrible feeling he did it on purpose, which again was just so totally unlike him. Maybe they could sit down and talk about what was happening, if she could ever catch him when he was alone and not harassed.

Adeline was sitting at the kitchen table having breakfast and reading the morning papers when Emily came down. The smell of fried bacon hung like a reproach and a challenge in that abstemiously red-meatless house.

"Good *morning*, sweetie!" Adeline sang out.

"Good morning, Adeline. Don't bother, I'll get my own, you just finish your breakfast," Emily said. She poured a cup of coffee and dropped a slice of diet bread into the toaster. Adeline had come to work for them five years ago, and had gradually exerted her power to where she ran everybody. She had Emily absolutely cowed and behaving like one of the children. Half black, half American Indian, huge, willful, and inscrutable, she seemed ageless and she wasn't telling, but Emily had to pay her in cash to stay. Adeline did all the cooking now, and Emily went to the supermarket with a list—she who had been such a gourmet cook and had taken so many courses in the cuisine of any country you could name was now allowed into her own kitchen only on Adeline's days off. Ken thought Adeline was a gem, Kate and Peter liked being spoiled by her, Emily couldn't stand her but no longer could do without her, and nobody ever knew what Adeline thought.

The kids were coming for dinner, and Emily could already see the long shopping list on the kitchen counter, and the cookie sheets laid out in readiness. She wished at least she could make the cookies. Cookies were love.

"You better go early before Gelson's get too crowded," Adeline said.

Oh, God, Thursday! Coupon day. The day when there were all those ads about specials in the newspapers. Adeline should have sent her yesterday . . . or she should have remembered and insisted.

"Maybe I'll go somewhere else," Emily said timidly.

"I like Gelson's," Adeline said, in a voice that clearly meant Emily was making a big mistake. Emily remembered that voice from her childhood, when she'd gone to buy clothes with her mother. Was that why she was so afraid of losing Adeline's good will that sometimes her throat closed up with anxiety when Adeline didn't agree with her? After all those years of analysis, wouldn't you think she'd be over her compulsive need to please everybody? She was the good child, the good wife, the good mother, and the invisible person.

"All right, I'll go to Gelson's."

By the time she'd taken a shower and washed her hair and dressed, and put on a little makeup because you never knew if you'd run into somebody who'd tell people you were looking awful, Emily knew it was already too late. She drove around and around the underground parking lot beneath the giant market, looking desperately for a space, and finally found one so far away it belonged to another store. Then the endless walk through thick carbon monoxide fumes from all those cars, trying not to breathe, knowing it would seem twice as long on the way back with a loaded cart. Adeline remembered everything Peter had ever liked to eat or drink and had put it all on the list, planning to send him home with a CARE package. Kate ate very little because she wanted to stay thin, and although she always very politely took cookies home, Emily was sure she gave them away.

Emily was sort of sorry both her children were coming to dinner on the same night, because when they were together they seemed to have secrets from which she and Ken were excluded. Elusive, smoky-voiced Kate, whose eyes held you at a distance . . . Emily had often wondered who, if anyone, was ever let into Kate's world, except for Peter, and she wasn't even sure about him. Peter was unfailingly polite and respectful to his parents because he felt that was the way one should be. It had little to do with feelings. Sometimes Emily wondered if he had any feelings at all, so deeply were they hidden. He refused to admit fear or vulnerability or even doubt of any kind. If he asked you a question, and he asked many, it was to learn. He was careful to tell you often that he wanted to learn as much as possible. He wanted to learn so that he could become a success. Neither Kate nor Peter ever touched their mother if they could help it;

they never kissed her. They of course allowed her to hug and kiss them if she wished to. That was the only polite way to treat one's mother. But they slapped each other on the back, they laughed and winked and cast each other shorthand looks covering a whole life from which other people were excluded. They were like two children who had to hold on to each other to keep from drowning. . . .

Two little wet heads, sleek as baby seals, bobbing above the surface of the water. A turquoise swimming pool . . . bare little tan arms, the bright orange life jackets locked away in the utility closet . . .

And a mother who never came when Kate screamed . . .

Emily cleared the visions from her mind and marched determinedly across the underground parking lot, pushing her heavy grocery cart. Tonight there would be a delicious dinner, and everyone would have a really nice time. All of that was a long time ago, when she was almost a child herself. Maybe they didn't even remember.

How could they not remember? Kate had been the one who told Ken. And then Ken had gotten a babysitter and driven Emily to the mental hospital and made her sign herself in. The children certainly remembered she had left them; she'd been gone six months. After that Emily had been so busy with her own problems, trying to get well, that it had never occurred to her to find out if what had happened had really hurt them. She'd been so busy being a good mother, driving Kate and Peter to the events of a crowded Southern California day; school, lessons, social life, sports—and trying to work out with her analyst why she still resented them, until she didn't resent them at all, not a shred of resentment remained.

Except for those few moments when she realized they had their whole lives ahead of them and hers was over. And that they were so much braver than she had ever been.

Back home, Adeline helped Emily unload the car. "God, it's hot," Emily said.

"Sure is. I can't stand the heat."

In the kitchen Emily drank a can of artificially sweetened iced tea and glanced through the mail while Adeline finished putting the groceries away. She didn't know why she always felt she had to stay in Adeline's presence, instead of having the tea by the pool or in her room; but something, that same unnamed guilt perhaps, made her follow Adeline around, trying to get on her good side.

"I forgot to write down butter," Adeline said.

Emily sighed. "Do I really have to go back?"

"Can't cook without butter. I'm sorry, sweetie."

Emily drove back down the winding road resentfully. *She does this all the time. I don't know why she does this to me. And I like my cookies better than hers anyway; hers are all greasy. Mine are soft and chewy and wonderful* . . . She stopped at the superette that was closer than the market and bought two pounds of butter, making sure it was Adeline's favorite kind, even though it wasn't *her* favorite kind. She didn't want to risk being fixed with Adeline's gimlet-eyed glare and listen to her banging pots around for an hour. By the time Emily got back to the house it was time to rush off to her job at the hospital.

Children's Hospital was new and beautiful, decorated in cheery primary colors to cheer up little children whose lives were filled with sickness and pain they could only partly understand. The other volunteers were mostly Emily's age, the nurses were young, and the Play Lady, Suzanne, who was Emily's boss, was twenty-eight. The Play Lady was allowed to wear street clothes, but Emily had to wear a silly pastel pinafore. The Play Lady was almost twenty years younger than she was. It was the kind of authoritative job Emily had had years ago, when she was first married to Ken and had been a psychiatric social worker, respected. Now she was just the general flunkey. But still, it made her feel fulfilled for a few hours to help the children act out their fears and anger, and to hope she'd made life a bit more bearable for them. They liked her and she got along well with them. If one was missing she always got frightened—you knew if they were going to be allowed to go home because they talked about it beforehand, but if they just disappeared you knew something terrible had happened. She was relieved today to see that everyone she knew was still here. There was one new small scared face, under a baseball cap pulled way down. Bald: chemotherapy. Cancer. She glanced quickly to see if he still had both legs.

"Hi! My name is Emily. What's yours?"

A sad little mumble. Emily hugged him.

"Emily, go get the paper and paints," Suzanne said. "We're going to play Matisse today. Or *Star Wars*. Depending." Emily went to the wall of cupboards and brought out the supplies. "Oh, we'll need a lot more than that," Suzanne said.

"I'm getting more," Emily said, trying to sound pleasant. Why did everybody order her around? But still, she was so lucky to be healthy and to have healthy children, and to be out of the house, she shouldn't complain about anything.

The hours passed quickly. The new little patient told her his name and she painted gold stars all over his baseball cap. She let him paint a monster on her arm and hair on her hand and claws on her fingers. Soon he was laughing. After the play session was over Emily and Suzanne went into the lounge to have coffee.

"Hey," Suzanne said. "One of the women told me you're Kit Barnett's mother."

"Yes." This was the first time anyone at the hospital had spoken to her in a tone of respect.

"I didn't know. The name's different."

"It's still Kate Buchman. She calls herself Kit Barnett professionally."

"I think she's terrific," Suzanne said. "I saw her in a couple of things on TV. When I read she's going to be in something I try to watch it." This was also the first time the Play Lady had spoken to Emily at such length. "What's she like?"

"Like?"

"In real life. What's she like?"

I'm not sure I know. She's my daughter but I don't really know her either. "Just a normal young woman," Emily said lightly. "Hard-working, dedicated. I'm very proud of her."

"Well, when you see her, tell her she has a fan."

"As a matter of fact," Emily said, "I'm going to see her tonight."

"Hey. Well." Suzanne nodded and smiled, and Emily nodded and smiled back, and then they went their separate ways. " 'Night, now," Suzanne called after her.

In the car, creeping along with the rush hour traffic, Emily thought: *I'm famous. I'm Ken Buchman's wife and Kit Barnett's mother. My freshman advisor back at Radcliffe would be thrilled.*

The kitchen smelled delicious. "Doctor Buchman called," Adeline greeted her. "He has to meet somebody and he says to start without him and save him something."

Emily's heart sank. "Did you remind him the children are coming?"

"He remembers."

The last several times Ken had had "meetings" they'd lasted until ten or eleven o'clock, and he'd come home surly and refusing to make conversation. She'd been so sure all that with his women was over, but now she wondered. What else could it be? Dermatologists didn't have meetings, and they didn't work until eleven o'clock at night. Maybe he was just having a drink with another man at the Polo Lounge, the way he sometimes did; but it was inconsiderate of him to do it when the children wanted to see him, too. They always ate at seven so Adeline could get home. A person could certainly have enough drinks by seven o'clock. Well, she wasn't going to argue with him. She would do her best to make it a pleasant evening for everyone.

"Hi, Mom! Hi, Adeline!" Peter, her tall, tanned, handsome son, smiling.

Adeline put her palms together and bowed the way Ed McMahon did on the Johnny Carson show. "The Little Prince!" Adeline said, and bowed again. Peter laughed and hugged her. He let Emily hug him.

"You're looking beautiful, Mom," he said. "What's for dinner?"

"Your favorite things and a surprise," Adeline said before Emily could answer.

"I saved you all the copies of *The Wall Street Journal,*" Emily said.

"I have my own subscription now," Peter said cheerfully. "The Little Prince is going to be the little tycoon. Or big tycoon someday, I hope. Where's Dad?"

"He's going to be late," Emily said.

"Something I said?" Kate asked, smiling, slipping into the room like a wraith. A head taller than Emily, but still fragile-looking, with a froth of dark hair and big gray eyes, she looked a lot like Emily did at her age, minus the fear. The shrill voice of her babyhood was gone—that piercing, demanding little voice that had driven Emily to distraction so many years ago—

replaced by an interesting husky tone. That was one of the things that distinguished her from other young actresses, but even more importantly it was her eyes; something mysterious and withheld, a challenge; even though her manner was friendly. Emily was aware of this on the screen, as was everyone else, but she also saw it in her own home, and she knew it was Kate's look; there was a place beyond which you could not go.

Kate gave Adeline a quick hug, suffered her mother to hug her, and put her arm around her brother. "Let's have some wine out by the pool," Emily said. "It's so pretty this time of the evening."

They marched out with a carafe of white wine, glasses, and a cooler, and arranged themselves in front of the sunset. Emily noticed for the first time that there was a bruise on the side of Kate's face, as if someone had struck her. "What's that?" she asked, alarmed.

"What's what?"

"Your face. It looks as if you hurt yourself."

"Oh, I have no idea," Kate said calmly. Her voice made it quite clear that she was not going to discuss it.

"How's work?" Emily asked quickly.

"I'm up for something, but if I tell anybody I'll jinx it," Kate said.

"Well, I have my fingers crossed. You tell me just as soon as you know."

"I will."

"I have a chance to sell my car to a girl at school,"

Peter said. He took a sip of his wine. "What kind of wine is this?"

"Just jug wine," Emily said.

"Oh. Anyway, I was thinking, then I could buy a used BMW and learn to fix it."

"You're too young for such an expensive car," Emily said. "We've talked about this already."

"But it would be good for me to learn how to fix a car. If it was my own car I'd have an incentive."

"I want you to spend your time studying, not fixing cars," Emily said.

Peter sounded pained. "I get all A's. You said if I sold my car I could have another one."

Where's Ken? she thought. *I hardly see him anymore. I miss him and I want to be with him and it isn't fair.* "I thought we decided you were going to get a Toyota," she said.

There was a silence while Peter mused on his fate. "Do you think a white car is too feminine?" he asked.

"Too feminine?"

"Yes. Girls have white cars, and so do fags."

"I go out with a man who has a white car," Kate said languidly. "He's not a fag."

"Maybe I'll get a white car and have the windows tinted black," Peter said. "That would really look great."

"How are you going to see?" Emily asked.

"You can see," Peter said.

"Oh, rub my back," Kate said. "It's killing me." She bent over double and Peter began kneading her shoulders. "Mmm . . . that's great," she said.

"I wish I had my own money," Peter said. "I wish I were phenomenally rich."

"You will be," Emily said encouragingly.

Peter smiled. "Then I'd get a glamorous beach house, a gorgeous live-in girlfriend, an expensive sports car, and a killer dog to protect it all."

"You'll get them," Kate said.

"Well," he said, "I'm trying."

"Dinner is served," Adeline called cheerily.

They went into the dining room, bringing what remained of the wine. Emily had put one of her white orchid plants in the center of the table, and around it had arranged small, fat white candles. She lit them now, and dimmed the light in the overhead chandelier to a faint golden glow. The room looked very pretty and she wished Ken were here to make the evening complete.

"I'm starving," Peter announced happily.

Adeline came in bearing a huge platter of her famous oven-fried chicken, surrounded by mounds of corn fritters. *I didn't know she was going to fry everything,* Emily thought in dismay. She noted with relief that there was a large glass bowl of salad on the sideboard.

A glare of bright light hit her like a physical assault. Adeline was standing by the dimmer on the wall, and had turned the overhead light on as high as it would go. "If I cook, you're going to *look* at what I cook," Adeline snapped. She stood there, arms folded, thin lips pinched in a straight line, waiting for any backtalk. Of course there was none. They all smiled at her and began to eat heartily in the blinding light until she was satisfied and went back into the kitchen.

Emily was furious, but she knew there was nothing she could do. Ken would never have let Adeline get away with it, but then, Adeline never tried anything like this when Ken was around. When Emily tried to complain to Ken he just told her she ought to be able to control her own help and was acting ridiculous. Kate was giggling. She thought Adeline was hilarious; the more outrageous Adeline was the more Kate loved it.

"Adeline, this is delicious," Peter called.

"When you're rich and have your beach house I'm going to give her to you," Emily whispered. Kate stifled another giggle and Peter just kept on gorging himself.

They had finished dinner and were having coffee when Emily heard the sound of Ken's key in the lock. "I'm here!" he called. He put some packages down in the hall and walked into the dining room. How tired he looked! He still had the boyish, sandy-haired looks that belied his age, but now instead of compact and athletic he seemed too thin. She wondered with a little start of fear if all this time there had been something physically wrong with him, some secret, almost unnoticed illness, and that was why he had been so irritable.

But he wasn't irritable now; he was charming with everybody. He pushed his food around the plate and ate nothing, but Emily pretended not to notice so he would stay this sweet.

Kate and Peter left soon after dinner, both with work to do; both carrying the boxes of food that Adeline had left for them before she went home. By the time Emily had turned out the lights and set the alarm system Ken was already upstairs.

"What did you buy?" she asked him cozily, as they were undressing for bed.

"What?" he asked—that strange, irritated voice again, like a stranger.

"Those packages," Emily said.

"Oh, just some socks."

"I would have bought you socks, Ken. You should have told me."

He turned quickly and glared at her as if he wanted to strike her. "Can't I even buy my own socks? Can't you let me breathe?"

She felt as if she were going to cry. "What did I do?"

"Stop whining."

"I'm not whining. If I'm whining then I'm *sorry* I'm whining. I'm just upset because you've been acting so weird lately. You're so unpredictable I don't even know how to talk to you anymore. Everything I say or do seems to make you mad at me."

"Go to bed," he said, dismissing her. He put on his swim trunks.

"What are you doing?" she asked stupidly.

"What does it look like I'm doing? I'm going for a swim."

"Ken, *please* talk to me. If something's upsetting you I want to help you. Do you feel all right? You look sick . . . I don't really mean sick, I mean . . . not well."

"I'm fine."

"Would you tell me if you didn't feel right?"

His face flushed with rage, actual rage. What had she done now? "Shut up," he said. He left the room.

Emily stood there with her arms wrapped around herself, shivering. Her teeth were almost chattering. Why did Ken act as if he suddenly hated her? Maybe there was another woman again, but maybe this time he was in love. It was possible. He was forty-seven, at the vulnerable age when men started to feel their own mortality. There were all those beautiful younger women everywhere he went, and who wouldn't want Ken? This time it might not be just cheating, not just a fling; it could be serious, and he'd want to get rid of her, the old, boring wife . . .

Maybe he was dying and didn't want her to know. But their family doctor would have told her; the wife had to be told, even the old boring wife he wanted to be rid of. . . . No, she knew Ken well enough to realize that if he loved her so much that he wanted to protect her then he wouldn't treat her the way he was now.

Their bedroom terrace overlooked the swimming pool. Ken had turned on the lights all around the pool and in the water. She went out on the terrace and looked down at him, a dark little figure in the water, tossing up glittering spray, plowing through the rocking waves he was creating, frantically doing laps. Back and forth, back and forth, seemingly tirelessly, as if he had to exorcise a demon. It was cold out here in the night; Southern California was desert country. Emily began to shiver in earnest.

He apparently had never noticed Kate's bruise, and she and Ken had become such strangers to each other that she hadn't even mentioned it to him after Kate left. What was happening to them?

Her husband was exorcising an unknown demon, and she was in the desert. She was all alone.

Chapter Two

ANNABEL HAD ALWAYS been blessed with beauty, intelligence, good health, and an almost euphoric joy in the anticipation of the possibilities of life. She loved people, parties, adventures, champagne, sentimental little objects, sex, and romance. All her life strangers had turned around to look at her, especially men; partly because of her striking auburn-haired looks, and partly because it was unusual and pleasurable to see someone who looked so happy.

So when she started her own business she knew that because it was going to be an enormous amount of work and take up nearly all her time, she determined to do it only if it was fun too. She had been earning enough for her needs working as a buyer at Bloomingdale's, but she had become bored. Walking to and from her job she would look at the little boutiques, particularly the ones on Madison Avenue, and think idly how she would have done that window differently, or carried more interesting merchandise; and eventually the idea took hold that she really wanted to have a boutique of her own.

There was one she'd particularly had her eye on, in the Seventies, which carried very expensive, very tacky evening dresses, the kind worn by old ladies who also wore henna-colored mink coats. When she saw a sign in the window that it was going out of business she wasn't a bit surprised, because she figured their clientele had probably all died off. She went immediately to the real estate person and embarked on the first business deal of her life.

Her father had left her a significant amount of money. She used it as collateral against a loan, named the new boutique after herself, and began demolition and renovation. She wanted it to be comfortable— the sort of place customers would stay in for hours. There were nice dressing rooms with good chairs to sit on, and plenty of hangers, and best of all, room to move around. Everything was done in white and no-color beiges, with slightly tilted mirrors to make you look tall and thin, but not so distorted that people would get home and decide the dress that had looked so chic in the store was really a mistake.

She remembered when she was a little girl her mother had taken her to stores where models actually came out and modeled clothes for you. At the time that had seemed very glamorous. Now it was an artifact of the past, but she intended to recreate it. And there would be tea served in the afternoons, with little sandwiches and pastries, and in the mornings of course there would be coffee and croissants. Never mind that the maid who brought these refreshments into the dressing rooms was the same kid who unpacked and hung up the stock, or that the model doubled as the salesgirl, or that Annabel hovered around giving all that nice personalized attention to the clients because she couldn't afford *two* salesgirls . . . when her boutique finally opened it was a success.

None of this would have worked if it hadn't been for the clothes, or Annabel's sense of style. The talent to put together a marvelous-looking outfit from a bit of this and a piece of that, which had started her on her career so long ago, was still Annabel's strong point. She could tie a scarf just so, add a belt, take something away, put an Anne Klein jacket with a Perry Ellis skirt and prove that the colors and patterns blended perfectly. Her stock was not large, but it was eclectic, from Chloe to unknowns from SoHo. She might show up at work in an Adolfo suit with a T-shirt under it. "Why not?" she'd say. "Fashion is to be enjoyed." And because she did enjoy it, and wore her clothes with such flair, people came out of her boutique having bought much more than they'd intended to but happy about it.

She had been right about the hard work. Annabel's was open six days a week, from ten to six, so she had to be there at nine in the morning to open the store and often couldn't leave until nine at night. At the beginning she did everything herself, from doing orders, reordering, bookkeeping, and even cleaning up. She did the window displays, and changed them every other day. She designed her own logo, the paper, the bags, the boxes; simple raised white on white. She'd discovered that—given a choice—people didn't particularly like carrying shopping bags with ads on them in the street, but if you gave them a neutral, good-looking shopping bag they'd reuse it over and over until it fell apart. So, in fact, her Plain Wrap was her own ad.

She was using an accounting firm now, and her two helpers looked as if they were going to stay around for a while. Maria spoke six languages, which was good because they often had foreign customers. Pamela didn't mind dressing up as the maid because she planned to open her own boutique some day and this was good experience. Since Pamela was only twenty-two and didn't have much money, Annabel didn't think she'd have to worry about replacing her too soon. The three of them saw so much of each other that they had become a sort of family. And Sweet Pea sat docilely in her basket, or took a nap in the window if the sun fell to her liking, adding a nice domestic touch.

Chris came by once in a while to say hello, even though she and Annabel spoke to each other on the phone almost every day. Annabel's daughter Emma, if she was in New York and between jobs, came by too, just to hang around. Chris bought clothes (Annabel gave her a discount), and sometimes Annabel managed to force a free outfit on Emma, but Emma's idea of high style still remained in the area of army surplus clothing.

It occurred to Annabel, as she was packing for her trip to Europe to look at the ready-to-wear collections, that the only thing that was missing from her life at the moment was a nice young man. It had been over two months, and surprisingly she hadn't even noticed! She wondered if that was a sign her taste was improving. She hoped it didn't improve too much. Maybe she'd meet someone in Europe, or better yet, on the plane coming home. That could be her little present to herself for all the hard work. . . .

When Annabel got to Paris after two days at the showings in Milan she was already over her jet lag. She checked in at her hotel, where the tickets for the collections were waiting for her. Rich buyers stayed at the Plaza Athénée, and a lot of others at the Meurice; Annabel was staying down the street from the Meurice at the St. James et Albany, where the year before she had discovered her favorite room at a price she could afford. It was actually a duplex suite, with a two story high ceiling, tall French windows looking out on a quiet courtyard garden, a small kitchen, and a dining table she could use for her paperwork. She unpacked quickly and went outside to the street.

It was late afternoon, chilly but beautiful. She loved Paris, even now when it was in chaos because of all the people who had come for the collections. She was too excited to be tired, and she began to walk through the city, her breath catching in her throat with joy. Two years ago all of this had been a dream. Now it was her work. She wondered if she should go to the Ritz for tea, and look at all the chic people, or right down the street to Angelina's, a tearoom that was enormously popular with the fashion buyers and where she might find someone she knew who would invite her to a party. Or maybe she should just have a quiet dinner and go to bed. Tomorrow she would be running around from early morning to late at night, going from one show to another, taking notes, trying to remember what she wanted to buy. She still had a limited budget and had to be careful what she spent for the boutique, and she couldn't afford to make even one mistake.

Who would have dreamed she would turn into such a serious person! The Annabel who never missed a party and a chance to get dressed up and flirt was now a woman preoccupied with lists and figures: dressing other people to go to their own parties. To tell the truth, she hadn't seen much around to flirt with anyway. There were a lot of attractive young men, but they were looking for men, not for her.

Finally she settled for window shopping, wandering, and a sandwich and glass of wine in a little café. She felt peaceful and content. Not that she'd given up the idea of a fling in Paris, but first she had business to do.

The next four days were as crazy as she had anticipated. Being a newcomer, she always had the worst seats, in the back row. Five thousand people, packed in a tent like sardines, trying to see over each other's heads. She could tell two of the models were on cocaine—they kept taking a reinforcement backstage between changes, until finally at the end of the day they were so glassy-eyed one of them nearly fell off the runway. Annabel went to almost every show; some to buy, others, like St. Laurent, just to drool. And she went to some just to get ideas of what was going to be happening. She would grab a bite to eat in stand-up bars between shows and appointments, fighting the mob of people and thinking how, for all of them at least, Paris was far from a gastronomic adventure.

Her last afternoon a woman she knew slightly from New York invited her to go to a disco that night with a group of people, but she said no. The next day she would have to get up early to go to London to see what the kids were wearing on the streets. Her head was spinning and she was tired. She just wanted to do something passive and relaxing, like go to a movie, so after the last showing she took a taxi to the Champs-Elysées, where there were a lot of movie theaters, and saw to her delight that *Gone With the Wind* was playing, in English with French titles. It was her favorite movie, since she had always thought of herself as Scarlett O'Hara anyway.

Waiting in line to buy her ticket, an attractive young man with touseled black hair and interesting topaz eyes smiled at her. She smiled back. He was wearing jeans and a leather jacket and looked as if he might be a university student.

"This is supposed to be a very good movie," he said to her in French. He had a merry voice which she liked.

"*Oui,*" she said.

"You're American," he said in English. He had a French accent.

"Oh, God," Annabel said. "I said only one word and you knew."

"It's okay," he said. "I have an ear. I go to a lot of movies. It's what I'm studying. It's my dream."

"Well, this is an *extraordinary* movie," Annabel said.

"You've seen it before."

She thought. "Eight times."

"It must be fantastic. You come to Paris to see *Gone With the Wind.*"

"Not exactly. I came for the *Prêt-à-Porter.* This is my relaxation."

He sat next to her in the theater. He didn't speak to her at all during the movie, which she appreciated, and when it was over he turned to her and smiled. "May I invite you for a coffee?" he asked.

Annabel smiled back at him. "Only if you liked the film."

"I loved it."

"I hope you're not lying to get on my good side."

"But if I am, that's a compliment, isn't it?"

"It is," Annabel said, and took his arm.

They went to a café on the corner and took a table inside because the night was chilly. His name was Mathieu and he was twenty-three. She wondered if

he was going to be her Paris fling. Frenchmen were
supposedly very attracted by the sophistication of an
older woman.

They talked for two hours about their lives and
their work, and had three coffees, and Annabel decided he was definitely sexy. It grew on you. The line
of his cheekbones above where he had stopped shaving was covered with pale down, almost baby fuzz,
which she found touching. He seemed tender, but
there was nothing childish about him; he was a
charming, sweet young man, and he seemed eager to
make a good impression on her.

She thought how truly inane the progress of a conversation with a stranger was; you revealed things
that were interesting but not too personal, just
enough so that he thought he knew you, and he did
the same. You couldn't share too much or you'd scare
each other off. And that was a date.

She told him where she'd gone to college; and she
admitted she'd hated it, because that was amusing.
She didn't tell him why she'd hated it, that she'd been
an outcast; that was all so long ago anyway. She told
him, when he asked, that she was divorced, that she'd
married the wrong man. She omitted the details of
just how awful it had been to be married to a fool,
because after all these years that seemed self-evident,
and besides it was boring. She didn't tell him that
she'd married the wrong man because before that
she'd been engaged to the right man, but he'd jilted
her. That could be made to sound dramatic, but what
was the point? If she'd married Bill he might have

turned out to be even worse than Rusty . . . you never knew!

She mentioned her daughter Emma, who was such an important part of her life, and told him how Emma was working in films as a glorified gofer, with dreams of becoming a producer and director, the same dreams he had. She commiserated with him about how hard it was.

She did not mention Max. You didn't say that there had been only one man in your life who had always been there for you, but that unfortunately he was murdered by a psychopath he'd picked up in a gay bar. No, that was definitely too bizarre. You did not discuss tragedies when you were talking to a potential one-night stand.

She was in Paris, at night, with a beautiful, affectionate-looking young man, and who could ask for more at this moment? She liked his voice, and his cat's eyes, and his mouth. She looked at his mouth and imagined kissing him. Yes, he was what she wanted. She glanced at her watch.

"It's late," he said, apologetically. "I'll get you a taxi."

"Would you like to come back with me and have a drink?" she asked.

"Oh, yes," he said, delighted.

Making love with him was even better than she had anticipated, and Annabel wondered for an instant why she had gone so long without this; the delight that was so great it always surprised her. He was hers: the hard, smooth muscles under the silky skin of his lean young body, all the energy and the tenderness of him, hers to touch, to share, to enjoy. She read him with her fingertips. The downy cheekbone that had been forbidden across from her at the tiny table in the café was hers, as was everything: nothing forbidden in that bed, everything giving more pleasure and excitement. They devoured each other with all the greed and yearning they had been hiding during their civilized mating dance.

Afterward he lay with his head on her shoulder and she stroked his thick hair. The sex had been terrific, and usually she felt marvelously relaxed and happy. But not this time. Annabel watched the sky go pale with morning through the double-height French windows and wondered why. For just a few moments, for no reason that had to do with him, she felt a little bit sad.

He was happy as a puppy in the morning, and that made her feel guilty and almost melancholy. She used to feel that way, not a care in the world, so pleased with herself. She shared her morning coffee and rolls with him, and then he watched her finish packing.

"I hope the next time you come to Paris I can see you again," Mathieu said.

"Of course," Annabel said.

"If I ever get to New York I'll call you." He smiled. "Maybe by the time I get to New York I'll be famous."

She smiled back; Annabel the Southern Belle, the flirt, the charmer. "I bet you will be," she said.

* * *

She was glad to be in London again. There was
something about London that always made her feel at
home, as if she'd been there in another life. She
stayed at a sweet little bed and breakfast place which
was much less expensive than the big hotels, and all
day she ran around the streets looking. Some of the
kids seemed to have nothing to do but try to look like
members of punk rock groups and hang out with
their other unemployed friends. It was a sign of a
depressed economy and lost young people, and it
disturbed her. But the beautiful old houses, the winding little streets, and the parks that were always
green, even in the winter, cheered her up again. She
had a very dignified, solitary dinner at The Con-
naught Hotel Grill, having carefully reserved in advance from New York, and the Scotch salmon, Dover
sole, and the solid, peaceful atmosphere made her
glad she had planned this special night out just for
herself.

She stayed in London only two days, and then flew
back to New York. Sitting next to her on the plane was
an unattractively loud man her own age, wearing a
wedding ring, who asked her if she would have dinner with him in New York, and when she said no he
spent the rest of the trip trying to make a date with
the stewardess. Annabel felt sorry for her, having to
put up with him and be polite. She busied herself
with her paperwork, looking forward to going home.

* * *

When she walked into her apartment, Emma was there, sitting on the living-room couch, wearing one of Annabel's robes, freshly washed hair up in a towel, Sweet Pea on her lap, both of them avidly watching an old black and white movie on television. "Emma!" Annabel cried in delight. "I didn't expect you till next week."

They hugged each other. "We're ahead of schedule," Emma said. "That's the only good thing I can say about Wesley Knoll, The Weaselly Troll, he shoots fast. I was going to call you, and then I thought I'd just surprise you. How was Europe?"

"It was wonderful," Annabel said. "I want to tell you all about it, and hear all about your job."

"I bought food," Emma said. "And I put a bottle of champagne in the fridge. We're going to be here a week, and I get the weekend off, which I desperately need, so we can spend a lot of time together."

"Oh, good. I have to take the girls from the boutique to dinner tomorrow night to tell them about the trip—I hope you can come too."

"I am totally at your disposal," Emma said.

"No boyfriend?"

"Well, of course there's a boyfriend," Emma said cheerfully. "But he has parents in Connecticut and he has to go see them. He wanted me to come too, but I said no I wanted to see you. Is it okay if he stays with us here next week? That way he can keep his per diem, because he's just as poverty-stricken as I am."

"It's perfectly all right," Annabel said.

She was already in jeans and a sweater from the plane trip, and didn't bother to unpack anything except the bottle of perfume she'd bought on the plane for Emma. They opened the cold champagne and sat in the kitchen, drinking it and eating sandwiches, happy and cozy together, just like all the old times. Emma had kept coming in and out of her life unexpectedly ever since she'd left Radcliffe after only one year because she wanted to go to the NYU film school and concentrate on movie making. She had lived with Annabel for a while, met some girls and decided to share an apartment with them because she'd never lived on her own like that; gotten bored with it, lived with a boy she thought she was in love with, got scared when he proposed, and came back to Annabel until graduation; and then off to California, because that was where the work was. Annabel kept Emma's room ready for her, just in case, and was always overjoyed to see her.

"Let me tell you about my glamorous life," Emma said. "I have to go to the set at five in the morning to tell the trucks where to park and tell the extras where to go. It was freezing cold and snowing all last week, and before that we had mud. Weaselly decided he wanted to use real convicts for extras because they were so real-looking. Ex-cons, I mean. I felt sorry for them because they thought they were going to be in the movies, and all it was for them was eight hours of standing around, and get paid thirty-five dollars and good-bye."

"Convicts!" Annabel said, alarmed.

"They were okay," Emma said, calmly. "At least they didn't make me get out of bed at two in the morning to go buy a pint of gin for the star, who was shacked up in the local motel with his girl friend. I mean, a pint of gin! Talk about gross . . ."

"You had to do that?" Annabel said, more alarmed.

"I have to pay my dues. I'm aware of it. But I'm twenty-two already, and I'm starting to wonder how long." Emma grinned, and Annabel realized with a little shock of pride how genuinely beautiful she was: the amused, innocent green eyes, the flawless skin with the faintest gilding of tiny freckles, the mane of auburn hair glinting with gold lights. She was her mother's daughter all right, with her mother's spirit too. "I've been making everybody I work for give me a letter of recommendation after each job," Emma said. "And I always make friends with the cameraman and everybody else I can on the set to learn things. My day will come."

"Soon, I hope," Annabel said.

"Not too soon to suit me," Emma said. Sweet Pea jumped into her lap again, and Emma fed her bits of turkey. "So how was Europe, anyway?"

"Hectic. Fun. Some of the clothes were really ugly. But by the time they get popular, in a year or two, people won't be able to imagine how they lived without them."

"Did you meet anybody?"

"Any men?"

"Yeah . . . any men?"

"Well . . ." Annabel said, and they both laughed.

"Was he cute?"

"I would say he was cute, yes."

"And . . . ?"

"It was just a date," Annabel said.

"Like me when I'm working on a movie," Emma said. "I get a big crush, and then when the movie's over, it's over too. We're still friends, and we run into each other sometimes, but we're both on to different things."

"It wasn't even a crush. It was attraction." For an instant Annabel felt again that little touch of sadness she had felt after sex with him.

"That's not so bad," Emma said consolingly.

"No . . . but I dread to think how many dates I've had in my time. I think in the natural order of things one gets to a saturation point."

"And then?"

"And then one becomes a serious person," Annabel said. "One looks seriously for another serious person."

"You mean you'd go looking for a man who's straight, single, unattached, terrific, and good enough for you? Oh, my God! There's nothing like that out there."

Annabel laughed. "Oh, Emma—do you realize a personality change like that could blight my whole life?"

Chapter Three

CHRIS'S OFFICE WAS a hermetically sealed place of peace and luxury in the middle of Manhattan, so high up she could see for miles. When she had first come to work there she had been a little squeamish about those enormous windows with their low sills, no curtains, and a view—if one wished—of cars the size of gnats. She'd particularly disliked the fact that her eminent position of Managing Editor, putting the magazine together, bore with it a corner office, so she was almost surrounded by air. Once she saw a plane that seemed to be on the same level as her window, and she was not happy about it. But she soon adjusted, and after a while even got to appreciate how pretty it was; the other office buildings all different colors, their windows glittering as they caught the light.

This good job had been an accident. When she'd still been working as a copy editor she had gone to a publishing party and met Bill Cameron, the financier who owned a lot of magazines, one of which was the new one he was going to start, *Fashion and Entertainment*. They were both quick-witted, and liked each other immediately. She knew he was about fifty, that he was married to his second wife, who was much younger, and that they had two small children. She thought he was very attractive; burly and dynamic, with bright blue eyes that missed nothing, thick gray hair, and, despite his expensively tailored suit, the manner of an old street fighter. She also knew right away he was very intelligent, even an intellectual, which she appreciated. He brought her another glass of wine, although people were trying to get his attention and talk to him, and then he asked her why she was wasting her time when she could be working for him.

The second glass of wine had made her brave, so she laughed merrily and said she didn't know. The next thing she knew she *was* working for him, in a difficult job that she really liked, and she realized he had been right: she *had* been wasting her time before.

Cameron owned other properties besides magazines, in other cities besides New York, so she didn't run into him often, but every time she did he made a point of having lunch with her, or a drink, and he always made her feel appreciated and special. He would ask her about her life, and although she never told him anything he shouldn't know, she felt that he was sympathetic and that he cared, even if it was just for the hour or two they were together. He was pleased with her work, and with his quick decision to hire her. He told her he always went by his first instincts, that they were usually right, and that she ought to be more assertive. It interested her that a man, especially her boss, was telling her to be more assertive. Most men, especially those his age, were made nervous by women who seemed too pushy. But Cameron (she never thought of him as Mr. Cameron, and she couldn't bring herself to think of him as Bill) seemed to have so much confidence that no one could make him nervous.

Chris realized that if she had been someone else, if she hadn't been so totally in love with Alexander, or if Alexander didn't exist at all, that she might have been attracted to this man. But she was safe, so they could be friends. And whenever she thought that, she was amused at her presumption; because a fifty-year-old man who was married to a beautiful (she'd seen the photo on his desk), much younger woman, in a second marriage (which were said to be the happy ones), after what she'd heard was an unpleasant first one, certainly wasn't going to be chasing *her*.

She gathered the work she had to take home, said goodnight to the few people who were still finishing up, and emerged into the crowded chaos of the midtown streets below. She was grateful it was neither raining nor snowing, since it was impossible to get a taxi at this hour. She began to walk uptown, glancing around but not really looking seriously for a cab, because she knew it was good to get the exercise. When she'd first started this job she'd had virtuous intentions of walking to work and arriving at the office glowing with health. But somehow she was always late and in a rush, so she took a taxi downtown, or a bus if there were no taxis; and then at the end of the day when she was tired was when she had to walk.

She remembered how when she had come back to live in New York the streets had seemed full of room for everyone. Now they were an obstacle course full of angry, hostile, even lunatic people. She could hardly wait to get home. A few blocks away from the apartment she began to have the warm, safe, happy feeling she always had when she knew she was going to see Alexander. Even if she got home first, it was the same feeling, like a golden glow that filled her and suffused the very atmosphere around her. Home from the wars. Safe with her love. Alexander . . . even the most ordinary things he did—sitting there reading the newspaper, watching the news on television, mixing a drink—were romantic to her. She would be embarrassed if people knew how absolutely besotted with love she was. And home too would be their son, Nicholas, fourteen now; a brilliant, lovely, handsome boy, not a man yet, still a shy kid, hanging around in a pack with the other boys from school, trying for two days to get up the courage to ask a girl for a date, and only if it was absolutely necessary to have a date at all. That made her a bit concerned, until she saw that most of the other boys his age were the same way. The girls they'd been so comfortable with when they were all little were suddenly scary.

The other boys' mothers weren't at all concerned that they were afraid of girls. It was said to be a natural phase.

But the other boys didn't have a homosexual father.

It was not really something to worry about—Alexander had been a marvelous father—but it was something Chris wondered about from time to time. She was sure Nicholas didn't know anything of Alexander's secret life. Kids were so sophisticated these days, but Alexander was extremely careful; so careful in fact that she didn't even know if he was still doing anything.

She let herself into their apartment and hung up her coat. She saw with joy that Alexander's coat was already hanging there. "Hello!" she called out.

"Hello!" Alexander called back, from the den. "Where are you?"

"Where are *you?*"

He came out into the foyer to greet her, smiling happily. They hugged each other hello and he picked up her tote bag of papers from the office to carry into the den for her. "This gets heavier every night," he said. "I bet you didn't get a cab either."

"It's aerobic," Chris said. She could hear the sound of Nicholas's new favorite dreadful record album seeping out from behind his closed bedroom door. "Do you believe he's doing homework with that on?"

"I don't think he can do homework without it," Alexander said. He put her bag next to his attaché case on the floor and poured her a glass of wine. They sat together peacefully on the sofa, talking about their day, sipping the wine, eating some *crudités*, finally deciding to turn on the TV and watch the news even though it was always bad. Chris was grateful for her luck in having good help so she didn't have to sacrifice this time with Alexander to rush around the kitchen cooking dinner. On weekends she still enjoyed making special meals, but then it was a kind of recreational activity. They both liked simple food and were careful about what they ate; Alexander because the fitness craze had finally gotten even to him, and she because she wanted to stay thin. Alexander played squash now, twice a week, at the New York Athletic Club, and was threatening to take up tennis in the summer.

After the news, Mrs. Gormley, their housekeeper, called them in to dinner, and Nicholas appeared. This would be the first summer that Nicholas would be away from them, and Chris knew she would miss him. He'd decided to go with a friend from school to something called The Wilderness Adventure, which as far as Chris could figure out was an adventure in risking your life, with white water rafting and mountain climbing, but he was all excited about it.

"I was thinking," Chris said, "that even though we have the country house, maybe we should take two weeks off this summer and go to Europe. Someplace not hot, and not full of tourists."

"How about Australia?" Alexander said. "It's winter in Australia."

"Is it cold? I don't want it to be cold."

"Japan," Alexander said. "How would you like to go to Japan?"

"Oh, don't go without me!" Nicholas said.

"But you're going to be having a wonderful time," Chris said encouragingly.

"Japan would be good for me," Nicholas said. "It would be an educational experience."

"True," Alexander said, amused. "Where *don't* you want to go, so we can go there?"

"I want to go everywhere," Nicholas said glumly. "Except the country."

Chris and Alexander laughed. "We like the country," he said. "We work hard all week, and the weekend house is just right for us. You have the entire summer off from school, so of course you should do something more constructive than hang around up there."

"I know," Nicholas said.

"Would you rather not go on a trip?" Chris asked Alexander.

"I want to do whatever you do, you know that. I'm going to take two weeks off anyway. Why don't we go to a place where this world traveler has already been, so he won't feel left out? How about the French wine country? It's hot, but it's beautiful, and Nicholas hates to drink."

They all laughed. "You have the wisdom of Solomon," Chris said.

Plans . . . they were still making plans. They lived their lives in a haze of pleasure.

After dinner Nicholas went back to his room to

finish his homework, and Chris and Alexander went to the den to do what they had come to call theirs. From time to time Chris looked over at Alexander, and once he caught her doing it and gave her a loving smile. *I'll get him to come to bed early,* she thought. *He won't be able to say he's too tired again. Maybe tonight . . .*

It was just like when they had been at college; wondering. She remembered those nights studying at the library together, and herself plotting and yearning to get him to make love to her—probably the only girl in the puritanical Fifties who had *wanted* to lose her virginity, without a thought for the consequences. And now it was happening all over again. She supposed some other married women had to go through this, from time to time; perhaps when their husbands were overworked or worried or had a girlfriend. But what about when your husband was affectionate and warm and kind, but just had no physical desire for you at all? *It's only been two months.* Maybe they should discuss it. *Two months is a long time . . .*

She glanced at her watch and began to pack up her papers from the office. "Let's go to bed," she said.

In bed with Alexander, she lay with her head on his shoulder. He had his arm around her. She ran her fingers lightly across his chest, then down his body, pretending to be casual, hoping he would get aroused. It gave her such pleasure just to touch him, how could he not like being stroked? "I love you, do you know that?" she said.

"I love you, too," he said. He kissed the top of her head, two quick little kisses, as one would kiss a cute child. Then he reached up and turned off the light beside him. "Goodnight, sweetheart. Sleep well."

"I'm not tired," she said. She sounded petulant, and that terrified her.

"Close your eyes and you will be," Alexander said. He was already curled up comfortably, his back to her, in case she had any more ideas of getting at him.

She had to say something, quickly before he was really asleep. "It's been a long time since we made love," she said.

"It's not been long," he said. Chris knew then that he knew exactly how long it had been, just as she did.

"Could we talk about it?" She tried to sound calm and reassuring, hiding how frightened she was. At least she didn't sound petulant anymore. "We've always been able to talk about things."

"I'm just tired," he said.

She sat up and touched him gently on the shoulder. "Please, Alexander. I don't know what you're thinking, and it scares me."

He turned around then and faced her, and the look in his eyes broke her heart. "I don't really understand it myself," he said. "I've thought about it a lot. I know you've felt left out, and I've tried . . ." He sighed, a deep, heavy sigh of pain. She knew whatever he was going to tell her would not be a lie, and she could hardly catch her breath for the fear of what it would be. "I can't sleep with anybody anymore," he said.

"Not numbers, not you; nobody at all. It's as if I've turned off my sexuality."

"When did this happen?"

"Look," he said, "I want you to know, first of all, that I love you more than I ever did, and that you and Nicholas are the most important things in my life. I think maybe this has something to do with love. I know that whenever I did something secretly, you knew—not exactly when, but you sensed it. I didn't want to be that way; meaningless sex with strangers, hurting you, and I felt guilty and hated myself afterward. And then one day I was with a number and I couldn't go through with it. I wasn't attracted at all. I couldn't wait to get away from him. And after that . . ."

She waited, numb. "After that, what?"

"I don't know what I am anymore," Alexander said. "I'm not gay, I'm not straight. I seem to have no physical desires."

"Can't I help?"

"No." He reached over quickly and gathered her into his arms, holding her tightly. "Chris, I didn't mean that to sound as heartless as it did. I'm sorry. What I mean was that *of course* I hoped you could help me, but it's all my fault. None of this has anything to do with you."

"Maybe it's a phase," she said.

He smiled, but his eyes were sad. "I hope so. I'll kill myself if it isn't."

"Don't you dare kill yourself!" she said in horror. "I'd rather have you this way than not at all."

"Are you sure?"

"Of course I am. Look, maybe we could go to a marriage counselor, or a sex therapist—privately, of course. I'm sure nothing is alien to them. It's not supposed to take long either. A few sessions . . . you talk about it . . ."

"I couldn't do that," Alexander said quickly. The muscle in his jaw twitched.

"Nobody would know," Chris pleaded.

"I would know."

"Maybe it's a phase," she said again, finally.

After she turned off the light they lay there for a long time sleeplessly. Her eyes grew accustomed to the dark and she could see that Alexander was staring at the ceiling. He looked so sad and she felt so sorry for him that she forgot to feel sorry for herself. She reached over and took his hand, and they lay there, side by side, and then he slid his hand from hers and turned over, away from her, and slipped into sleep. He had finally gotten it out, and now it would be better for him. At least now she understood.

They had been through worse things. Well, perhaps not worse, but different. They loved each other. She had always waited, and somehow things had always worked out eventually. She had to believe that again.

But three months went by and nothing changed. It was June, and the evenings were light. They were spending weekends in their country house in Connecticut, inviting friends to come with them, filling the long days with pleasant things. The stars were brilliant at night, the air smelled of fresh green life, and the days of sun left Chris feeling sensual and pulsing with desire. Her ripeness seemed an affront to Alexander's dry celibacy. He was neither charmed nor attracted, and she wondered if other people could see how she felt. It made her ashamed; and sometimes angry, at herself and even at him. Then she would feel guilty about resenting him for a problem he didn't know how to solve, and tenderness would rush through her until her eyes filled with tears. He was so kind and thoughtful—and so vulnerable. But his affection for her was playful, never sexual, and she wanted more.

She had discussed it with Annabel, but Annabel's idea of a solution was not hers. "I think you need a lover," Annabel had said. "Some charming, marvelous man who makes you feel happy. Nothing serious. Just a fling."

Chris was annoyed. "You act like it's nothing. 'Have a fling,' like 'Have dessert.'"

"That's all it should be," Annabel said cheerfully. "How about Cameron?"

"My *boss?*"

"Why not? You talk about him enough. He's married, so he's safe."

"He certainly is safe," Chris said. "He has a young wife."

"So what? I hear she's totally vapid. A little of that goes a long way."

"Forget it," Chris said.

A lover: what a joke. She would not even allow herself to imagine it.

The sales conference for all the Cameron magazines, including the one Chris worked on, was being held in Scottsdale, Arizona, this year. Chris flew there with several people from her office, all of them looking forward to a change of pace even though it would still be work. There would be meetings and presentations, but also time to sit around the pool, cocktail parties, a barbecue, and, the last night, a banquet. Spouses, roommates, and dates were not allowed. Since part of the sales conference fell on the weekend, Alexander was going to the country as usual, having invited some friends. In a way, Chris was relieved to be away from the tension that had pervaded their lives these past months.

Unpacking in her motel room, she realized she had brought too many clothes, which was out of character for her, but she'd been distracted lately. The motel was a large, sprawling compound in the middle of what seemed to be the desert, surrounded by mountains and ringed with tall palm trees. It had been built to appear to be many small bungalows, although they were really just rooms. Each one had its own patio in back, covered with Astroturf, leading out to real lawn. There were tennis courts, a pool, a Jacuzzi, a poolside bar, and a large main building which housed the meeting rooms as well as two dining rooms. Chris reread her schedule and then went out to find the pool.

She joined a small group of people she knew, and stretched out in a metal chair. It was late in the afternoon, but the sun was warm on her face. Everyone was talking about how the mountain in the distance looked like a camel. She glanced around to see if Cameron was anywhere. She really didn't expect to see him, and she didn't. On the other side of the pool she saw his secretary.

When it started to get chilly Chris went to her room to dress for dinner, and the phone rang.

"Chris? Bill Cameron."

She was surprised, and yet she was not. "Hi," she said.

"I'm taking a few people to a restaurant near here tonight at eight o'clock," he said. "I wondered if you'd like to join us."

She had already planned to have dinner at the hotel with the group from the pool, but she knew they wouldn't care if she changed her mind. She hoped they wouldn't be jealous when they found out she had been invited to dinner with the brass. No, they'd think it was a command performance. Besides, she didn't care what they thought, or what anybody thought, and she never had. "I'd love to," she said.

Cameron had invited four other people. They drove to a Mexican restaurant that looked like an old mansion, and when he told everyone where to sit he put Chris next to him, which pleased her, because she liked to be near him. She noticed the look of interest and amusement he had when he looked at each of his guests, much the same way he looked at her when they had their lunches or drinks alone together—the good host, the good friend, someone who cared about their futures. They were all executives, like herself; two men and two women. It was a relaxed, totally pleasant evening, and ended later than she'd expected. By the time they got back to the motel it was midnight.

Chris sat on the edge of her bed beside the phone and wondered if it was too late to call Alexander. She didn't want to wake him up. Besides, she felt so calm and mellow, all alone, away from the object of her desire and her frustration, that all she wanted was to crawl under the covers and fall peacefully asleep. It was a moment in a capsule, out of time, and she wanted it to last. She didn't call.

The next day was spent in meetings. Cameron made a speech. For their lunch break they had a buffet in the main dining room, which was annoying, because everyone was looking longingly at the pool area, where the desert sun was shining brightly. After lunch there were more meetings, and then they were let out at four o'clock, like kids from school, and everyone rushed for their swimsuits and suntan lotion. When Chris walked into her room the phone rang.

Oh, it's Alexander, she thought.

"Chris? Bill Cameron."

"I know your voice," she said.

"Just habit," he said. "Tonight is the big cookout."

"I know."

"Colored lights, waiters dressed in costumes, a mariachi band, a live donkey wearing a hat, big greasy steaks . . . let's sneak away."

She laughed. "It does sound horrendous."

"Seven o'clock," he said. "They'll all be drinking their margaritas. I'll drive by your room and you jump into the car."

"Shall I wear a black veil?"

He laughed. "Jeans will be okay. See you at seven."

After she hung up she realized how excited she was. It was going to be an adventure. There was just enough time to wash her hair. She wondered where they were going. Some dump, probably, where no one would find them. She was glad that she looked well in jeans, and changed her sweater twice before finally deciding on a silk shirt. She hummed along to the music on the radio while she put on her makeup. Then she called Alexander in the country to be sure everything was all right. He said it was, and that he was having drinks on the terrace with his weekend guests.

Chris heard the crunch of tires on the gravel outside her front door. "Oh, then I don't want to keep you," she said lightly. "Goodnight . . . I'll talk to you tomorrow." Her heart turned over at the deception. What deception? That she hadn't said she was rushing off to have dinner with someone? Alexander knew she was having breakfasts, lunches, drinks, and dinners with people all this time. What in the world was she feeling guilty about?

As she ran to Cameron's car she heard the sound of music drifting over from the pool area where the party was in progress. He was alone, and he smiled at her as she slid in beside him. "You look very pretty," he said.

"Thank you."

The car sped off down the road into the desert evening. There was soft music on his car radio, too; but something old, from her past, from one of the many college dances she'd never gone to. She glanced at him and realized she was unaccountably nervous. He looked freshly shaved and smelled faintly of lime cologne. His shirt was crisp and white, and he was even wearing a silk scarf knotted around his neck like a cravat. For some reason she found it touching that he'd gone to these preparations for her.

"Where are we going?" she asked.

"An oasis."

It was. Off the highway, in the middle of the desert, with not a shopping mall to be seen; the sky filled with big stars like glittering flowers, the scent of sagebrush rising around them, the mountains dark purple shapes in the distance; a very clean little restaurant surrounded by palm trees. Inside it was cool and dimly lit, with nice leather booths. Cameron ordered a bottle of wine.

"How did you find this place?"

"It's famous," he said.

"Oh." She who had always had a million things to say to this man, or to anyone, couldn't think of a thing to say. She who had been on only one date in her entire life, except for Alexander, felt like a girl on a date. She busied herself with reading the menu, so he wouldn't sense how totally at a loss she was.

"What do you think you're going to have?" he asked comfortably.

"The barbecued chicken," Chris said, because it was the first thing she saw. She thought if she ate anything at all she would probably choke.

"Cheers," he said, raising his glass, and drank.

"Cheers." She sipped the wine. *Did Annabel feel this way when she was starting an adventure?* Of course not; Annabel was never nervous. And besides, Cameron wasn't one bit interested; she was just somebody who was fun to have dinner with. Well, hardly fun tonight, just sitting here trying not to look at him.

And then she noticed his hands were shaking, just a little.

The young Chris, the one who had been known for her sharp-tongued honesty, would have said: I don't do this. Do you fool around, and if so, why are you so nervous? Or are the people who *don't* fool around the ones whose hands shake when they start to think of it? But this adult Chris, who moved smoothly through her world and Alexander's, never said things like that.

He must think she was boring tonight. He was probably sorry he had thought of this escapade and wished they were back at the party. She couldn't move; she felt as if she were melting.

"Enjoy your dinners," the waitress said, putting huge platters of steaming food in front of them.

"Thank you," they both said in unison.

And then he started to talk. Chris was so relieved and grateful she began to relax. The moment of danger seemed safely over. She drank another glass of wine and allowed herself to admit how attractive he really was, now that she knew he would never know she felt that way. His hands weren't shaking anymore. She leaned back peacefully against the leather. It was too bad the two of them hadn't met at some other time in their lives. But then, at what time of her life had she ever been available in her heart, even when she was alone? It was a shame she was so woefully unable to handle something like this. Another woman in her place would have thought she was lucky to have the chance.

After dinner he drove back through the desert under the sky full of stars. She had her hand on the seat between them. He put his hand next to hers, innocently, but the air between them seemed to vibrate. If either of them moved just a little they would be touching. . . . She clenched her hands together in her lap and stared straight ahead out the windshield. No, it wasn't over.

When they reached the motel Chris could still hear the music from the party, and the sound of people laughing. Cameron stopped the car at her door. "Thank you," she said. "That was wonderful."

"Yes, it was fun, wasn't it." He was looking at her, waiting to be invited in for a drink, afraid to ask, afraid even to touch her, because then she would know. But she already knew.

"Goodnight," she said quickly, and was out of the car and gone.

The next day Chris sat through the meetings with her heart pounding, thinking of nothing but him. They passed each other going to lunch and he smiled, and she knew that even though tonight was the final banquet which they would both have to attend, there was afterward, and her room, and their last chance. In the afternoon she saw him watching her when he thought no one was looking. "See you at the cocktail party," he said, his voice too casual, when they passed again.

"Right." She went to her room and put her dress for the evening on the bed. She looked at the king-size bed, and the drapes at the windows that could be pulled tightly against the world, and at her wedding ring. Then she called Cameron's room.

"It's Chris. I'm going to have to rush back to New York tonight because my son isn't feeling well." She hoped he would mistake the tension in her voice for concern. Then she fled.

She was alone in the apartment. Alexander was still in the country, as was Mrs. Gormley, and Nicholas had been away for ages. It was very late. *Oh, God, I'm safe*, Chris thought. But she knew Cameron would be back in New York tomorrow, and so would Alexander, and nothing would have changed with either of them; so she was not safe at all. She took a shower and looked at herself in the mirrored wall of the bath-room. This was the body that one man wanted so

badly, and another man—although he loved her—did
not. It was so stupidly unfair. She sighed, and then she
put on a robe and went into the kitchen. She hadn't
even remembered she'd missed dinner.

She made a sandwich of whole wheat pita bread
with melted cheese and alfalfa sprouts, and drank a
glass of wine with it. She found some cold chicken and
ate that. There was a half container of butter pecan
ice cream that had been hanging around because nobody liked it, so she finished it up. Then she saw an
entire pint of chocolate chip ice cream, which she did
like, so she let it soften on the counter while she had
some crackers and creamy Valembert with another
glass of wine. The ice cream was nice and soft then, so
she took it to bed with her, eating it slowly and sensually in front of the television set. She was starting to
feel a little nauseated. When she took the empty container back to the kitchen to throw away she started
in on the cookies. Before she had finished everything
in the cookie jar she was already tearing open a new
package of cookies with her teeth, dumping some of
them into the jar and eating the others with a glass of
milk, dipping them into the milk to soften them, then
sucking at them and finally letting them melt on her
tongue. She was beyond nausea; she couldn't stop.
There was an empty, starving place deep inside her
stomach, and no matter how much she ate she
couldn't seem to fill it up.

She ate toast with butter and peanut butter and
jam when there was nothing else to eat. She even
took Mrs. Gormley's awful supermarket coffee cake,

and ran her finger around the inside of the tin when it was finished, to get every last greasy crumb.

When she had finished eating, Chris went back to the bathroom and brushed and flossed her teeth carefully to be sure she wouldn't get any cavities. She cleaned off whatever makeup might still be left after her shower, put on moisturizer, and combed her hair. Then she put on a nice, fresh nightgown, got into bed, and fell asleep instantly, as if she had been drugged.

It was the first time that she had forgotten to call Alexander. It was the first time in all the years of their marriage that she wasn't where he thought she was.

Chapter Four

EVERYONE SAID THE Caldwells were a perfect family; attractive, bright, rich, charming, social, athletic, and Daphne was also artistic. Their four well-behaved sons would be a source of pride to anybody. They had lived in Greenwich, Connecticut, for a long time now, and the few people who remembered things in their lives that were not perfect would certainly not mention them. There was, for instance, Richard's first, unfortunate marriage, when he was barely a teenager; nothing really unusual about it except that his wife had been a roadhouse waitress and he a socialite, and their son (who was also named Richard Caldwell, so you couldn't avoid the coincidence) was a rising star in liberal politics, who was written about in *People* magazine, and he and Richard had had nothing to do with each other since he was an infant. And there was Daphne and Richard's youngest child, the daughter, the "different" one who lived away from home. No one ever mentioned her, either, and by now people had either forgotten about her or had never known.

There was about those perfect Caldwells a certain blandness that was a kind of denial of anything that was disruptive or weak. They gave enough of themselves to make you think you knew them, and for their circle of friends that was certainly enough. It never occurred to anyone that they kept as much secret from one another as they did from the world.

Daphne was aware of this only in relation to herself. She knew she would always be the Golden Girl she had been at college, simply older. She knew Richard always gave away anything that wasn't perfect. She had seen it, and denied it, and made excuses for it, just as he had. Richard's whole life was *Rashomon*. He always had a persuasive reason for anything he did, and seemed bewildered, even annoyed, at the evidence that he had caused anyone pain. A gentleman was someone who never did anything hurtful by accident, and a Caldwell never would do it on purpose either. He tiptoed considerately through lives he had wrecked, smiling his glittering, winning smile. Daphne loved him. There was nothing else to know.

It was another lovely summer. The boys were home from school: Matthew, sixteen, Sam, fifteen, Jonathan, fourteen, and Teddy, twelve. The huge old trees around their house were rich with cool leaves, her rock garden was filled with tiny colorful flowers

Rona Jaffe

which she arranged with pleasure in little vases, there were days filled with water-skiing and swimming and laughter, weekend picnics, friends, entertaining, movies, some jaunts to the city to the theater or a special restaurant for just her and Richard alone. The mirror in the dining room reflected six golden heads, Richard's a little graying at the temples now, only making him more attractive. Daphne didn't find it so attractive on herself, and had been coloring her hair for years. The boys all had her patrician, delicately sculpted face. She looked at them sometimes with awe that she had been able to create such wonderful creatures. They were her immortality, hers and Richard's. This life—a comfortable home, happy children, and Richard—were all she had ever wanted. Although she did volunteer work for the Junior League, because that was what one did, she would have been quite happy staying home reading, running with the dogs, and sketching, her new hobby.

Today was Sunday. Two couples were coming for an early dinner. Steaks were marinating; Richard would grill them later outdoors on the barbecue. He still enjoyed cooking as much as ever, but now he only had time to do it on weekends, and during the week they had a cook. Daphne had given him an ice cream maker, and he delighted in inventing new and exotic ice creams and sherbets, several of which they were going to have for dessert tonight. Sam and Matthew had gone jogging, Jonathan was up in the attic in the photography studio they had outfitted for his special interest, and Teddy was in his room doing who knew

[70]

what. The two older boys and the two younger ones had paired off for years now, the older ones more outgoing, the younger two more interested in quiet, solitary pursuits, although all of them could keep up a conversation and were properly charming to adults.

The evening was as nice as she had expected. There was only one tiny, unexpected sting of pain. After dinner, when the boys were playing touch football on the lawn in the last rays of the dying sun, the adults were talking about their various children, and Dan and Janet Mason, who were new to the neighborhood and had a precociously sexy and beautiful fifteen-year-old daughter, were complaining about the older boys who took her out. They gave her drugs, Janet was sure. It was so hard to control a girl who looked like a woman and acted like a child. They were thinking of sending her to a strict all-girl boarding school, but what would they do about vacations?

"No matter what anyone says," Richard commiserated, "the double standard still exists."

Everyone nodded. "The idea of a college girl trying to corrupt Sam or Jonathan . . ." Dan said, and laughed.

"Matthew would love to have one corrupt him," Richard said, and Daphne smiled.

"You're so lucky to have only boys," Janet Mason said.

"Yes, yes," Richard said genially, and Daphne felt the stab.

We have a daughter too, she wanted to say. But, of course, she didn't.

And that night in bed, when she and Richard were alone together at last, she didn't mention it either. There were things they hadn't talked about for years, and Elizabeth's existence was one of them.

"Another wonderful weekend over," Richard said. "Oh, tomorrow night I have a dinner meeting in town. Just wanted to remind you."

"I remember."

"I won't be home very late."

"All right."

He'd had quite a lot to drink, but still he made love to her. Or perhaps that was why. But Daphne, who was still addicted to Richard's sexuality and her own, thought they were lucky that after all these years their passion for each other was still special. She had so little to complain about in her marriage. Other people had so much less happiness. She could see it on their faces, and they told her things she would have been embarrassed to tell to anyone. Now that she thought about it, it had surprised her a little that the Masons would talk that way about their daughter, even though everyone really knew.

The next day, when Richard was in New York working, and the boys were amusing themselves, Daphne got into her car and drove on her semimonthly pilgrimage to see her own daughter.

The road was so familiar by now that she drove it by rote. So many years had gone by, and yet she always had the same image before her eyes: the baby being carried away by a stranger, herself turning and driving home alone. Elizabeth, nine years old now, going on three. The baby, the little girl who would be another Daphne, the one Richard had persuaded her to have even though she was afraid she was too old, too tired, had pressed their luck too far. But Elizabeth was not epileptic like her mother. Elizabeth was retarded. And Richard, who had so begged and cajoled for her arrival, had with the same sweet reasonableness made Daphne put her into a very nice home for "special" children.

Richard always gave away anything that wasn't perfect.

That's why I was always afraid he would give me away.

How many hugs and kisses she had stored up for her daughter, the only one of her children she was still allowed to cuddle. . . . Daphne lit up another of her too-frequent cigarettes. Her boys were "little men" now, and hugs and kisses were reserved for reunions and farewells. Sometimes she allowed her hand to linger for a moment on Teddy's silky hair, her youngest boy, or touched Matthew's broad shoulder lightly when she gave him money to go out with his friends and told him to drive carefully in her borrowed car. But Elizabeth would always be a baby; her feelings open, her needs direct, and her understanding limited to the world she knew, which did not include the tall, kindly woman who called herself Mother when she came to visit and bring presents. To Elizabeth, Mother was Jane, her cottage mother; the woman who took care of her at the home and showed her the most kindness. Other children sometimes were adopted, or went to foster homes, but Daphne would never allow that. Elizabeth would stay in this very expensive place, and when she was eighteen she would go to a group home with her friends. That time was so far away that Daphne could not even allow herself to imagine it.

The home looked like a large country estate, with a main house and several small ones, painted in pale, cheerful pastel colors. They were expecting her; Elizabeth was wearing one of the many party dresses Daphne kept bringing. Jane had cut her blonde hair in bangs. Daphne felt a stab of resentment. *I didn't tell her she could cut my child's hair.* But Elizabeth looked so cute. She was small for her age now, and the dresses Daphne chose, decorated with flowers or ducks or rabbits, were always for a child much younger. Since the physical therapists had trained her to hold her tongue in, it sometimes occurred to Daphne in a flash of optimistic madness that Richard would accept her. You could see she was Daphne's and Richard's child. The coloring was the same. There were Daphne's slanted cornflower-blue eyes, but the telltale eyelid flap made them not really Daphne's eyes at all, but a sort of sad parody of them. Years ago, in the hospital when she was born, Richard had asked angrily if Daphne thought normal meant being toilet trained at eight. Well, Elizabeth was toilet trained at nine, and could feed herself with a spoon, drink from a cup, and spoke in short phrases. To Daphne, who had seen the way she had been at the beginning, it was a miracle of progress. But Richard would find nothing to take pride in.

"Look, here's your mother!" Jane Baldwin said happily.

"Say what?" said Elizabeth, and laughed.

"Her favorite TV program," Jane said. "Don't you think she sounds like George Jefferson?"

"I don't know," Daphne said, embarrassed. "I don't watch much television."

"She's become addicted to reruns. Do Mork. Elizabeth, what does Mork say?"

"Na-noo, Na-noo!" Elizabeth said.

"Good God," said Daphne, and gathered her into her arms.

The small body was soft and warm. Elizabeth wriggled away after a moment and pulled Daphne off to look at her dolls. They were perched on the pillow of her neatly made bed, and lined up on the bookcase filled with picture books. "Doll," she said, as if patiently explaining, slowly putting her finger on each one. "Doll." It was still difficult to understand her speech.

"I know. They're so pretty. I gave them to you, do you remember that?" Elizabeth smiled and didn't answer. "And guess what I brought you today," Daphne continued brightly. She held out a brightly colored package, and helped Elizabeth open it. "Another doll for your collection."

"Say 'thank you,' " Jane said.

"Thank you."

"How much she's learned," Daphne said wistfully.

"It used to seem so impossible. Sometimes I wish . . ."

"That you could take her home?"

"Or that we'd kept her. But it was all so impossible."

"You ought to remember," Jane said kindly, "that this is a stubborn little girl and she's her own person. She needs a lot of time, and sometimes she's difficult. But mainly, she's happy. She has friends. We're her family."

"But I'm her family too," Daphne said. "I was a stubborn little girl, and I'm sure my mother thought I was difficult when I insisted on doing things even though she was frightened to death because of my epilepsy." How easily the word came out here . . . epilepsy. Nothing was embarrassing or forbidden here.

"Why don't we have lunch?" Jane said.

In the dining room Elizabeth ran in her awkward little gait to sit with a favorite friend. Daphne followed her and sat beside her. Every time she came here she went through the same mental list: the pros and cons, why Elizabeth was here instead of with them, and always she had the distinct feeling that when she left it was she who grieved and never the child. And, of course, it was easy to be the visitor, not responsible. She could go away, and she always did. Life went on. You did the best you could. You did what you thought was right. The majority ruled. She had other children to worry about.

But her other children seemed to require so little

worry. She supposed Richard would say that was because she *had* done everything right.

After lunch she had to leave. It was a long drive. She kissed Elizabeth good-bye and watched her go off cheerfully with Jane. Just like the first time. It would always be as painful as the first time . . . her smiling baby in a stranger's arms. But then, at one point on the way home, as the scenery changed it seemed life changed too, and Daphne returned to her other world. Everybody was so happy in that other world, and it was she who had made them so.

Richard came home very late. "How was your day?" he asked her.

"Fine," Daphne said. "Uneventful. And your business dinner?"

"The only thing more boring than having to go through it would be having to describe it."

Neither one knew the other had lied.

The days went by peacefully in their safe haven. It was Friday again, an extraordinarily beautiful summer afternoon. The sky was a brilliant, cloudless blue, and sunlight splashed on the polished wood floors of Daphne's house and washed the pale, carpeted stairs in a golden glow. From the kitchen came the scent of a cake baking, and from the open windows the perfume of freshly cut grass brought in on the light breeze. Everything was clean: the silver-framed family photos with their dustless glass on the rich mahogany baby grand piano, the rows of books in their bright jackets in the large bookshelves, the polished silver coffee service that she often used. Those Radcliffe evenings so long ago flashed through Daphne's mind; the demitasse served in the dorm living room after dinner, poured by the House Mother and whichever trembling girl had been chosen to help that evening, and she thought how without even being conscious of it her life had turned out to be the "Gracious Living" they had been taught. She had laughed at the idea at the time, but it had happened to her, and she liked it.

It was very quiet. The boys were all occupied elsewhere, the dogs were asleep. Daphne went upstairs to her bedroom to read, feeling the security and peace of the house around her.

When Richard came home and had changed into casual clothes the family gathered for dinner. All except Jonathan, still working in his attic photography studio. The dogs were barking at his door.

"Stop that racket," Richard called out, as if the dogs knew he was talking to them anyway.

"Teddy, go get your brother," Daphne said. "And put the dogs outside if they won't behave."

"Yes, Mom." Teddy was out of the room in a flash, up the stairs two at a time, twelve years old and overflowing with energy. The others went into the dining room and began to sit down at their places. And then they heard Teddy scream.

"Mommy! Daddy!" He hadn't called them Mommy and Daddy since he was four.

"What the hell?" Richard said, frightened. They all ran up the stairs.

The dogs had stopped barking. The attic door was open. Teddy was standing there, his small face drained of color. And inside the room . . . The first thing Daphne saw was Jonathan's blue running shoes, dangling four feet above the floor, then his clean white socks and faded jeans, and all of his body, up to his fragile bent neck and distorted face; her son hanging dead from the noose he had made of a rope and tied around one of the ceiling beams.

It was no longer Jonathan they were staring at, but her. She was lying on the floor, in a pool of her own bodily wastes, and she knew what had gone before: she had had a major seizure. She remembered that look on young faces—half horror, half revulsion—from her childhood, when the faces were those of her classmates, not her children. She had been writhing and groaning, eyes sightless, mind asleep. Her children had never seen this happen to her, neither had Richard, for it had been so long . . . For an instant she forgot what had made it happen, and then she remembered, and Daphne wished she could stay unconscious forever.

No one touched her. Richard went over to Jonathan and very gently cut him down, holding his body in his arms as though he was not heavy at all. Then he put his son on the studio couch and carefully arranged a cushion under his head, as if he was not dead at all either. But he *was* dead.

"Call the doctor," Richard said. Matthew and Sam ran down the stairs.

"Mom . . . ?" Teddy said, in a scared little voice.

"I'm all right," Daphne said. Where had the courage come from, to speak, when she felt as if hands were squeezing her throat, choking her? That innocent white neck, bent and broken . . . Jonathan . . . "It was the shock; I'm all right now." Teddy was afraid to touch her, and so, apparently, was Richard. Then Teddy walked over slowly and held out his hands to help her up.

"Who's the doctor for?" he asked.

Who indeed? "Jonathan," she said.

Richard turned and walked out of the room

She could not believe he had done it; she felt as if he had stabbed her in the heart. She went over to where Jonathan was lying and put her arms around his body, and then she turned to look at Teddy. She knew she was still in a kind of shock because she had not shed a tear; she was holding on, denying it while she knew it was true, trying to keep Teddy from falling apart. The tears would come later. Perhaps they would never stop.

"I'll wait with you," Teddy said.

"You don't have to," Daphne said gently.

"I'm not scared," he said.

"Thank you."

Holding her dead fourteen-year-old son, rocking his body as if he were a drowsy infant, Daphne thought how many years it had been since she had shown this depth of physical affection to any of the boys, and how long it had been since they had let her do so without embarrassment. Her busy, boisterous, healthy boys. Who had made them all so formal, so damn proper? Richard? Was it her fault? *Jonathan,* she thought, *why did you leave us? What did I do to make you go? I didn't even know you were unhappy.*

Richard hadn't looked at her; he'd just run away. Was he overwhelmed by emotion because of his son, or repelled by his wife? At this moment, holding her dead child in her arms, Daphne didn't even care. Teddy walked over, slowly, noiselessly, and put his hand on her shoulder.

And so that house, that safe, pretty house, was forever transformed into a house of horror; and the sun-splashed stairs would forever after lead upward not to restful rooms but to the memory of dark, terrible surprises.

Chapter Five

My name is Teddy Caldwell and this is my secret journal. Nobody in this family ever talks about the things that really bother them or the things that really matter. I used to be able to talk about things with my brother Jonathan, but last week he killed himself, and now I have nobody to talk to, so I decided to start this journal and talk to it. The funeral was yesterday. It was the first funeral I ever went to, because when some relatives I didn't really know well died I was too young to go. I think people should be able to go to minor funerals before they have to go to a big one, so they can get prepared. The funeral of my favorite brother was an awesomely horrible event for me. I kept thinking it wasn't really happening, and I kept hoping it wasn't, but I also knew it was. I felt dead too. Of course, I don't know what dead is really like, but Jonathan does. I wonder what he thought it would be like to be dead before he killed himself. I'm sure he thought about it a lot. He wasn't the kind of person who would kill himself on an impulse. We talked about a lot of private things but we never talked about either of us being dead. We didn't like to talk about anybody we cared about being dead. Dying means your parents. At least that's what I always thought it meant before.

At the funeral we all tried to act calm and not cry. Afterward my father told us we had been "good." I don't know what's so good about that, but it was what he and my mother wanted. Everybody in this family pretends to be perfectly happy all the time, even when they're not, and if they can't be happy then at least they have to be brave. I know that even though he won't admit it my father hates that my mother has epilepsy. She told me about her epilepsy after I saw her have a seizure, and she told me that I don't have it and never will. I asked her if my father knew she had it before he married her, and she said that was a funny question. I said I didn't know why it was so funny, and then she said he didn't know for years. Right away I could see it all. It's just like he is with us. We have to be the best. The best in school, the best in sports, and be popular and happy and healthy. It's as if he doesn't care about us being that way for us, but for him. He would be embarrassed if we weren't what he calls "winners." One day we all went swimming and he yelled "The last one in is a loser!" I kept thinking there always has to be a last one unless it's a tie, so there always has to be a loser, and that isn't fair. I wonder if Jonathan thought he was a loser?

Jonathan was a genius. I don't just say that because he was my brother. His photos were brilliant. He did scenery, and empty rooms, but he didn't like to take pictures of people. He said they never looked the same to the camera as they did to him, and he couldn't figure out if the way they looked to him was the way they really looked or if the camera was right, or if maybe he just wasn't a very good photographer. Jonathan worried about things like that, but he was really a happy person, and I don't understand how he could kill himself. I mean he had everything. Everybody liked him. And if something was so terrible that he wanted to die, why couldn't he have talked to me first about it?

I have to stop now because they're calling me for dinner. If dinner is anything like breakfast and lunch were, everybody is going to talk about things that don't matter, and they're going to pretend Jonathan never existed. But that makes it worse. He's sitting right there at the table, in his usual place, and he's never going to go away. That's the worst part, that he's never going to go away but he's not here either, and I need him.

Chapter Six

THAT FALL THE results of the questionnaire that had been sent to their class appeared in *The Ladies' Home Journal*. Emily was a little disappointed that after spending a whole week trying to frame proper responses she was not even quoted by name. There were some quotes, but they were credited to "a housewife in Seattle," or "a college professor in Vermont," and the rest of the article was divided between a compendium of the kinds of information that had been gathered and six interviews in depth with women the author had found interesting, or perhaps typical. Emily thought how ironic it was that if she had written the truth about herself and her life all these years she probably would have been one of the six women who was chosen. Marriage immediately after graduation to the perfect catch, followed by a perfect home and family life, and then a nervous breakdown! A woman who had wanted two perfect children and then had wanted to kill them! What a story that would have made for all her classmates.

She was back at the analyst, but this time it wasn't because of herself so much as it was because of Ken. Dear old Dr. Page, who had been middle-aged when they started her analysis. Emily felt as if they were two old warriors together, they had been through so much. She sat down in the worn brown leather chair facing Dr. Page across the huge, scarred desk. Years ago she had wondered if patients had stuck knives in it to make those pits and marks, but now it just seemed like a symbol of comfort. They were all scarred and recovered, in some way.

"You know, it's so unfair," Emily said. "Ken is still sexy and attractive to me. I remember his wrists, when I first went out with him. He wore his watch on the inside of his wrist, and he had that sandy hair on his arms . . . I thought it was so sexy I got a weak feeling in my stomach. In those days I thought hands and mouths were the sexiest parts of a man, and I guess I still do. It doesn't matter to me if his body gets older. We're all human. But it doesn't seem to count for a woman. We have to stay young and firm and never change or else the men complain."

"Not all men feel that way," Dr. Page said.

"But Ken does. It's funny . . . you remember how I used to be my own worst enemy, how I always thought I was so ugly. It was part of my craziness, always inspecting myself and being so critical, never knowing what I really looked like. And when I finally got over it and Ken was so happy, and we did things together, and he was supportive . . ." She choked back the lump in her throat and tried not to cry. Dr. Page silently pushed the box of tissues closer. "No, I can't," Emily said. "I'll look a mess and then he'll say something." And then she did cry.

"It sounds as if Ken needs some therapy," Dr. Page said. "He's gradually turned from Dr. Jekyll to Mr. Hyde."

Emily giggled through her tears. "Doctor Buchman." There was a pause while she gathered herself together and wiped her eyes. She wore waterproof mascara to her analyst's sessions. "He's always putting me down lately. And I'm not so secure that I can deal with that. I don't think I ever will be totally secure, just like some people will never be fast runners. I'm just not built that way. But I don't need the person who is supposed to be my helpmate and best friend tearing me down all the time. Last night we were getting undressed for bed and he looked at me with this absolute distaste and said: 'You've got a fat ass.' And I *don't*. Do I?"

"You know you don't," Dr. Page said gravely.

"I swim, I play tennis, I do my exercises, I watch everything I eat. My women friends say they envy me because I look so well. They're kind to me. Ken seems to hate it that I'm not twenty. I don't know what it is he wants. I think he's great, I tell him so all the time, but he just looks at me as if he wishes I weren't there."

"Do you think there's another woman?"

"Who knows?" Emily said. "Ken never could handle that. But this time it's worse."

"What about drinking?"

"Well, lately it seems to put him in a bad mood instead of cheering him up."

"What about drugs?"

Emily looked at her aghast. *"Ken?"*

"It happens in the best of families."

"I used to worry about the kids. But they seem all right. Ken is an adult. He's not a rock star or one of those movie people. I know a lot of them take things."

"Ken has constant contact with that world," Dr. Page said. "And it's also easy for him to get drugs if he wants them."

"Ken is a nice Jewish boy," Emily said, insulted.

"And you are a smart girl from Radcliffe," the doctor said.

"If it were a brain tumor or one of those diseases that changes the personality, his doctor would tell me, wouldn't he?"

"Not if Ken swore him to secrecy to protect you because you couldn't take the stress of knowing. But it doesn't sound as if Ken cares that much about your feelings."

"Oh, who *knows* what Ken cares about," Emily sighed.

Even though her name wasn't actually mentioned in the article about her class, Emily left the magazine prominently displayed on the coffee table in the living room, opened to the article, so people would see it. Adeline was very pleased and made Emily buy her a copy. Emily's tennis group was coming over on Monday, because it was her turn to have them at her house, and Emily knew it would be a good topic of conversation. They'd gotten to be pretty good tennis players over the years, especially since they all took tennis lessons and some of them even went away to tennis camp (to get away from their husbands, she suspected), but the real reason for their weekly tennis-and-lunch meetings was companionship and talk. They were her friends, and they were nice to her, but Emily still secretly thought of them as frivolous women. Their husbands were all successful, and they introduced new members of their group as the wife of so-and-so, as if the woman herself had no identity. Their conversation revolved mainly around clothes, new gyms, trips, and gossip. They read whatever new books you were supposed to read, and they wouldn't be caught dead reading a magazine for housewives, but the article might make them talk about their own dreams and expectations, and it would be a different kind of day.

On the Friday before the Monday tennis lunch Emily sat at the kitchen table planning the menu with Adeline. *"Please* don't make pasta salad again, Adeline. Everybody's on a diet. How about Chinese chicken salad?"

"Everybody *likes* macaroni salad," Adeline said. She refused to call it pasta even if it was shells.

"Well, they left it over last time and I was embarrassed," Emily ventured bravely. "There's a nice recipe in my file for the Chinese chicken salad, and go easy on the soy sauce." She smiled. "Maybe it would be funny if I put a dish of diuretics on the table on the side of the salad. They'd all laugh. They're going to go home and take one immediately, they always do."

"I'll make chicken salad with mayonnaise," Adeline said grimly. "Those pills are bad for you."

"Vinaigrette?" Emily said. "Please?"

"I don't know why you all want to watch your weight anyway," Adeline said, disgusted. "You're all too thin."

"Fruit salad and cookies for dessert," Emily said briskly, ignoring her. She was working her way up to the tradeoff. Any negotiation with Adeline took sly diplomacy because it was a battle of wills, and Adeline always managed to win or at least destroy your victory.

"Too much work, sweetie," Adeline said. "I can't clean the house and make lunch and dinner too. If you're on a diet you can't have cookies."

"All right," Emily said pleasantly. She wrote the menu as she talked. "Chicken salad with vinaigrette dressing—*very light*—and fruit salad for dessert. Make a lot because we'll have the exact same thing for dinner. I don't care, and Dr. Buchman likes that."

And on Sunday afternoon I'll make the cookies. Me. My own special cookies. Not yours. Mine. And you'll serve them.

It didn't matter that at Friday dinner Emily's piece of fish which she had requested dry broiled without any butter because Ken had said she had a fat ass was served by Adeline as a white, rubbery, and repulsive mess without any seasoning either, because Adeline's nose was out of joint about the no butter. That was a minor skirmish. The real victory was coming Sunday, when Emily could bake her butterscotch chip cookies in peace and bliss.

On Sunday Ken was out of the house right after breakfast, claiming a tennis game. He didn't bother to invite her, either to play or to watch, but by now she was used to it. It was like the bad old days, when she was beginning her nervous breakdown, when he used to vanish for hours on end because he couldn't stand to be with her. But now she was perfectly sane, and she had something to do if he left her home alone. She was beginning to think of the happy time they'd had together when she was well again as simply an interlude, not their life. Even their years together at college, going steady, and the early years of their marriage when she was still working, had taken on the aspect of a brief, happy vacation from reality. Those were two other people; young, idealistic, trying to conform. They had chased happiness with the dedication of two kids studying for an exam, armed with their research gleaned from the media and public opinion. Emily didn't even know what happiness was supposed to mean anymore. She knew what made her happy, and she also knew it wouldn't mean a thing to someone else. But maybe that was what happiness was: what Kate called "doing her own thing." God knows, she had no idea what made Ken happy, or Kate. Peter, she suspected, wanted nothing more than success and money and material things, and perhaps his own idea of love. She didn't even know what Peter thought love was. He talked about his imaginary future beautiful live-in girl friend the same way he did about owning an expensive car. But she wasn't going to think about any of them now. This was her day.

She got out the cookie sheets, the mixing bowl, and the ingredients she had bought the day before. Adeline never left the cookie sheets clean enough for Emily's taste, so she scrubbed them until they shone, and then she began to mix her secret recipe for what she thought were the best, chewiest, melt in your mouth butterscotch chip cookies in the world. They were not too sweet and not too greasy. Nothing in them tasted artificial. It had taken her years to get the recipe exactly right, with Kate and Peter as her willing taste testers. When fickle Peter finally pronounced them addictive, Emily knew she had it.

While she baked her special cookies her mind was wiped free of everything that bothered her. She had music on the kitchen radio, but she hardly listened to it. She felt warm and creative as she put everything together, even though it wasn't difficult, and then when the cookies were baking Emily sat in the kitchen waiting because she loved the way they smelled. She could almost tell by the smell when they were exactly ready. But she enjoyed going over to the oven and peering in through the glass window to watch those pale little blobs of batter rise and move and bubble and start to turn their golden color. How could she ever have allowed Adeline to deprive her of this?

When the cookies were ready and had cooled off enough Emily took one, just one, and put it on her best plate. She poured a glass of skimmed milk. Then she took her milk and cookie out to the pool area and sat in the shade at the metal table under the umbrella and tasted her handiwork very carefully. It was perfect, as usual.

She put the others neatly into her cookie tin, the layers separated by waxed paper, and knew that with the magazine article and the nice lunch, her tennis group day would be a success.

It was. Aside from a remark that idle hands find busy work, an obvious malapropism, Adeline served the cookies without a murmur, and Emily's friends devoured them. The article set them reminiscing about their lost young dreams and quickly realizing that they'd gotten exactly what they'd wanted. Emily began to think maybe it really wasn't their fault they were so frivolous; they had never been told there was anything else for them.

At dinner she tried to tell Ken about her pleasant day. "Hookers," he said disdainfully. "Your friends are nothing but hookers and parasites, living off their husbands."

"They are not!" Emily said. Her throat hurt. Why was he spoiling everything again? "They don't have to work; their husbands are rich. But they do charity things. They help raise money for Share . . ."

"Only because they want to go to the parties and see movie stars."

Emily was brave from her feeling of accomplishment and allowed herself to be angry. She wondered if Dr. Page would approve. "You see movie stars. You get to look at their pimples and who knows what else."

"What exactly does that mean?"

"I don't know what it means, but I don't want to know either."

Ken's face got so dark with rage she thought it would pop. He got up from the table and threw down his napkin. "You're just as bad as they are," he said in that voice, congested with hate, she had come to know and fear, and then he left the room.

Adeline entered the room silently and began to clear the table, knowing the meal was over before it had even begun. Emily wondered what Adeline must think about their arguments, and then decided she didn't care. She heard Ken's car roaring out of the driveway and went up to the bedroom to cry.

Later she heard Adeline's car chugging away. It was dark already these days, and soon it would be standard time again and then it would be dark really early. Then they would turn off the heater in the pool because Ken said it was too expensive. Then, when he had stopped swimming his laps, what would he do to work off his anger? Hurt her? Stay out all night? She'd rather he stayed out all night than ever lay a hand on her. Sometimes, like tonight, he looked as if he were actually ready to do her harm.

Maybe she should leave him. But where would she go? What would she do? People like her didn't get divorced; they just kept working on their marriages and hoping things would get better. She knew she was a boring married woman now and if she left Ken then she would only be a boring divorced woman. Nobody but her analyst seemed to think she had any worth. Maybe she should get a dog. A dog adored you no matter what. But dogs shed and jumped on things, especially you and your bed. No, she was not even meant to have a pet. Emily washed her tear-swollen face and wondered what in the world she *was* meant for.

She ought to try to keep up her scrapbook of Kate's press clippings. She had been keeping scrapbooks for years, at college and then since she was married, but she never looked at them obsessively anymore because the past was the past. But still, if your daughter was a successful actress, you had reason to be proud and keep a record of what she had done. Emily had a whole folder of clippings and photos that she'd been meaning to sort and paste into the new leather album she'd bought. They were in her walk-in closet in the bedroom, on the shelf.

There was Ken's tennis bag right outside her closet door where he'd left it instead of putting it away in his own walk-in closet where it belonged. He'd just dropped it down when he came home for dinner. It reminded her of that movie *Gaslight*, where the husband kept trying to drive the wife crazy. If Emily tried to put Ken's things away, or do things for him, he would turn on her and say she was smothering him, and if she left his bag where it was he would come home and accuse her again of being a parasite. She marched right over to it and picked it up, and then, for no reason she could think of, she opened it and looked inside.

There was his tennis racquet, of course. And there was also a plastic bag of fine white powder, and a great many Polaroid photographs.

Emily sat down on the rug, this bizarre and terrifying evidence in her hands, and stared at it. She was so horrified she didn't know which to look at first. The pictures were all of the kind of girls you saw on the covers of filthy magazines, more naked than dressed, in the same sort of obscene clothing, in the same sort of lewd poses; but they were not always alone. Sometimes they were with Ken.

In some of the pictures the girl was standing with her arm around Ken, and he with his around her, and they were smiling at the camera. In one photo they were both wearing army officer's hats, which for one terrible distorted instant Emily thought were actually Nazi hats, but they weren't, and the hooker or whatever she was was wearing a black garter belt and black stockings and nothing else at all. Ken was wearing nothing at all either. His penis was right there for the world to see, half erect. Emily felt like throwing up. What had they used, a time setting, or was someone else there? And the worst photo . . . the worst . . . was the one of Ken having sexual intercourse with the girl, and they were both still looking at the camera and smiling their heads off.

Then Emily opened the plastic bag and looked at the white powder. She had never seen cocaine before except in photographs, but she was sure that was what it was. She was afraid to taste it, and besides she didn't know what it was supposed to taste like. She certainly wasn't going to smell it; snorting was what made you high. It was a tremendous amount of cocaine for one person to have unless he was an addict or a dealer. Maybe Ken was giving it out to his friends, to show off how rich he was.

She understood it all now—the erratic behavior, the anger, the irritability, the loss of weight, the endless nervous energy, the lack of appetite. It wasn't Ken, it was the drug. Dr. Page had been right, and she had been blind and stupid. But why the sex with those trashy women? Did cocaine do that too, or simply free Ken to do what he had secretly wanted to all his life?

Emily sat there like a statue, cold and nearly not breathing, the evidence in her hands, waiting for Ken to come home.

At midnight she heard his car, and then she heard him walking around downstairs. Then she heard him on the stairs, and then he came into the room, a drink in his hand. She could see that he was already drunk, and also—she now knew—stoned out of his mind. They stared at each other; the kind, considerate man who had become a malevolent stranger, and the fluttering, self-abnegating woman who had become a cold statue; and then he spoke. He actually sounded relieved.

"So you found out," Ken said.

Emily nodded.

"I'm glad," he said. "I wanted you to know."

"So I could help you?" she asked, finally finding her voice.

"Help me?" He laughed, more of a snicker really. "I don't want help. I like my life."

"Then what?" Emily said. "Did you want me to forgive you?"

"Forgive?" he said. *"Forgive* me? Who are you to forgive me for anything?"

"I'm . . . your wife."

"I am more than aware of that," he said. He finished his drink. "Did you enjoy the pictures? Did you learn anything? You're such a prude and a bore in bed you might learn something from them."

"I'm not!" Emily screamed, even though she thought he was probably right. "I would do whatever you asked, but you never asked. How could I know anything? I was a virgin when I married you and I learned everything from you!"

He stormed into her closet and began to pull her clothes off their hangers and rip them. "Look at these things," he said with disgust. "Who could get aroused looking at a woman who dresses like this? You're a dowdy old housewife, a frumpy old bat with cottage cheese for thighs and a fat ass and saggy tits."

Automatically Emily glanced at her thighs and ran her hands over them. "I'm not!" she cried, "I'm not twenty, but I'm not disgusting either! Let go of my clothes." She was so angry she wanted to choke him, and so terrified that she wanted to run away, so she just stood there like a rabbit frozen in front of headlights. Ken was ripping her things to shreds; her beautiful silk party dress that she'd worn only once, her favorite white linen suit, all her at-home robes; tearing them with his drug-crazed strength.

And then he rushed to his night table, and took from the drawer his gun—the gun that was supposed to protect his beloved family from burglars and intruders—and pointed it at her.

At her.

Her heart was pounding so wildly she thought she was going to faint. She tried to run but Ken stepped between her and the bedroom door, still holding the gun aimed right at her. She glanced from it to his eyes, trying to read some sanity there, but all she saw was hate.

"They're not your clothes," he said. "They're mine; I paid for them. I give you money and you buy ugly, sexless, hausfrau clothes to humiliate me. Is this what I worked for so hard all my life—to come home to something like you?"

She felt cold again now, calculating, wondering if she could distract him and make it to the door before he shot her. She had never been devious or clever. Nothing in her life had given her any training in anything but trying to please. But apparently everything she had learned had been for a different Ken, one who had vanished in a puff of white powder.

"Please let me go . . ." Emily whispered.

"Let you go?" Ken said.

"Please . . ."

"Nothing would give me more pleasure," he said. "Get the hell out of here and don't come back."

She ran down the stairs, trying not to stumble and break her neck, praying he wouldn't shoot her in the back. Her car keys were in the little silver dish in the kitchen where they all left their car keys, and she grabbed them as she ran. She fled out the door and into her car. The brightly moonlit night was chilly and she was shivering and sobbing with fear. Her hand was shaking so badly it took a few moments before she could fit the key into the lock. She locked the car doors. The windows were already up, but a bullet could go through a window. *Oh, start . . . start . . .* Then the engine turned over with a welcome growl, and Emily careened down the narrow winding road without even putting on her seat belt, something that ordinarily she would never omit. Glancing into the rearview mirror, she looked back at her house, and Ken wasn't anywhere in sight.

She had no handbag, no money, no credit cards, not even the key to her own house. No, not her house; Ken's house. California community property laws or not, he thought it was his house, just as he thought those were his clothes he had torn up. As for her, she never wanted to go back there again. Tears were streaming down her face and she could hardly see. Then she realized she had forgotten to turn on the headlights. She could easily have been killed . . .

Ken would be so glad. . . . The thought made her cry harder. She hadn't the faintest idea of where to go in the middle of the night in such a state, with such an embarrassing story. Even now, shocked and terrified, almost hating him, she couldn't hurt Ken's practice. The scandal of an incident like this could do irreparable harm. Let him destroy his own life, but she wasn't going to do it.

Without having realized it, she discovered she was heading toward Westwood, to Peter's apartment. Her calm, calculating, stable son. Even if he wasn't home to let her in, he had all those roommates. She could sleep on the couch. She could hide at Peter's. She didn't want to go to Kate's. She didn't know why, but she didn't feel she would really be welcome. No, she would go to Peter.

So Emily, former victim and now fugitive, drove off to a destiny which an hour ago she could not have imagined, and which would turn out to be something she could never have dreamed.

Chapter Seven

KIT BARNETT, WHO was Kate Buchman to her family, and Emma Buchanan, the product of Annabel Jones's brief marriage to Rusty Buchanan, were sitting in Kit's small living room in Laurel Canyon getting drunk together on jug wine. They had become friends on a picture, and unlike most friendships formed during the encapsulated world of making a movie, they had remained friends. At the moment both were living alone, were between jobs, and were hoping to get on the new Zack Shepard film.

Kit's rented house was one of many strung together along the winding canyon road that led up and through the mountain that separated her two lives: Beverly Hills, where her parents lived, and The Valley, where most of the work was, and where she took acting classes, voice lessons, and yoga. Her house consisted of the small living room, a smaller bedroom, a kitchen with a dining area, and a bathroom; and there was a great deal of glass from which you could see the other houses, and beyond them the lights of the world which she intended to conquer. Like almost everyone else she had a security system, but because of the glass she slept with a can of mace under her pillow whenever she didn't have a live-in boyfriend.

"I would kill to get that part," Kit said. "It's perfect for me. I would do anything. I would sleep with Zack Shepard."

"Ha, ha," Emma said. She poured herself another glass of wine. "First of all, that would be no sacrifice, since he's gorgeous and sexy and brilliant; and second, you've got no chance, since he likes older women."

"How much older?" asked Kit, refilling her own glass.

"The one he lives with now is supposed to be thirty-five."

"Big deal. He's forty-five."

"I mean older than us, not older than him."

"You've got lousy grammar for somebody who went to Radcliffe."

"I didn't go that long," Emma said.

Emma had brought the magazine article her mother had sent her, but it turned out Kit already had it because their mothers had gone to school together. I hope you don't hold it against me, Kit had said when they found out, and Emma had laughed, but Kit had meant it. You couldn't trust the past. "Was your mother like those women?" Kit asked.

"No, I think she was ahead of her time," Emma said. "She slept with guys, and the other girls hated her for it. They made her miserable. Then she got engaged in senior year, like everybody wanted to do, but he dumped her right before the wedding. So she married my father. Then she set the house on fire and took me and our cat and ran away to New York."

"Set the house on fire?" Kit said. This was turning out to be a very interesting evening.

"Not on purpose. She was smoking, and she'd had too much champagne, and the curtains caught fire."

"Smoking what?"

"Just cigarettes. Nobody she knew did drugs in those days."

"God, my father certainly does now," Kit said. It didn't bother her to tell Emma; Emma was trustworthy.

"Your father?"

"Yeah. I found coke in his dresser drawer about a year ago. My mother doesn't know."

"What were you doing in his dresser drawer?" Emma said.

"Snooping."

"Ah . . ." They sat there for a while in companionable silence, sipping their wine.

"So why did she run away?" Kit asked. "Was she afraid of what your father would do to her?"

Emma grinned. "No . . . she went to bed with the fireman who rescued her. She said he was beautiful and young and sexy. Anyway, she didn't want to be a wife who cheated, and she knew the marriage was over, so she ran away and got divorced. My mother has a very strong sense of morality, in her own way. She's a decent person. When I was growing up she was very protective of me. Once, when I was in high school, she had a boyfriend who was much younger than she was—my mother likes younger men—and she caught him letting me try some pot he had, and she threw him out of her life forever. I think she felt badly about it too, because she liked him."

"She told you about the fireman?" Kit said.

"Sure. We're really good friends."

"Interesting," Kit said. "My mother and I are not friends." She realized how drunk she was getting and thought about what she was going to say next. Then she thought the hell with it. Nothing shocked Emma. "When my brother and I were very little we were drowning in our swimming pool, and my mother was sitting right there in a chair beside the pool, and when we screamed for help she didn't lift a finger."

Emma looked aghast. "What do you mean?"

"I mean she just sat there."

"She would let you *drown?*" Apparently something could shock Emma; not sex—Kit could tell her anything—but betrayal.

"You got it."

"But why?"

"Apparently she was having a nervous breakdown. I don't want to talk about it anymore. It's stupid really, to be so upset about something that happened when you were a child. But I always felt that if your mother wouldn't save you then nobody would. I mean, who can you trust? I trust my brother, and I guess that's it."

"You can trust me," Emma said. She had round, innocent green eyes, and they were soft now with protectiveness and sympathy.

Kit thought about it. "I know," she said finally. "Are you hungry? Do you want some cheese or celery or something?"

"Sure. Anything you've got."

They went rather unsteadily into the kitchen and piled the limited contents of Kit's refrigerator onto two plates. The rest of the refrigerator contained a few diet sodas, which they left. Then they went back into the living room and sat on the floor. Kit reached over and made the music louder. She had rock music playing all the time, even quietly when she was going to sleep. It made her feel safe.

They ate the food and drank some more wine and Kit began to feel better. "I want that part," she said, again. "Nobody can do that part like I could. I know in the beginning I got parts because I looked sixteen when I was eighteen, but now I've worked hard and really learned a lot and I know I'm good. My agent says there's a chance."

"You'll get it," Emma said encouragingly.

"Thank you. My friend."

"And if I could get to be his assistant . . . Imagine, Zack Shepard's assistant! I'd be his gofer, I'd be anything. As long as they gave me enough money to pay the rent."

"They'd be lucky to have you," Kit said, and meant it.

"*My* friend."

They drank to friendship. The level of wine in the jug was considerably lower than it had been when they opened it. "I love sex," Kit said. "If I was at college when your mother was I would probably have been like her and the other girls would have detested me too. I hate not having a boyfriend. I miss sex."

"But you were never really in love, were you?" Emma asked.

"No, but sometimes we were friends for a while. I'll put up with a lot of annoying traits in a man if he's a good lover."

"What's your concept of a good lover?" Emma asked.

"I'll tell you if you tell me."

"Okay."

"Considerate," Kit said, thinking about what she liked. "Asks me what I want him to do. Inventive. Willing to try new things. And, although I don't want to be gross . . . well-endowed. What do you like?"

"The same."

"Did you ever do it in a Jacuzzi?"

"No," Emma said. "Is it good?"

"Fantastic! You have to do it in a Jacuzzi. The water or something . . . it's the greatest. Did you ever do it in a bathtub?"

"Yeah. The water slopped all over the floor."

"But wasn't it wonderful? All warm . . ."

"Stop," Emma giggled. "You're making me horny,

and I'll call up Bob and I told him I was through with him."

"How about in a plane?" Kit asked.

"You didn't!"

She smiled triumphantly. "I did!"

"The Mile High Club?"

"You got it."

"When?"

"Coming back from New York after I had that reading. There was this actor I met when we read together, and we were very attracted to each other, and we came back on the plane together, so . . ."

"You did it in that tiny little smelly bathroom?"

"It's not so smelly," Kit said.

"But do you do it standing up, or what?"

"You sit on the sink and he stands up."

"But the sink is so high," Emma said.

"It's not how high *it* is, it's how high he is."

"How do you get up there?"

Kit started to giggle. "Well, if he's any kind of a gentleman he'll help you up."

They were both giggling now and couldn't stop. "If he's any kind of a gentleman . . ." Emma repeated, laughing until there were tears in her eyes, "Oh . . . oh . . ."

The idea of him having to be a gentleman in a situation that was so gross and disgusting and outrageous made them both hysterical. Kit was gasping with laughter. As she remembered the incident it hadn't been so great, but she liked talking about it, and she liked having done it. "It's just fantastic in a plane," she said. "Something about the air."

"You're an exhibitionist," Emma said. "What if somebody tried to come in?"

"You go in right after the movie starts," Kit said. She remembered how scared she had been that someone might catch them, and she wondered if she was an exhibitionist after all. Part of her was, showing her outside as an actress, wanting to be famous, liking to have sex in dangerous places; but another part of her—her feelings and thoughts—was intensely private. "Anyhow, I am a member of The Mile High Club, and it's something I always wanted."

"I think you are totally weird," Emma said, still weak with laughter. "What was the movie?"

"What was the *movie?*" Kit said, totally incredulous. "Only you would ask a question like that."

"Well, I'm interested."

"Emma, I think you like movies better than sex."

"It depends," said Emma, "on which movie and which man."

"No, I think you like movies better anyway."

Emma thought about that for a while. "You can't compare them. They're two different things."

"Truth . . ."

"Okay, at this point in my life if I had to give up one or the other I'd stay with movies. My career, I mean. But I don't have to decide because I can always have both."

"I didn't ask which you'd give up," Kit said, giggling again. "I asked which gave you the biggest orgasm."

"Oh, you asshole," Emma laughed, taking a swipe at her. "You are totally sick."

They lay on the floor, weak with laughter and tired from the wine. Finally Emma said, "I'm too drunk to drive. I'd better call a cab."

"Oh, stay," Kit said. "You can sleep on the couch. I don't mind. If you take a cab you'll have to get someone to drive you back here tomorrow to get your car, and that's so much trouble."

"I don't even have a toothbrush."

"I have hundreds. Besides . . ." Kit thought about the creepy guy again, as she did from time to time, and it scared her in a way that was not fun, not exciting, not sexual. "There's a strange boy in my acting class who has a crush on me. He keeps hanging around. He wants me to go out with him but I won't. I think there's something not right about him."

"Did you tell anybody?" Emma asked, concerned.

"What's to tell? He didn't do anything yet. Just looks at me. Sometimes he sits in his car outside my house. I'd feel better if you stayed."

"I'll stay," Emma said.

Kit felt relief flooding over her and went to get her extra quilt. "Good," she said.

"You realize that when you're a famous actress this sort of thing is going to happen a lot," said Emma.

"When I'm famous I'll be able to afford to live in a house with big gates."

Emma poured the last of the wine, trying to divide

it fairly and spilling a little in the process. "You're an interesting, uh, what's the word I'm looking for? Contradiction. Lots of times you've taken dangerous chances with men you didn't even know, and you weren't worried at all, and then something like this really scares you."

Kit felt the familiar choking sensation. She moved it around inside her psyche until it became something she felt much more comfortable with: rage. "*I* pick the men I have anything to do with," she said. Her voice was still low, but it was filled with a lifetime of hidden emotion. "They can't pick me—I pick them. *My* choice. *My* decision. Nobody is ever going to have power over my life but me."

Not ever again, she thought.

Chapter Eight

ANNABEL, WHO HAD never wanted to become a businesswoman, who had always wanted only to have a good time, discovered now that her work had become her life. It was her own choice, but a choice by default; she was not happy with it and it did not satisfy her. That summer in New York, after her business trip to Europe, she'd had two more one-night stands, and after each felt the same unaccustomed sadness. She knew what it was from: she had grown beyond that form of recreation. She wanted a man to love and live with, to read the Sunday *Times* with and then take a walk, to be there for her, to share her life. Not the temporary, part-time live-in lovers she'd had while she was raising Emma; for no matter how fond she'd been of them she had never deluded herself that she was madly in love with them. No, now finally, at forty-six, Annabel wanted what she hadn't wanted since she was twenty.

More and more often lately when she walked home from work in the autumn early darkness, carrying her lonely dinner from the neighborhood Korean salad bar, Annabel thought about Max. Dear Max, her best friend, her stability, the person she could always run to with her troubles and know he would cheer her up . . . dead now five years, never coming back. She had always realized that as you got older people you cared about died, but nothing had ever prepared her for Max's murder, and nothing would ever make her get completely over it. It was Max she had gone to when she thought she was pregnant in college, Max she had run to when she left her miserable marriage, Max who had been like a father to Emma as meaningless lovers drifted in and out of Annabel's life. And Max had truly loved her, just as she had loved him. If only Max hadn't been gay, she could have married him and all of them could have lived happily ever after.

It was pointless to dwell on what might have been. Even if Max were alive she would not be reading the Sunday *Times* with him. She could hear him in her head, just as if he *were* alive. Annabel, he was saying, now that you know what you want, you know what to go for.

Or perhaps it would come looking for her. She cheered up when she thought about that. She had the confidence and the optimism of a beautiful woman to whom romantic adventures came easily. She only had to choose a man with some depth.

When the young man walked into her boutique to

buy a birthday present for his girl friend he was so gorgeous Annabel's breath caught in her throat. Much too young, of course; about twenty-six. Therefore just right for her. Over six feet tall, with a beautiful body, thick black hair, brilliant blue eyes, a face that had it been a shade craggier or a shade prettier would have been all wrong, but as it was was perfect. Even Maria and Pamela were standing there gaping at him. He ignored the effect he had on them, since he was obviously used to it. But when he saw Annabel he stared at her for just a moment too long, and she realized that some combination of luck and chemistry was causing him to have exactly the same reaction to her that she was having to him.

She said perhaps a dress was difficult to buy for someone else and a sweater might be better. Or a handbag was always safe. She wanted to see just how personal a present this was going to be for the girl friend who suddenly stood between them. They settled on a very nice shoulder bag. During these negotiations Annabel cleverly found out the size and shape and age of the girl friend (his age, twenty-six; she had guessed correctly, tall and slim; so she, too, was his type) and after he had made the purchase Pamela brought in afternoon tea and he lingered.

His name was Dean Henry, and he was a very successful commercial artist who had done covers for *Time* magazine, as well as many ads Annabel recognized as soon as he mentioned them. He was a prodigy, the combination of talent and a single-minded determination to become an artist ever since he was a child. She liked people in the arts, and one who was also making money was an improvement on the young men she usually chose. It was late now, finally time to close the store. He seemed ready to hang around forever.

"My card," Annabel said, handing him one although there was a whole glass bowlful of them on the counter.

He took it, and then he looked into her eyes and she felt younger than he. "Could I take you to lunch tomorrow?" he asked.

"That would be lovely," Annabel said. She didn't tell him that she never took time off for lunch; for him she would.

"I'll come get you at one o'clock, all right?"

"Perfect."

He left then, with the gift-wrapped birthday present, and Maria helped Annabel pull the metal safety gates down over the front display windows and lock them. "I never saw such a good-looking man in my whole life," Maria said. "He really liked you."

"We shall see," Annabel said, hiding how excited she felt.

"I wonder what the story is with the girl friend."

"We shall see that too," Annabel said sweetly. "Goodnight."

The next morning she got up early and washed her hair. As she applied her makeup, music playing softly on the stereo, she felt the way she had years ago getting ready to go to a dance. It was the promise of something new, romantic and wonderful. And now that she was an adult, and free to do what she wanted, it was also the promise of something intensely sexual. Ordinarily, in the mornings getting dressed, she would have the news on, but today she didn't want to hear about a single tragedy, and that seemed to be all the news was lately. She even stopped to straighten up her apartment, and made the bed, just in case . . .

Dean came to pick her up at the shop promptly at one, and took her to Le Metropole, a small French restaurant where he had reserved a table in the corner by the window. Light filtered softly through the lace curtains, gilding them both, touching the crystal vase of red and blue anemones, glinting off their prudent glasses of Perrier.

What had happened to her good resolutions? This could only be a one-day stand, or a brief fling at best, since he was not only already taken but cheating. She was acting like a loon. But he was so exceptionally good-looking, and so sexy, with the bonus of being talented and successful, and perhaps even intelligent and interesting . . . she couldn't believe she'd be depressed after him.

"Let's have champagne," he said. "I just feel like it."

"I always feel like it," Annabel said, and laughed.

They toasted each other with their champagne glasses and looked into each other's eyes and then looked away, embarrassed. "I want to tell you about my situation," Dean said.

"In case I'm wondering."

"Yes . . ."

Shorthand. They both knew what was happening to them. Annabel wondered why she had always been so astute about physical attraction but unable to read men's minds about other things. Perhaps the men she chose had no minds to read. No, that wasn't fair. Most of them were bright, most were sweet, nearly all of them well-intentioned.

"Do you want to know her name? Her name is Monica. We've been living together for five years. Since we were both twenty-one. That's a fifth of our lives. She wants to get married and have children. I want to leave her because I'm not in love with her anymore. I'm very, very fond of her, but I don't love her, and I don't want to get married and have kids. Not yet, anyway, and not with her. I feel really badly about this. She and I were going in different directions for quite a while. I know this sounds totally cruel. But isn't it better to break up before we cause each other any more pain?"

"Damage," Annabel said. "Before we do any more damage to each other—or to ourselves. That's what I said to my husband in a note I left him. I was married to *him* for a fifth of my life. At the time I thought it was a slightly pompous note, but as I look back it did have a lot of truth in it."

"I want to wait until after her birthday," he said. "I'll tell her then. There's never any right time, but I'm doing the best I can."

And when will this unforgettable birthday be? Annabel wanted to ask, but stopped herself. That was the sort of too-sharp thing Chris would say, but she would only think. She was always charming. And it was true; there was never any right time for leaving someone who didn't want to be left. She nodded.

"I'm telling you all this," he said, "and I don't even know if you're free, or if you're even interested in me."

"Yes you do," Annabel said lightly.

"Well, I hoped," he said, and then they both laughed, giddy with their discovery of one another.

Lunch passed in a fog. They ordered without caring and ate about two bites of it. They held hands under the table, which Annabel had not done in years. As soon as they could decently pretend (for whom, the waiter? the patrons?) that they'd had a normal lunch date, they rushed off to Annabel's apartment. She didn't even bother to call the girls at the boutique. They would figure it out, and she would see them when she picked up Sweet Pea at closing time.

He was not only insatiable, but romantic and loving. He acted as though he had been waiting for her all his life, and although Annabel knew better, she liked pretending it was true. It was dark when they lay together, exhausted, and she waited for that little pang of sadness, but all she felt was contentment.

She glanced at the clock on the bedside table. "I have to go get my cat."

He wound her auburn hair around his fingers and then let it fan down in a shower of golden lights, like a magician doing his magic act; looking at it as if he were also the child watching the magician. "Can I see you tomorrow?"

"I have to work," Annabel said. "What about Sunday?"

"Lunch on Sunday?" he said.

"Perfect," she said. "Why don't I get some food and we'll have a picnic here."

They had three dates, if you could call them that. Three picnics where they ignored the food and went to bed to devour each other. He told Monica, who wanted a husband and children, that he wanted only to be free, to "find himself." And then he asked Annabel if he could stay with her while Monica was looking for her own apartment.

It took Annabel about two minutes to say yes. She had never been a person who worried about consequences until afterward. Dean was not what she had been looking for: he was too young, it was impossible that it could last. But she was interested in *him* now, not some unknown someone else. She knew she was falling in love with him, and that it was insane. Their relationship was mostly physical—not that he wasn't bright and talented and fun to talk to—but they had no shared history. Even when they read the Sunday *Times* together they would be looking for different things, seeing them through different eyes. But wasn't that often the way with people who weren't twenty years apart in age? She didn't want a soul mate any more, she just wanted to be with him. She liked that he was not like her, that they came from a different place in time. Whatever someone else might consider a flaw in their relationship she found interesting, a challenge. His extraordinary good looks still stunned her. That proved he wasn't a boring person, because you got used to beauty so quickly. Didn't you . . . ?

Chris, speaking of a person who had fallen in love with beauty, had stopped coming around the boutique, although she and Annabel still spoke on the phone almost every day. Finally Annabel had to make a lunch date with her in order to see her.

"Don't get shocked when you see how I look," Chris said on the phone.

"Shocked how?"

"I'm fat."

"You could never be fat."

"Well, I've gained quite a lot of weight since you saw me last. But I don't want you to talk to me about it, okay?"

"I won't say a word," Annabel said cheerfully. She couldn't imagine Chris, whom she'd known ever since they were eighteen, through frumpiness and chicness, as being anything but lean.

She was wrong. They met at Chatfield's, a little restaurant that looked like a country inn and specialized in plain grills and good salads, with a few mandatory substantial items included for men who made business lunch their main meal. Chris was already seated at their table, but even sitting down it was obvious how much she'd changed. *No wonder she's been avoiding the boutique,* Annabel thought. First of all, Chris was wearing a black muumuu. It billowed around her, making her look dumpy and matronly. But her face . . . it was her face that shocked Annabel, because it was puffy.

"I declare, Christine, you certainly have made yourself a stranger."

"You said you wouldn't talk about how awful I look," Chris said defensively.

"I said you've been acting like one, not looking like one. You can't be too busy at the office to spare a little time for me."

"I'm going through a difficult . . ." Chris said, and stopped, her eyes filling momentarily with tears.

The waiter came over and they both ordered white wine. Chris put ice in hers and began methodically to devour the entire contents of the basket of crusty peasant bread, slathering each slice with butter. Annabel pretended not to notice. "Tell me about it," Annabel said.

"It's too boring. Tell me about Dean."

"He's living with me at the moment. I'm very fond of him."

"Are you in love with him?"

"Maybe," Annabel said.

"You look like you're in love," Chris said. "God, you're so lucky—you always do exactly what you want."

"You could too, you know."

"No. I can't. I just eat."

The waiter came over to announce the specials. Grilled shrimp, and a pasta with porcini mushrooms, cream sauce, Gorgonzola cheese and walnuts. Annabel was on the verge of making a face at the richness of the latter when Chris ordered it.

"Chicken and vegetable salad," Annabel said. "And another glass of wine, Chris?"

"Not at lunch," Chris said. "I need my wits at the office. I'll have an iced tea."

"Two," Annabel said. She was relieved that only food and not alcohol too seemed to be Chris's problem. The bloated face, she decided, must be from too much salt.

"Is all this because of Alexander or Cameron?" Annabel asked when the waiter had left.

Chris wiped up the last of the dish of butter with the last bit of crust. "Oh, Cameron doesn't look at me in the same way anymore, and who could blame him? And Alexander hasn't looked at me in ages. My son, of course, thinks I'm a beast. He's ashamed of me. He nags me to go on a diet. Alexander says nothing, but I can imagine what he thinks."

"Are you ever sorry you didn't go to bed with Cameron?"

"I guess I am. After I ran away and started to stuff myself, I couldn't stop. I'm hungry all the time. I'm *starving.* And even when I'm full I can't stop because there's a little place inside of me, which I think used to be my heart, which is still starving."

"Maybe it's not your heart," Annabel said.

"Maybe not." They smiled at each other. "Do you remember how many years I waited for Alexander?"

"I do."

"I'm still waiting. I couldn't even handle the thought of an affair. I know I'm trying to make myself unappealing to Cameron so I won't have to make a decision."

"Well, you obviously don't need an analyst," Annabel said.

"An analyst would probably say that's just the top layer," Chris said. "Then there are layers and layers that make me obsessively in love and also so ambivalent."

"It sounds pretty simple to me," Annabel said.

Chris polished off all her pasta and ordered carrot cake. She demolished that, too, including the sugary icing, in quick, methodical bites that were without any pleasure at all. Annabel felt like grabbing the plate away from her, but what good would it do?

"One thing I'm still smart about though," Chris said. "I'm very good at my job. Cameron is still glad he hired me. He respects me as a colleague and a friend, so I have that. Do you know, he asked me once if I was all right? He thought I was sick. He thought all this . . . was some disease."

"Oh, Chris," Annabel said, wondering why Chris was so stubborn, and always had been. She remembered the time at college when she'd made Chris get out of bed and dressed her up to go to the Freshman Mixer, and how Chris had refused to have any fun at all and had left early. "I suppose Alexander is still claiming to be celibate."

"What do you mean, 'claiming'? I know he is. He's

home every night, works all day, and plays squash. That's all he does."

"Sounds unnatural to me," Annabel said. "I think you should have an affair with Cameron. *That* would be natural. And it would be a lot more fun than indigestion."

"I can't," Chris said. "I look too awful."

That night Annabel told Dean about her lunch with Chris, and he listened with the concentrated awe and pleasure of a child hearing a story. She realized that nothing in his life or experience so far had made him able to understand the complexities of how Chris really felt. Or her own concern and empathy either, for that matter. He believed in acting on his feelings, as she did, and trying not to hurt people too badly; but a person like Chris was a mystery to him.

"She's ruining her health," he said. "I thought you told me she was brilliant."

"She's one of the most intelligent people I've ever known," Annabel said.

"Then she doesn't care," he said. "I have friends like that."

"Where?"

"I haven't let you meet them."

Drugs, she thought. "Dean, do you have a secret life?" she asked him, half kidding and half wondering.

"No, but I have some friends you haven't met; people I knew before you, when I was young and silly. Don't you know people from before, who you wouldn't want me to see?"

"Lots," Annabel said cheerfully. "But I've forgotten them."

She was, however, to see the rejected Monica, since Dean's agent had gotten an art gallery to put together a showing of his work. There would be some originals of his magazine covers and ads, and also some new paintings. There would also be drinks, canapés, publicity, critics, and, hopefully, buyers. Dean had already, at his young age, sold a painting to a museum.

The party was at Glass II, the frisky new SoHo addition to the staid Glass Gallery on Madison Avenue. Annabel was very proud of Dean. Because of the rush hour lack of cabs and the honor of the occasion she had hired a limousine to take them there, wait, and then take them on to dinner. Limousines charged a two-hour minimum anyway, she said when Dean protested the expense. He actually felt comfortable on the subway. It was one of the things that made her conscious of his youth. And of course, other people would be conscious of it too, since much of the talk tonight would be about how amazing it was for an artist so young to have done so well. He could have hired his own limousine, if he had cared, or even thought of it.

Annabel was aware that she was twenty years older than he, but it didn't bother her. She knew the happiness she was feeling with him made her radiant. She dressed in black, her favorite and best color, which showed off her own bright coloring of auburn hair, creamy skin, and green eyes. She made Dean wear a dark suit. He deferred to her in many ways lately, which she found touching. When they entered the room she thought they made a splendid couple.

The gallery was just crowded enough to make the party a success, but not so crowded as to be uncomfortable. Annabel had been there with Dean the night before to see the pictures all hung, but even the second time she was struck with admiration for him. His agent, who looked like a gypsy fortune teller, was thrilled, and Annabel hoped she had the gift as well as the outfit. People kept coming over to meet him.

"This is Monica," Dean said. "Monica, Annabel."

So this tall, slim, sad-faced girl was Monica. She was wearing the shoulderbag he had given her before they parted, the present that had brought him to Annabel. She was sweet-looking but not very pretty; she had probably been comfortable to live with, devoted, a good friend. There were girls like her all over, having their hearts broken, thinking they weren't beautiful enough, wondering what they had done wrong. Annabel wanted to take her aside and tell her it wasn't her fault, that when she was young she'd been spectacularly beautiful, and all it had brought her was more men to break her heart. But of course she would do no such thing. Monica was not a "girl," she was a woman of twenty-six, and she wanted a grown-up life. So did Annabel. It was only Dean who did not. *I'm not your rival,* Annabel wanted to say; *the world is.* But knowing it was also true for herself, she simply smiled and shook hands.

Then more people came over to be introduced to

the guest of honor, and they were all three separated.
A pleasant-looking slim woman with blonde hair and
a green suit came over to Annabel and smiled.
"You're Annabel Jones, aren't you," she said. "You
don't know me. My husband pointed you out. He
recognized you. He used to go out with you at college."

"Oh?"

"I'm Ann Wood. You might remember him—he
was at Harvard Law School. Bill Wood?"

Remember him? Her fiancé, who had jilted her just
before the wedding? Used to go out with him? What
about slept together for a year? "Where is he?" Annabel asked, trying to sound casual.

"Oh, do come over and I'll reintroduce you," Ann
Wood said. "And thank you for not marrying him.
Because otherwise I wouldn't have met him, and
we've been very happy all these years."

Annabel was so dumbfounded she couldn't think of
an answer. You're welcome? Obviously this woman
thought Annabel could have caught him if she'd a
mind to; what in the world had Bill Wood been saying? Not much of the truth, she was sure of that.

She was led over to a tall, lined, gray-haired old
man. Only the eyes were the same, Bill Wood's eyes,
or she would never have recognized him at all.

"Well, I declare!" Annabel said cheerfully. "Bill
Wood! I always did think you would grow up to look
like Abraham Lincoln and you didn't disappoint me."

They shook hands. She could see from his eyes that
he was absolutely stunned with admiration, and she

wanted to kick him in the ankle. "You're looking wonderful, Annabel," he said, in that drawl that used to
remind her of Jimmy Stewart—oh, she was a great
one for making people famous—and now moved her
not at all.

"Thank you. And are you a judge? I always thought
you would be."

"Nope. Just an Indiana lawyer."

"A quite eminent one," his wife said. She smoothed
his lapel and Annabel noticed on her finger the very
same little diamond ring that Bill Wood had once
given to *her*. It had to be the same ring. She would
never forget it, and how proud of it she'd been, letting no opportunity pass to show it off. The little diamond engagement ring she'd dropped in his martini
after he ditched her at the airport. *Good-bye, Bill.
Have a nice life.*

"And are you having a nice life?" Annabel asked.

"A very nice life," he said. "And you?"

"Excellent."

"I'm pleased. Ann has an art gallery back home.
That's why we're here. We travel quite a lot, looking
for paintings. It's interesting for me, having that in
addition to the law."

Bill Wood, with the life he'd wanted, living it happily without her. Annabel had often wondered what
he would be like now, and here he was, and he moved
her not at all. He looked so old! He carried himself
like an old man. But he wasn't that old; only forty-
eight or so. It was just that she'd always remembered
him the way he had been twenty-five years ago. She

didn't look the same either. But she looked better. She tried to remember if he had been amusing or interesting and realized he had not. He had been an intellectual, an idol, an image: The Serious Lawyer. She had wanted to bring fun and humor into his life, as he would bring stability and honor to hers. If he had married her, perhaps she would be the one standing here now smoothing his lapel, saying how eminent he was.

"And what brings *you* to this opening?" Bill Wood asked, by way of conversation, since she looked like his idea of a sophisticated New York woman who went everywhere.

Annabel smiled sweetly. "I live with Dean Henry," she said.

Bill Wood's mouth dropped open. His wife looked at Annabel with something approaching awe. Twenty-five years later, women like her were no longer The Harvard Whore.

Thank you, Bill, Annabel thought. *You always gave me a great exit line.*

Chapter Nine

CHRIS, TAKING A bath, cursed the day she had put a mirrored wall into the bathroom to make it look large and luxurious. Her image—distorted, soft, with obscene rolls and lumps of dimpled fat—mocked her in those mirrors now, and she avoided looking at her ugly naked body. She had filled the tub with bubble bath so she would not have to look at herself through the water either. She was not simply stout, which might have been all right, but she was like someone who had been force-fed, some diseased Strasbourg goose, and she had been the one who had force-fed herself. The food looked as if it had not even been digested yet but was simply hiding under her skin, bite upon bite, like a monstrous impressionist sculpture of a fat woman. She hated herself for having done this, but she could not stop.

Her scale had been relegated to the back of her

closet because she never weighed herself anymore. Her Thin Clothes, the ones from her other life, were in another closet, and the closet in her bedroom held her Fat Clothes, the shapeless tents she had bought to cover this new body. They were always black, for she was in mourning for the person she used to be, and because black was said to make you look thinner. She bought a great many handbags lately—in fact, she might be said to be obsessed with handbags—because handbags didn't have to fit. Everything else did, even shoes.

She also bought lovely things for her handbags: wallets and makeup cases and pens and appointment books. She was neat and organized. She was also clean. Her house was clean, her face and body and hair and clothes were clean. Her stomach was always distended, and she thought whatever was inside it (and there always was a great deal inside it; she felt as though she never digested fully before she was stuffing herself again) was filthy. She often thought of stopping this madness, of going on a diet, but the resolution never lasted even for a day.

Tonight Alexander was playing squash after work, which he did twice a week lately. His physical fitness made her inactivity and appearance seem even worse. He would come home at eight, and then they would have dinner. He played squash and she took a bath. To each his own form of relaxation.

Out of the tub she dried herself quickly, avoiding the mirrors. Body lotion, scented powder, a touch of perfume, some makeup. Her at-home muumuu, one of a large new collection. She wanted everything to be nice, even though it wasn't.

"Hello! Where are you?" Alexander called out the same thing he always did. He wanted everything to be nice too, even though it wasn't.

"I'm here." A glass of wine in the den, and then dinner, a normal dinner with normal food and conversation, Chris eating little, making sure she ate less than he did, as if she were fooling anybody.

Nicholas emerged from his room in time for dinner. He had changed from his school clothes to jeans and a sweatshirt, and Chris noticed that although she had bought them for him only a few months ago, he was already growing too tall for them. He looked like a combination of her and Alexander; the best of both of them. Alexander's intense, dark eyes and Heathcliff face, her own warmth and humor. Alexander's handsomeness had always been unique, so spectacular that it seemed almost a tragic beauty; with always something withheld, mysterious; but Nicholas's teenaged good looks were more accessible, friendlier; he smiled easily and had ready laughter in him. The laughter she used to have. . . . Naturally he was very popular.

They had decided to spend Thanksgiving weekend in the country. Nicholas was not going to be there; he was going to Disney World in Florida with a friend from school and the friend's parents. It was the first time he was not spending Thanksgiving with her and Alexander, and Chris wondered if it was the normal process of growing up or if he was anxious to be away from the sight of her. She did not intend to mention this.

"I must tell you, Nicholas," Alexander said, "that your mother and I are a little offended to be rejected this Thanksgiving for Mickey Mouse and Goofy."

"*And* Minnie Mouse," Nicholas said, grinning.

"Well, we'll miss you," Alexander said. "Not that I want you to be overwhelmed with guilt and have a miserable time, but I just thought I'd say so."

"Thanks, Dad."

"And you know you can invite your friends to the country," Alexander said. "Remember when you were young and always had kids up?"

Nicholas nodded. "It was great then, but . . . I'm too old to run through leaves."

Alexander laughed. "When you're older and less jaded you'll like it again." He turned to Chris. "The house won't be too empty though. I've invited the banker I play squash with to come to the country for Thanksgiving and bring a date. You'll like him, I think."

"What's his name?"

"James Riss the Third. But he's not as stuffy as that sounds. Although he insists on being called James, not Jim."

"You insist on being called Alexander, not Alex," Chris said. "And you're not stuffy."

Alexander smiled. "Well, thank you. Although sometimes I think I am."

"What about his date; separate rooms or together?"

"I don't know how well he knows her. How about separate rooms and let them sneak across the hall."

"Fine," Chris said.

Nicholas looked amused, obviously storing away the antics of grownups for future blackmail when *he* was old enough to bring home a date.

It was an ordinary family dinner. But no, it was not an ordinary family dinner, because as always lately, there was the thing that totally possessed her: the food.

Dessert was a plain cake. Alexander did not eat it, saying he was full. Chris, therefore, did not eat any either. Nicholas had one piece, as always. He was slim and active, and had never been obsessed with sweets. As soon as dinner was over he went to his room to do his homework, and Alexander and Chris went to the den to do some work from their offices before going to bed. Mrs. Gormley cleaned up the kitchen and went home.

It was a normal evening. But no, it was not a normal evening. Chris thought about the cake that was left over, she thought about nothing else. Not Alexander and how much she loved him; that was too painful. Not the work from the office, although she tried. Not even the pleasant Thanksgiving weekend and what she should serve with the turkey; that was too far away. The cake was right in the next room, and she could taste it and feel it against her tongue.

She and Alexander watched the eleven o'clock news in bed, and he was asleep before it was over. He had forgotten even to kiss her goodnight. He always came home from the Athletic Club exhausted, freshly showered and virtuous from his hour of frantic physical activity. She suspected that it was his sublimation, just as she had hers, but his was constructive and hers was bad.

Bad . . .

She turned off the television set and lay there in the dark sleeplessly, thinking about that cake. She wanted to roll over and lie against Alexander's back, put her arms around him for comfort, smell his skin, coordinate her breathing to his until she, too, fell asleep. But he had taken to wearing pajamas now, as she had begun to cover herself with nightgowns, and she felt if she pressed her body to his it would be an intrusion. He was as kind and sweet as ever, but no longer physical at all. He patted her and kissed her, but as if she were a beloved relative or best friend, not his wife. And she had to be careful about the way she touched or kissed him, to be sure it didn't seem like a sexual invitation and therefore a reproach. Besides, if she put her arms around him now she might disturb him and wake him up.

She got out of bed quietly and went into the kitchen.

The cake was put away in its white box, tied with white string. Chris cut a large slice and ate it out of her hands, standing up over the sink to catch the crumbs. Then she washed her hands and rinsed the crumbs down the drain, closed the cake box, and tied it again neatly as if no one had touched it at all. As soon as she had, she opened it again. Her hands were shaking with impatience and desire. *No*, she thought. She closed it, and threw the whole box of cake into the garbage, there with the crumpled damp paper towels, the empty soda cans, the remains of Nicholas's bedtime snack. She went back to bed.

She couldn't sleep. She watched the green numbers leap and change on the digital clock beside her and wondered what Cameron was doing. Sleeping beside his young, pretty wife, of course, as he probably always would. That was never the issue. But he had desired *her* once, and she had wanted him. Chris wondered what would be happening now if she had said yes. Then she got up again and went into the kitchen to get at the cake.

She took it out of the garbage and she ate it all, the whole thing, sitting at the kitchen table, methodically slicing off hunks and jamming them into her mouth. She didn't even bother to put it on a plate, just devoured it right out of the food-stained box on the theory that she would stop before it was gone. But then it *was* gone, and she went out into the service hall and threw the empty box into the incinerator so no one would know.

Then she brushed and flossed her teeth carefully, as she always did, and went to sleep. Alexander had never noticed she had left.

As Thanksgiving approached it seemed pointless to start a diet, because the Thanksgiving feast in the middle of a diet would be so demoralizing. Perhaps afterward . . . She was always making these good resolutions, and she realized now that she had no intention of doing anything about them. She hoped James Riss the Third, and his no doubt slender date, would not wonder what in the world Alexander saw in her.

She and Alexander went up to the country the night before, to be sure everything was ready for guests. Chris was going to do the cooking herself. That morning, in the crisp autumn air, she and Alexander went to buy firewood together, and flowers, and then the food, comfortable and happy in each other's company as they hadn't been for a long time. It was doing things, she realized, that saved them. Activities, plans; the fabric of their marriage. They were loving companions, but that was not enough and never would be, for her at least. Yet it was better than some other marriages. She would try not to think about it.

Their guests arrived on Thanksgiving morning. There was a fire in the fireplace, and Alexander had mixed a pitcher of Bloody Marys. Chris had put fresh flowers in their bedrooms and all over the house, piles of new books and magazines lay beside comfortable chairs, and the delicious smells of holiday food emanated from the kitchen. The young woman was named Kimberly, Kim for short, and she was one of those Muffy Buffy whitebread girls. She was even wearing penny loafers. She had that accent Chris remembered from Daphne the Golden Girl at college, but she wasn't nearly as attractive as Daphne had been. James, the squash partner, was cute, and just saved from being whitebread by something Chris couldn't put her finger on. She decided she liked him.

As soon as the couple had deposited their overnight bags in their respective rooms, they came down and everyone had drinks together. Then Alexander showed them around the grounds while Chris attended to the dinner. James came into the kitchen after a while to ask if he could help with anything.

"No," Chris said, "but you can sit there and talk to me."

He seemed quite pleased to do that. He seemed anxious that she like him, and she found it appealing. He was only thirty-one, but he said Alexander was a good squash player and the age difference didn't matter. He was relatively new at the firm, having been there nearly a year, and he told her how hard it had been to find his Sutton Place apartment, which was a sublet in a co-op and cost a great deal more than he had wanted to spend. Alexander came in after a while and opened a bottle of champagne.

"Where's Kim?" James said.

"Running."

"Oh God," Chris said.

James cast her an innocent, curious look. "Is there something wrong?"

"No," Chris said. "It's just the thought of all that energy."

"I know," he said, and smiled at her. Alexander handed him a glass of champagne and they looked at each other, James and Alexander, and James smiled his thanks, and suddenly she knew. Her heart felt like an icy stone and she stood there staring at them for what seemed like a long time but she knew it was just an instant, just as the look that had passed between the two men had been only an instant—but she knew.

James and Alexander.

It was a look of love, on the face of the man she loved who claimed he loved only her, and he was bestowing it and everything it meant on someone else. Alexander and James. She wondered if they even played squash at all.

The rest of the day passed in a mist of shock. Chris managed to get the dinner on the table, not burned, and made conversation. She drank more champagne than usual but did not get drunk. She ate almost nothing, not because she was pretending but because she thought if she ate she would gag. She remembered that other November, so long ago now, in Paris, when she had finally found out that Alexander was gay, and she wondered if the Thanksgiving season was destined to be for her a time of horrible revelations. All she knew was that she would manage to get through this weekend somehow, and on Monday, which was "squash night," she would go to James's apartment building and hide outside and wait to see.

Perhaps it was bizarre to spy on them. Another woman might simply have confronted her husband and asked. But Chris knew Alexander too well to do that. He had said he was no longer interested in sex with anyone. He had not said he was in love. She knew she could have weathered the discovery that he was cheating, because she was used to it and had accepted it, but love was different. It had never occurred to her that he could fall in love with someone else . . . with a man. She could survive anything, but she didn't know if she could survive his being in love.

Who was this obese, middle-aged woman hiding in the shadows, at five forty-five of an autumn evening, staring at the house across the street? It was she, Chris; still young, still slim, still desperately in love. Nothing had changed. Only exteriors changed, but her heart remained the same. She remembered how years ago, when she was first pining after Alexander, Max had tried to tell her she was too young to throw her life away, and she wondered what he would say to her if he were still alive. That she was too old to behave like a fool? All of that was nonsense. She had never gone along with the herd, and she never would. It was cold, and she was shivering, more from emotion than chill. She waited . . .

A cab pulled up to James's building, and James and Alexander got out. The doorman nodded at them familiarly. And when the doorman turned away again towards the street, so they were unobserved except by her, Alexander looked at James with that look of love that broke Chris's heart. Then the two of them disappeared into the lobby.

She stood there for an hour and a half, waiting and remembering when it was she whom he loved. That drab room where Alexander lived at college, and that night when at long last he invited her there . . . her-

self standing looking at the photos on the wall, and
Alexander coming up behind her and kissing her on
the back of the neck, a gesture she found so sexy and
romantic she could hardly breathe . . . and then he
turned her around and kissed her on the mouth for
the first time . . . that miracle that ended with the
two of them in bed together, and then finally . . .
no, not finally their lives together. Never a happy
ending. Only the hope of one, the period of bliss and
trusting, and then the betrayal. Betrayal yes, but
never the ultimate one of being in love. Chris held
her breath and prayed to die.

Finally Alexander came out alone. The doorman
hailed a cab for him and he disappeared on his way
back to his happy home where he expected her to be
waiting. Chris walked to the next block and found a
taxi and went home too.

She walked into their apartment silently, no cheerful call of hello. Alexander was in the den pouring
himself a glass of wine, acting as if nothing had happened.

"How was your game?" she asked.

"Great."

I'll bet, she thought.

"And who won?"

"He did." Alexander poured her a glass of wine.
"He always wins."

"Does he?" Chris said. "Does he always win? Is he
going to win this time?"

He stood there looking at her, still holding the glass
of wine she had refused to take, and then he put it

down on the bar very carefully. "What do you mean, Chris?"

"What you think I mean. I know about you and James."

She watched his face change almost imperceptibly, as if he wanted to lie and then changed his mind. "How did you find out?" he asked, finally.

"Do you mean are people talking? Do you mean you might be *caught?* You don't have to worry, Alexander. Nobody knows but me. I only want to know whether I still count."

"Oh my God, Chris." Alexander's face was ashen. He drank his wine in one long gulp as if it were water. Then he looked at her with such open terror that she began to be afraid, not for herself but for him. "I've ruined everybody I ever loved. I ruined your life, all these years. I ruined Max's life—he *died* because of me. Don't you understand, if I hadn't cheated on Max, made his life so unbearable that he couldn't stay with me anymore, he wouldn't have been living the life he did. He wouldn't have gone to that bar, he wouldn't have taken that psycho home with him, he wouldn't have been killed. He would have been home with me. I killed Max. Don't you realize I've always known that? And you . . . look at you. Look what I've done to you."

"I don't look in mirrors much anymore," Chris said.

"And I ruined my own life," Alexander said. "The one person I didn't love."

Chris felt the chill and began to shiver again. "And what about James?" she asked.

"I love him," Alexander said, very softly. "I don't know what to do about it. Maybe he'll ditch me. He's younger than I am, he'll get tired of me. That's all I hope—that he'll want to get rid of me—because I can't . . ."

The chill had entered her body and mind completely now. It was not like the old days when she had been sick with conflicting emotions, wanting to throw up, wanting to cry, alternately angry and melting. All the old anger was long gone. The knowledge that Alexander would always be the center of her life was still there, and she could do nothing about it. "I suppose I'm to wait," she said coldly, knowing she would.

Alexander's eyes filled with tears. "I love you," he said. "You're my life . . . my life. You're my love and my best friend. I love our son, you know I do. I'll never leave you. Please don't leave me. You *should* leave me, you should escape. I don't deserve you. But please don't go."

"You want me to wait until he falls out of love with you. You never said 'until *I* fall out of love with *him.*' Does that mean you think you'll love him for all eternity?"

"What a terrible thought," Alexander said.

"Yes," Chris said. "Isn't it."

And so, in the end, it was not resolved. They sat through dinner for Nicholas's sake, although he knew everything was wrong. Again, Chris could hardly eat. And even while she was mourning what was happening to her marriage, a thought started coming up in the back of her mind. Her magazine had often run articles by that famous diet doctor . . . what was his name? Dr. Michael Fields. He was right here in New York. He believed in sound nutrition and no drugs or pills. He was said to be kind, sensible, and supportive. She would call his office tomorrow and make an appointment.

Maybe when she was back to her old self she would have an affair with Cameron; maybe not. But one thing she knew now: she was through being a coward. She loved Alexander and she would never leave him. But she was going to go on a real diet and she was going to succeed at it.

And then she was going to have a life of her own.

Chapter Ten

IT WAS ALMOST four months since Jonathan had hanged himself; four months of denial, realization, anger and grief. Daphne did not know which was worse, the times when the other boys were away at school so she could pretend they were all away, or when they came home and she knew that now and forever more there were only three. No, not "forever more." She could never believe in her safe little world again, that world where children grew up and did not die.

Richard didn't want to discuss it anymore. He wanted to forget, to hide. Her friends pretended nothing had happened, never asked her how she was feeling, never talked about the disaster, because they felt uncomfortable and were afraid to cause her any more pain. No one knew how to treat her. She didn't even know how to treat herself.

There were other teenage suicides that winter, and someone wrote a feature article for the Sunday *Times* about children from affluent, suburban families who inexplicably chose to end their lives. Some of them had been withdrawn, depressed: Jonathan had not. Others had been seeing therapists: Jonathan had never seemed to need to. A few had been upset over broken romances: not Jonathan, who was popular but not in love. And there were even the ones who had seemed perfectly normal, like Jonathan. His name was in the article even though she had refused to talk to the reporter. He had spoken to people who knew Jonathan at school, who were willing to tell everything they could remember. Her son had become an anecdote.

The article upset Richard a great deal. He seemed ashamed, which was typical. Daphne read it with the eye of a detective, trying to find some clue to solve the mystery of her loss. But there were no answers. And that was perhaps the worst thing, to have someone you loved kill himself without ever giving any reason, so that for the rest of your life you could only wonder why.

At night she dreamed about Jonathan, and sometimes about her other children. Often now she dreamed about Elizabeth. Sometimes Jonathan and Elizabeth were the same age—not their real ages, but both of them about three. They would be running away from her in the woods, in a park, a playground; running into some unknown danger that paralyzed her with fear while she shouted after them in a voice that refused to come out of her throat. She would awaken with hot tears pouring down her face . . . she had no idea tears could be so scaldingly hot. And one morning, while she was lying in bed trying to compose herself so that she could go downstairs and face the world, Daphne heard a voice inside her head, probably her own voice, and it said: *Children are not disposable.*

It was then she knew she wanted Elizabeth back.

She had started to visit Elizabeth more often; twice a week instead of twice a month. Richard was absorbed with work and spending more evenings in the city. Daphne didn't have to rush back to an empty house nor invent excuses. She knew she had to tell him eventually, but she wasn't sure how. And as if it were part of some giant conspiracy to thwart her loving instincts, the home was reluctant to give Elizabeth up.

Her own child! Jane Baldwin, Elizabeth's cottage mother, acted as if Elizabeth were *hers.* "She's happy here," Jane said. "She doesn't really know you. This is a big responsibility. You have no experience with these children. She's not as easy as she seems."

"I'm her mother," Daphne said.

"She doesn't know that. She's been here all her life —this is her home."

"Are you telling me I can't have my own child?" Daphne said, holding in the outrage and anger, acting cool and well-bred as always, a woman who knew she would win.

"Of course I'm not," Jane said. "I'm only warning

you. Start with a day trip, a visit. See how it goes. Don't just uproot her. That would be cruel to any child."

"If it's so cruel, why do children always want to be adopted?" Daphne said. There was a long silence. "I'm taking her home for Christmas," she said.

"That would be nice," Jane said. "Christmas is fun."

"I hope it will be," Daphne said mildly. She did not add that Christmas was only going to be the beginning of Elizabeth's new family life, and her own.

Richard was horrified. He thought Daphne had lost her mind from grief. He had never seen Elizabeth since she was an infant, and Daphne wondered if perhaps he would not be impressed with her progress at all, but only shocked at where she was now. It didn't matter. Daphne was firm, adamant, unmoved by all his pleading and logic, and even, finally, his thinly disguised threat.

"This family can't take any more stress," he said.

"It's only for Christmas," Daphne lied. "Christmas is going to be so painful . . . this will be a distraction . . . like having a baby around. She's so sweet, Richard. You'll like her. You will."

"And if I do say no, you'll bring her here anyway, won't you," he said.

"How could you say no?" Daphne said gently, as if he were so good, kind, and loving that it was unthinkable.

"I think I'll spend the Christmas holidays drunk," Richard said. Daphne threw her arms around him and kissed him. She knew it was as close as he could get to saying yes.

She spent the next week in busy preparations, making Elizabeth's old room into a haven for a little girl. She hoped Elizabeth would not be frightened sleeping alone.

"Why are you making such a big fuss if she's just coming for a visit?" Teddy asked, passing by the room one day and glancing in. The boys were home for the holidays now. They were used to having four friends at a time all sleeping on their bedroom floors in sleeping bags.

"I thought it would be a nice thing to do," Daphne said.

She had prepared them, but she didn't think they really understood. The imminent arrival of a sister they could barely remember, who was "different" and would need special patience, was not of great interest to them. They had their social lives, and there was the tree to choose and decorate, the presents to buy. Daphne decided to bring Elizabeth home on Christmas Eve, when the giant tree was glittering with ornaments and tinsel, the holly strung up the stairs, the whole house looking like a wonderland. And also, because she was aware there would be problems with a baby in the house, she wanted the boys to be able to trim the tree alone together with her and Richard the way they always did, to have something traditional to cling to, because they would be missing Jonathan particularly during this season of alleged joy. She wanted Elizabeth to be a holiday visitor, not a distraction, and then gradually fit into the family.

Elizabeth was waiting docilely for her at the home, the little suitcase Daphne had bought her all packed. She was holding her favorite doll, but Daphne had brought a large shopping bag and put all her other dolls into it too. "I want her to feel comfortable," she said in answer to Jane's questioning glance.

"That was thoughtful," Jane said. "Be a good girl, Elizabeth. Have a nice time with your mother."

"Good-bye," Elizabeth said pleasantly, and climbed into the car.

That evening, which had given her some qualms, went as well as Daphne had hoped. Even though Richard waited until the last possible moment to make his appearance, he behaved—if not like a father —like a gentleman. Elizabeth loved the Christmas tree, the packages piled under it, and the holiday music. Daphne unpacked her suitcase and arranged her dolls on top of the dresser. Elizabeth even seemed to like her pretty new room. At dinner she fed herself, spooning up the pieces of food Daphne had cut for her, drinking neatly from her cup of milk. She seemed to think she was at a party, and since it was Christmas Eve and her welcome home dinner, why not? Although Richard drank quite a lot he did not get drunk as he had threatened.

When dinner was finished Elizabeth yawned. "Home," she said.

"Yes, you're home," Daphne answered, and hugged her.

"No," Elizabeth said. "Out—car."

"You're going to sleep here tonight," Daphne said. "In your pretty room. And tomorrow we're going to open our presents. You're going to get all sorts of presents."

Elizabeth looked at her, thinking. "Okey dokey," she said.

Day one, Daphne thought.

But day two did not work the same way. Elizabeth looked at her new toys, watched some television, and then she wanted to leave again. "For God's sake, Daphne," Richard said, annoyed, scowling at last.

Elizabeth scowled, looking just like him. Daphne laughed. Then they had Christmas dinner and Elizabeth put her hands into the food instead of using her spoon. "Don't do that, darling," Daphne said, trying to help her. But Elizabeth pushed Daphne's hand away and began to smear her mashed sweet potatoes into the lace tablecloth. This time Daphne did not laugh. "No," she said firmly. Elizabeth deliberately knocked over her cup of milk.

"She's a savage," Richard said angrily. "I told you it wouldn't work."

"She's just upset," Daphne said.

"Well, I'm upset too," he said, tossing down his napkin and getting up from the table.

"Richard, don't . . ."

Elizabeth reached out her hand and patted Daphne's arm. "No," she said in a consoling tone. She looked at Richard. "No fight."

Daphne's heart broke. She looked at her sons, who

were looking as if their sister were an intransigent pet, and at Richard, who was ready to leave the room. "She's right," she said. "Please let's not fight."

"All right," he said. "Because it's Christmas."

That night Elizabeth did not want to go to bed. Daphne realized she was homesick, and wondered if she should sleep in the room with the child. But Richard would be furious. She didn't dare. She held her daughter in her arms and rocked her, crooning to her. "You'll get used to us. You'll like it here, I promise. I love you. We all love you." Finally, when Elizabeth fell asleep, Daphne went back downstairs. Richard was sitting in front of the fireplace, looking at the fire, a bottle of brandy beside him, a glass in his hand.

"Is she really staying for the whole Christmas holiday?" he asked.

"That's what we planned," Daphne said. The fact that it was longer than he had planned, and much less than she was planning, remained unsaid.

"But not after New Year's, when we go skiing?"

"It's still the holiday. We'll take her with us."

"Daphne, are you crazy?"

"I'll take care of her. And during the day, when we're on the slopes, I'll put her into the beginners' group."

"What about at night?" he asked, his voice tight. "When we go to restaurants."

"She'll be good by then. She knows how to behave like a little lady, you saw that last night. Tonight she was tired and cranky. You know how babies are."

"Daphne, she's not a baby! She's almost ten years old."

Daphne was thankful that she'd been on her medication ever since her seizure after Jonathan's death. She would be strong and healthy and work this thing out. "Please, Richard, let's not talk about it just now, all right?"

He looked at her for a long moment, and Daphne realized he was thinking about her seizure too, realizing what stress could do to her, not knowing she was safer than he thought. She let him remain concerned, knowing it would help her achieve her victory. "All right," he said quietly, and poured her a glass of brandy.

They sat there together, gazing at the fire, sipping their drinks, walking the fragile tightrope of conciliation . . . perhaps because they loved each other, perhaps because they had been part of each other's lives for so long . . . perhaps because it was Christmas.

The next morning when they went downstairs for breakfast Elizabeth was sitting beside the front door, all dressed, her dolls and messily packed suitcase beside her.

"Home," Elizabeth said.

"She's just like E.T.," Matthew said, laughing, coming in from the kitchen.

"You stop that!" Daphne said.

"Well, she's been there for hours, going 'Hoome . . . hoome.'" He shrugged, disappointed that his joke was unappreciated.

"This is your home, sweetheart," Daphne said gently. She took the suitcase. "Let's put this back in your room and have some breakfast."

"No."

Finally Daphne tricked her by leaving the suitcase by the door and taking Elizabeth into the kitchen, and while Elizabeth was eating, under the watchful eyes of their cook, Ina, Daphne sneaked the suitcase and dolls upstairs, unpacked Elizabeth's clothes, tried to start all over again. In the kitchen she realized that Elizabeth had eaten everything with her fingers, and what was worse, had smeared jam and oatmeal on the walls.

"Ina!"

"I couldn't stop her, Mrs. Caldwell. I told her no, but that made her do it more. I was afraid to grab her —I thought you'd mind. It's only washable wallpaper and tiles."

"Next time you grab her," Daphne said. "But not hard. Just so she knows we don't want that kind of behavior." She turned to Elizabeth. "Elizabeth, you don't do that at . . ." She sighed, and continued. "At home, so I don't want you to do it here. All right?"

Elizabeth sulked and refused to look at her.

"It will take her a while to get used to things," Daphne said.

But everything only got worse. Every morning when the family came downstairs, Elizabeth was already sitting beside the front door, her suitcase packed, her dolls by her side. She was so awkward that Daphne realized it must have taken her a long time to do all this, go up and down the stairs, bring the dolls one by one, then the suitcase. She must have slept very little. Jane Baldwin had been right; Elizabeth was stubborn. But she would get used to them, grow to love them . . . she had to. They were her family. Before, when Daphne had visited her, Elizabeth had been so cheerful and sweet. Now she never smiled anymore, and hardly spoke at all. Daphne didn't know what to do. She tried closing Elizabeth's bedroom door firmly, but Elizabeth managed to get out, and that night for the first time she soiled herself.

"Oh, no," Daphne cried, annoyed and guilty. Was this a sort of punishment for being shut in, or a regression? All she knew was that saying no was absolutely the wrong thing to do. Once that "No" had escaped her, it was as if she had said "Do it more."

Elizabeth was no longer toilet trained. Daphne had to keep her in diapers. She seemed to have forgotten everything she had ever learned, and did whatever she could to annoy everyone. Richard stayed away from the house as much as he could. He spent a lot of time with the boys, taking them places, when he wasn't working. Daphne knew he was counting the days. Only kind-hearted Ina kept making excuses for Elizabeth along with Daphne, for which Daphne considered herself blessed, because any other cook would probably have threatened to quit over the mess. The only one of the boys who paid any attention to Elizabeth now was Teddy. Sometimes Daphne saw him watching her closely, as if she were some sort of curiosity. He also played with her, and Elizabeth seemed to like him. In fact, Teddy seemed to like her, too.

Jane Baldwin called. "How is Elizabeth getting along?"

"Fine," Daphne lied.

"I hadn't heard from you, so I wondered. When are you bringing her back?"

"Well," Daphne said cheerfully, "we're going skiing for a week right after New Year's. We're going to take her with us."

"She'll enjoy that," Jane said. "She likes to play in the snow because she knows snow. But don't take her on the ski lift. She'll be terrified of open spaces."

That woman must think I'm an idiot, Daphne thought. "They don't let little children on the ski lift," she said. "It's too dangerous."

"Well, then, I'll see you when you get back. You're really lucky there haven't been any problems."

"I know," Daphne said.

Chapter Eleven

JANUARY, 1983

I'm beginning to think that if anybody finds this
secret journal there is going to be real trouble in
this house. Not that there isn't already. Ever since
my sister Elizabeth came here things have been
very strained. It's strange to think that she's my
sister, because I don't know her. I guess it's sort of
like somebody bringing home an orphan from
Vietnam and saying "Here's your new relative."
Then you all get used to it together. But Elizabeth
doesn't want to be here, and my father doesn't
want her here, and she IS my long lost sister. The
whole thing seems upside down.

It's sad because she can't tell anybody how she
feels. Nobody in this family is allowed to express his
real feelings, and Elizabeth doesn't know how.

Also, I noticed that even though she sulks, she never cries. We never cry either, because my father doesn't like it. It's a strange coincidence that we do the same thing for different reasons. I don't know why she doesn't cry. The truth is, she's pretty devious and not as dumb as everybody thinks. The minute you tell her not to do something she realizes you don't like it, and then she does it even more on purpose to annoy you. Her table manners are horrible, and she messes up everything, and she's not toilet trained anymore, which is really gross. Living with Elizabeth is like living in "Animal House," which was my favorite movie after "E.T.," but I wouldn't want to live there. I know she does all this so my parents will send her back, because that's where she really wants to be. I feel sorry for her, because my mother is pretending she's a little baby and that she can replace Jonathan. Nobody can replace Jonathan, ever, so what's the point?

New Year's Eve everybody went to parties except me (and Elizabeth, of course). I was supposed to go to my friend Mike's party, but then his mother found some joints in his underwear drawer and his parents canceled the party. Mike has been drinking and smoking dope since we were all eleven. I don't know what took them so long to figure out why their son was so spaced out all the time. We wanted to have another party somewhere else but nobody could get any plans together. Also, everybody's parents started to be really nosy and strict, and suspicious of all of us, even mine. I am only thirteen years old and have my whole life ahead of me, and I never do drugs and I hate liquor, but anyway there was no New Year's Eve party. Sometimes I get really depressed about the injustice of my existence.

So there I was alone at home with Elizabeth and the baby-sitter, which was Ina actually, since no one else wants to baby-sit for us anymore. It turned out to be a good experience, because I had a lot of time to be with Elizabeth alone. I always keep looking at her, trying to figure out what's in her head, and I ask her, but she can't tell me. So that night I sat down with her and stared into her eyes and she stared back, and I tried to get on to some other sphere, like a psychic thing, and read her mind. She just thought it was a game. She's an excellent mimic, so what I did she did. I kept thinking there was more in there than we knew, and if she couldn't get it out then I would go in and find it.

It didn't work. I felt very close to her, and I even loved her, but I didn't find out any secrets. Maybe there aren't any. Maybe she's just what she seems. She's telling us what she wants the best way she knows how, and we're the stupid ones.

I miss Jonathan all the time. While he was still alive I should have thought of trying to get inside his head. Maybe then I could have stopped him. Nobody in this family EVER talks about him anymore. His birthday is coming up soon. He would have been fifteen. I guess nobody will mention it. I would like to go out to the cemetery and put some flowers on his grave, but we're all going to be away skiing.

Chapter Twelve

EMILY, SITTING IN her friend's chalet in Vail, watching the snow fall prettily outside her window, thought how strange it was that she was here. Who would have expected it? She didn't even know how to ski. But then, who would have expected all the other strange things that had happened to her in the past few months? The night she fled from Ken's madness —and his gun—she went to Peter's apartment. She stayed only two days. Ken was phoning everybody, trying to find her, saying he wanted to make up. Emily was terrified. Of course he called Peter, and she made Peter lie and say he didn't know where she was. But she was such a creature of habit; her volunteer work, her tennis group, that it was only a matter of time until Ken would track her down, unless she became a recluse. She had tried to protect him from scandal and he was calling all her friends, saying she had left him. He implied it was her fault, that she'd had a tantrum. She finally had to tell a few best friends the truth, and swore them to secrecy.

Her friends rallied around her. Karen lent Emily her beach house at Malibu, since it was no longer beach weather and the house stood empty. Karen and Sue practically dragged Emily to her former home, when Ken was at the hospital, to pick up some clothes and her credit cards. "You're still married to him," they told her. "He has to pay the bills. And if you get divorced it's community property here in California, you know. He'll try to make up and get you back, just wait and see."

Why didn't any of them say Ken loved her? She supposed they didn't think she was dumb enough to believe such a thing after what he'd done.

But when she finally called Ken, from a public telephone in a restaurant because she was so scared of him she was getting paranoid, he was very sweet, just the way he used to be before all this happened. He asked her if she'd been to see a lawyer. No, she said, and had he? No, he didn't want a divorce. He wanted her to come home and try again. He would get off the coke, but he needed her to help him. Her friends had been right, but Emily didn't want to go home. She told him she would keep in touch but that she needed some time alone to think.

Who would believe she would turn out to be so brave? No, not brave . . . frightened. But she had Dr. Page, and she had her friends. Dr. Page convinced her to go back to her volunteer work, that Ken wouldn't confront her at Children's Hospital and make a scene. She gave Emily an extra hour of analysis every week during this crisis.

And then winter came, and the storms and high tides. People watched their oceanfront homes floating out to sea on television, million-dollar piles of wreckage. The roads were blocked and flooded. Emily had to move back to Los Angeles, renting a furnished security apartment near Beverly Hills. She called Ken once in a while, only to keep him at bay, and they had civilized conversations. During the holidays she went to her friends' parties, and he went wherever he always did when he wasn't with her. She tried not to think about it, because now it not only made her sick but very angry. Dr. Page said the anger was good, a sign Emily was giving up her ingrained role of victim trying to please.

Sue and her husband had a condominium in Vail, this pseudo Tyrolean chateau where Emily now sat in splendor. After New Year's Sue and Karen and another friend, Linda, all decided that it would be fun to get away from their husbands for a few days and go to Vail to ski and relax, just "the girls." It didn't matter that Emily couldn't ski—she certainly needed a vacation. So here she was, happy and grateful, in this beautiful place that looked like instant Switzerland, surrounded by gorgeous snow-covered mountains, smelling of wood smoke, full of rich people and celebrities and snow bunnies. During the day she walked around and looked at everything, breathed the fresh air, window-shopped. She was afraid to use her credit card, for which Ken paid the bill, for anything as frivolous as shopping. Food and shelter were another matter. At night she had dinner in restaurants with her friends. They knew so many people; everybody seemed to know everybody here.

So this was skiing. She remembered many years ago, when she had gone to that snobbish society party with Richard Caldwell at college, and Daphne the Golden Girl had been standing there with all her fancy friends talking about the best places to ski. How left out Emily had felt then, how insignificant and insecure, because that wasn't her life at all. The party where she had met Ken . . . Maybe she should blame Richard Caldwell for that, instead of being thankful to him.

It was the most extraordinary thing that this morning, when she'd been having her walk, she had actually seen Daphne the Golden Girl on the street, with a little girl who was obviously her daughter, and obviously retarded. Daphne was just as beautiful as she had been at their twentieth reunion; she would always be special. This morning was the second time it had occurred to Emily that without her ever thinking it was possible, all kinds of terrible things had been happening to Daphne. Oh, and to Richard too, of course, although it was Daphne who had always awed Emily so, and who had seemed destined to live in protected, perfect bliss. The first time was when she read about Daphne's son's suicide: he had been mentioned in *The New York Times*, which Ken always had flown out to them on Sundays. And now this little girl.

Daphne seemed very protective of her. Poor Daphne. Emily had almost had the courage to say hello to her, and then had not. Daphne didn't even recognize *her*.

This was a perfect place for families to come with children. Everywhere there were groups of kids together, and groups of parents, and the parents and kids together; and then at night the kids went to the pizza place to play video games and eat kid food and the parents dined with their friends in expensive elegance. That night Emily went to The Left Bank for dinner with "the girls," who knew all the best restaurants, and there was Daphne again, at the next table, this time with Richard and two other couples. Daphne was dressed all in white, and she was glowing.

"You see that woman?" Emily whispered. "I went to college with her. And her husband, too."

"What an attractive couple," Sue said, and went back to reading the menu.

"They were college legends," Emily said. "I was terrified of them, they were both so sophisticated and glamorous."

"She's got a great lift," Karen said. "Ask her who her doctor is."

"No, she hasn't," Emily said, indignant for some reason she couldn't explain. "She's always looked like that."

"That proves it," Karen said, and laughed.

Emily and her friends were in the middle of dinner when there was a minor commotion. An adorable blond boy of about thirteen, who was apparently Daphne's and Richard's son, came in with the little retarded girl in tow. The child was soaking wet and shivering with cold, and crying, and the boy was looking upset and scared. Daphne stood up immediately, her face pale with concern. But Richard . . . Emily could hardly believe it . . . he just looked annoyed that his lovely dinner was being interrupted.

"Teddy!" Daphne said. "What happened?" She was wearing a jacket flung over her shoulders, and she took it off and wrapped it around the crying child.

"We were fooling around and she fell into the creek," Teddy said.

"But where were the other boys?"

"I don't know. They went off someplace and they took the key. Otherwise I wouldn't have bothered you. I'm sorry."

"I'll go back with you," Daphne said.

"Just give him the key," Richard said wearily.

"She could have drowned!" Daphne said.

"Oh, no, it's shallow," Teddy said. "I fished her right out. I'm sorry, Mom. Really."

"I sorry I cry," the little girl said.

"Oh, Elizabeth . . ." Daphne said sadly, shaking her head.

"Daphne, where are you going?" Richard said.

"I'm going to put her into a nice hot tub," Daphne said. "You all enjoy the rest of your dinner. I'll catch up with you later."

"Don't hold your breath on that," Richard said. The other two couples smiled politely, pretending to be unaware of the tension. Daphne smiled back, and then she went off with the two children.

"Just another happy marriage," Karen said.

The next day Emily looked for Daphne on the street, and when she finally saw her, with the little girl as usual, Emily went up to her. "Daphne?" she said, although she knew quite well who it was. "I'm Emily Applebaum from Radcliffe . . . Emily Buchman now. Remember?"

"Oh, yes," Daphne said politely, and smiled.

Emily realized Daphne didn't remember her, hadn't remembered her at the reunion, probably had hardly even noticed her in the dorm all those years. It didn't matter anymore. She went determinedly on. "I hope your daughter didn't catch cold after last night," she said. "I was in the restaurant."

"Ah," Daphne said. "No, thank you, she's fine now. She just had a bad scare."

"That ice can be treacherous," Emily said. They looked at each other. "Would you like to come and have some hot chocolate with me?" Emily asked. "The Alpenrose Tearoom has lovely pastries."

There was a pause. "I have to warn you," Daphne said, finally. "Elizabeth's table manners leave something to be desired."

"I don't mind."

"Then let's go," Daphne said, and this time when she smiled the smile was real.

They sat across the table from each other in the European tearoom and talked. Emily, who was used to unhappy children from her work at the hospital, gave Elizabeth warm and friendly looks and ignored it when she smeared buttercream filling on her snowsuit. After a while Elizabeth stopped.

"I used to be so scared of you in college," Emily said.

"College seems a million years ago," Daphne said.

"I know. You had a camel's hair coat. I thought it was so chic and sophisticated. I had a fur coat and I hated it. I wanted one just like yours."

"I probably would rather have had a fur coat," Daphne said, smiling.

"Do you remember Ken Buchman?"

"Sort of."

"We went steady at college and got married right afterward," Emily said. "And nothing was the way I thought it would be. I'm here because my husband threw me out. I should have left him a long time before that, but women of our generation don't do that, do we? We keep trying to make the happy ending happen."

"Happy endings," Daphne said. "Ha. Some days I find it very difficult to believe in anything at all."

"I'm sorry about your son," Emily said. "I read about it in the paper."

Daphne burst into tears.

Oh God, what had she done? The Golden Girl, her idol, sitting here weeping; discreetly, but definitely weeping; in a public place, her heart broken, so unlike Daphne to fall apart—what had she, Emily the idiot, done?

Elizabeth was patting her mother's arm. "No cry," she said. "No. No cry."

"Don't mind me," Daphne said. She stopped, finally, and wiped her eyes. "It's just that everybody has been pussyfooting around the whole subject for so long, pretending it's going to go away, and it was such a relief when you said something."

"Are you all right?"

"It would have been his birthday today," Daphne said. "We all got up, and nobody said a word about it, and the rest of them went skiing as usual, and I took care of Elizabeth as usual. . . . I don't know whether there's so much emotion lying dormant that if . . . Oh, I just don't know."

Emily reached across the table impulsively and took Daphne's hand. "I'm sorry," she said.

"Thank you. Tell me . . . did you have a happy life before Ken left you?"

"Not really," Emily said. She wondered if Daphne would end what was starting to look like a possible friendship if she told her about the nervous breakdown. Then she thought: If she runs away she wasn't worth knowing in the first place. "I was married too young and I couldn't deal with the realities of what marriage and children actually were. I had a fantasy of perfection for everything in my life, which was really silly."

"Ah, yes," Daphne said. "Perfection."

"Ken was away a lot, and I was alone a lot, and then I found out he'd been cheating, and I cracked up. I'm all right now, but it was rough for a while."

"You cracked up because he was *cheating?*" Daphne said.

"No . . ." Emily thought about it. "I think it was because I wanted to go back and do it all over again differently, and I didn't know how."

"You didn't know how because it's impossible," Daphne said.

"I know that now."

Elizabeth was asleep with her head on the table. "You're good with children," Daphne said.

"Except my own," Emily said lightly. There were some things that were too delicate to discuss, even though she was feeling quite warm and comfortable sitting here with a totally different Daphne than the one she'd known so long ago. "I really enjoyed talking to you," she said. "Maybe you'll come to California some time. I'll give you my address. And I'll give you my friend Karen's phone number too. I seem to be living in a lot of temporary places lately, but she'll always know where to find me."

"Maybe you'll come to New York," Daphne said. "I go into town a lot. We could have lunch."

"I'd love that," Emily said. "I really would."

Chapter Thirteen

As it turned out, Kit did not get the part she coveted on the new Zack Shepard film, although her friend Emma did get to be his assistant. Not Assistant Producer, of course, but Assistant *to* the Producer. Credits were regulated by the unions in Emma's line of work. In Kit's they were negotiated by agents. And so, as if life had offered her a good consolation prize for losing the movie, Kit landed a juicy part in a miniseries that was to run an entire week on network. Her billing read: And Kit Barnett as "Angel."

The miniseries was full of stars, and former stars whose names still looked pretty good in an ad in *TV Guide*. There was "starring" and "co-starring" and "with" and "featuring," and one actor got a box around his name. Kit could just imagine all those agents fighting over who got what, and the actors at home complaining that if they were going to take a cameo at least they wanted big print in the ad. She loved her billing, and sent her agent flowers.

The part was not very interesting: a congressman's daughter who was a hooker, but Kit was aware that her complex personality would make it interesting. As she studied and worked and grew more in control of her craft she also realized that she had an innate something on screen that gave her an edge. Sometimes she was afraid to get too close to that part of her, because she was afraid she would spoil it. She didn't want to dissect herself too much. She was neurotic? Good, she would just let it flow out into the work and enrich the character, give it layers.

The creep from class had stopped hanging around outside her house. He had found someone else to be in love with, and was actually living with her. Kit was relieved. But now that the filming was over, and it was the boring drag-end of winter, she was restless. She went to a lot of parties, had a lot of sex. She hadn't met any man she wanted to settle down with, but she was sort of looking. Her parents were still separated. They seemed to have joint custody of Adeline, or, more likely, Adeline had custody of both of them. Adeline trundled back and forth, one day a week to her mother, who only had a small apartment, four days to "The Doctor," who was still living in their big house. Now Kit and Peter had two duty dinners to go to every week instead of one.

Tonight would be the seventh night in a row that Kit had gone to a party. They started late and sometimes ended days later, depending on who was giving them, but Kit always went home before the sun came up, always with a man. If he wanted to hang around all day and come to the next party with her, that was fine. But it was understood that if she met someone else she liked better, she was free. He was free too, of course, but they never seemed to want to be. Why did so many people only want what they couldn't have? She hoped that never happened to her. She was nearly twenty-two, and she supposed she was long overdue to have her heart broken, but so far she'd been lucky.

The guy she'd brought home last night was gorgeous but stupid. His name was Rick, and she'd forgotten his last name, if he'd even told her, and after fucking him all night it would be gross to ask now. While he was in the shower she looked at his driver's license. That was when she discovered he was only seventeen. He had told her he was twenty-six, and he could have passed for it. What a liar. Kit supposed he was also not in real estate. He was probably in high school. What a jerk. Still, it was kind of amusing to have had a much younger man.

As usual, they drove to the party in separate cars. The house where the party was given was high in the hills, and there was valet parking, which was nice. A producer was giving it. Kit had never worked for him, but she hoped to someday, and in the meantime she was pleased that he had invited her when they'd met earlier in the week at another party. There were a lot of expensive cars here, and the house was beautiful, all glowing with pinkish light; reflected back on itself it seemed to be swimming in its own swimming pool.

Kit wandered around the living room looking at the people. There were candy dishes full of various kinds of pills, and several with cocaine in them, and there was food and liquor and champagne. It was a terrific party. Most of the people were attractive. Kit dipped into the candy dishes several times, as casually as if she were taking souvenir matches, and loaded her little evening bag with drugs to take home. By now she could identify everything. Daintily, like a princess, she partook of a little bit of coke, a glass of champagne, rejected a proffered joint, danced with Rick to the music that was booming loudly all over the house, tried to decide with whom she would replace him.

She noticed one of the actors from her recent miniseries; Jed Soames, the one with the box around his name. He was totally drunk, and had never been attractive in the first place, besides being too old. He came weaving over to her. "Dance?" he said.

"Mmm." She just kept moving, and he lurched along in front of her. Rick was already dancing with someone else.

"What's your name?" Soames asked. She realized he didn't recognize her.

"Kit Barnett. We were in *The Monument* together. By the way, you were very good."

He peered at her. "Did we fuck?"

What a creep! She looked at him coolly, trying to

think of the ultimate putdown. "I don't remember," she said, and walked away.

There was a projection room, where people were watching one of the producer's old movies, lounging around on soft, deep couches, and there was a game room where other people were shooting pool and playing video games. Very, very nice, very, very chic. And upstairs there were bedrooms where couples and groups repaired to have sex if none of the other diversions appealed to them. Kit accepted another glass of champagne from a waiter and smiled back at a totally adorable blond guy who was smiling at her. He had on tight jeans, a tight T-shirt with Mickey Mouse on it, and a terrific body. The Mickey Mouse put her off a little, but at least it didn't have sequins.

"Hi," he said. "I'm Mac."

"I'm Kit."

"You're beautiful."

"Thank you."

"I'm not in est, I'm not a vegetarian, and I won't ask your sign," he said.

"I hate Rodeo Drive, I don't jog, and I won't ask what kind of car you drive," she said.

"I think I love you," he said.

"I hope so," she said. They both laughed. She held up her glass of champagne and let him sip from it. He put his arm around her waist and kissed her. She kissed him back. He was a marvelous kisser, slow and sensuous and not too aggressive. He acted as if he were tasting her. She started to feel it all through her body, and she decided he was what she wanted for this evening. She wanted him right now. But it was too early to go home, and this was a good party. They were standing outside one of the bedrooms, and Kit opened the door with her free hand and then she drew back and looked into his eyes and smiled. He looked so cute and pleased. He followed her into the bedroom. Her heart was racing, and she knew his was too.

It took a few moments for her eyes to get used to the dark. There were gleaming naked figures intertwined on the huge bed; what finally seemed to be a man and two women. The three of them were very busy working on each other, and then the man groaned with pleasure and sat up to change his position. Kit was looking right into his face. It was her father.

All he saw of her was a silhouetted shape because she was standing in front of the open door. But she saw him. She had never heard him make sexual sounds, but she recognized the timbre of his voice. There was no doubt. It was her elusive daddy, the almighty hotshot doctor, in bed with two women he'd probably just met, fucking in front of her very eyes. A wave of nausea hit her, rising from the pit of her stomach into her throat, and she fled to the bathroom and locked the door.

Safe behind her barricade, on her knees, Kit gagged and vomited into the toilet as though she could never stop. She was shuddering and sweating, throwing up all the hate and fear and anger that had been hiding inside her all her life. And in spite of the champagne, and whatever she'd eaten, all it tasted like was pool water.

She tasted the chlorine on her tongue, and thought for a moment she had gone insane. Gallons of swimming pool water were inside her, coming up, and she was a child again. How could this be happening? Inside her head she was screaming to be rescued, and no one ever came.

Finally she stopped, and sat on the cool tile floor resting. The people outside probably thought she was just another drunk. She flushed the toilet, and washed her hands and mouth and sweaty face, and neatly combed her damp hair. The most important thing on her mind now was how to get out of here without her father seeing her and realizing that she knew what he was up to. It was of no importance that she was at this particular party. She had a right to be. This was *her* life, until she decided she wanted some other kind of life. But her father had no right to be here, fucking strangers in front of her. As far as Kit was concerned, he had violated the incest taboo. It was disgusting, and it frightened her. It was a betrayal.

She opened the bathroom door noiselessly and looked out. Her father was still on the bed doing whatever he had been doing with the two women, totally oblivious of her, so she sneaked out of the room. Mickey Mouse was nowhere to be seen. Ah well . . . She sort of hoped he would be in the hall waiting for her, or in the living room just below, but no. Sex was the last thing on her mind right now, but he had seemed nice and she wished she had a friend.

She wandered around for a little while looking for him, and then realized he had found someone else to tell he loved, so she went outside and had the parking guy bring up her car.

Driving home, Kit sang aloud to cheer herself up, to the tune of "Rudolph the Red-Nosed Reindeer." "Snow nose, the cokehead doctor, has a very runny nose. When he goes out to parties, he likes to take off his clothes." She parked her car in front of her house and went inside and changed to one of the T-shirts she slept in, and then opened a bottle of wine. Her ever-present music was playing on the stereo. She put a nice little bowl on the coffee table and poured all the pills she had taken from the party into it. Very nice, very chic, just like the party she'd left. She tried to think of someone she liked enough to invite over, but couldn't. "Here's to me," she said, toasting herself.

Should she take an upper or a downer? She wasn't sure what her mood was. When in doubt take a Valium. Kit took three. She finished the bottle of wine and felt perfectly foul. What would happen if she died? Would anyone care? Would *she* care? She took a Quaalude and waited to feel better. She only felt worse; fuzzy, light-headed, nauseated again. She was afraid she was going to black out, so she lay on her bed, propped up on all her pillows because she felt so sick. There had to be an easier way to commit suicide. She thought about it for a while, trying to decide what she really wanted to do. She was miserable and lonely, but she didn't want to die. She reached over to the phone beside her bed and called the police.

"I took too many pills," she told the cop on the phone. "A whole bunch of stuff."

"Who is this?"

"You'd better send someone over. A male cop, not a woman. And be sure he's cute."

"I can't send anyone over unless you tell me where," he said. It was obvious from her voice that she wasn't kidding, and from his that he knew it.

"I don't want this in the papers," Kit said. "I'm a famous actress and it would be bad publicity."

"It won't be in the papers. Just tell me your name and address."

She did. In what seemed like a very short time two cops arrived; both young, both attractive, one black and one white. She wondered if they always traveled in a mixed set or if the man on the phone wanted to be sure she got what she liked. She managed to get up to open the door for them, and then fell on the floor.

They asked her questions, but she was absolutely incapable of speech. Then they were talking about her, trying to figure out what she'd taken and if it would be lethal. One of them was walking her around the room. She didn't remember much after that until she woke up to find it was midmorning, and that one of the cops had tucked her teddy bear into bed with her before he left.

Being young and very healthy, she didn't even feel particularly rotten. She rolled over and went to sleep again, and then sometime later the phone rang.

"How do you feel?" the man's voice said.

"Who is this?"

"Tip Weiner. One of the police officers who saved you last night."

Weiner? A Jewish cop? "I feel okay," Kit said.

"I put your teddy bear with you so you wouldn't feel lonely," he said. "Did you find it?"

"I haven't slept with my teddy bear since I was seven," Kit said, "but it was very thoughtful of you anyway."

"I didn't know," he said. "We didn't take you to the hospital because you seemed okay. Do you remember drinking coffee?"

"Nope."

"Do you remember me?"

"I remember both of you," she said.

"I'm the blond one."

"I hope this isn't going to be in the papers," Kit said.

"It's not. We took pity on you."

"Thank you."

"Listen," he said, rather hesitantly. "It's my day off today, and I thought I'd come by to see if you were all right, if that's okay."

"That's okay," Kit said.

"I'll bring some food. You haven't got any food in your house I noticed."

"That's because if I buy it I'll eat it," she said.

"If you keep drinking and popping pills on an empty stomach you could die by accident," Tip Weiner said. "I'll be there in an hour."

He arrived in a civilian's car, with two armloads of groceries. He was tall and blond and as cute as Kit remembered, and he was wearing a T-shirt and faded jeans. He had bought orange juice and milk and ice cream and lots of salad things and a barbecued chicken, and bagels and eggs for her breakfast. He scrambled the eggs while she made coffee and then they ate together and talked. He was single, and he was going to law school in his free time. He was a lot brighter than most of the guys she'd been seeing lately, and he was also obviously very kind. It interested her that he hadn't come over only to get laid, although that was probably on his mind, unless he thought it was a big deal just to have breakfast with a rather well-known actress, which she doubted.

Around six o'clock she was feeling almost normal, so she excused herself and took a shower and dressed. She realized that her house was filthy. She'd been on such a merry-go-round that she hadn't even noticed. She was embarrassed that he would see the mess, because she was basically a clean person. They had the chicken and salad for dinner, and afterward she took him to bed. He was a very good lover, as she had hoped he would be. He stayed all night, and after that they started to go together. Kit really liked him, as much as she was capable of liking anybody, and he seemed to be in love with her.

She wondered what Emma would make of this adventure when she told her. It was just like Emma's mother being saved by the fireman who came back the next day to go to bed with her, except of course

Emma's mother had been married and had run away afterward. But Kit had no intention of running away, at least not for the time being. *What is it about us,* she thought, *that makes us want to get saved?*

Chapter Fourteen

FOR A WHILE now, Annabel had realized she was in love with Dean Henry. It was a bittersweet feeling, full of complications. He was twenty-six—soon she would be forty-seven. He would be twenty-seven soon, and already she could see he was fretting that his youth was passing by too quickly. What was she to say; that being young was a state of mind, that when he was thirty he would look back at this time and think he'd been a baby, that youth was highly over-rated anyway? Any more platitudes? She had allowed herself to fall in love with him after years of protecting her feelings, and while she spent her days in moments of happiness and excitement, she also knew there would be no forever for the two of them.

She could console herself by thinking that judging by the marriages she'd seen there was no forever for most people. It was small consolation. She had never been like "most people." She only wanted Dean; she had him now; she wanted their happiness together to last.

It was spring again, and she went to Europe to the collections. This time she did not look for any young man to have a fling with, and she phoned Dean several times just to hear his voice. With the time difference and his erratic schedule she caught him only once. She was impatient to be home with him again. She wondered if he was cheating while she was away, and chided herself for being jealous and silly. If he were so anxious to cheat, he could do it while she was in New York. She worked such long hours, and his time was flexible enough to do what he pleased. That was the trouble with being in love . . . you cared too much. You wanted your love object to be happy, but only if you were the one who made him so.

He seemed happy. He was thoughtful and romantic. He continued to be insatiable in bed. After they made love he almost purred, like Sweet Pea. When Annabel stroked his thick black hair Dean moved his head in her hand, the way a cat did, sensually, to feel the touch of her palm, to push into her, to be cosseted. She loved the unabashed selfishness of his sensuality because there seemed to be a vulnerability in it too. He was so open. He wasn't afraid to show his need. He knew she wouldn't refuse him, or leave him.

They had been living together six months, and her life had changed in so many ways she wondered if she could ever bear to be alone again. She had someone to talk to, and to be quiet with, to read the paper with and have meals with, to take walks with, to go to the movies with on the spur of the moment. Her apartment was filled with the sounds of a human being she loved. His clothes and favorite objects were there. One day she left a note taped to the refrigerator: "Going to the supermarket. Write down anything you want." And he wrote back: "Love."

For his birthday Annabel took him to The Four Seasons for dinner. They sat side by side on a dark brown leather banquette facing the pool in the high-ceilinged, airy, tree-filled Pool Room, and ate gigantic crisped shrimps with mustard sauce, and drank champagne; and held hands under the table the way they had on their first date. She'd had the chef make a little birthday cake for a surprise. Dean's present was a vastly extravagant six-foot-long cashmere scarf with a fringe at each end, in a wonderful shade just lighter than navy blue that matched his eyes.

She'd given a scarf like that to Max, on the last birthday of his life, but his had been white. When she chose the scarf for Dean, Annabel hesitated for a moment, remembering. She had loved Max, and she loved Dean, in a different way. She decided it was neither macabre nor sentimental to have given them both the same present. Both of them had more panache than any man she had ever known.

On the card she wrote: "Just another way of tying you to me." It was the kind of thing she would never have dared to write a few months ago, but now she knew he would like it, would be flattered, not feel she was moving too fast or assuming too much. He *wanted* to be tied to her. She found herself thinking of famous couples who had lived together happily despite a great age difference, and at last allowed herself to believe.

Back in their apartment that night Dean took his birthday scarf and wrapped it around the two of them, drawing her tight against him. "This was the best birthday of my whole life," he said. "I love you so much."

How could she not allow herself to believe it would last?

Once in a while on Sundays they drove up to Chris and Alexander's house in the country. Dean got along with all of Annabel's friends and she with his. Chris was going to a diet doctor now, and had lost some weight. The puffy look was gone from her face, and she looked much better. She was resigned to the fact that her diet was going to be a long haul, but she was enthusiastic about Dr. Fields; so enthusiastic that she reminded Annabel of those women who got a crush on their gynecologist when they were pregnant because it seemed as if the two of them were working together to create a new person.

"I love Dr. Fields," Chris kept saying. "He's so kind. He really understands me."

"My rival," Alexander said, chuckling.

Alexander hadn't meant anything cruel, but it was the first time Annabel was really angry at him. Her eyes met Chris's across the table, and then they both looked away. Annabel knew about Alexander's big love affair with James, although Alexander never invited him to the country anymore now that Chris had found out. Still, the romance was going on, and Chris was bravely trying to cover it up and pull her life together. Annabel wished there *were* a rival. Cameron, or even Dr. Fields . . . anybody.

Dean was very pleased about Chris's diet and loss of weight. He couldn't understand why she wanted to stay with Alexander; such loyalty to someone who seemed, in his opinion, a hopeless case. "You wouldn't do that," he said once to Annabel, when they were discussing it.

"No. But I'm not like Chris."

"You would never let any man walk all over you."

"I hope not," she said.

"But of course, you could get any man you wanted," Dean said.

"Well, thank you."

Perhaps instead of taking it as a compliment she should have looked at it as a warning. Didn't men tell you that you could have any man you wanted when they were thinking you might have to look for a replacement? But how could she think that? She was lulled with her happiness and contentment.

Sometimes now Dean was moody, even seemed sad, but when Annabel asked him what was the matter and he said it was just his nature, she believed him. Most of the time he was happy. Whenever he seemed restless she thought of things they could do together that would amuse him. She was busy with the boutique and her business responsibilities. He was working on a new series of pictures in his studio downtown. They talked about the possibilities of a short summer vacation. She had left the shop with the girls before, when she went on business trips. The fact that she and Dean couldn't seem to set a suitable time didn't worry her. . . .

On Annabel's birthday Emma phoned from location and sent flowers to the shop. Chris took her to lunch, ate very spartanly, wrote down everything she had eaten on a little list she carried in a plastic holder in her handbag, and presented Annabel with a needlepoint pillow she had made herself. She had embroidered on it: *Redheads have more fun.*

"I'm doing a lot of needlepoint these days," Chris said. "It keeps my hands busy doing something besides putting food in my mouth."

That night Dean took her for her birthday dinner to the same place she had taken him for his: The Four Seasons. For an instant it occurred to Annabel that this was unlike him. The Four Seasons was her world, not his. His world was cute little bistros, SoHo, TriBeCa. Part of the charm of their relationship was that each brought the other into a different life, adding variety. But then she dismissed the thought as being ungracious and ungrateful. He had been so impressed by his birthday dinner that he simply wanted to do the same for her. The present he gave her was much more typical of Dean—a very modern black plastic necklace with clear lucite stars that looked like crystal hanging from it. He said one of his friends in SoHo who made jewelry had made it specially for her, and Annabel was very touched. It looked beautiful with her coloring. It was perfect.

"This was my best birthday," Annabel told him happily. "My best ever."

"I'm glad," Dean said.

Sunday, which they always looked forward to because it was their one day together, Dean wanted to go to the zoo. When they got to the zoo he wanted to sit on the terrace outside the cafeteria and have coffee. That was all right with her, although a bit strange because they'd just finished an enormous breakfast. But it was a pretty day, and she was happy to be with him, even though sitting in the midst of a throng of strangers, mostly families with noisy children, was not very romantic.

"I have something to tell you," he said. He looked down at the paper cup of coffee, which he had not even tasted, and then he looked at his hands. Anywhere, except at her. Annabel felt a sharp, remembered fear.

"What?" she said.

"I'm going back to Monica."

She felt as though his hands were squeezing her throat. The pain was so great that she shut it out, tried not to gasp, although she could hardly breathe. "Why?" she asked stupidly. *You said you didn't love her,* she thought. *You said you loved me.*

"I realize I should marry her."

"What do you mean?" Annabel said. "This isn't nineteen hundred. *Why* should you marry her?"

"Because . . . I love her. And I want to settle

down and have kids. I've thought about it a lot. You've helped me a great deal. This was a very important period in my life, the time you and I spent together. I want you to know I really loved you. But I want to go back to Monica."

Bill Wood, she thought. And all those other men, all through college, who decided they didn't love her anymore. Her rotten marriage to Rusty . . . Mistakes, mistakes through the years, until finally she'd settled not for love, but only for wary convenience. And now, just when she'd thought she was safe and smart and had allowed herself to fall in love again, here he was, calmly tearing her heart out. Men always took you to a public place to wreck your life because they were afraid you would make a scene. Except, of course, for the worst cowards, who just disappeared.

"Say something," he said.

What was there to say? That it was convenient that Monica had never managed to find her own apartment? That she was sure he'd had plenty of chances to see Monica when he was supposedly so madly in love with *her?* That maybe he never really loved her, but he damn sure didn't love Monica either, and probably couldn't love anybody? That soon he'd have his marriage and his kids, and his nice, settled family life, and then he'd be cheating? She remembered all those times when she'd wondered how a man could love you one day and then suddenly decide he didn't love you anymore, and the times she'd even asked them why this was, but never got any kind of an answer at all.

Oh, Dean, she thought, you loved me. You loved me. I was so happy. I was so sure you loved me. I love you so much that I can't even hate you for using me as a vacation.

"It was nice of you to wait until after my birthday," she said.

"If you're going to be clever you're much better at it than I am," he said.

"I know," Annabel murmured sweetly.

He was packed and gone by that night. He didn't even say he hoped they could remain friends, and Annabel didn't suggest it. He was going back to his friend, with whom he had spent a fifth of his life and now hoped to spend the rest of it. Annabel felt so filled with tears that she was raw inside, but she could not cry. A few tears filled her eyes, and her voice was unsteady, but the sobs and the anguish had been buried so deeply inside her for so long that she couldn't get them out. Her apartment was unnaturally quiet. Where Dean had been there was empty space. She had been used to the sound and feel of his presence, and now the home where once she had so enjoyed her independence and freedom was only a place where she felt lonely and bereft.

She put on music, but could hardly hear it. She sat staring at the wall, a glass of wine in her hand, Sweet Pea cuddled in her lap. She dialed Chris's number, but there was no answer; they were probably on their way back from the country. There was no Max to call. Even though she had known from the beginning that Dean would not be hers forever, she hadn't been prepared for the shock and pain of his leaving her.

Young men wanted different things for their lives than she did. A young man wanted a wife and a child; she had been a wife and she had a child—she didn't want that anymore. She probably couldn't even have a baby now if she tried. But why was it that the only men she was ever attracted to were so young, so impossible, so impermanent? She never even glanced at a man her age; it was as if they were all invisible.

Younger men were so sexy, so beautiful, so hypnotized by the joy of lovemaking. Their bodies were firm, their minds were leaping every which way, easily bored, impatient to find what was ahead of them.

Young men were so safe.

Chapter Fifteen

FOR THE FIRST time since she was eighteen years old, or perhaps ever, Chris was the most important person in her own life. And the most important man in her life was her diet doctor. Here she was, at seven o'clock in the morning, walking briskly to Dr. Fields's office for her weekly appointment before she went to work, trying to be first so she wouldn't have to wait so long; glancing at her reflection in store windows for the first time in months. She was looking better, almost normal again. *Soon*, she thought, *soon* . . .

They sat on opposite sides of his big desk, he in his white doctor's coat, she in her new khaki dress that she'd bought for the interim period between her old black muumuus, which were much too voluminous for her now, and her Thin Clothes, which were still too tight. Her new dress was of the lightest cotton because Dr. Fields insisted on weighing his patients in their clothes. Chris didn't think it was fair. She always took off her watch before she stepped on his scale, and of course she didn't have breakfast until after she'd left his office.

He was looking at the list of everything she'd eaten that past week, which she had written down according to his orders, and she was looking at him. He had nice blue eyes, wavy brown hair with gray in it, and aristocratic features. She assumed he was slim because he had to be a good example to his patients, but since he always wore that loose white coat no one knew for sure.

There, on top of his desk like miniature Claes Oldenburg sculptures, were a plastic steak, a lump of plastic spinach, an empty cottage cheese container, and an empty three-ounce can of tuna fish. Dr. Fields taught portion control as well as permissible and forbidden foods, and he did not allow patients to count calories. After a while you could judge what something weighed just by looking at it on the plate. If it weighed more than you were allowed you had to leave it over. That was not difficult for Chris, since at the end of a meal she felt satisfied. The hard part began about an hour afterward, when she began to feel starved. By four o'clock in the afternoon she was famished, and the small piece of fruit she was allowed was a joke. Sometimes, around midnight, she was so hungry she couldn't sleep, and stayed awake thinking about food and drinking numerous glasses of water until sheer exhaustion put her to sleep. She was constantly starving. It seemed particularly ironic since she had eaten herself into this obesity not out of hunger at all.

She had never needed to be taught which foods were fattening; she knew. She had always been careful what she ate, and had always been thin. Her need was moral support, psychological fortification; someone who cared as much about her weight loss as she did, even more, and who would be a kind of benevolent coach, not a policeman. She didn't want someone to control her; she'd had that. She wanted to control herself.

Dr. Fields was looking at her nearly perfect list. "A chocolate chip pound cake?" he said, peering at her, his eyes showing more amusement at the absurdity of this item than censure for the infraction. "A whole one?"

"Well, most of one," Chris said. She remembered sitting in the living room in the dark with the cake in her lap, digging at the center of it with a spoon. She'd finally thrown away the ragged edge. It was on one of the nights she knew Alexander was with James.

"Why?"

"I felt that my blood sugar was low," she said.

"Your blood sugar is fine," he said. "You just wanted it."

"I was depressed."

"And after you ate it, did you feel better?"

"Yes and no."

"When you're on maintenance you'll be able to have desserts in moderation," Dr. Fields said.

"I know."

"Is there any particular time you get these cravings?"

Chris shrugged noncomittally. "When my husband is out playing squash." She and Alexander still kept up the pretense of "Squash Night," although now he saw James almost every night, often going out after dinner to meet him. Chris knew, and Alexander knew she knew, and they both lied to their son.

"Doesn't the needlepoint help?" Dr. Fields asked.

"Oh, yes. My house is full of it. I make presents for everybody."

"Except for that cake, you did very well last week," he said. "You're losing weight at just the rate I want you to. The Three S's: Slowly, steadily, and sensibly; which is the best way to keep it off."

"The Three S's," Chris said. "Starvation, starvation, and sublimation."

He laughed, and handed her another blank list with the name of each day printed at the top of each column. "This week I'd like to see you be perfect. Try, okay?"

"I'll try," Chris said.

She always felt better, though, after she left Dr. Fields's office. She felt she had a future again. She would stop at home for her meager breakfast, and then go down to her own office. Usually she was so cheerful that she walked.

She had made certain changes at home which reflected the transition she was making to her new, independent life. The first thing she had done was to move out of Alexander's bed. She bought one of those upholstered beds that looked like a couch, but when you removed the cushions (and her many needle-point pillows) it was a comfortable three-quarter bed, and she put it into the den. Nicholas had his own television set now, in his bedroom, and Chris moved the bar things into the living room. When she and Alexander had their wine before dinner—if they ever did anymore, since she was dieting and he usually had his somewhere else with James—they did so in the living room. If they had guests, they entertained in the living room and dining room, and no one thought anything of it. Chris's personal things were in the bathroom off the den, the few clothes she could wear hung in the den closets, her books and work were on the tables. It was her own space, her own self-respect.

It was Chris's Room.

How long ago, that secret room Alexander had kept in his Paris apartment, called Alexander's Room, where he lived his hidden life . . . How innocent she had been, following him to Paris, waiting . . . And the day she had arrived unexpectedly at his apartment and had seen the boy, and Alexander's Room, that other terrible November. It was so long ago they were two different people now, she and Alexander. Now she had her own private place. There was nothing forbidden to hide there, but it didn't matter.

Alexander didn't mind that she had her own room now. It took some of the strain off their relationship. Nicholas worried, of course. Chris told him she and Alexander kept such different hours it was easier for her to have a room of her own—for her work. She said she and Alexander wanted separate lives for a while, but that they were still a family and they loved each other. It didn't fool Nicholas a bit. He waited for the divorce, like someone waiting for the other shoe to drop, and nothing Chris and Alexander said could reassure him.

The irony was that they had no intention of getting a divorce. They were just trying to survive.

At Chris's office Cameron seemed to be around more often. He would come in to say hello on his way to or from meetings, and then finally he invited her out to lunch. It secretly amused her that their lunches were starting again now that she was looking like her former self. When she ordered her chef's salad with only turkey and cheese, no ham—and without dressing—and then wrote down what she had eaten on her little list, he watched with interest.

"You've lost a lot of weight," Cameron said. "It takes a lot of courage."

"And a high threshold of pain," Chris said, laughing. "I sit in my doctor's office and talk to other patients sometimes, and they say they're not hungry after a few weeks. It never happened to me. I don't remember being hungry when I was thin, except before meals and that's normal. But apparently by the time you get thin you're used to this deprivation, and maintenance seems like an enormous amount of food."

"You should write an article about it for the magazine," he said.

"Me? I don't write."

"You could write this. It's your own experience. Besides, you do rewriting on things, I've seen your work. It's good."

He was so enthusiastic Chris began to think she could really do it. She remembered how he'd hired her, in an instant of instinct, and how he'd been right about what she could do. Maybe she *could* do a diet article. How brilliant did it have to be? She could get some anecdotes from Dr. Fields, and she certainly had plenty of her own.

"We've used my doctor a lot before, though," she said.

"Don't try to weasel out of it. This is going to be your story, not his. Besides, he's a good doctor, and I don't care how often we use him."

"Okay," she said.

In the long evenings, struggling with her piece after dinner, while Alexander was out, Chris was both frightened and happy. She wanted to please Cameron and not look like a fool, but he was so sure she would succeed that there was more warm anticipation of his approval than fear. He had become a sort of mentor. Perhaps he always had been. She allowed herself to think about how nice he was, and then at last the sexual feelings started to return, and she sat there gazing into space over her typewriter like a schoolgirl. The only thing that could bring her back to her work was remembering it was for him.

This wasn't what she had planned. She didn't want to be dependent on any man again. It was crazy. But

she had always liked Cameron—he wasn't just a
haven she was running to. She had run *away* from
him. Somehow she managed to finish the article.

Cameron loved it. He said it was not only informa-
tive but wickedly funny, and that other women
would identify with it. Just as Chris was breathing a
sigh of relief, he gave her another assignment.

"But I don't write!" she said again.

"You do now," he said.

He took her for a drink after work. They went to a
small, dark pub near the office; no place special, just a
quick, casual drink, not a date. They sat at the bar on
those uncomfortable high stools, instead of at a table.
Chris looked at the bowl of peanuts and salivated. She
ordered a glass of white wine because she was allowed three a week and this would be one of them.
You couldn't give up everything in life. Besides, being
with Cameron was like a party; even in this place.

"My wife is having a formal dinner tonight," he
said. "I have to rush home and get dressed up. Otherwise I would have taken you to '21' for drinks."

"Your wife," Chris said. "That's an odd way of saying it. Not, '*We*' are having a formal dinner."

"But we aren't," he said blandly. "She is. She loves
to give dinner parties. Her friends are all boring. I
would rather go to bed and read."

The wine had gone to Chris's head immediately
and it made her brave. She thought how ironic it was
that when she was young she had said outrageous
things because she couldn't stop them from popping
out of her mouth, and then she had become a circum-

spect adult who now needed a little help before she could be herself. "You never struck me as hen-pecked," she said.

"I'm not," Cameron said, not at all offended. "I'm gracious. I go to her boring social events and she leaves me alone."

"Are you happy?" Chris blurted out.

He smiled. "Are you?"

"I asked you first," she said.

"I suppose so. I love my kids. They're very young. I was married before, but never had children. I could be my kids' grandfather. I guess that's why I enjoy them so much; I can afford expensive nannies to take them away."

"You're awful," Chris said.

"Half kidding, half awful," he said. "And you?"

"What?"

"Are you happy?"

"If I were, do you think I would have turned myself into a blimp?" she said lightly.

"Other people have been ecstatically happy doing it," Cameron said. "I didn't know."

"Well, now you know."

"I never give up," he said.

"What does that mean?"

"Just that." He looked at his watch and asked for the check. "If you don't want it to, it doesn't have to mean anything at all."

Oh God, she thought.

She thought about it at home that night, and in the office during the day, and she knew he meant that he was still interested in her. It was June again, and the sales conference was coming. This year it was to be in Los Angeles. If anything were to happen, it would be there. She couldn't imagine cheating on Alexander in New York—it was just too close to him—even though being close to her had never stopped *him.*

Now that they were spending every weekend in the country, she had taken over one of the guest rooms in their country house for her own. Their physical separation was now complete. Alexander was friendly and warm with her, much the way he had been all those years ago in Paris when she had discovered his secret life, and it occurred to Chris with a heavy feeling of sadness that they had come full circle. They should have been best friends, like Max and Annabel; not lovers, not married. But Alexander was never like Max, and could never accept himself or his life. And she was not like Annabel, resilient, open to change. She was doomed to be in love with one man, forever, no matter how he treated her.

She was, however, allowed to have a crush on another. She had decided that, and knowing it made her feel alternately terrified and euphoric. She had never had so much energy. She was doing extra work at the office between her regular duties as Managing Editor and the articles she was now writing, she was walking both there and back, she seemed to need very little sleep. Nicholas had decided to spend the summer away from them again, at tennis camp with some friends from school, and Chris thought it was probably best. Alexander suggested that instead of he and

Chris taking a trip during the summer they wait until Nicholas came home and then the three of them could go somewhere together.

"Just like the old days," he said.

She wondered if he wouldn't rather be able to take his vacation with James. "Yes," she agreed kindly. "Just like the old days."

She had lunch with Annabel, who was still alone, still gamely trying to recover from being ditched by Dean.

"Los Angeles with Cameron, eh?" Annabel said. "Are you going to run away again?"

"Maybe he won't want me."

"You never think any man will want you."

"Do you realize it's been a whole stupid year?" Chris said. "Can I consider this a long courtship?"

Annabel laughed. "If it makes you feel less guilty, by all means."

Chris thought about it. "I don't know *if* I'm going to feel guilty, or *how* guilty, and I don't care," she said finally. "All I know is, this time I'm not going to run away."

Chapter Sixteen

AFTER THE CALDWELLS returned from their ski trip to Vail, Daphne brought Elizabeth back to the home as she had promised. The child had to go to school, didn't she? Elizabeth was all smiles and bubbling glee. She unpacked her suitcase, hugged Jane Baldwin and her friends, and ran around making sure nothing had changed during her enforced absence. Daphne watched with a sinking heart. This place was where Elizabeth's school was; but it was apparently where everything else she cared about was too.

Daphne continued to bring her home every weekend. After a few months Elizabeth realized that her visits were only temporary; she was not a prisoner; and she became less unhappy and less obstreperous, but she still packed her suitcase and sat by the door every morning, not knowing exactly when she would be allowed to leave. Despite Elizabeth's improved behavior, Richard absented himself more and more, saying he had business in the city. Daphne realized he was forcing her to make a choice; and that was unfair. The boys were all away at school and she was alone. She began looking for a good day school in Connecticut for a retarded child.

It was June now, time to make a decision for the fall if she intended to keep Elizabeth at home. The boys were back for summer vacation. The house was filled with their activity, their friends. None of them seemed to mind Elizabeth—they were too busy. It was Richard who minded, who made excuses when Daphne wanted to invite people to their customary summer barbecues, who finally agreed to a social life only if Elizabeth would not eat with them. Daphne refused to leave her out, and so a "compromise" was reached: the boys would not be there either.

Daphne felt as if she were always juggling everyone's social life, trying to keep them all in the right places on schedule. Luckily now both Matthew and Sam were allowed to drive. Richard bought them a car to share. It was only Teddy who needed to be taken to meet his friends and brought back. She had wanted to live in the country with Richard and a houseful of happy children. Instead she was Mussolini trying to make the trains run on time.

And for what? For a fantasy? Richard had turned into a stranger. Even his lovemaking was mechanical, almost as if he might as well have sex with her since she was there. For Daphne, who was stung and saddened by this new difference, she would have told him not to bother, but it was her only way of communicating with him now.

And what did everyone talk about when they finally did have an evening with other adults? Drugs. Problems with their kids. Even one of Teddy's friends —so young!—had been caught with drugs. Ever since that incident, the parents, without wanting to admit it, had taken up a sort of subtle spying. When you were in your child's room, putting away clean clothes perhaps, you looked around. You paid attention. Better now than later. Even though it could never happen to *your* child . . . could it?

It was a Saturday, hot, quiet. Richard had gone to a friend's country club to play golf. In the perfect life of the Caldwell family, which seemed so long ago now, they were their own country club, and needed no other. But now they were scattered. The boys were at the beach. Elizabeth was playing morosely in her room. At the home she would have had other children to play with. Daphne felt guilty and selfish. Maybe all of this had been a mistake. She wandered into each of her sons' rooms in turn, looking casually, hoping to find nothing illegal or destructive.

If she had looked in Jonathan's room while he was alive, would she have found some clue to what was to happen? She refused to let herself think about it again. But she did, she thought about it almost all the time, at the back of her mind while she thought she was thinking about other things.

And then, poking about in Teddy's dresser drawer like a thief, Daphne found his secret journal.

She really didn't mean to read it, just glance into it to see what it was. But when she saw the first line she was struck as if by a blow to the heart, and she sat down on his bed to read on. She read it all, all, and long before she was finished tears were streaming down her face.

"Nobody in this family ever talks about the things that really bother them or the things that really matter."

It was true.

She had only done what she thought was right, but everything had been all wrong. How deeply she had hurt Teddy, and probably all of them, as had Richard, by their unreasonable demands that everyone pretend they were having a normal life. She had only wanted to protect her family. What had Richard wanted? Daphne didn't know anymore. They should have talked about Jonathan instead of each of them grieving silently. Teddy was right: she was using Elizabeth as if she were a new baby, a substitute for her dead son, and that was both wrong and impossible. She had hurt everyone, even the little girl she had made sad.

They should have talked about everything.

Daphne closed Teddy's journal and put it in its hiding place where she had found it. She went to her bathroom and washed her face. On Sunday evening she would take Elizabeth back to the home as always, but this time it would be for good. She would visit Elizabeth, but Elizabeth would not have to come here any more to be used as something she was not.

And then they would talk, all of them. They would start all over again, and if they could not be completely happy, at least they would try to help one another.

No more lies and secrets.

She couldn't tell Richard at dinner that this was probably the last time he would be seeing his daughter, because he had called to say he would be eating out with a client he had met at the club. She did tell the boys. They nodded solemnly, agreeing it was for the best; not showing how relieved they were, or how sorry they were—if indeed they were sorry. Daphne thought that their feelings about the whole incident might be one of the things they would all discuss in the future, since they would be talking about everything that happened to them. She wondered what Teddy would write about this tonight in his journal. But she wasn't going to look in it again. She was on her own.

They had eaten early so she could bring Elizabeth back in time for her bedtime. It was a long drive. Elizabeth was happy in the car. She had her suitcase, her dolls; she knew she was going home. "I won't make you come back with me anymore," Daphne said. "I love you, and I'll miss you, and I'll visit you just the way I used to. I'll bring you presents."

"Jane," Elizabeth said happily.

"Yes, you're going to see Jane."

So much for presents.

Daphne hadn't told Jane that she was secretly planning to keep Elizabeth, so there was no need to tell her she had changed her mind. She merely said she was changing the schedule. Jane understood. It was not the first time this had happened with a family, and in this particular case she had long expected it. Daphne kissed Elizabeth good-bye and stood for a moment alone under the star-filled night sky, breathing the summer country air, listening to the sound of chirping. Then she drove home.

Richard still wasn't there. It was unlike him to be so late on a night when he knew he had to get up early the next morning. Daphne wondered if he had gone to a restaurant or stayed at the club, but in either case, even though she was a little concerned, she would never call looking for him. The boys were watching a horror movie they had rented for their VCR. She went upstairs to the bedroom to read.

At one o'clock she was really concerned. Richard hadn't even called. Thoughts went through her head of auto accidents, drunk drivers . . . but someone would have phoned. Teddy had gone to sleep, and Matthew and Sam were watching yet another movie. They would stay up all night if you'd let them. She was tired and would have loved to go to sleep, but the moment she undressed and got into bed she was wide awake. She wasn't used to sleeping without Richard. Maybe he was having such a good time that he'd forgotten how late it was. She hoped that was all. . . .

When the phone on her bedside table shrilled in her ears Daphne jumped. "Daphne?" It was the nasal, laconic voice of their family doctor. "This is Dr.

Price. I have Richard here. He's had a slight heart attack, but he seems to be in good shape. We're keeping him in the CCU for observation."

She felt herself turn icy cold with terror. "Heart attack? Where is he?"

"New York Hospital."

"Why did you take him all the way to New York?"

"He was *in* New York."

That was odd. "What time did it happen?" she asked.

"About eight o'clock. He's been quite stable for a while now, but I do want to watch him for a few days."

"I'm coming in," Daphne said.

She told the two older boys, trying to make it sound minor, and then dressed quickly and was in her car, driving to the city. Richard had always been in good health, but at his age he was a prime prospect for a coronary. She remembered his warning: This family can't take any more stress. Had he been hinting about something he wouldn't tell her? Then it was her fault. . . .

She was chain-smoking as she drove, thinking about the irony of it—she should have been the one who had the heart attack, not he. But Richard kept his tension inside, not losing his temper, not provoking fights, just staying out of the house whenever he could, trying to make the best of things. Daphne felt like a villain. She didn't know anyone her age who was a widow. She would have been the first of all her friends . . . it made her too aware that they were getting older. *Oh, Richard,* she thought, filled with love and fear and regret, *I'll make it all up to you. Things will be better now.*

At the hospital a nurse told her she would have to wait because Richard had just had a visitor and he had to have quiet interludes. "But I'm his wife," Daphne said in a reasonable tone that implied the nurse was being ridiculous.

"Oh," the nurse said. What was that look that flashed across her face and then was gone? She checked her watch. "Just sit down in the waiting area and I'll come get you in a few minutes."

Daphne chose instead to stand in the hallway outside the Coronary Care Unit. There was a big sign: *Oxygen. Do not smoke.* She paced.

Another woman had brought a chair into the hall and was sitting on it, right in front of the CCU. She was in her early or mid-thirties, blonde and very beautiful, and something about her was disturbingly familiar. A former model? An actress, perhaps, or a movie star made unrecognizable out of context? The woman was watching her, too, and Daphne noticed the same glance of puzzlement cross her face. Then she realized why the younger woman looked familiar: they both looked alike. She was Daphne ten years ago —how strange. Daphne smiled at her to apologize for staring. The woman gave her a polite little half smile and then turned away.

"Mrs. Caldwell," the nurse said, walking down the hall. "You can go in now."

The other woman, the younger Daphne, drew in

her breath in the faintest, almost imperceptible, gasp of pain, and then looked away again. Daphne rushed in to see Richard.

He had a little pronged thing in his nostrils that was supplying him with extra oxygen, and he was hooked up to monitors, but otherwise he didn't really look sick. It was hard to tell if he was pale under his carefully tended tan.

"Oh, Richard," Daphne cried, "are you all right?"

"Sure," he said, to cheer her up. "Just that it scared the hell out of me at the time. I'm sorry you had to come rushing into town."

"Sorry?" Daphne said. "Did you think I'd leave you here all alone? You know I love you. I was terrified. I really blamed myself, sweetheart. There's been so much pressure on you lately. But everything's going to be different now." She took his hand and he returned her grasp.

"I love you too," he said.

"Elizabeth isn't going to come home anymore," she said. "I realize it was a mistake."

He nodded. "But you didn't have to decide that for my sake."

"I did it for all of us." There was more she wanted to tell him, but it would have to wait until he was better and home again. Little by little she would repair their marriage, as he repaired his health. "You look uncomfortable attached to all those gadgets," she said.

"I am." He smiled. "But I'm here."

"Thank God for that."

"Yes . . ."

She stood there holding Richard's hand and looking at him with concern and tenderness until the nurse came in to say that he needed to rest. "Why don't you go home, Daph," Richard said. "I'm only going to sleep anyway."

"We'll see," Daphne said noncommittally. She leaned over and kissed him on the forehead. "I love you," she said.

"I love you," he murmured, and closed his eyes, dismissing her.

Daphne walked quietly out of the room. As she passed the young woman who was still sitting in the hall, the woman spoke to her.

"Mrs. Caldwell?"

"Yes?"

"I'm Melissa. Melissa Loring?"

The woman thought Daphne was supposed to know her. "Yes?" Daphne said again.

"Could we talk?" Melissa Loring asked.

Before Daphne could answer she was out of her chair, propelling her gently down the hall to the visitor's lounge. Then they were facing each other on the couch, looking to anyone who might happen by like two sisters, an older and a much younger one.

"If it would be more comfortable for you," Melissa said, "we could arrange to visit him at different times."

And then of course she did know who this woman was.

No false step, no real clue, had prepared her for

this, but then she had not been prepared for anything that had happened to her lately, and she had not been looking. Richard's girl friend . . . lover . . . mistress . . . whatever it was called. Apparently Richard, too, had secrets. *I can't bear it,* Daphne thought; *I just can't take another thing.* She lit a cigarette, her hand shaking, and said nothing. She thought if she opened her mouth to speak she would start to scream and never be able to stop.

"Look," Melissa said. "This is difficult for me, too."

Daphne finally found her voice; it came out of her in a calm, controlled manner, the way she had been trained to speak since her earliest childhood, the way her would-be replacement was speaking to her now. "I'm sorry, but I don't know who you are."

"I thought Richard told you."

"I would like *you* to tell me."

"We've . . . been seeing each other."

"You must have been the one who called the doctor." She had to know if Richard had had his heart attack in this woman's bed. She didn't even know why she wanted the truth when it might be so terrible, or if it would ever be offered, but she had to know.

"I knew he shouldn't have gone bicycle riding in this heat. So much exertion. He didn't feel well."

"In the park?" Daphne asked coolly.

"No, he was fine in the park. It was afterward. We were getting ready to go out to dinner. He complained of chest pains and shortness of breath, and I of course, immediately, called his doctor."

Getting ready to go out to dinner. Having gotten out of bed. Possibly not. Possibly simply after taking a shower before dinner. After bicycle riding. After making love. Daphne closed her lips in a little Mona Lisa smile to hold back the screaming.

"How long have you been . . . seeing my husband?" she asked.

"He said you knew," Melissa said. "I'm sorry this had to happen here . . . now . . . I believed that you knew."

"How long?" Daphne asked again, in that same calm voice.

"A year and a half."

Before Elizabeth came to live with us. Before Jonathan died. Before anything that could have been considered an excuse: guilty by reason of insanity. He chose her before any of it happened. "Are you married?" Daphne asked.

"No."

"Do you have children?"

"No."

"What do you do?"

"I'm a lawyer." She mentioned the firm. It was one of the most prestigious in the country. Of course.

"I would prefer it if you didn't come here anymore," Daphne said.

"I'm afraid that would be impossible." Melissa's voice was as controlled as her own. "The doctor said Richard is not to have emotional turmoil of any kind. Richard asked me to stay. If I don't come to see him he'll be upset. I would be glad to set up my schedule to accommodate yours, as I said before."

"All right," Daphne said. There was one more question. No, there were two, but she would only ask one. "Are you in love with Richard?" she said.

"Very, very much."

She was not going to ask the other.

Driving home in the predawn darkness Daphne still refused to allow herself to fall apart; she was waiting for the safety of her own bedroom, behind locked doors. You did not have hysterics at the wheel of a moving vehicle when you had children who still needed you. She felt raw with the pain and humiliation of the encounter, and the shock of Richard's betrayal, but she wouldn't let it take over yet. She would have loved to kill that woman. Perhaps the woman felt the same way about her, but Daphne really didn't care. She drove on doggedly, teeth clenched, waiting for her house. Finally she saw it, rising up out of the trees, familiar and solid, silhouetted against the purplish-black sky.

She was home. This was what she had wanted all those years and thought she had achieved: to live in the country with Richard and a houseful of happy children. She had never wanted more. Now she thought she had wanted too much.

Here she was, home. Her home, once a refuge of safe tranquility, then a place of always to be remembered horror, and now only a beautiful shell.

Chapter Seventeen

AT THE END of May Emily was still living in her own apartment. She didn't like that it had other people's furniture in it, but she did like that she was accountable to no one but herself. She was still not sure what she wanted to do with her life. Ken kept asking her to come back to him, promising that everything would be better. A part of her knew he only wanted to avoid an expensive California divorce with its disastrous (for him) community property law, but another part of her refused to believe something so painful, even though he had made it abundantly clear that he had no use for her and couldn't stand her. She kept remembering the old, nice Ken, their happy times, and wondered if she could salvage something again; and then she would tell herself to stop living with long-dead dreams. Dreams had been her undoing.

If she did divorce him, she could find a permanent

place to live, and fill it with her own things: a concrete admission at last that she had a new life. She didn't know . . . All she knew was that she wasn't lonely, and that was a surprise for someone who had never been alone before and had always dreaded it. And yet hadn't she been totally alone so often while she supposedly had a family?

Kate had landed a part in a movie—a theatrical she called it, as opposed to a television movie, and seemed excited about it. Peter was looking for a summer project, preferably a job that would pay more than a pittance, but there seemed to be nothing for college students, even one who had gotten an A for his paper on "Starting a Small Business." Adeline showed up once a week to clean Emily's apartment, but Emily would not let her cook, saying she was hardly ever home lately anyway. When the children came for dinner Emily cooked, usually something simple, always followed by her famous cookies, and when she was alone she ate whatever and wherever she pleased, at whatever time suited her, and felt free.

Before, when she had been living with Ken, she had been in limbo much of the time, waiting for him to come home. Now that she wasn't responsible to anyone (except the children at the hospital) she found there were a lot of things she wanted to do: go to the movies, to a new play, to lunch or dinner with a friend. She was no longer either waiting for something or waited for. She wasn't unhappy but she wasn't really happy either—it was more as if she were on vacation, letting her bruised ego heal.

Her son was being unusually attentive lately, and Emily wondered why. Peter never did anything without a well thought out reason. One day he called and asked if he could bring a friend to dinner that week, and if Emily would be sure to bake her butterscotch chip cookies. She was so surprised and flattered that she made enough cookies for both Peter *and* the friend to take home afterward. His friend was a polite, clean-cut boy from Peter's class, who obviously had rich parents: he drove the same kind of little two-seater Mercedes convertible that Emily owned, but his was new. Peter always chose rich friends.

Three days later Peter called and asked if he could come over again. "You don't have to go to any trouble cooking, Mom. I'll bring a barbecued chicken. I want to talk to you about an idea I have."

He wanted something; she should have known. Oh well, she could always say no. She had become much better at saying no lately.

He arrived at six, handsome, sleek, and charming, carrying not only the barbecued chicken, hot in its paper bag, but a chilled bottle of Dom Perignon (from his father's refrigerator she supposed) and a folder filled with papers. When she kissed him hello he actually put his arm around her.

"I am about to change our lives," he announced triumphantly.

"Oh?"

"*I* have a terrific summer job, with the possibility of it becoming a permanent job, and *you* have a career."

"I do?" Emily said, amused. He was virtually glowing. "And what is my career to be?"

"You remember my friend Jared who was here the other night. Have you ever heard of the Mills Tool Company?"

"Not unless I play tennis with the wife," Emily said.

"Well, that's his father," Peter went on. "His father invented something, some little thing you can't send up a plane without. He's got millions. Anyway, I wrote a prospectus and took it to his father, and I brought your cookies, and we now have a loan to start our own business."

"What business and who's 'we'?" Emily asked. "You and I?"

"You, me, Jared, about a dozen kids from school . . ." Peter sat on the couch and put the folder of papers on the coffee table in front of him. "Sit down, Mom."

She sat.

"This is the prospectus and some papers you have to sign," he said. "You can look them over tonight after I leave, but I'm coming back to get them early in the morning. Meanwhile I'll explain everything to you simply, because this is written in language that may be a little confusing—it's got charts and stuff, and lots of figures. Number one: You make the best butterscotch chip cookies in the world. Everybody says so. Number two: You have a genius for a son." He smiled. "I found us a location for a small cookie factory . . ."

"Factory!" Emily cried, concerned.

"That's just a term for a place with an oven and mixing machines, so don't panic. We'll sell right out of the store while they're nice and hot and gooey. This is not a shelf product. We will also have kids handing them out in shopping malls, and we're going to sell them in the school cafeteria during summer session to start. All my friends who need summer jobs are going to work for us." He gave a grin that was downright wolfish. "Everywhere they go they get offered crummy wages. Well, now you and I are going to pay crummy wages and my friends are thrilled."

If I don't sign anything, Emily thought, *he can't get involved in this crazy thing.* But Peter's excitement was contagious, and he seemed to know about business—at least his school thought so. And that millionaire person seemed to think so too. "I don't want to sound like a spoilsport," she said, "but why can't you and Jared just work for his father?"

"Mom!" If Peter hadn't been twenty his voice would have cracked, such was his outrage. "Haven't you heard of free enterprise? The American way? We want to do this on our own."

"Jared's father has no jobs."

"Oh, we could do something dumb that he invented for us, but he's very impressed that we're doing this. He's lending us the money. You don't even want to hear about it."

"I do so," Emily said.

"Okay. Now you may have the idea that the market is saturated, but people will always eat cookies. All you have to do is write down your recipe, and then I'll adjust it on the computer for our huge machines. The kids who are doing the baking will have to follow the recipe *exactly*. Naturally I will have copyrighted it so nobody can steal it."

"Naturally," Emily said. She felt a little numb, but also quite pleased. Maybe it would be possible after all. . . . She didn't know anything about business, but she knew how good her cookies were. She'd always known that. "But Peter . . . what's going to happen in the fall when you have to go back to college? Who's going to run this thing?"

"Maybe I won't go back to college," he said calmly. "We'll see. I might take a leave of absence. The only reason I'm going to college anyway is to learn how to be a success in business, and who knows, maybe this will be my success."

"But the other kids will have to go back . . ."

"Mom, why do you always worry about everything? There are always kids who need jobs. Not everybody in the world goes to college, you know."

No, that was true; and as she thought about it she wondered what college had ever done for her except overeducate her for the life she had been told to want. "Peter, do you really think we can do this and make it work?"

"Of course I do."

She knew now, she knew exactly what she wanted and why she wanted it. "I'd like to name the company myself," she said, with a firmness she could not remember ever having mustered before.

Peter's face lit up again. "You're saying yes!"

"I'm saying yes if I get to name the company."

"Of course you can. You're a partner. You're the creative one."

Emily took a deep breath. "I want to call it 'Emily's Cookies.'"

"Perfect!" Peter said. "It sounds like home. It sounds real."

"It *is* real," she said, mildly insulted. "I'm real. And we have to have a cute tin to put the cookies in. In case somebody wants to buy more than just one to eat on the spot."

"Riiight."

She was thinking fast now, the adrenaline flowing. "They're butterscotch chip cookies, so it should be a butterscotch and white tin. Gingham. Little checks. With 'Emily's Cookies' written on top of it. Maybe in orange, maybe brown. We'll try both and see what we think. We'll look at different styles of lettering too."

Peter grinned and held up his hand; thumb and index finger making a circle of approval. "Perfect!"

Emily smiled back, feeling close to him, the way she had for that brief happy time so long ago, when she had come home from her class reunion thinking how much they all loved one another.

"Let's open the champagne," she said.

It was hot that summer; ninety-five almost every day, day after day of blindingly sunny unremitting heat. Emily worried that when Emily's Cookies opened no one would want to go out into the street and therefore wouldn't know about her store and her cookies. She was thinking of it as hers now, even though it was a group project. The place they had rented was in Westwood Village, where things were always lively. There were first-run movie theatres, record stores, bookstores, a big department store, and lots of restaurants for the students from nearby UCLA and other young people who lived in the area or came there because there were things to do. There were actual streets you could walk on, and people who used them. It wasn't like Beverly Hills, where she could never afford to rent anyway, but which was so dead on a hot day it looked like an unused movie set.

The analysts were away for the month of August, so by some ironic coincidence Dr. Page was going to disappear just when Emily was about to face her first step toward real independence. "You're ready," Dr. Page kept telling her. "You can do it. You've always wanted a career."

"This isn't exactly a career," Emily would say one minute, and the next minute she would be terrified again, because it could become one, and she wanted it to be.

She told all her friends to come on opening day and bring their friends. She had quit her volunteer work at the hospital with some regrets, but before she left she promised that if the store was a success she would send someone by with hot cookies once a week for all the sick children.

"Great gimmick, Mom," Peter said when she mentioned it to him.

"I didn't mean it to be a gimmick," Emily said.

She had decided on the orange lettering for the cookie tin, and had also chosen their slogan: "Cookies Are Love." It was something she had often thought when Adeline had refused to let her make the cookies at home. Adeline pretended to be pleased about the new turn in Emily's life, but Emily could tell she felt ambivalent about it.

"I could have done that with my cookies," Adeline said. "Gone into business. Just never thought of it."

Mine are better, Emily thought, but said nothing.

She had suddenly become extremely competitive. She sampled all the major brands of freshly baked cookies and found something to criticize about every one of them. They were too dry, too greasy, too small, too sweet, too salty . . .

Workmen were working overtime to finish the store. It was to be a simple, utilitarian place, with the ovens in full view of the customers, emitting their mouth-watering cookies-baking smell; the rest of the machinery in view too behind a glass wall, the kids who were doing the baking dressed in white T-shirts, butterscotch-colored jeans, and white aprons. Best of all, you could see the cookies rising and starting to bubble and turn golden, just the way they had in Emily's own kitchen. It was the part she had always liked best, and she wanted it for the child in everyone.

She waited for some reaction from Ken. He had

accused her of being a useless woman. Now what would he think? Did she care? No. Well, yes, she did care a little. She supposed he would say that she couldn't have done it without Peter, that Peter was a man, again a male taking care of her—that she was just a figurehead. Sometimes Emily worried it was almost true. But she had invented the recipe, and the packaging; the tin and the little butterscotch and white gingham paper bags, and the slogan; and she had thought of the idea of giving away the cookies at the hospital, and she was Emily, after all, THE Emily. The hell with what Ken thought.

On opening day it was blazing hot. Emily lettered a sign and put it in the window: Take some cookies to the beach. There was also a banner that said: Grand Opening. On the window was lettered, *Emily's Cookies,* and underneath in smaller letters, *Cookies Are Love.* The store was sparkling clean . . . and empty.

Ken had sent flowers. He had even written Good Luck on the card. The flowers and card were for all of them, his son included, so while Emily was pleased she was not touched. Besides, she was too busy worrying. Where were the customers? The new ovens were baking like mad anyway. By lunchtime Peter had to deliver an order to the UCLA cafeteria, but they couldn't live on that alone, and after lunch the cookies would continue to be baked in hope someone would buy them, and if no one came they would all be wasted. Emily pictured hundreds of love-filled cookies, all just lying there getting cold and hard.

Around noon her friends started drifting in. They

looked around, spread compliments, bought cookies, wished her luck, and went away. She waited.

At the end of the first day of business they had sold cookies to exactly four people.

"Tomorrow I'm going out to a mall too," Emily said. "I can't just sit here, I'll be too nervous. I'll take Century City."

"You have to be quick, Mom," Peter said. He had been debriefing his troops. "There are other cookie stores there and if they catch you they chase you away."

"I'll be quick."

So here she was, walking around the huge outdoor shopping center in the heavy heat, carrying a basket full of her cookies, approaching total strangers as they hurried from one air-conditioned store to another, or from their air-conditioned offices to an air-conditioned restaurant or take-out place at lunchtime, smiling sweetly and forcing cookies on them. She was too desperate to be frightened or even embarrassed.

"Have a nice fresh cookie," she would say brightly, as if they were the children at the hospital. "They're good. Try one. They're free."

There was a sign on her basket with the name and address of her store, and she handed each person a cookie wrapped in a paper napkin with the name and address of the store printed on it too. There were lots of those napkins back in Westwood, still unused. She moved around a lot, watching out for anyone who would chase her away. She knew the Century City mall well; she'd shopped there for ages, and she knew where people liked to buy food to eat outdoors. Even on a day like today there were a few sun-loving die-hards, mostly young tourists, scantily dressed. She knew they would appreciate something free. "Here's dessert," she would say, with her mommy smile.

Every hour one of the kids from the store (Peter called them The Couriers) would come by with freshly baked replacements. There was a courier assigned to every mall. "Are they selling anything?" Emily would ask.

"No."

"Oh God."

At the end of the day she was exhausted, and although she had long before lost count of how many cookies she'd given away she knew there had been a lot. She drove back to the store to meet with Peter and Jared.

"They loved them at the school cafeteria," Peter said.

"They seemed to love them at my mall," Emily reported. "I looked in the trashcans before I left and nobody had thrown any away. I think people thought I was a bag lady." She tried to sound cheerful, but the truth was when she had seen all those empty paper napkins crumpled there she had wanted to cry, and she didn't know why. Perhaps a combination of pride and frustration.

"If things aren't better tomorrow we can go out in the street and give them away here," Jared said.

"We can't give them away forever," Emily said, frightened again. How could they be a failure before they'd even begun? How long could they afford this? She didn't even want to ask. To cheer the boys up she took them to dinner in a restaurant.

That night she couldn't sleep. She had allowed herself to think all this could be possible, and now real life had intervened. Real life, for most other people, was hard work followed by success. For her, it seemed, it was her college advisor all over again, telling her she had been improperly prepared. *If you're so interested in medicine, Emily, you marry a doctor.* If you think you can sell cookies . . . What was that awful old joke? "If you want bread, go fuck a baker." She felt miserable.

The next morning the radio weather report said it would be just as hot. Emily drove to Westwood with dread, her car air conditioner already on. When she got to her block she saw people in the street. What was happening? Then she saw that they were standing in line.

They were standing in line waiting for her to open the store.

They were standing in line for Emily's Cookies.

Emily held back the tears of joy, excited and happy and unbelieving. She wanted to laugh, to sing, to hug all of them. Peter was already there, inside the locked store, supervising the kids who were doing the baking. Even with the door closed you could smell the delicious aroma. He came to the door when he saw Emily get out of her car, and he held out his hand in a gracious gesture. She had a key too. She mimed "Me?" and he nodded. She took the key out of her handbag with a flourish and opened the door to the shop to let the long line of customers in.

She felt as if she were a celebrity cutting the ribbon.

Chapter Eighteen

BY THE BEGINNING of summer Kit realized her relationship with Tip was going nowhere but down, at least as far as she was concerned. He still thought they were "in love." But she was bored and restless and lonely because he was hardly ever there. It was bad enough to be going with a cop, who was working all the time, but a cop who was going to law school on the side . . . He might as well be just another date, but his clothes were there, and he kept bringing food, and he showed up faithfully to sleep, as if this were his home too. He had started talking about the future. Where they might go for a vacation, how if they kept on getting along so well maybe one day they might get married. He said he had a great career ahead of him.

The whole thing made her feel like she was choking.

She would be starting her movie soon and she wanted to be free. She tried to tell him that once and he got really upset. He said he'd never found a girl as wonderful as she was and he didn't want to lose her. He said that even though she'd been patient enough not to mention it he realized being his girl friend at this time in his life wasn't the easiest thing in the world for her, or for anybody, but when she was making the movie she wouldn't mind that he kept long hours because so would she, and it would be so nice to spend their time off together. It sounded as if they were already married.

One thing Kit didn't want to be was married. Sometimes in conversation she would say: "When I get married," but it was a phrase that just popped out of her and had no relationship to how she actually felt. Oh, maybe sometime eventually she would try it. Marriage was probably something you had to try along with all the other experiences in life, particularly if you wanted to enrich yourself as an actress. But she certainly never wanted to have kids.

She thought of her mother, already married at her age. And then going crazy . . . Nobody had ever sat down and tried to explain it to her and Peter—it was always that her mother had gotten sick, period. But her mother had been alone all day with two little kids, their father away most of the time becoming successful; and even though no one ever told her, Kit understood that part of it, intellectually at least. Being locked up with two kids, as active as they had been, must have been hard. But emotionally Kit could not condone her mother's behavior at all. *She* was the child her mother would have let drown, not some abstract person you read about in a case history. She thought of herself as having been adorable; nice little Kate, lively and curious. How could you kill your little Kate? You shouldn't scare her. You should love her.

It was a lucky thing Kit had no feelings at all about either of her parents. Otherwise she would really feel hurt at the way they had betrayed her.

Her mother was going to start a cookie business with Peter. He was all excited about it, already planning how to spend the money he was going to make. Kit thought there was a good chance he would do well. Peter was very clever. Their father wasn't being too gracious. He called her mother "The Cookie Monster" behind her back, but he said at least she wasn't trying to produce movies like those other rich Beverly Hills wives. He was also trying to get her to come back. Ah, domestic harmony.

Kit's script had arrived. It wasn't a huge part, but it was a good one, with some good lines, and she actually got to be funny. She played a kind of tough, wise-talking teenager—yecch, a teenager again!—but she also had a scene where she was emotional and cried. A range of emotions to show off what she could do. She knew there would be lots of rewrites coming, but she had already memorized her part anyway. God knows she had enough free time.

Emma's movie was being shot in California and New York. She came by one afternoon on her day off. Tip was there, but he was asleep because he'd worked all night. Emma had never seen him, so Kate opened the bedroom door and they tiptoed in, Emma looked at him sleeping, and they tiptoed out.

"Cute," Emma said.

"Not bad." Kate grinned because Tip really was good-looking and she knew it.

They sat in the living room and drank coffee. "He leaves his gun right there in the bedroom?" Emma said.

"He has to take it home. He's a cop."

"Doesn't it make you nervous?"

"I'm used to it."

"So is it looove, or what?" Emma asked cheerfully.

Kit shrugged. "He loves me."

"As usual. And you?"

"I'd like to start seeing other people."

"What's wrong with him?"

"Bad timing I guess."

"You always say that," Emma said.

"When do I say that?"

"Always. Ever since I met you."

"I think I'm in for about ten more years of bad timing," Kit said. "Why do men get so serious?"

"Lots of men don't."

She thought about it. "Yeah," she agreed. "How's the movie going?"

"It's terrific. Zack Shepard is a genius. I'm right by his side all the time learning a lot."

"And . . . ?"

"And nothing. He's not interested in me. All he does is work. He doesn't even have a girl friend on the set. He might still have that one at home, but she didn't come to New York with us. Or maybe she did but she was shopping or something."

"I've decided it would be just as boring to be married to a famous man as to some jerk," Kit said. "Except the celebrity might give better parties."

"You'd have to give the parties," Emma said. "The wife entertains. The wife brings the Porthault pillowcases on location to put on the drool-stained pillows in the hotel."

"You still have the same disgusting turn of phrase," Kit said affectionately.

"I have to be observant. It's my job."

"Like noticing Tip's gun," Kit said. "There must be a million things in that room and you zeroed right in on it."

"My talent," Emma said calmly.

"Did I ever tell you that my father chased my mother out of the house with a loaded gun?"

"My God," Emma said. "And you're still not scared?"

"What's there to be scared of? He's not my father and I'm not my mother."

On the other hand, she thought, it gave rise to a lot of interesting possibilities. . . .

When Tip woke up he insisted on taking her and Emma to dinner, at a Mexican restaurant down by the Marina. They drank margaritas, hers and Emma's without salt because they didn't want to get bloated. Tip said they were ruining the drink by having it that way. *What a civilian,* Kit thought, irritated. *He really doesn't understand anything about me.* Everything he said or did was beginning to annoy her lately. It was her usual reaction to feeling trapped.

After dinner Emma had to go right home because she had to get up early. Kit and Tip went back to her house and had sex. That, at least, was still superior.

"You were strange tonight," he said afterward.

"Strange when?"

"At dinner."

She didn't answer.

"Were you mad at me or something?" he asked.

"No."

"Did you mind that I invited your friend to come along on our one night alone?"

"Emma?" she said incredulously. "Why should I be mad? She's my only friend."

"I'm your friend," Tip said, hurt.

"That's like apples and oranges," Kit said distantly. She wished he would go away.

"I start working days next week," he said. "Then we'll have nights together. Except the three nights I'll have class, but then I come home early."

She nodded.

"I'll be studying my law books, you'll be preparing your scene for the next day, it'll be nice. I'll take care of you."

You make me sound like a geriatric case, she thought, but said nothing. She wanted to scream.

The next day she made a couple of phone calls, surfacing for air. She found a party. When Tip was at work Kit went out, testing her old social life and find-

ing it surprisingly exhilarating after all these months
as a hermit. At first, walking into the beautiful house
where the party was being held, she had the fear that
she might run into her father again. But he wasn't
there. She decided that if she ever did catch him
again she would let him see her, and then he would
be so intimidated that he would be the one who had
to lay low. She wasn't going to allow him to ruin her
fun.

She saw Seth from class standing by the bar, holding a glass of something nonalcoholic and looking
over the women. He was a combination of gorgeous
and adorable, and incorrigibly priapic. Kit thought
she was probably the only girl she knew who had
continued to say no to him so far, but she was saving
him for a rainy day. This was the rainy day.

"Hi," she said.

"Kit . . ." He put his arm around her, murmured
her name, nuzzled her hair, the way anybody else
would have shaken hands.

"How are you?" she asked.

"I want to go home with you," he murmured, giving her a winsome look. Sometimes she wondered if
he knew how goofy he was and did it on purpose,
acting outrageous when other people only felt that
way and tried to cover it up with a semblance of pre-
fuck conversation.

"Dance with me," she said, "and maybe I'll say
yes."

They danced, she had a glass of white wine, and he
had his hands all over her. He had a nice touch, he

was cuddly, and the girls from class said he was a terrific lay. It would be easy to find yourself aroused by him, she thought, and then allowed herself to be.

"I just want to lick you all over," he said in a little-boy voice. "Please . . ."

"Okay," Kit said.

She gave him her address and he followed her in his car. At her house he put on some soft music, lit some candles. Then he took her clothes off, just like people were always doing in books and movies but never in real life, or at least not in her experience, which had been considerable. Then they went into the bedroom and he did indeed lick her all over, very slowly and patiently, with obvious enjoyment, until Kit decided she should have said yes to a session with him a long time ago. Then he did a lot of other things which she enjoyed just as much.

After her fourth orgasm she was beginning to get a little sore. She glanced at the clock on the bedside table and figured Tip would be home in three hours. "How about we get some sleep?" she said.

"Sleep?"

She wondered if he was one of those guys who sneaked out in the middle of the night when you were sleeping. Nobody ever said he was; they said he was absolutely terrific. Guys who sneaked out were not terrific; they were total shits, and she had only met one of them and she thought he was probably bisexual. "Just for a while," she said.

He rolled over and put his arms and legs around

her until she nearly disappeared. "Can you fall asleep like this?" he asked. "I want to hold you."

"I'll try."

He was nibbling gently on her ear, but Kit was so tired she drifted right off to sleep. She slept lightly but pleasantly, dreaming she was sailing away in a balloon.

She woke to the sound of Tip's car pulling up, and then she heard the front door opening and closing quietly. The bedroom was softly golden from the morning sun seeping through the thick tan linen shades. Seth was still asleep and so was her arm. She curled up into a little ball and waited. She was excited, but she was not afraid. Her heart was pounding the way it did just before the camera started rolling. She closed her eyes and pretended to be asleep.

She opened her eyes and saw Tip standing in the doorway, still in his uniform; with his gun in its holster, big, black, and phallic. She didn't say anything. He didn't say anything either, just stood there looking at her with an expression on his face she couldn't read. He glanced at Seth and then looked away again at her, as if her bed partner were completely beneath contempt but she was the one with whom he was concerned.

Then Seth woke up and turned dead white. The poor jerk thought this was some kind of a raid. He sort of gurgled.

Then Tip just turned around without a word and walked out of the room and out of the house.

And, it turned out later that day, out of her life. He

came back when he knew she was at her yoga class (there was a hang-up on her answering machine and she knew it was him) and took all his clothes and stuff. He left her a note on the kitchen table. All it said was: *You don't want to be happy.*

Amateur psychiatrist, what did he know? She was rid of him and his dependency and demands and she felt perfectly fine. It was just what she wanted.

It was only later that night, when she noticed her teddy bear propped up on the bedroom chair, that she got a lump in her throat. It was sad that things changed. She didn't know what to do about it. She hid the teddy bear in the back of the closet and went out to meet Emma and a couple of guys who were friends of hers on the picture for dinner.

Chapter Nineteen

IT WAS NEARLY summer in New York, and Annabel found herself counting her blessings; not because she was happy but because it was the only way she could keep herself from becoming despondent. She felt she had come to a turning point in her life, as she had often before, but this time there was no action she could take. She could only wait.

Now it was Chris who was going to be starting an adventure, when the sales conference came up in late June. Emma was working, loving it, learning. Annabel saw her own summer looming ahead of her; planned, busy . . . lonely. In July she would start her summer sale. Then she would go to Europe for the collections. She could spend Sundays in the country with Chris and Alexander whenever she wanted to, and pretend with them that they had an ideal marriage. Other people might envy her for being beautiful and free, able to travel, to earn her own living, make her own choices. She wondered if they knew how limited her choices really were.

The young girls came into the boutique to splurge on "something sexy" to wear for their summer weekends in the Hamptons, where they shared communal rented houses and looked for boyfriends who might last all during the week. The wives came in, many of them Annabel's age, looking for something new to wear to the summer parties they would go to with their husbands, also in the country or at the beach, also on weekends. New York was a different city in the summer; everyone who could afford to escaped. The streets were filled with tourists in shorts, and the poor. Annabel thought of closing on Saturdays in August, but then she would have nothing to do. She didn't want to become a fixture at Chris's.

She had never had a lot of friends. She'd always had Chris, and then Emma, and Max, of course. There had always been young lovers. There were the girls in the store to keep her laughing during the day, but Maria was married and Pamela was living with a man now, a hairdresser who sent her to work every week looking like somebody else. Max was gone. Emma was away, eagerly pursuing her own life. Chris had always been busy. There were no more young lovers. Annabel wasn't sure she wanted another one. Wasn't it enough to have a job and one best friend? Did other people have more?

Yes they did: they had families.

People with families, who often envied her inde-

pendence, did not have long empty evenings.
Neither did those young girls who came into the boutique for a dress some man would want to charm off
them. Annabel knew it was possible for her to fill
every evening with social events if she wanted to—
she knew a lot of people; a lot of gay men, a lot of
divorced and single women, and they went everywhere, enjoying the things the city had to offer.
Maybe they didn't want to stay home alone either.

Sometimes she did go to publicity parties, or to
dinner with someone she saw twice a year, but she
couldn't see it becoming her life. When she had been
at Radcliffe she had gone to parties and dances to flirt
and find romance, then when she was married she
went to the country club because that was what everyone did, and then when she got divorced and
moved to New York she lived every day as if it were
an adventure, the way Emma did now. She had
changed. She had finally become that Serious Person
she had half-jokingly threatened Emma she would
become, and although it had been the disaster she
had predicted, she didn't know what else to be.

"I wish you would meet a divine man," Emma said
on the phone.

"So do I," Annabel said, pretending to be cheerful.

"You always have a man whenever you want one,"
Chris said when they were alone together.

"Maybe I don't want one," Annabel said lightly.

All she knew was that for the first time she wanted
one her age. She wondered what kind of older man
she would like. He would have to be attractive and

sexy, bright and interesting. She saw dozens of men walking briskly up Madison Avenue after their work day, getting out of taxis, going into large apartment buildings and expensive townhouses. She saw them when she closed the shop for the night, and when she walked home. Some were well dressed, attractive, in good shape, the right age. All had the purposeful look of a man who has somewhere he wants to go. They were going home to their families.

The men were her age, but unless they had married their college sweetheart their women were mostly younger. She saw those women with their husbands, and their children, and the women were always much younger. Younger than their husbands, younger than she was. Annabel wondered if they were second wives.

She would be too old to be the second wife for a man her age. But who wanted a man her age who had never been married? A man could marry almost anybody. A nice-looking, successful man of forty-seven who was still a bachelor was always suspect. But if he was divorced after giving some woman a horrible life, society didn't seem to mind. Her ex-husband had remarried a long time ago.

Annabel supposed she had become fixated on much younger men after her bad experience with Bill Wood, and her rotten marriage. She had been afraid of permanence, or even the promise of it, because there was no such thing, and when you believed in it you got hurt. Even when you didn't believe in it you got hurt.

The evenings were longer and lonelier in the summer because it stayed light so long. In the winter you could hide at home and feel snug, cook something good, watch television. In the summer she was filled with an almost crazed nervous energy. So although she hated athletics, she began working out at a gym three evenings a week. At least it made her tired, and it was supposed to be virtuous.

And even so, walking up Madison Avenue alone with her exercise bag in her hand, she still saw all those men going home. Some of them had been to their own gyms, some had been at business drinks, or perhaps out cheating on their wives; but they all had one thing in common: now they were going home to their lives.

Chapter Twenty

CHRIS, UNPACKING IN her hotel room at the Beverly Wilshire Hotel in Beverly Hills, could not believe it had been only a year since the last sales conference of the Cameron magazines, the one where she had fled. It seemed an eternity, so much had happened to her. She looked around her room with the half-nervous, half-happy anticipation of a virgin bride. It was one of the special corner rooms in the "old wing," which was actually the new wing now since it had been redecorated with central air conditioning, marble bathrooms, and flowered fabric on the walls. Her main view was of Rodeo Drive with its expensive shops, and the mountains beyond, purplish in the smoggy haze. She had a dressing room with a second telephone in it, and in the bedroom there was a king-size bed, an armoire with a television set and radio hiding inside, some other furniture, a small refrigerator, and a half bottle of champagne in a cooler with two glasses, and a basket of fruit, both sent by the management.

The sales conference was to be held downtown, a half-hour's drive away, and everyone could stay wherever they wished. People who wanted to play tennis or be seen at the Polo Lounge stayed at the Beverly Hills Hotel; for romantic privacy it was the Bel-Air; if you were a dedicated New Yorker who wanted to be able to walk around in what passed for a city you stayed at the Beverly Wilshire; and if you wanted to fall out of bed and get right to the meetings you could stay downtown in the new Bonaventure. Chris had asked Cameron what he recommended, and he said he liked to stay at the Wilshire, so she said she would too.

How much more obvious could she get? And yet, she told herself, he knew Los Angeles and she did not; it was a normal question. She hoped he would know she was being devious . . . she hoped he wouldn't. She looked at the champagne and decided to save it for him, just in case . . .

She had finished unpacking and had taken a shower when the phone rang. "Chris? Bill Cameron."

Instant replay.

"I know," she said, smiling.

"I'm taking a few people for an early dinner at Chasen's tonight at seven o'clock, and I wondered if you'd like to join us."

"I'd love to," she said.

Instant replay continues. But this time maybe a different team would win.

Again, Cameron had invited four other people, and again he seated Chris next to him. No one could read her mind. They were relaxed and jolly. She was in a fog. The restaurant was all wood paneling and pink and glowing, there were celebrities, it was very expensive. Cameron had brought his guests there in a limousine. He said his magazines had done so well that he was going to start a new one, called *Fashion and Entertainment West,* and that he would talk more about it at the meeting tomorrow. He seemed so excited and pleased, so confident, so totally in control. Chris found it terribly attractive. It had been a long time since she had seen him with a group of people, taking over and leading them in that charming, interested way of his.

She ordered dry broiled fish because she was still on her diet, and then she couldn't eat it anyway because of all the emotions swirling around inside her.

"Jet lag?" Cameron said kindly, noticing.

"I guess so," she lied.

"We'll make it an early evening. Everybody's tired."

"I'm not," she said bravely.

"You will be. Trust me."

Yes she did, she trusted him. If this was to be an affair, she would let him orchestrate it. He had said he never gave up, and that it meant whatever she wanted it to; all she had to do now was indicate that she was ready.

After dinner he took them all back to the hotel in the limousine. Everyone was feeling the three-hour time change, and tomorrow the meetings started at nine o'clock. Their rooms were on different floors (she knew Cameron had a suite), and he got off the elevator before her. "Goodnight," he said cheerfully to everyone who was left. *One flight below me,* Chris thought. *Easy to use the stairs.* But she knew it wouldn't be tonight.

She had no messages, and it was too late to call New York. She didn't want to anyway, in case Alexander had decided to stay over at James's apartment. If he had, she didn't want to know. A maid had turned down the bed and laid a breakfast menu on the pillow. She had also closed the drapes. Chris opened them again so she could see her view. Twinkling lights, mountains, a place far away from New York. A place where her adventure might begin. She wondered if Cameron would call. No, he wouldn't, not tonight, but she hoped he was thinking about her. She got into bed and suddenly realized how exhausted she was. She was asleep in an instant, and her last thought was that he had been right as usual.

At the opening meeting in the morning Cameron spoke about the new magazine he was going to start. It would be based here in Los Angeles, and would be like the New York based *Fashion and Entertainment*, and also different, as the lifestyles of the two Coasts were different. Some of the features and articles would appear in both magazines; others would be specially written for the local audience. Each editor would coordinate with his or her counterpart to see which material would be suitable for both, and the Managing Editors would serve as consultants to both editions.

At the coffee break Chris cornered Cameron. "I like your new idea," she said. "Does it mean I'm going to get a raise?"

"I knew you'd say that," he said, amused. "How about lunch?"

"Instead of a raise, or besides?" she said, smiling at him. She was flirting! She who had never flirted in her life was suddenly flirting.

"Besides, if you pay for lunch."

"I like that deal," Chris said. They both knew lunch was free anyway.

At lunch he deliberately sat at a large table so they could be joined by other people, and soon was deep in a business discussion. He would be hiring the new staff immediately. He had already taken more office space in the building he now used for his West Coast headquarters. Several of the people at the table had suggestions for possible editors, capable colleagues who were out of work because of the squeeze in publishing.

After lunch they went back for more meetings. On her way, Chris was stopped by Cameron's light touch on her arm. "Remember the party last year that we didn't go to?"

"Of course," Chris said, her heart beginning to pound wildly. "The mariachi band and the donkey wearing a hat."

"This year it's a buffet indoors. Harder to sneak away. But I thought after the cocktails, when everybody's still milling around, I could give you a look and then you could head for the door and I'd follow, and then we could have dinner together someplace decent."

"I'd love that," Chris said.

He nodded and walked away. She sat through the rest of the meetings in the same fog she had been in last night at Chasen's, frightened as well as determined. She knew the decision was still hers. But she also knew she had made it back in New York. She wanted him.

In her room—bathed, perfumed, carefully made up, dressed for the party—she phoned Annabel. "I'm scared," Chris said. "I feel like I'm a kid again."

"I don't know why that scares you," Annabel said cheerfully. "As I recall, back in college when it was considered a major sin to go all the way, you couldn't wait to do it with Alexander."

"That was Alexander. And this isn't. I've been married for fifteen years and never . . ."

"It's not a marriage anymore," Annabel said.

"Besides Alexander I've only slept with two men in my entire life—both before I was married. One was when Alexander went to Paris for all those years. And the other was a one-night stand."

"This isn't a lifetime commitment, you know," Annabel said. "Cheer up. Maybe it'll be a one-night stand too."

"Oh God."

"Why are you groaning?"

"Because I *like* him. Cameron's too good for a one-night stand."

"Just take it one lay at a time," Annabel said.

This time Chris really did groan. But when she hung up she was feeling better.

The cocktail party before the buffet dinner was so crowded that Chris found it easy to slip away unnoticed. Cameron had a car waiting, and he drove to a restaurant that looked like a tiny roadhouse, called Dominick's. The neon sign in front was out and it looked closed, but he drove right into the parking lot and entered through the kitchen in back, giving the woman cooking in the steamy little kitchen a hug. It was dark inside the restaurant, with red leatherette booths, probably not even ten, checked tablecloths, a Reserved sign on every empty table, a bar, and a jukebox playing old Sinatra records. It all reminded Chris of the kind of places people had gone to on dates when she was young; other people, not she. She had gone to the library to pine over Alexander.

Then her eyes got used to the darkness and she recognized some movie stars sitting in the booths. It was not exactly like the places of her youth, but then neither was she the same person. They ordered white wine and the waitress brought them an enormous carafe.

"Addie, you're going to kill us," Cameron said.

"It's closing night, Bill. Liquor's on the house."

"They always close for the summer," Cameron told

Chris. "Nobody knows when they'll open in the fall, so you just keep calling."

"Is that why the light in front is out?"

"No, it's always out. Dom didn't want people he didn't know. They didn't have to be celebrities to get in; he just had to like them. One night I saw him keep a famous movie star waiting at the bar for hours, getting angrier and angrier because all the tables were empty—and just because Dom had decided he didn't like him."

"This is a strange city," Chris said. "Ma Maison has an unlisted phone number, this place turns out its sign."

"I'm beginning to see an article for you to write."

"Oh no . . ."

"Oh yes."

They sipped their wine in silence, looking at each other. Chris's heart started to pound again and she looked away. "Do you always leave your company parties?" she asked.

"If possible. I'm paying for them, so I don't have to go to them too. Life is too short to waste at parties."

They ordered broiled chicken and mixed green salad. Chris didn't bother to ask them to leave off the dressing; she knew she wouldn't be able to choke down a bite anyway. Cameron had the ability to make everyone comfortable, and he could have made her comfortable too, but sex always messed up everything. She had repressed her sexuality for so long she wondered if it was dead forever. A year and a half

. . . What would happen if she let go and gave vent to all those feelings she had locked up inside her?

They both pretended to eat. Chris kept dropping things. She knocked all the french fries off her plate and felt like a fool as she tried to put them back. Then she gave up.

"I don't know what's the matter with me tonight," she said.

"I'm in love with you," he said.

She stared at him. Warmth washed over her, and she felt something begin to flutter faintly inside her— her dead heart.

"Why me?" she blurted out. He laughed.

"You shouldn't say 'Why me?'" he said. "You should say 'Why not?'"

"I have inappropriate responses," she said. "Someone told me that a very long time ago, a friend. He said I had the most inappropriate responses of any girl he knew."

"I don't get involved with people I work with," he said. "With other people, sometimes. But I couldn't help this happening. And I want you to know that I would never do anything to threaten either of our marriages."

"Does that mean no?" she said in dismay. It was out of her mouth before she could stop herself. The old Chris, open, honest, outrageous. He was laughing again, a hearty, happy laugh, looking at her with genuine affection.

"Of course it doesn't mean no," he said. "I'm just

trying to cover all the important points." He stopped laughing. "Does what you just said mean yes?"

She nodded.

They left the restaurant and went back to the hotel. The elevator was empty so they both got off at his floor. They walked side by side, discreetly apart, into his suite.

He had a large living room and a bedroom, and he had set up a bar. There was a king-size bed, already turned down for the night. When he came close to her she smelled his cologne again, the cologne that had so touched her the first time they went out to dinner, that night in Arizona. He put his arms around her and kissed her for the first time, and he seemed as desperate as she was. Chris held him tightly, almost sighing with the relief of being held, of being so wanted, feeling how aroused he was—and Alexander sailed into her mind like the moon over the treetops, flooding her world with pale, baleful light.

She tried to will Alexander out of her head. She brought up anger, resentment. She tried to push away the love and the guilt, and concentrate on the kissing. She was betraying Alexander, who did not want her, and she was betraying Cameron too, who did, and who had no idea what she was thinking. He led her into the bedroom.

He was a perfect lover; tender and passionate, considerate and not shy. He was much better than Alexander. She had always been the aggressor with Alexander, hoping every time that she would succeed, but here she was the one being wooed. She was appreciative of it, but she might as well have been anesthetized. *I'm wasting all this,* she thought in despair. *I'm so lucky, I never thought I'd have this, he's trying so hard; and I might as well be somewhere else.* She was sure he must know, but then she realized he didn't, and the knowledge made her feel so tender that she loved him.

She remembered the first time with Alexander, so long ago at college. It had been a total disappointment except for the moments afterward when he held her lovingly. And she remembered thinking that the first time was always said to be strained. But not for Annabel, not for other people. Only for her, trying to make love to one man with another man inside her head.

But of course he knew—he had to. He wasn't a fool, and she wasn't a faker.

"It will be better next time," Cameron said afterward. "We have lots of time."

How could they have? There was only tomorrow, and then they were going home to New York, where he had promised nothing would threaten either of their marriages.

Chris sneaked back to her room in the middle of the night, using the stairs. She hoped Alexander hadn't called, and when she saw that the red message light on her phone wasn't lit she breathed a sigh of relief. She would have to call him tomorrow morning; they had never gone this long without one of them phoning the other. Then she was annoyed. Had they become this estranged without even noticing? But she had to smile at the ridiculous humor of it. They had separate rooms, they both had lovers now—what was that if not estranged?

She got into bed and thought about Cameron, and her phone rang. *Alexander,* she thought, concerned. But it was Cameron. Warmth and happiness seeped into her.

"I just called to say goodnight," he said.

"I conjured you up," Chris said.

"Good. Tomorrow night . . . the dreaded banquet. We have to go because there are place cards, but can we meet afterward?"

"Of course."

"I love you," he said. "Sleep well." He hung up before she could say that she loved him back, and she wondered if he was afraid she wouldn't say it. She dialed his room.

"It's Chris."

"I know."

"How did you know?"

"Who else would call me at this hour?"

"I just wanted to say that I love you too."

"Good," he said.

After they hung up she realized what she had done. She had cheated on Alexander for the first time, but more importantly, she had told another man she loved him, and had meant it. She didn't love Cameron in the same way as she loved Alexander, but love itself was the real betrayal. Alexander had shown her that.

She wasn't going to think about it anymore tonight.

She wanted to keep on being happy for as long as she could.

The next day at the final meetings and in the evening at the banquet she tried to act normal. It was easier than she had expected. After the banquet people went back to their hotels to pack, or to have a final drink with friends, and in the confusion Chris found it simple to disappear into Cameron's suite. He had given her his extra key, but he was already waiting for her.

Then she was in bed with him, and she knew this was her last chance for a long time, and Alexander was still in her mind. She spoke to herself again, this time with perfect logic. *There is no point in being here if I'm not here.* And now, finally, for the first time, she concentrated totally on what was happening to her body instead of on Alexander, and suddenly Alexander was gone. She was in a world of sensations, and nothing else mattered. It was easy now, everything was easy, and she never wanted to stop.

"You see?" Cameron told her afterwards.

"Don't gloat."

"I'm not gloating," he said innocently.

"Well, I am."

He poured a glass of brandy and they shared it in bed. He was to stay on in California for several days on business and she was to leave the next day at noon for New York. Chris wondered what would happen to them.

"Why do you look so sad?" he asked.

"I can't do this in New York and then go home every night to my husband. I can't handle it."

"Are you ditching me?" He smiled, but she could see from his eyes that he was upset.

"No, of course not," she said. She really did love him; and she could never have believed it was possible to love two men at the same time. "I just don't know what . . . how . . ."

"I have it planned," he said. "First of all, I want you to know that I never do anything in New York that would hurt my wife. It's really a small town, and people talk. I certainly don't want to do anything that would make you uncomfortable either. I told you I will never jeopardize our marriages. I travel a great deal, as you're aware of. Now you're going to have to travel too. Did you think you could be a special consultant to the new magazine on the telephone?"

"I didn't really think about it," Chris said.

"You'll have to fly out to California once a month for a day or two of meetings. It's a tiring trip, so I could arrange for it to be over a long weekend."

"And you'd be there?"

"Of course I would. I run the meetings."

"I think I could handle that," Chris said.

"I know you can."

"So much sneaking around," she said. "So much planning."

He smiled. "You'll begin to find it makes our relationship much more romantic."

She thought how ironic life was, and that although it was the antithesis of what she had always thought of as romance, he was probably right.

Chapter Twenty-one

IT WAS FALL. In Connecticut the leaves were turning color, the children were back at school, people wore warm sweaters. Pumpkin time. The weather changed and changed back as the seasons changed, but people like Daphne whose lives had been irrevocably altered could not. She knew now that she had become a different person, and that she no longer loved Richard.

He had recovered from his heart attack but was still taking it easy; going into the office for half days. She knew he saw Melissa in New York. His half day at the office was in the morning, but he hardly ever came home to Greenwich until dinner time. Daphne no longer wanted to kill her, but only felt sorry for her. Richard was not such a prize—he was merely charming.

Over and over, like picking at a sore, she relived

the tender scene at the hospital when she had told Richard she loved him and he replied that he loved her, while the other woman he had been making love to and lying to waited outside. She and Melissa were both The Other Woman. He had lied to them both.

It was not his cheating that had made Daphne stop loving him; it was everything. He was no longer someone she could respect or love. For decades now, he had sat at the very core of her life, like some benevolent-malevolent monarch, arranging festivals for his subjects, withholding what they needed the most. He could give you a million reasons why he wasn't doing anything wrong to anybody, and he believed them. She had believed them once, too.

She remembered her good resolution to discuss everything now, and how quickly it had been thwarted. Whenever she tried to have a frank talk with Richard about their lives he told her she was going to upset him, that he was still convalescing, his health unstable. So he would not even allow her that.

At the beginning of November she telephoned Dr. Price. "How was Richard's last checkup?"

"Just fine," the doctor said. "Didn't he tell you?"

"Of course, but sometimes he forgets little things. You know Richard, he wants to be as healthy as a horse and it's more convenient to forget."

"I told him he could resume a normal life. I do want him to watch his diet though; cut down on fats and red meat, a little less drinking. I want him to walk every day, or swim at the club, or whatever he enjoys. His weight is fine."

"And sex?" Daphne said casually. "Is it all right for him to have sex?"

Dr. Price sounded surprised. "I told him yes a long time ago. Has he been afraid . . . ?"

"Oh, no," Daphne lied, although Richard hadn't touched her since he came home from the hospital and she wouldn't have let him if he had tried. "I just wanted to be sure."

"Richard can have a normal life now," Dr. Price said.

"And what about stress?"

The doctor laughed. "Stress, unfortunately, is an unavoidable fact of a normal life."

That evening when Richard came home from the city she was waiting for him. She had a glass of white wine beside her, but no cigarettes. She had stopped smoking in his presence, even though it was hard for her, and tonight if she gave him another heart attack she didn't want to blame it on her smoking. "Sit down," she said graciously. "Let's talk."

"Daph, will you let me unwind?"

"Of course."

While he was upstairs she finished her wine, smoked several cigarettes next to the open window. She waited. He came down at seven fifteen, because they always had dinner at seven thirty. He went directly to the bar and poured himself a drink. She said nothing about it. From now on his health precautions would be his own concern.

"Well, now," she said, in that same gracious tone.

"The doctor gave me a very good report today. You're as good as new."

"I do feel a little better every day," Richard said.

"I'm glad," Daphne said. "Because now we can discuss our divorce."

He looked at her in surprised distress. "You want to divorce me?"

"Yes. Now you can be with Melissa full time," Daphne said with a tiny smile. She couldn't believe she was acting so cool and in control, but inside she felt dead so all this came easily.

His face paled, just slightly. "I can't believe you would divorce me because of one little meaningless affair."

"I doubt Melissa thinks it's meaningless," Daphne said. "And anyway, that's not the reason I'm divorcing you."

"But you love me."

Daphne smiled.

"It was a lapse," Richard said. "These things happen. I'm not perfect."

"Neither am I," Daphne said.

They sat there looking at each other for a long time in silence.

"What do you want?" he asked.

"A divorce."

"And what else?"

"The house. You'll be better off in an apartment in New York anyway. Child support, of course. The boys' tuition. Elizabeth's home."

"You're asking for a lot."

"My lawyer will discuss it with yours."

"You have your own money," Richard said. "A great deal as I recall."

"I'm not asking you to pay my bills. The house is paid for. The boys need a place to live. So does our daughter, even though she's not with us. They all deserve an education. Consider it a settlement."

"A settlement for what?" Richard said. "For my affair?"

"For my life," Daphne said.

"I don't understand," he said. "What did I ever do to you?"

Poor Richard. She thought of all the good times, their youth, their love. They had created their own make-believe world; eroded bit by bit, and finally simply collapsing under the weight of truth. Poor Richard. Poor Daphne. Poor Jonathan. Poor all of them.

"I did it to me, too," Daphne said quietly. "And no, you don't understand."

He left two days later. He moved into a hotel. He said it would be inappropriate to move in with Melissa, but Daphne suspected he wasn't ready either for a commitment or for a hard-working young lawyer's small apartment. Daphne and Richard agreed that she would wait to tell the boys until they came home for Thanksgiving. It would be easier face to face. Her divorce lawyer's father had known her father, and was said to be excellent. Everyone was extremely civilized. They were, after all, still Caldwells.

But she wasn't. Not anymore.

Chapter Twenty-two

By fall Emily's Cookies was an established local success. She had worried that in this city of fads it would be only another fad, but instead business got better and better. People told other people about her. She was even filling orders for some restaurants, The Couriers rushing them there every day, fresh and warm. And now the most amazing, flattering thing had happened: she was going to be interviewed for the new magazine *Fashion and Entertainment West;* by Christine Spark English, whom she'd known at Radcliffe.

Chris Spark, who had always been so smart and talented, and who had finally married Alexander English, that handsome boy she'd had such a crush on all through school. Emily wondered if Chris's marriage had turned out better than hers. The piece was on California women who had started their own small businesses. Chris had written to her, and then phoned, and was coming out for several days, staying at the Beverly Wilshire Hotel. Emily was sorry she didn't have her old house so she could have invited Chris to stay with her. But of course, if she had her old house she'd still have Ken, so she wouldn't have dared to invite Chris. They were meeting at the store, and then they were going to go to Emily's rented apartment to talk.

Peter was practically delirious with joy. He kept saying what a great publicity break this was, and telling Emily to be terrific. She didn't even want to think about it, but of course she thought about nothing else. She had never in her life expected to be interviewed, and besides being flattered she was scared to death. So what else was new? She was always scared to death. But she was beginning to get over it in a lot of ways.

Chris arrived in the morning as soon as the store opened, looking chic and very New York. They'd seen each other at their twentieth reunion six years ago, so they recognized each other immediately.

"This piece is for our December Christmas issue," Chris said.

"Oh, good," Emily said. She had prepared a little promotion package for Chris, with their Christmas tin—thin red and green lines in the butterscotch and white checks—and the matching Christmas paper bags, and the nice-looking flyers they were sending out to a large mailing list they had bought. Of course there were hot cookies for Chris to taste, and Emily had brought in coffee to go with them. She introduced Chris to Peter and Jared and the kids who were working in the "factory"; and did a guided tour, which took all of about five minutes.

"I have to tell you I'm very honored," Emily said. "What made you pick me anyhow?"

Chris grinned. "My boss said, 'There's a cookie lady in California who went to school with you.' When I heard it was you I thought it was a great idea. I wouldn't have suspected you would turn out to be a successful businesswoman—the last time I saw you, you were exactly what we were brought up to be."

"A dishrag," Emily said, and grinned back. "But I'm not so successful yet, just getting there."

"Wait till you're in the magazine," Chris said.

"I still can't believe it," Emily said, shivering with pleasure as she remembered. "Everything happened so fast. First I thought we were going to be a total disaster, and then . . ." She told Chris the story of their first few days. As they talked, the store was already full of customers, as it always was now. "Why don't we go to my apartment where we can talk in peace?"

They went in Emily's car so Chris wouldn't get lost. Emily had bought flowers, and there were books and magazines all over, so the place didn't look so temporary and unlived in, even though she was hardly ever there. They sat on the living room couch and had more coffee, and Emily talked about volume and orders and their future plans.

"But how did you get started?" Chris said.

"Oh, God. It was almost an accident. My husband threw me out. My son was looking for a summer job. I had always been sort of famous for my cookies . . . No, don't say that about Ken throwing me out. I wasn't poor—I had money and credit cards—it isn't as if I was on the street, destitute or something. Actually I didn't have to *do* anything." She was sure she was screwing up the interview and felt like a fool. Then she pulled herself together and went on. "I guess I'm sort of jabbering, but I was never interviewed before."

"That's all right," Chris said. "You're doing fine. You and Ken are separated now, I gather."

"Yes. We might get back together, I don't know. But this business is my life now, and even if I do go back to Ken it won't be in the old way. I mean, I won't just be filling up time, and waiting for him. Maybe you shouldn't say that either."

Chris laughed. "If you keep making me take out the interesting parts we won't have any interview."

"Do you think this is interesting?"

"It is to me. We weren't educated to go into business. Or to take care of ourselves if our marriages ended. We were to be the helpmeets of powerful men and live happily ever after."

"Yes," Emily said. "That's absolutely true. Education for Education's Sake. I got it all mixed up with being a perfect person. Maybe we were supposed to. Remember that Gracious Living nonsense we were taught at Radcliffe? Some of us laughed at it, but I believed all of it. The house mother pouring the demitasse in the living room after dinner. No jeans allowed in the dining room; we had to dress. And we couldn't wear slacks in Cambridge, even in the snow. We had to freeze to keep our ladylike image."

"Yes," Chris said, nodding and smiling.

"And remember Curfew?" Emily went on. "And the sign-out book? Social Pro for breaking the rules, for coming in late, remember? And we couldn't let boys even peek upstairs, *ever*. It was a sexy, forbidden seraglio—full of girls in curlers and pimple cream." Now that she'd started, she couldn't stop: it all came pouring out. Chris just kept silently nodding agreement, fixing her with bright, sympathetic eyes. "I remember when the girl on Bells would say: 'You have a caller,'" Emily said, "and how I'd come down like a princess, all fixed up. And the phone messages from 'Mr. X' . . . We couldn't call a boy back, remember that? It was considered too pushy. The grown-ups, society, told us we were so smart and intellectual and special, but then they told us not to let anybody know it or we'd scare the men away. We were supposed to be perfect ladies, virgins, compliant hypocrites; and the future wives of Harvard men if we followed the rules."

"Yes," Chris said; rather sadly, almost mysteriously, Emily thought. "The Rules."

"We judged people by how they followed the rules," Emily said. "The Saturday night date . . . if he was a gentleman he'd call you on Monday for Saturday, Tuesday at the latest. Ken did. We both followed all the rules. Always. And we started to go steady so soon after we met, because we thought we knew each other, because we both followed the rules and that was supposed to be the way you knew what a person was."

"So many secrets . . ." Chris said, in that same odd tone.

"And you know what?" Emily said. "Ken and I did have Gracious Living when we got married. Fresh flowers all the time, lovely food, beautiful things, I read the right books . . ."

"A house in the country for weekends," Chris said. Her voice sounded dreamy and ironic. "A fire in the fireplace . . . good wine . . ."

"I wonder about some of those other women like me," Emily said. "Under all that Gracious Living I bet they're living the same kind of lonely, stunted lives that I was."

"I'm sure," Chris said.

"I certainly made a big speech, didn't I," Emily said with a little laugh. "This is the first time anybody ever listened to me."

"You give a terrific interview," Chris said.

"Was that my interview?" Emily asked, a little taken aback. "I thought we were just talking."

"That, too."

"But I don't want you to print everything I said! The part about my life being awful. And how circumstances just kind of threw me into this at first. Because I'll tell you the truth: all my life I was a wimp and a terrified doormat, and I don't want to be that anymore. I want to be independent. I don't want it to look like I had to do this; I want it to be that I chose to do it."

"But you did choose to do it," Chris said. "That's what you told me."

"It's true."

"And you worked hard."

"I did. I still do. I'm going to keep on."

"I'll give you some good advice, Emily," Chris said. "The next time you do an interview, be careful what you say. I'm a friend, and you can trust me. But nobody reads the Miranda Act to a celebrity."

"Oh, a celebrity!" Emily laughed. "I'm never going to be that."

"You never know," Chris said.

"Tell me about your life now," Emily said. "I bet it's terrific."

"It's interesting," Chris said mildly. "I never expected to be this involved in a career either."

"And are you still as happy with Alexander as you used to think you would be?"

Chris smiled. "I didn't have the faintest idea about anything back then. I was simply obsessed."

"And now?"

"Let's just say . . . I'm older and more realistic."

Poor Chris. Emily understood. She had been unprepared for life too, as they all had been. But maybe nobody could ever prepare you for the things that happened. "Are you free for dinner?" she asked. "I thought you might be alone, and I know a lot of lovely places."

"Can you give me a raincheck?" Chris said. She didn't look like somebody who was alone at all.

"Of course."

"Do you ever come to New York?"

"I'm hoping to," Emily said.

"Then we'll definitely have dinner in New York. Or lunch. Whichever you prefer."

"You have a deal," Emily said. "I know two people in New York now. I'm really going to have to get there."

Chris's article appeared in the magazine at the end of November, and Emily's life changed overnight. There was an order for five hundred tins from IBM. Mail and phone orders came pouring in, and cars jostled for space outside in the street all day, double parked while their owners rushed in to buy the cookies that were newly chic. The ovens were going day and night, and she had to hire extra help; luckily there also seemed to be an unending supply of college kids who wanted part-time jobs during this holiday season. A lot of them wanted to stay on for good, and it looked as if she would need them to. Peter was negotiating to get the lease on the pizza place next door, so they could break through and expand.

"Maybe we're being premature . . ." Emily said. "I mean, Christmas is cookie season."

"It's always cookie season," Peter said. "Let's lock this deal in now, before they find out we're rich and charge us double."

"We're not rich yet," Emily said, but she was pleased, and secretly thought they would be soon.

She introduced a new recipe: butterscotch chip marshmallow, making sure it wasn't too sweet and cloying, which wasn't an easy feat, and it did well as soon as it appeared. She sent the kids out to the shopping malls again on the day she revealed her new flavor, and this time instead of having to cajole people to take free cookies they were mobbed.

Peter was looking for a good press agent now, and had stopped even mentioning going back to school. He had given up the apartment with all those roommates and now had one of his own; his first step on the way to the beach house, the expensive sports car, the gorgeous live-in girl friend and the killer dog.

It was at this moment that Ken invited Emily to dinner.

She thought: Why not? He had been phoning her regularly and acting civil. If she entertained thoughts of going back to him they should at least discuss their future face to face.

He picked her up at her apartment, looking distinguished in a suit and tie, and took her to Chasen's. She thought he looked a lot better than when she'd last seen him; not so thin and wasted. He ordered a very expensive white wine, saying he thought she would like it, and was polite and charming. "Come home for the holidays," he said. "We'll go to a little off island near Hawaii for Christmas. A deserted island where we can get to know each other again."

"But Christmas is our busiest time," Emily said.

"The boys can run the business."

He was saying it gently and persuasively, but it hurt. Why did Ken always think she was useless? She could take a vacation if she wanted to—she was only as far as the nearest phone, and whenever things were running smoothly she was actually the figurehead, even though she was also the famous Emily. "I don't know," she said.

"I'll hire a boat," Ken said. "We can go to several islands. Would you like that?"

She thought about it. She didn't like boats, and she didn't sit in the sun much anymore. Ken had accused her of being fat and flabby and old, and now he intended to look at her in merciless sunlight in a bathing suit? She preferred Chasen's in a dress. Besides, even though Ken looked a lot more like his former sane self, the idea of being alone on a boat in the middle of nowhere with him was more frightening than romantic. "I'd rather go to one island," she said. "You pick it."

"All right," he said, looking pleased. "Christmas week. It will be like a second honeymoon."

They hadn't had a dinner like this, where he actually talked to her, the way he talked to other people at dinner parties but never to her, in ages. She could see why everyone liked Ken. The wine and the roseate atmosphere of the restaurant relaxed her, and she began to look at him as a man again instead of the unpredictable monster she had once lived with. He was still so attractive . . . She had never stopped thinking that, even when she liked nothing about him at all.

After dinner, she thought he would drive her back to her apartment, but instead he took her to their house, the home they had once shared. "I don't think . . ." Emily began, but he stopped her.

"Just for a drink," he said.

They sat on the couch and he poured her a glass of wine because he knew she didn't like brandy. He had music playing on the stereo. It was just like a date, but they were married . . . it seemed strange. She liked it better than marriage.

He looked at her winningly, and then he leaned over and kissed her lightly. "I missed you so much," he said.

"Oh, Ken, I wish that were true."

"It *is* true," he said. He kissed her again, this time more seriously. Despite her reservations she found herself enormously flattered. "Stay," he murmured. "Please stay."

"I . . ."

"I'll drive you back in the morning."

She stayed. She was back in her room, her bed, with her husband, and it seemed both different and familiar. They made love the way they always did, perhaps better, perhaps more lingeringly, because he was trying. And while it was happening Emily realized that she had never really liked sex very much with Ken. She had liked the idea of it, because it was supposed to mean they loved each other, but often he had stopped before she was satisfied, and often she had faked an orgasm because she didn't want him to think it hadn't been rewarding for her, or to offend him. They had never really discussed their sex life, and she wouldn't have been able to tell him the truth even if they had tried.

He had told her she was a boring lover, but so was he. At least for her. Maybe he was better with those other women, or perhaps she never *had* been very highly sexed. She might have been frightened right out of her sexuality by her mother's warnings. Emily sighed, and Ken took it for a sigh of relaxation and bliss. He pulled out, and she wished she could go home.

The next morning he drove her back as he had promised, and she said she would go away with him for Christmas. She told herself that sex wasn't everything, but that maybe on their "second honeymoon" it would be better.

She had only two weeks to get ready for her departure. It should have been more than enough, but she was beginning to feel a sort of excited anticipation, as if she and Ken might really have a second chance. She spent a whole day finding two bathing suits that were both sexy and flattering. She had her hair cut, and a manicure and pedicure. She had to make sure that Peter could run the business without her. It no longer was a concern to her whether or not Peter and Kate would miss being with either of their parents at Christmas: she knew they would not. Kate had made one token visit to the store, one day when Emily was at their accountant's office, and Peter had reported afterward with gleeful sibling rivalry that she'd seemed more taken with the help than the product.

"Attractive sales people never hurt," Emily said.

Her friends were not surprised she was going to try it again with Ken. This was a difficult town for single women of their age. For all its Hollywood pretensions, it was really the suburbs; spread out, isolated, early-to-bed; a place for couples, for being at home at night. The other life here, the one Ken lived without her, was one Emily could not imagine and had neither the wish nor the qualifications to enter. Her friends believed in compromise, especially when it came with the trappings of "romance."

Ken was busy too, getting ready for their trip, because he had so many patients who were upset that he was going to leave them, even though it was only for a week, and his time was fully booked. He phoned Emily every day, but he said it would be more like a second honeymoon if they didn't see each other until the night they left. She knew he meant not sleep together, and she was amused. She wondered if he suddenly found her so irresistible that to take her to dinner would mean he couldn't keep his hands off her, or if he was just trying to recapture something from their engagement. Wouldn't it be wonderful if they could recapture something . . . anything . . . She intended to try. If it didn't work, if it was a disaster, she could break off with him afterward. She refused to think that far ahead.

She arrived at his house—their house!—promptly

at six o'clock, suitcase in hand. He opened the door, a drink in his. He seemed neither drunk nor surly, so Emily was reassured, and when he offered her a glass of wine she thought it was festive. He gave her a warm kiss hello and told her he wasn't finished packing, so she went into the bedroom and sat on the bed, sipping her wine, watching him pack, and feeling pleased with herself for not offering to do it for him the way she would have in the old days.

"I hope you brought books," he said. "There's really nothing to do there. Lie on the beach, drink, talk . . ."

"I brought two," she said, "but I'll read yours when you're through with them."

Ken went into the bathroom to get some more things and she walked idly to his suitcase to see which books he had packed. Good; all the new novels she hadn't had time to read. She picked one up, and underneath, slipping out from inside a folded beach robe, she saw the edge of a plastic bag of cocaine. Her heart crashed.

She took the bag out and looked at it. There was enough dope there to keep Ken out of his mind for the entire week. When he came out of the bathroom she was still standing there, but she had put the cocaine back in his suitcase, right on top of the books so he would know she had seen it.

"Oh," he said, as if it was nothing. "I told you it's totally deserted and peaceful there. This is just for a little recreational high."

"You said you had given it up," Emily said, trying to sound calm.

"Am I acting stoned?"

"No . . ."

"Well, I am. Just a little. I told you I'd get it under control."

"Then why do you have to bring so much?"

"I'm a respectable citizen. I don't intend to run around a strange place trying to buy this stuff."

"Why do you need it at all?" She didn't even know why she'd asked. Whatever answer he gave her would be the wrong one.

"I don't *need* it," he said, sounding irritated suddenly, like the old, feared Ken. "I *want* it."

"So you can stand me," she said dully. She should have known. Miracles were limited. She'd already had her share. Ken wasn't going to change.

"Don't be stupid," he said. "I want it so we can have fun. Don't you want to have fun?"

She wondered if he had a gun in there too. She walked to the door. "I was willing to compromise," she said. "I was willing even to dream again. But not this way. It's not going to work. Not if you bring that stuff with you."

They looked at each other. She wished he would take the coke out of the suitcase and say he would go away with her without it, but she knew he never would. He didn't. "Don't you tell me what I can and can't do," he said.

"I don't intend to," Emily said. She walked down the stairs, trying to hide her fear, and picked up her suitcase. Ken had followed her. She glanced at him and saw he had no gun. It was not going to be a repeat of the last time. Not in any way. This time she had a place to go. "Enjoy your trip," she said coldly. Then she walked out the door, leaving him standing there.

She drove away, but this time she was not crying, not shaking, no longer frightened: feeling only a deep, sad disappointment. And then, as she drove back to her own apartment, even the disappointment melted, and left the beginning of what she recognized as a shell of strength. She smiled. She would leave Ken with that damn house with all its memories, and his drugs, and his lies, and while she was cleaning out her life she might as well also leave him Adeline.

Yes, she would definitely leave him Adeline.

Emily laughed, feeling strong and free, and, for the first time, a little crazy in a way she knew was not crazy at all.

The next morning she showed up at work. Everyone was surprised to see her. She got Peter aside. "Your father is back on cocaine and we're getting divorced," she said gently. "I'm sorry."

"That's life," Peter said. "Do you want to meet the potential press agent this week, as long as you're here?"

"Sure. The sooner the better."

"His name is Freddie Glick."

"Oh good," Emily said. "Like Sammy Glick."

"Who's that?"

"Never mind. It's from a novel."

The press agent wanted to meet them at the Polo Lounge for breakfast. He was wearing an open-necked red shirt, a black sport jacket, three gold chains nestled in his chest hair, and he looked like a middle-aged Las Vegas comic. He ordered two fried eggs and slurped them up while Emily and Peter drank coffee. She thought breakfast meetings were barbaric: people should eat breakfast alone at home in peace. While Glick drank his coffee he recited an impressive list of his celebrity clients and revealed his expensive fee. "But I don't think I can do anything for you," he said.

"Why not?" Emily said.

"So you make cookies. So what? What's the gimmick? You're not a sweet old granny, you're not a glamorous young thing in her twenties like Mrs. Fields. You're a normal, average, real person. How am I going to get you on television? Even newspaper and magazine interviews? I can start with the local papers, but eventually I'd want to go national. How am I going to sell a real person? I'll be perfectly honest with you, I'm not going to waste your time."

"How glamorous do you want me to be?" Emily asked.

"Hey, Mom, you're fine," Peter said. "Let's go."

"No. I'm asking a question."

Freddie Glick looked at her appraisingly. "Sort of a Joan Collins type might suit you. Could you do that?"

"Could you give me two months?"

He nodded slowly. "You really want this, don't you?"

"If I look the way you want, can you get me publicity?"

"Sure. I read that piece in *F.E.W.* You do a good interview. I wouldn't be here if you didn't."

"We have a meeting in two months," Emily said, and called for the check.

When she and Peter went back to the store Emily disappeared into the little office they'd opened in the rear. She started to make phone calls. First to her friend Karen, to find the name of the best plastic surgeon in town for a facelift. Karen was an authority on such matters, including the best hair colorist, the best makeup artist; but first things first. Karen said the best plastic surgeon this year was Dr. Harley Winthrop.

"I thought you were in Hawaii with Ken," Karen said.

"Change of plan. Call you later."

Next Emily called Dr. Winthrop's office. Even though it was Christmas week there was an appointment nurse there. "The first appointment for an interview would be at the end of February," the nurse said.

"I need it right away," Emily said.

"I'm sorry."

She took a deep breath. "I'm Dr. Kenneth Buchman's wife."

"Oh. Well then, just hold on a minute and let me see if we have any cancellations."

The nurse was back in a few seconds with an appointment for the beginning of the first week in January. Doctors' wives always got preference, especially when they were the wives of doctors as well known as Ken. "And I can schedule your surgery for the week after that," the nurse said in a new, very friendly voice. "I'll book the hospital room too. You want a private room, of course?"

"Of course," Emily said. "And private nurses."

"Fine, Mrs. Buchman. See you in ten days."

She had two months. That was more than enough time for everything. Emily looked in the mirror of her compact and imagined herself looking like something on the order of Joan Collins. She wondered if Ken had gone to Hawaii alone, or if he had taken someone. She couldn't care less. Fine, Mrs. Buchman. Of course, Mrs. Buchman. I've just found a cancellation and can fit you in, Mrs. Buchman. Aren't you lucky, Mrs. Buchman!

Emily smiled at her image in the mirror. *This is the last time I'll ever have to say I'm Ken's wife to get what I want,* she thought. *The next time I'll get it because I'm Emily.*

Chapter Twenty-three

AT THE BEGINNING of December Kit found out that Zack Shepard was casting a new movie. She made her agent get her the script, and as soon as she read it she knew that she had to have the supporting role, she had to be that girl; if she couldn't have that part she would die. It was her. It wasn't one of those airhead bimbos she was always playing, or those smartass teenagers—it was a real person, with layers and layers of complexity, strengths, weaknesses, everything. When she read the script she almost cried she wanted that part so much. Before, she'd always had to improve a part with her own complexities, but these were right here. Even the movie she'd finished last month was shit compared to this.

The truth was she was a little disappointed about the last movie. She wondered what would happen when it was released. The director had kept cutting her part because the fat bitch star she had most of her scenes with was jealous. The bitch kept saying: "Oh, I can't say that line. What's my motivation?"

Your motivation, Kit wanted to say, *is that you're here.*

But the director was a weakling who wanted everybody to love him, especially stars, and he kept letting the bitch change the lines, or making the screenwriter do it. The poor screenwriter kept chewing Maalox, and he always had a white rim around his mouth. When the scene was rewritten to everyone's satisfaction (except Kit's, of course), it naturally turned out that Kit's best lines were the ones that had to go so the star could have her motivation.

On her list of the things she would have when she herself became a powerful star, Kit added "Approval of cast, director, and script at all times." Well, she could dream, couldn't she?

Right now her dream was that new Zack Shepard movie. She wondered if he remembered her from the part she'd read for but didn't get. He probably saw thousands of actresses. He was reputed to be thorough. She remembered *him* very well. He was dark: dark hair, dark crackling eyes, and slim but very nicely built, with an intensity that was intellectual and sexual and something else she couldn't quite read. She thought it might have to do with his dedication to his private artistic furies. She liked that idea. He was only about five feet ten, but that was because he hadn't grown up in California. He was extremely attractive, in a way you wouldn't get easily tired of.

She thought she could be perfectly happy living with him. He would make her a star, and their life together would never be boring.

She would even marry him . . .

Her fantasies were, she realized, getting out of hand. She wouldn't mind fucking him, anyway. That, at least, was plausible. But more vital was getting a reading. Her agent arranged it without any trouble.

Everyone was auditioning the same scene; a confrontation between mother and daughter. It was the confrontation Kit had never had, but was certainly prepared for. She had been prepared for it all her life. In the short scene the two women talked about how they had betrayed each other, the mother doing it when the girl was a child, the daughter doing it to her in return when she grew up. Kit was aware that she wasn't a very loving daughter in her own life, but it was something she had never bothered to think about until she began rehearsing this scene. What a part! It was the supporting role, but it was just as important as the lead. She knew that if she got it and some egomaniac got the mother's part, Zack Shepard wouldn't let that actress start messing around with the script. *He* had balls.

She arrived at the reading looking fantastic. Zack Shepard seemed to remember her right away; he smiled and stood up to shake hands and said it was nice to see her again. He made her feel comfortable and talented. Kit knew that was probably one of his own talents, and that she didn't mean anything to him, but it worked just the same by making her loosen up and do what she thought was her best work. Afterward he said, "Terrific!" and smiled again when he dismissed her, but Kit knew most of them did that. It was the same kind of polite, meaningless shit like kissing people hello and good-bye. Still, she felt high. She'd been good, she knew she had been good. She drove home in a fog.

She wished Emma was working on this picture too so she could ask her how she'd done, but with the credit from the last Zack Shepard film Emma had gone right into a low-budget picture as Production Manager. She wanted the big credit. You had to make choices: you could stay with one person and work your way up if that person liked you, or you could keep moving around and move up that way. Emma was impatient. Besides, she said Zack Shepard told her she could always come back another time.

Now the hard thing started: the waiting.

Kit called her agent every day. He liked her or he wouldn't have put up with it. Had anybody said anything about her reading? Had the part been cast? Were there going to be call-backs? No, no, and he didn't know. Kit told herself Zack (she was thinking of him as that now, "Zack, my friend") had to cast the mother first before he could cast the daughter. The mother was the starring part, and they had to be a good mix.

But she was so perfect—she'd be perfect with anybody.

Maybe he didn't like her after all.

Maybe she should have dressed for the part, like a

frump, instead of looking like herself. The actress who had read before her was wearing a sloppy dress with embroidery on the yoke and had long hair under her arms. *Red* hair. Maybe they wanted a redhead, not someone with dark hair like her. But she had such fair skin, and gray eyes; she could color her hair if they wanted that. What difference did it make? It was the quality that counted, wasn't it?

Kit thought it was a good thing she was between boyfriends because she was so irritable and single-minded these days that she wouldn't have been able to stand having anyone around. Whenever she needed some recreational sex she found it how and where she always did; easily, and at parties. Seth from class had told everyone about the cop walking in on them in almost flagrante delicto, but it hadn't dried up her source of supply there either. Maybe they were hoping to get shot.

In the midst of this anxious musing about her career, Kit received an invitation to a fancy poolside brunch party in Bel-Air given by a producer she knew. Everybody was pretending it was winter, just because Christmas was coming. Santa Claus and silver stars were flying over Rodeo Drive. Kit knew there would be poinsettia plants beside the pool, and that the water would be properly heated so they could swim. She wore her bikini, with a gauzy sarong wrapped around her waist.

She walked out to the pool, and there among the Christmas decorations and the pâté and champagne and fresh fruit and glossy turkey the size of a small child, and the fifty people who had been chosen for their fame or ability or beauty or charm, was Zack Shepard.

She had never seen him in real life, since she considered auditions not real life at all but simply an extension of that other dimension which was the movies. Here he was, right in front of her, in his tiny little swim trunks: both the god of the casting office and the mortal with his clothes off. The people he was talking to turned away to greet some other people, and in that split second when he was alone and looking at her, Kit smiled. He smiled back in a friendly way. She walked over to him. Not only did he not have a girl friend hanging on his arm, she didn't see one who was talking to anyone else with her eyes darting around in that aggressive, paranoid way girl friends had whenever their tenuous property talked to someone attractive.

"Hi," she said.

"Hi."

A waiter came by carrying a tray of glasses filled with champagne. She took one. Zack put his empty glass on the tray and took a full one. He looked perfectly sober, but relaxed. "I'm Kit Barnett," Kit said.

"I remember."

For just an instant she panicked. She had never had to go after a man who was very important to her life. Then she remembered that no man had ever rejected her either, unless he was patently worthless and she hadn't wanted him much anyway, and she drew herself together and proceeded to be herself. "Those plants are said to be poisonous," she said, gesturing at the red-flowered poinsettias.

"I didn't plan to eat them," Zack said.

"No," she said. "You wouldn't." Then she met his eyes with a look that plainly said she could think of something else he would much rather eat, and if he wanted to it was available.

"Kit Barnett," he said noncommittally, almost to himself.

"Yes," Kit said. She let her eyes travel down his body and back to his face. "Are you having a good time?"

"I don't know yet."

They sipped their champagne, still looking at each other. She was standing very close to him.

"Do you want to go swimming with me?" she said.

"Now?"

"Why not? Can you swim?"

"I can swim," he said, looking amused.

She dropped her sarong and kicked off her shoes. Now he was looking at *her* body; good. "I'll race you," she said. They drained their glasses and walked to the edge of the pool together and dove in.

She was giddy from the champagne and the euphoria of her conquest. His hair was streaming out under the water, and his long, lean legs moved sinuously as he swam, edged with tiny bubbles. They surfaced, shaking the water from their faces, and went for the other end of the pool. She was planning to let him win, but she didn't have to; he was fast.

"Gotcha!" he said.

Kit smiled.

They began swimming again, but this time slowly. She dove under the surface of the water and swam through his moving legs, graceful as a porpoise. When she surfaced again she could see that he was impressed. She let her hair fan out like a mermaid's, and then she did a back flip and swam underneath him again, breathing out slowly, feeling the sensuality of the water and their movements together, and the beginning of arousal. Ah . . . She really wanted him now, not just as Zack Shepard, but as a man. She put her hand out and gently cupped his cock.

He swam away. Not just away as in a game, but really away: he left her and climbed out of the pool. Kit looked at his trunks and he wasn't the slightest bit aroused, and then she looked at his face, and the expression there sent her into terror. *It was disdain.*

He was looking at her as if he'd had every beautiful girl in the world and she was nothing but some kind of sleazy hooker. He looked as if she were not attractive at all, and worse; pushy, inept, unwanted. He looked at her as if she were a kid. Then he picked up a towel and turned and walked away.

Kit felt as if she'd forgotten how to swim. Her arms and legs felt heavy, the water was getting into her nose and mouth, she was sinking, out of control. She thrashed in that terrible terror, soundlessly, afraid to scream, and knowing it would do no good anyway because she was alone. And then the moment passed, and she rose up safely, sputtering, her heart pounding wildly. They were all still eating and drinking there at the side of the pool and they hadn't noticed anything unusual at all.

She swam to the edge and held on until her heartbeats and breathing were under control. She looked up and saw Zack standing drying his hair, talking to a group of people, nodding and even laughing, accepting a glass of champagne. She had blown it. She would never get the part now. It was over. He might have entertained some thoughts of using her once, but now he never would.

She got through the rest of the party because the thought of going home by herself to brood on how stupid she had been was intolerable. She avoided Zack Shepard, which was easy because everyone wanted to talk to him and he didn't want to talk to her. She wrapped her hair in a towel and let the sun dry the rest of her, and was nice to the producer who was the host. There was nobody there she wanted to have sex with: she felt completely empty and without desires of any kind. When people finally started to leave, Kit did too.

She went home and huddled in front of the television set all night, wrapped in her quilt, watching *MTV*. In her head she rewrote the scenario of her scene with Zack Shepard, who was no longer, and never would be again, "Zack, my friend," and in this new script they swam and laughed and played innocently, and she never touched him. She swam through his legs and ran away. No, better, she didn't even do that at all—they just had a race and he won.

Of course he won. She should have known before

she even started to try to get him that he was way out of her world and she was a damn fool. *How could she have been so unprofessional?*

The next day, thank God, was Monday, and she could go back to her normal life of classes that filled up her time and kept her fit when she wasn't working. She did not call her agent. She kept her ears open to hear about other pictures that were casting or about to.

On Tuesday her agent called. "Are you sitting down?" he asked.

"Yeah."

"You have the part in the new Zack Shepard film."

"What? You're kidding!" She started to scream with joy. "Oh, I can't believe it! Oh, my God!" She was so excited she forgot to listen when he told her how much money she was getting and then she had to ask him all over again. "What did he say about me?"

"What did he have to say? Obviously you were the right one for the part."

Obviously. In spite of everything else.

"Who's the mother?" Kit said.

"Sit down again."

"I'm sitting."

"Sarah Very."

"Wowww . . ." she breathed. Sarah Very: two Academy Awards. What a break to be able to work off *her.*

"Oh, yes," her agent said impishly, as if he'd just remembered it. "Zack Shepard did say something about you."

[293]

"What?"

"He said he thought this movie would make you a star."

Kit's eyes filled with tears. She had always known it would.

Chapter Twenty-four

NEW YORK IS an enormous candy store filled with tantalizing things to buy, and at no time more than the period between Thanksgiving and New Year's, when love, you are told, means the purchase and giving of presents. Merriment screams at you from every shop window. Of course it is the worst time to be alone. So Annabel, who *was* alone, was grateful that Emma was working on a movie in New York and was staying with her instead of at a hotel.

It was so good to have Emma to talk to on their rare times together, and to see her things scattered around; to be able to buy food for two again, even to care that there was food in the kitchen at all. They always had part of Sunday together, even if Emma had a date, and it saved Annabel from going into a complete holiday depression. They had fun with each other—they always had.

Annabel had invented and commissioned a novelty item to sell in her boutique for Christmas. In the supermarket, looking at the shelves of soda with no sugar; soda with no caffeine; soda with no sugar *and* no caffeine; soda with no sugar, no caffeine, and no saccharin; and finally, soda with no sugar, no caffeine, no saccharin, and no salt either; Annabel had decided the inevitable next step was no soda. She had a company make an empty white polka-dotted can with plain white letters on it that read: *No Soda;* and underneath it said: *Minimalism Is Everything.* She made a pyramid of the cans in the window next to the clothes, which were also white, and were for parties. Other than that, she made no concession to the holidays, except for thin slices of fruitcake she was planning to serve with the afternoon tea during Christmas Week.

Emma loved the No Soda, and brought cans of it to the set to put on the buffet table with the real food they served to the cast and crew.

"It's the middle of December already," Emma complained. "Mom, please take next Saturday off and come with me to pick out your Christmas present."

"Why don't you surprise me?"

"Because if you don't like it you'll have to spend time returning it, so you might as well more productively spend time choosing it."

"What did I do to deserve a logical daughter?" Annabel asked happily.

"So does that mean yes?"

"It does."

An actual day as a buyer instead of a seller, out in the world! But more importantly, a day with Emma, to wander the streets and stores, to have lunch together, to talk. Emma had already chosen her own Christmas present from Annabel: a selection of designer sweaters from Annabel's boutique; which was an improvement on her usual casual taste, although Annabel had been unable to persuade her to accept a skirt to go with them. As far as Emma was concerned, everything went with jeans, and jeans went everywhere.

Saturday was bright and beautiful. All over there were families shopping, crowds pushing, and today Annabel didn't mind at all. She drew out the process of choosing her gift because she didn't want the day to end. Finally, after a leisurely and festive lunch, Emma dragged her into Tiffany's.

"I know what you have to have," Emma said.

It was an Elsa Peretti necklace: a very thin gold chain with a tiny diamond in the center. "It's too expensive," Annabel said.

"It is not. You'd go blind trying to see that diamond. And anyway, I've been saving my money. I want to give you jewelry. Jewelry is forever."

Annabel looked away, remembering Dean's birthday necklace, and then she looked back at Emma and smiled. "Then it's just what I want," she said.

Emma made her walk to another part of the store while she bought the necklace, paid for it, and had it gift-wrapped. She was still a child, sentimental and funny . . . Like me, Annabel thought. There is a part of each of us in the other, and it's the best part, even though mine is hidden away.

They went out to the street again, Emma looking triumphant, and struggled against the crowd of holiday shoppers towards home. Then Emma shrieked and waved, and was hugging a handsome, dark-haired, intense-looking man in a sheepskin jacket.

"Mom," she said, as if she had discovered something miraculous, "this is Zack Shepard! Remember, who I worked for? Zack, this is my mother."

They shook hands. "Emma has never stopped talking about you," Annabel said.

"She talked about you, too," he said.

"About me?"

"Oh, yes."

"Well," Annabel said. They smiled at each other, pleasantly and a little carefully. He was so intense, she thought. Like there was an engine turning away inside of him all the time. And on top of that an overlay of loose-limbed relaxation. It was an interesting combination. Emma's god in person. Well, well.

"I can't believe you're right here in New York," Emma said. "What are you doing here?"

"Some meetings with the studio people," he said. He smiled at Emma in a fatherly fashion. "Your daughter deserted me," he said to Annabel. "She wants my job."

Emma actually blushed. "No, I don't," she said.

"I am not a jealous person," he said mildly.

"You don't have to be," Emma said. "Not of anybody."

"Where are you two going?" he said. "Do you want to have a drink?"

"Why not?" Annabel said. She suddenly felt wild again, the person who believed life was full of unexpected adventures. "Where shall we go?"

"There used to be a place on the East Side . . . the Metropole or something. Sort of a bistro. I liked it."

"Le Metropole," Emma said.

"Oh, no," Annabel said. The place she'd had her first date with Dean. Why did people you'd had a bad experience with keep hovering over your life and ruining everything: presents, restaurants, new encounters?

"Is it no good anymore?" Zack Shepard said.

"It's great," Emma said. "It's fun."

"I don't mind," Annabel said.

Zack Shepard peered at her; those director's eyes, taking in everything. Emma had said he was forty-five. Almost her age. She would exorcise Le Metropole with her daughter and this interesting man; she would have a nice afternoon. He took each of them by the arm, himself in the middle, and marched them there.

The restaurant was still full of people; exuberant holiday shoppers having a late lunch, or an early drink. It was quite noisy and jolly; not the romantic place it had been when Annabel went there so long ago for her lunch with Dean. The three of them wanted white wine, so Zack ordered a bottle. He had a warmth and spontaneity about him that Annabel liked, and she began to relax and enjoy herself, and let Dean float away right out of her head. Zack was talking enthusiastically about the new film he was going to make.

"I have a good friend in that movie," Emma said. "Kit Barnett. Her mother went to Radcliffe with you, Mom—Emily Buchman."

"Oh, yes, Chris interviewed her," Annabel said. "The cookie lady. She was Emily Applebaum and we all had rooms on the same floor in Briggs Hall."

"She always writes to the alumnae bulletin about *her* daughter," Emma teased. "You never write about me."

"I don't even read the thing," Annabel said. She smiled at Zack. "I do not have the fondest memories of my college years."

"I had very little to do with mine," he said. "I spent most of my time in the dark like a mole."

"Doing what?"

"Either editing film or going to the movies."

"And were you popular?" Annabel asked.

"I don't think I noticed."

She laughed. "I wish I had known you. You seem more level-headed than I was."

"I think I was a nerd," he said, smiling.

"You could never be a nerd," Annabel said.

She was flirting again, she was happy. He made her feel wonderful. No wonder Emma was so fond of him. She had never met anyone with so much energy.

"Do we have time for another bottle of wine?" he asked.

"Of course," Annabel said, without even looking at

her watch. They had nowhere to go, and this was like a party. What a shame that such an attractive man had to live all the way in California, where she was sure he had someone. Everyone seemed to have someone. She wondered if he thought she did. Emma was sitting there quietly, looking pleased, no, impishly self-satisfied, at the way her mother was getting along with Zack. The matchmaker. It occurred to Annabel that before Dean she had never wondered for an instant whether a desirable man who liked her had another woman waiting for him at home. If he had, she wouldn't have cared. She would not have thought of herself or the other woman as any kind of a threat to each other.

But now she had found herself vulnerable, and that changed everything. Not enough, however, to keep her from thinking that Zack Shepard was extremely sexy.

Emma went to make a phone call and left them alone together. He looked at his watch. "I have a meeting in half an hour," he said, "but I was wondering if you were free tonight for dinner."

"As a matter of fact, I am," Annabel said.

"About eight?"

"That would be lovely. How should I dress?"

"The way you are now is fine," he said. "I was just going to go to a little Italian place I like downtown. It's my secret place and I don't tell anybody about it. You make a restaurant famous and then you can't get a table."

"You don't look like a serious eater," Annabel said.

"I am a serious everything," he said.

Emma was thrilled. "Don't come home tonight, Mom," she said. "If you come home I will consider this evening a failure."

"Are you living vicariously through me?" Annabel said.

"No, no, he doesn't want me, he wants you. We had a purely professional relationship. You two are perfect for each other. You'll have a wonderful time."

"And what are you going to be doing?"

"I *should* sleep, but I got talked into going out dancing with some of my friends who I haven't seen for a while."

Zack arrived fifteen minutes late, apologized, and whisked Annabel down to the Village in a cab. They sat at a large table in a small, brightly lit little restaurant, and he ordered an enormous amount of food. "You don't have to eat it all," he said. "Just taste it."

Ah, garlic, she thought after the first bite. *There goes romance.* But it was said that if both people ate garlic neither one noticed. Besides, since Emma had banished her for the night she had taken her toothbrush along with her makeup. Zack was looking at her.

"I just have to tell you," he said, "that you are absolutely knockout gorgeous."

"Thank you," she said, amused and moved.

"Now eat," he said. "Isn't this great?"

"It is." The veal was so tender she could cut it with

her fork; the salad crisp and fresh, the pasta perfect. She remembered her first meal with Dean. They had not eaten anything. It had been instant, crazed, moonstruck, adolescent passion. With Zack she had the feeling that he enjoyed each moment in its own time. He had meant it about being a serious everything. She wondered if he were a serious lover.

"Have you been married?" she asked.

"Once, when I was young. Neither of us wanted children, and by the time she changed her mind neither of us liked each other enough."

"And did you change your mind too?"

"No. Never."

"How refreshing," Annabel said.

"Most women would have said selfish," he said.

"I'm not most women."

"That's obvious from hello," he said. They smiled at each other. "I think you were right; I wish we *had* known each other twenty years ago. I might not have been able to handle it, you would have scared me, but you would really have enriched my life."

"It's twenty-five years," Annabel said, "and I wouldn't have scared you. I never scared anybody."

"I can't imagine why not," he said.

"I was always too accessible," she said calmly. "And I was different from everyone else."

"You don't think that's frightening?"

She thought about it. "Maybe it was. Coming from that stiff, totally priggish time right out of the Middle Ages . . ."

"You know what scares people the most?" he said.

"I mean, not counting things like the neutron bomb, or being poor, or sick, or dying; you know what people really can't deal with?"

"What?"

"Thinking they made the wrong choices."

"Or knowing they did," Annabel said.

He was staying at the Carlyle Hotel. After dinner they went there together quite naturally, not wanting the evening to end. He invited her up to his suite for a drink. It was a very big suite, the living room French, the bedroom English, and she never did see his bar.

He was a serious lover. Annabel was delighted: that was the best kind. She had not been so happy in a long, long time. He had given her back the joy in the moment, and even though she was aware he would be leaving, she wanted to keep it as long as she could. He obviously felt the same way.

"I'm going to be here for five more days," he said. "Let's see a lot of each other. Let's saturate."

"Yes . . ." Nourishment. Water for the desert to come.

They were together every night, all night, and during the day whenever he didn't have a meeting. He came to the boutique to take Annabel away, or phoned and asked her to meet him. The store was busy with Christmas shoppers, but Maria and Pamela were experienced now, and able to handle things.

"We're talking about shooting part of the movie in New York," Zack said. Her heart leaped like a trout.

"We've decided against New York," he said the next night. She felt as if she had been abandoned.

Annabel was falling in love with him. It was foolish, she knew. She had discovered there was no woman in his life right now, no one waiting at home to take him away from her, and therefore she felt even more vulnerable; because there was nothing to keep Zack from loving her in return except the fact that he just didn't feel that way. The days were going by so fast; only three more, then two, then one . . . It was the beginning of Christmas Week. He was going back to California for Christmas. There was no real necessity for that. He could stay here, or he could invite her to come to spend the holidays with him. But he never said a word. He seemed to assume that she had her life and he his, and while what was between them was marvelous, it was only an interlude.

She didn't want any more interludes. She didn't want any more partings. She didn't want any more pain. Dean was too fresh in her mind, and all the men who had betrayed her through the years were hovering at the edges of her memory like so many hateful ghosts. It seemed she was always saying good-bye and smiling, tossing off the perfect exit line, going home to hide her broken heart. What would her last line to Zack be? Have a nice trip? Merry Christmas?

Call me the next time you're in town, if you don't mind making sequels?

"What are you giving Zack for Christmas?" Emma asked her.

"Why should I give him anything?"

"Well, I mean . . ."

"I'm not even going to be with him for Christmas," Annabel said.

"Yeah, that's sad," Emma said. Then she brightened. "You could give him something to remember you by."

"He has enough to remember me by," Annabel said sweetly.

"I don't understand why the two of you have never discussed what's going to happen next," Emma said.

"Do you think my life is different from yours?"

"I think it is now," Emma said.

"No," Annabel said. "It's just that the little romances are farther apart."

It was such a flippant thing to say, and she wished she didn't have to believe it. But tonight was their last night together, and Zack had suggested dinner in his suite with room service. She supposed he felt it was the ultimate saturation. She found it too painful to contemplate.

The two of them had shown love in every act and word, but neither of them had ever said it. She had to give him credit for not trying to deceive her. Dean had said he loved her, over and over, and yet he had left. Zack would leave with integrity.

Knowing he had integrity was not much compensation for falling off a mountain.

She was to meet him at his hotel at half past six. At five o'clock Annabel called. His suite didn't answer. She didn't trust herself to call a second time. "I want to leave a message," she said. "Please tell Mr. Shepard that Annabel Jones will not be able to see him tonight; something came up. Thank you."

Then she called Chris. "Can I stay at your apartment tonight? I have to hide, and I need moral support."

"Sure," Chris said.

"I'll meet you at the office in ten minutes."

And then she ran away to her friend, who would understand.

Annabel sat in Chris's kitchen, drinking screwdrivers. It suited her furtive and mourning mood. The housekeeper had taken the night off, Alexander was out, as involved as ever in his love affair with James, and Chris's son Nicholas was staying with friends from school for part of the holiday, as well he might with such a bizarre home life.

"You can sleep in Nicholas's room," Chris said.

"Thank you. Isn't it strange—you were the one who ran away, and I told you it was silly, and now I'm the one who's running away."

"Do you want me to tell you it's silly?"

"No. I just want you to give me another shot of vodka in this thing."

"You'll have a hangover tomorrow and feel worse," Chris said, bringing the bottle.

"I couldn't feel worse."

"Why didn't you just see him tonight and then feel worse the next day?" Chris said.

"Because it would have been more *worse* than I could stand."

When Annabel was good and drunk Chris put her

to bed. "Are you happy with Cameron?" Annabel asked fuzzily.

"Yes."

"And do you tell each other you love each other?"

"All the time."

"Do you mean it?"

"Yes," Chris said.

"What about Alexander? Does he say he loves you?"

"There's been no occasion for it lately, but I know he does."

"What's his idea of an occasion?"

"Go to sleep," Chris said.

"I wish Zack Shepard loved me, the son of a bitch," Annabel said, and slept.

The next morning she did not feel wonderful. Chris had left for work before Annabel got up, but there was hot coffee in the coffee maker and a bottle of aspirin next to it, with a note: *Come back for dinner if you're still alive.* Dear Chris. Annabel pulled herself together and went home to change her clothes.

Emma was in the apartment, and when Annabel opened the door Emma got a strange look on her face, almost as if Annabel had done something to hurt her.

"Hi," Annabel said. "Night shooting tonight, huh?"

Emma nodded. "You look like you got drunk last night," she said.

"As a matter of fact, I was."

"That was a really mean thing you did."

"What did I do?"

"Dump Zack his last night. Cheat on him."

"Cheat? Are you saying *cheat?* My health is too fragile to listen to this standing up." Annabel went into her bedroom and Emma followed her. "What did he do, call?"

"He was here."

"Ah." It hurt. He had cared enough to come looking for her. Or perhaps he didn't have anyone else to have dinner with at the last minute.

"He came at midnight," Emma said. "He wanted to know if you were back yet. I said I thought you were out with him. I felt like a fool. Your stuff wasn't here—I knew you were out for the whole night. I just assumed it was him. You always bring everybody else home. I tried to cover it up, but he knew. He knew you weren't coming back."

"How did he know?"

"He asked me and I told him," Emma said sheepishly. "I felt terrible, but he was going to wait. He thought you were at a business meeting. He honestly did. He just couldn't imagine that you'd go out with someone else on his last night."

"I was at Chris's," Annabel said. "I was too afraid of another good-bye."

"Well, look on your dresser," Emma said. She didn't wait for Annabel to get up, she ran over to the dresser and grabbed something that looked like an envelope. "He said to give it to you, that it was your Christmas present. I guess he was going to give it to you at dinner. He looked really upset; he just dropped it on the table and walked out." She put it into Annabel's hand.

It wasn't an envelope; it was a folder containing an airline ticket to California, made out in Annabel's name.

Annabel called his hotel, but he had checked out. She called the airline club and had him paged, but he wasn't there. That night she began calling his house in Los Angeles. He either wasn't in or wasn't answering his phone. She called again early in the morning, and then got the phone number of his office from information and called there when business hours began. They said he was out of town. She called his house again that night, and the next. She called his office. Still out of town. "Where?" she asked. They didn't know, but he would be calling in. Annabel left a message. He never called her.

How could he not call her, when she wanted to apologize, to explain? But he didn't know that. She'd blown it.

Emma and Chris didn't have to tell her; she knew it too well. She got through Christmas somehow, trying to pretend she wasn't miserable for Emma's sake. Even if Zack had gone to a desert island for the holidays he would have to come back to start his picture. Misery held her in a vise, and she went through her days, hours, minutes, by rote. Once in a while, at night when she couldn't sleep, she telephoned his house, just to hear the phone ringing in a place that was his. She wondered what his house looked like.

She would have been there with him now if she hadn't been such a coward.

Wherever Zack had gone, she wondered if he had brought another woman with him. Probably. He certainly had a choice. And maybe he would begin to care for that woman, the way he had cared for *her*. He and Annabel had had only six days. No, five . . . Five days did not make a life. But it had been a beginning, and she had ruined it.

She had the plane ticket. Maybe one day she'd just show up on his doorstep. The young Annabel, the wild one from years ago, would have done just that. She would be standing there with a bunch of roses in her hand.

But this was the older, wiser, wounded Annabel, who probably would not. The Annabel who had run away from one good-bye too many would never risk being thrown out of an ex-lover's house.

For her Christmas present Zack had wanted to surprise her with the invitation she had wanted more than anything; to stay in his life. She had not even gotten him a Christmas present. If he accused her of not understanding him at all, he would be right. But why did he have to wait until the last minute to surprise her? She was not the maiden in the tower waiting to be swept away by the noble knight. She had a life, a career, feelings. He didn't understand her either.

What did he think life was, anyway; one of his movies? Adults made plans, adults did not play games. But she knew he could as easily say that to her. Being angry at him only made this time of not knowing more bearable.

Chapter Twenty-five

THAT YEAR, 1983, Christmas came on a Sunday, so most offices closed early on Friday and stayed closed until Tuesday for a long holiday weekend. For people with something to do and somewhere to go it was a pleasure; for those with nothing and no one the weekend would seem endless. For people who were in love with people who were married to others, it meant they would probably celebrate Christmas at Friday lunch on the twenty-third.

Chris's office closed at noon on that Friday, and she and Cameron were going to have lunch together. After some deliberation she had bought him gold cufflinks. They were simple and dignified, and if his wife asked any questions he could say he had bought them for himself. On Thursday he took Chris to Cartier. If anyone *else* asked questions they could pretend they were choosing a surprise for his wife. In actuality, he had told Chris, he was giving his wife a fur coat. He bought Chris a bracelet made of three gold rings attached together; one white, one yellow, one pink. It was expensive, but she would tell Alexander, if he asked, that she had received it from Annabel.

James had left New York early for the holiday, to spend Christmas with his parents. Alexander was wearing new gold cufflinks. Chris did not ask him anything.

Ah, she thought, *La Ronde*.

She was giving Alexander a new attaché case; black, of fine leather, elegant. And she knew he was giving her the same thing, because he had asked her what she wanted. Hers, however, was tobacco brown. Identical, functional presents seemed to suit their new relationship. They were as close as twins, loving but platonic, dependent on each other . . . and, although Alexander did not know it, each in love with someone else.

She was still amazed that she was able to be in love with two men at the same time. And she knew she could never have been able to deal with Cameron if she didn't have Alexander, nor with Alexander if she didn't have Cameron. She had tried. But she was different now. The dream she'd had all her life of perfect love was gone forever. The strange thing was that she was often quite happy lately anyhow.

"Merry Christmas," Cameron said at their holiday lunch. They tried to ignore the fact that their Christmas, and probably all the other important holidays, would always occur on a different day from the rest of the world's.

"Merry Christmas."

He had brought her quite naturally and openly to the same kind of restaurant he used to before their affair started. They did nothing differently in New York. They slept together only on their business trips to California. He called her at home whenever he wanted to, since he was known to be a workaholic. She did not call him at home because she was only his employee, although of course she would have called him if it were a business emergency.

They had champagne because it was Christmas, and because they were in love. They exchanged their presents. With the gifts they had each written a cryptic message on one of the small white cards stores like Tiffany's and Cartier gave out; those dignified little white cards so suitable for every occasion, to write something short and trite, or something secret and incriminating, to hide in your wallet and reread when you were alone.

Each of them had written: *Thank you.* It meant the world.

"Sometimes I wish things had been different," Cameron said.

"So do I," Chris said. "But they can't be, so I don't think about it."

"What we have works," he said. "It wouldn't work any other way."

"Why not?"

"Because both of us want what we already had, *and* each other."

"All I know," Chris said, "is that I'm very happy with you."

"I'm glad," he said. "Because I love you."

"I love you too." For a moment they held hands under the table. It felt alien to her here, uncomfortable, where there were different rules. Then she relaxed and let the warmth of his hand seep into her skin. "I would die without you," she said.

"You won't ever have to be without me."

"Good."

She had told him once that her husband was in love with someone else. She had not said it wasn't a woman, so of course Cameron had assumed it was. He never asked her personal questions about her marriage, nor did she ask him any, since they both felt such things would be not only painful to discuss but a betrayal of the others. Besides, they liked to keep their private world encapsulated.

They finished lunch at half past three. "I still have to buy some presents," he said. "I always leave it till the last minute. I'll call you over the weekend."

She would have liked to ask if she could come with him, but she didn't. In the street they kissed each other good-bye lightly, as friends and colleagues did everywhere, and said Merry Christmas again. Then they set off in different directions. She turned around once, but Cameron was gone. She went home, hoping Alexander would already be there waiting for her.

They had decided not to go anywhere this Christmas. Nicholas would be with them for a week, and then right after New Year's he was going away again, skiing with a friend from school and the friend's parents. She and Alexander had gotten theater tickets to some of the hit shows, for the three of them and whomever Nicholas wanted to bring along. They had all been invited to a party on Christmas Day. At least at home they could pretend things were normal, despite the fact that she and Alexander had separate rooms. At a resort or a hotel they would have to make an issue of it. She would not sleep in the same room with him; she couldn't. Even as friends. Their relationship was still too complicated for them to be such comfortable friends as that.

Alexander came home soon after Chris did, and so did Nicholas. Every time she turned around the boy seemed to have grown; he was nearly sixteen and already as tall as his father. And he had grown emotionally too—always busy, ever pulling away from them. Other mothers could think of it as normal for that age, but Chris couldn't help wondering if he was avoiding the oddness of his home life. . . .

"When I go skiing with Steve I'll have to bring his parents a house gift," Nicholas said. "What should I bring?"

"Well," Chris said, "what are they like?"

"Rich," Nicholas said. "They have everything."

"They're not too rich to read, are they?" Alexander said. "How about books?"

Where was the little boy who went to Africa with his parents to see the animals; who trekked with his parents all through Europe; as close to her as a papoose? Buying a hostess gift for someone else's mother. Had she and Alexander driven him away?

"Will you help me pick some?" Nicholas asked him. "I don't know what they would like."

"Absolutely," Alexander said. "And if they already have them or don't want them, they can exchange them."

"Can we go tomorrow?"

"It'll have to be early; it's Christmas Eve and the stores will be mobbed."

"How early? I have a party tonight."

"You also have a curfew," Alexander said.

Nicholas ignored that. "The three of us could pick the books and then we could go out to lunch."

Alexander looked at Chris and smiled. "Chris?"

She smiled back. "That will be fun," she said.

He was too old to be her papoose, and she didn't want him to be, but he still needed the family time they spent together, and that was good.

That evening they trimmed the tree. It looked quite wonderful. Although Chris and Alexander had each bought the other only one thing, there were extra presents underneath for friends who would drop by during the weekend. And of course there was a huge pile of gifts for Nicholas. He kept shaking the wrapped boxes, trying to guess what was in them; still a child, at least for Christmas, no matter how strange his parents were.

Chris wondered whether Alexander was thinking about James, and whether he missed him a great deal.

She knew James wouldn't call the house for fear she would be the one who answered the phone, but Alexander would probably call him. Just a friend calling to wish him Merry Christmas. James's parents probably didn't know their son was gay.

When the tree was finished Alexander opened a bottle of champagne. Nicholas left for his party, leaving them alone together. Chris wondered what Cameron was doing right now. She and Alexander sat there looking at the little lights twinkling on their tree, listening to Christmas carols, sipping the champagne. It could have been lonely, but it was cozy and nice.

"We did a good job," he said.

"Yes, we did."

For some reason she remembered the night so many years ago in Paris, the first time she had seen Alexander's apartment, and all those glass objects glittering on his coffee table in the semidark. She remembered the constant, empty yearning she'd had for Alexander then, and for all those years afterward, wanting so much to be a part of the special mystery of his life. They were two such different people now . . .

Glittering objects, tiny lights . . . She had never wanted things, only him.

"What are you thinking?" he asked.

"How comfortable we can be together, when everything's quiet."

"We're not so badly off, are we?" Alexander asked. "It's not a bad life."

It was as close as he could come to daring to ask her if she was happy. And, in fact, she wasn't unhappy at all.

Chris smiled at him. "You're my best friend," she said. "And you always will be. I love you."

"I love you, too," he said. "You know that."

She wondered if she and Cameron would ever be best friends.

The first day she was back at work after the pleasant Christmas weekend Chris got a phone call at the office from Emily Buchman in California. "Remember you said we should get together when I came to New York?" Emily said. "Well, I'm coming tomorrow night. Could we have drinks together on Saturday afternoon?"

"New Year's Eve . . ." Cameron was going away with his wife and children. She and Alexander were going to a late dinner party. She was to meet Annabel at the store for a New Year's Eve drink at four. She supposed she could bring Emily. "Sure, that would be fine."

"Oh, great!" Emily said. "I'm going to the theater that night with Daphne Caldwell. She got tickets to *Cats.* Do you remember her from college? I thought we could all have drinks together."

"Daphne the Golden Girl?" Chris said in horror.

"No, she's really nice now," Emily said. "She's had a lot of grief in her life. And the latest thing is that she and Richard just got divorced."

"Well, that says something good about her anyway," Chris said. "Getting rid of Richard, I mean. I'm having drinks with Annabel Jones that afternoon and I was going to bring you. I don't know how she and Daphne would feel about each other. They never liked each other at school."

"Do you think *I'm* different?" Emily said. "Do you think you're different? Well, wait till you see how different Daphne is."

"I guess Annabel is too," Chris said, and gave Emily the address.

It was almost dark at four o'clock. Chris got to Annabel's early to spend some time with her alone before the others came. Annabel still hadn't been able to reach Zack, and was putting up a good front the way she always did, but Chris knew she was grieving. Between her job and her family and her affair, Chris knew she was more of an absent friend to Annabel during this holiday season than she would have liked to be. Their little celebration this afternoon was not only to see each other on the last day of the old year, but to cheer Annabel up.

Annabel opened a bottle of champagne. There were no customers expected on this late afternoon just before New Year's Eve, and the boutique was for all intents and purposes closed. Pamela and Maria had been allowed to go home. Sweet Pea was asleep in her basket. There was a plate of thin smoked salmon sandwiches on the tea table for their private celebration.

Annabel raised her glass and touched it to Chris's in a toast. "Another year and we've survived," she said.

"Always," Chris said.

They drank to both past and future survival. "Funny to be seeing Daphne and Emily," Annabel said. "Odd that they'd even like each other. I wonder if Daphne and I will get along. If not, just so it won't be a complete waste of time I can always sell her some decent clothes. Do you remember that *gold* dress she wore at our twentieth reunion? Daphne the Golden Girl, in case we forgot. Happy Halloween."

Chris laughed. "I wonder why she divorced Richard."

"Maybe *he* divorced *her*."

"I never thought of that. I just assumed . . . I mean, Daphne always seemed so in control. She was the sort of woman who if her husband got out of line she'd just walk away."

"Mmm."

The door burst open and there was Emily with Daphne, both of them smiling—Emily enthusiastically, Daphne politely, in that same cool, self-sufficient way she'd always had. "Oh, you're having champagne!" Emily said. "Do you know what that reminds me of? The first day we all met at Radcliffe, when we had champagne in Annabel's room. Do you remember? It was *warm,* and we drank it out of our toothbrush glasses, and I was scared to death we'd get into trouble because it was against the rules to have liquor in our rooms."

"Well, this time it's cold," Annabel said, and poured some for each of them.

"What a beautiful boutique you have here, Annabel," Daphne said. She wandered around, looking at everything, murmuring enthusiastic little remarks. Chris remembered that Daphne had always been artistic.

"Oh, yes it is," Emily said. "And the clothes are so great. Annabel, do you know what I'd love? I'm doing a total makeover on myself for my new business, because I'm going to have to do publicity, and maybe you could help me create my new image."

"I'd be delighted," Annabel said.

"I want to be glamorous, like you. I mean, I realize I'm shorter . . ."

"You mean you want to be glamorous like *you*," Annabel said. "That will be easy."

"I'm going back Tuesday night," Emily said. "Could we do it Tuesday morning?"

"Of course."

"What a nice bonus," Emily said. "I thought we were just going to have our own class reunion."

Daphne isn't being aloof, Chris thought suddenly. *She's uncomfortable. It's as if she's lost all the things she always believed in, and now she has to find something else.* She didn't know why she was so sure Daphne felt that way; a reporter's instinct perhaps, or just her own.

"We're all working," Daphne said. "Imagine. I'm back at the gallery. I didn't think they'd give me my old job, but they did. Being single in the suburbs, especially with all the children away, was a big mistake."

"It must be boring," Annabel said.

"It's deadly, actually."

"Being single in the city can be pretty lonely too," Annabel said.

"Yes," Daphne said, smiling. "Lonely was really the word I meant."

They smiled at each other. *Annabel smiling at Daphne with friendliness,* Chris thought. *Well, well. And Daphne smiling back, making a new beginning.* Daphne, she had just noticed, wasn't smoking anymore. She'd always remembered Daphne with a cigarette in her hand, until it became almost part of her persona. Maybe after saying good-bye to Richard Daphne had decided to clean up her act altogether.

They ate the sandwiches and drank more champagne, and began to talk about their lives. Chris told them how she'd become so fat, and then had finally managed to lose the weight. She didn't discuss her love life, nor Alexander's, but simply said she'd been unhappy. Daphne talked about her children; the one who had committed suicide, and the one who was retarded. Her divorce from Richard was certainly the least of her troubles. Emily told Annabel how the paradise she thought she'd attained after graduation had become a hell. And Annabel (who still didn't totally trust them after what they'd done to her at college, and so had to make it sound like a funny story) told how Bill Wood had ditched her before the wedding and how she had finally gotten her revenge on him years later at the art gallery with Dean.

But despite the stories withheld, and the truths evaded, to protect the men the others all knew; as

Chris listened she saw something strange happen: they began to know each other in this brief time a hundred times better than they ever had in the four years they had gone to college together. Perhaps that was because way back then none of them had really known herself either.

"God, we were such babies at Radcliffe, weren't we!" Emily said. "To think we were allowed to make lifetime decisions . . ."

"Forced to," Daphne said. "Expected to. And we were sure we knew what we were doing."

"You realize we have lived more of our lives now, since we've been out of college, than we had when we graduated," Annabel said. "We've been paying for mistakes we made as mere children. If this was a court of law we'd get a parole."

"I think we should give it to ourselves," Daphne said. "I want you to forgive me for being such a total shit to you at Radcliffe, Annabel. It's just that I was jealous that you slept with Richard before I did."

Annabel grinned. "You should have thanked me," she said. "How did you think he got so good?"

They all laughed. Annabel opened another bottle of champagne to celebrate the truce and their new-found friendship. The lights were bright in the store, and the door was locked against unwelcome strangers. Outside it was dark and cold, but inside it was warm and they were all feeling very good. Anyone passing by in that dark winter street would not have known what ghosts had been laid to rest, nor that this was in fact a reunion of infinitely more importance than the one they had celebrated six years before on the grounds of their old school. All the passerby would have seen was four attractive women, obviously having a wonderful time together.

Chapter Twenty-six

This has been a very strange holiday for all of us.
My parents got divorced. My father came to see us
and brought presents for me and my brothers, and
a bottle of wine and a fruitcake for my mother. She
didn't give him anything. They treated each other
in a polite and careful way, as if they were a little
afraid of each other. It was a different kind of ner-
vousness from the way it used to be around here
when everybody was so tense and trying to be
jolly. He took a lot of snapshots of us and then he
went away again. We didn't have to play touch
football with him because he's still talking about
his heart attack, and I was secretly relieved because I don't want to play sports with him. It's
never real fun because he gets too serious about
everything.

My mother and I have been having some good talks since I came home for vacation. We never did this before. We talk about Jonathan a lot, and how much we miss him, and the things he used to do. We talk about me, and how I feel about things. When I tell her my personal opinion about something she really pays attention. I told her I don't want to go back to boarding school next year. She asked why, and I told her the truth, that our family has been falling apart lately and I'm afraid if I go away something else bad will happen. She said it was always expected that we would graduate from St. Martin's because our father and grandfather did, but if I didn't want to it was okay. She said it would be nice to have me around for company. I was so surprised that I said I would think about it. Now she probably thinks I'm crazy.

I'm fourteen now and Jonathan was fourteen when he killed himself, but I still don't understand any more about why he did it. For a while I was scared that the same thing would happen to me, but now I know it won't. My mother asked me if I wanted to go to a therapist to talk about all the shocks we've been having around here lately, but I said no. Can you imagine anyone in *our* family going to a THERAPIST??? My father would really have a heart attack over that. But that isn't the reason I said no. I feel okay. For the first time in my life she's become like a friend to me, instead of that distant person My Mother, and I think I'm a help to her too. I used to think I was just a pest, but now I feel I have value.

I have also decided what I want to be when I grow up. I want to be a writer. It's a great relief to get that decision out of the way. St. Martin's has a very good English department, so maybe I should stay there. I'll see.

While I've been home this holiday I could see how lonely it is for my mother now that my parents are divorced. Some of the people she thought were her friends don't call anymore. But she likes her job. The only bad thing is that the woman she works for won't let her take a week off to take us skiing, because she just started there, so we can't go this year. My father won't take us because he's going to the Caribbean with his girl friend. Matthew and Sam are going skiing with their friends because they're old enough, but I just have to hang around.

I guess I will spend the time reading some good books and trying to prepare for my future career. Of course I'll also see my friends. It won't be so bad.

This year we'll be here for Jonathan's birthday. I asked my mother if we could go to visit him, his grave I mean, and she said yes. I can't believe that she and I are able to have these conversations now. I just can't believe how far we've come.

Chapter Twenty-seven

IT WAS FEBRUARY. The store windows Daphne passed on her way up Madison Avenue to work were filled with Valentine's Day decorations and gifts: candy, cards, ruffled pillows with sentimental inscriptions. It always made her think of when she was a child. Even after she'd had her own children, some holidays reminded her of herself more than of them. She was certainly nobody's valentine these days.

Since the divorce the women she'd thought were her friends seemed afraid of her. She knew why. She was single now, and too attractive; therefore a threat. And her "perfect" marriage had fallen apart, which threatened theirs. If it could happen to her . . . They probably thought their husbands would want to start something with her, now that she was alone. They said how sorry they were that they didn't know any nice men to introduce her to, and then excluded her from their dinner parties because she was no longer half of a couple. She supposed she should entertain, and then they would feel guilty and have to invite her back, but she wasn't sure she liked them enough anymore to bother.

The weekend before Valentine's Day there was a huge blizzard. Everyone was snowed in. For her it was just another weekend alone with the dogs and her books and sketch pad. The only difference was she couldn't drive to the supermarket for her weekly shopping, but since the boys had gone back to school her own needs were very small.

Teddy sent her a valentine. He had made it himself. Daphne carried it in her handbag for days. It had never occurred to her to send valentines to the boys because they were too old for that now, and when Teddy sent her one anyway she cried. She had to keep remembering how sensitive and loving he was, her genius son of the secret journal, carefully disguised as a carefree All-American Boy. She was finding herself in tears often lately, having opened herself up to the vulnerability she had denied for so many years.

If she was friendless in the suburbs she had new friends in the city. Chris and Annabel, and Emily even though she and Emily hadn't seen each other since Emily went back to California. And now Chris had invited her to a dinner party; without a date, without a husband, and with no utilitarian ulterior motive of finding her a new one. It was tonight, Friday, and Daphne had driven in instead of taking the train. All the guests would be coming directly from work, so the dress she was wearing would be suitable. She had brought makeup in her handbag, and prepared herself for the party in the employees' ladies' room at the gallery. It was a rather wretched little bathroom, and reminded her of the one at college, and that depressed her. . . .

That was the last time she had been unattached, and getting ready for a party or a dance had been an occasion filled with excitement and the promise of adventure. She had been so popular. She always met new men at parties then, and they took her to football games, and out dancing, and to other parties, where she met more men who pursued her. But tonight all she felt was relief that she didn't have to go home yet, that there was somewhere to go where she wouldn't be alone. She no longer expected anything particularly exciting at all, and that made her feel old.

Chris and Alexander lived in a very elegant Fifth Avenue building. Daphne hadn't seen Alexander since college, as he hadn't come to the reunion, but she recognized him right away. He was still extraordinarily handsome, perhaps more so. She had never really known him well at college, but she remembered he had always seemed so grumpy and gloomy; now he was urbane and charming. And he seemed very devoted to Chris. Their apartment was both attractive and comfortable. A uniformed maid opened the door and took Daphne's coat, another offered her a drink and some small hot hors d'oeuvres. Chris took her around and introduced her to people. There were nine. Annabel was there, and Chris's former diet doctor, Dr. Michael Fields; Chris and Alexander, two other couples, and herself. Nine. *Somebody doesn't have a date,* Daphne thought, *and it's probably me.*

She had a glass of white wine and talked to Annabel, feeling shy. Annabel seemed subdued, not the flirt Daphne remembered. But that was so long ago. "Dr. Fields is attractive," she said quietly to Annabel. "Is he with you?"

"No. We're all here alone. Chris, thank God, is beyond the stage of giving parties that resemble Noah's Ark."

He had brown hair with gray in it, kind-looking blue eyes, and chiseled features. Not like Richard's, so picture perfect, but more accessible, more human. And she noticed he was lean and nicely built, an encouraging example for his patients, but with none of the gristly look of the fanatic about him. It had been a long time since she'd looked at a man that closely, but then of course there hadn't been any close enough to look at.

"He's available," Annabel said. "Or at least he isn't married. I don't know about the available part. His wife died last year. He's probably got a few twenty-year-olds tucked away; most of them do, don't they?"

"Or thirty-year-olds," Daphne said, remembering Melissa.

"He also has two children," Annabel said. "A son and a fat daughter. Poor thing—a diet doctor with a fat child. And it must be hell to have a diet doctor for a father. They probably haven't got a thing in their refrigerator but skimmed milk."

Daphne laughed. "How do you know all that?"

"Chris told me. When she was going to him she had a major crush on him. She found out all about him from his nurse."

"But not quite all . . ."

"No," Annabel said. "If we aren't disgraceful, hunting him down like he was the last living man on earth."

"I'm not hunting him down," Daphne said. "I haven't even spoken to him."

"You will. Chris has seated him between us at dinner. If you like him, please feel free to whisk him away, because I am still in love with someone."

"Oh?" Daphne said. "Where is he?"

"I have no idea," Annabel said lightly. "Just another broken heart, the story of my life."

"The story of mine," Daphne said.

She was so safe and content fantasizing about Dr. Fields and making a joke of it that when he saw them standing there and came over it was almost an intrusion.

He smiled at them. "I'll just stay here for a while so those other people can eat their hors d'oeuvres," he said, glancing at the couple he'd just left and looking amused. "People are always afraid to eat in front of me just because I'm a diet doctor."

Daphne looked over and saw them accepting small stuffed mushrooms from the maid and popping them into their mouths with a look of starved relief.

"They're not even overweight," she said. "Are you such an ogre?"

"Not at all. *I* don't care what people eat as long as they're not my patients."

The maid came to them and she and Annabel took cheese puffs just to prove they were not intimidated, and then they both looked at each other and at him and laughed, because they *were* intimidated. "How awful," Annabel said. "It's like meeting a psychiatrist and trying to pretend you're normal."

"You should see what it's like when I go to restaurants with friends," he said. "Everybody's afraid to order until they see what I'm having. Or else they ask for dry broiled fish. These overweight people who you know never ate a piece of dry broiled fish in their lives." He smiled.

"I wonder what Chris will offer us tonight," Daphne said.

"I'm sure whatever she wants," he said. "Chris and I have laughed about this. The funniest story is the carrot cake. Hostesses always serve carrot cake for dessert when I'm there because somehow they think it's healthful or dietetic because it has carrots in it. Actually it's one of the richest, most fattening things you can eat. If I have to go to another dinner party where I have to look at another piece of carrot cake . . ."

"That *is* funny," Daphne said. She looked at him. He was the first man she'd found attractive in so long that she couldn't even remember how long it had been. She hadn't bothered to think about other men that way when she had been married to Richard. And now she would have to stop thinking about the years of Richard; they were over, and she didn't want them back. She smiled at Dr. Fields. "Do you prefer being called Michael or Mike?"

"Michael, please."

"Dinner is served," Chris said.

"That's good," Michael said to Daphne and Annabel. "Because I've just run out of all my best anecdotes."

He was shy . . . And yet he covered it nicely, and could even admit it. She hoped he wasn't dull. Well, if he was, she was experienced at small talk; she'd been a good hostess and a good guest for so long.

He wasn't dull. At dinner Daphne discovered he knew about art, was widely read, and had a sense of humor. She felt comfortable with him, and was also beginning to be attracted to him. Because there were only nine people everyone talked to each other and it turned out to be a good dinner party. There was roast rack of veal, very tender and juicy, without sauce and not needing any, and an enormous green salad with feta cheese in it. And then . . .

Carrot cake. Chris looked at Michael and he at her, and both of them collapsed into laughter. The other two couples didn't know what was going on. "This is for you," Chris said to him.

"Thank you."

"Oh, poor thing," Annabel whispered, and then the maid came out with a crème brûlée.

They all lingered at the table, and then they went

into the living room for brandy. Daphne didn't have
any because she was going to have to drive back to
the country. Suddenly, in that warmly lit room filled
with pleasant people, the thought of going home
alone to her empty house hit her with a jolt of desolation.

She felt the dangerous imminent presence of tears
again. Pretending she was looking for the powder
room, she went blindly down the hall until she found
a private room that seemed to be the den, and then
she began to cry.

She couldn't bear any more loneliness. It was worse
after being with people. It was like being handed a
life preserver for just one moment and then having it
yanked away. She didn't know what was wrong with
her. Actually she hadn't been alone for a very long
time, but it seemed like an eternity. Nothing had
prepared her for a life like this.

Michael was standing in the doorway looking at
her.

"Are you all right?"

"I'll be fine," she lied.

She glanced at him, embarrassed, her nose running, her eyes red, her mascara streaked, making a
scene; and she saw that he was gazing at her as if she
were the most beautiful creature in the world. "Is
there anything I can do?" he asked.

Yes, don't leave me, she thought. "No . . . thank
you," she said.

"Everyone's leaving," he said. "May I take you
home?"

"I have my car. I have to drive to Connecticut."

"Then why don't I drop you off at the garage?"

"Thank you," Daphne said. "That would be very kind."

She repaired her makeup in the bathroom off the den so no one would ask questions, while he waited for her in the living room. But all the other guests were gone. She thanked Chris and Alexander for the lovely evening, and then she and Michael took a taxi to her garage.

"I really enjoyed meeting you," he said.

"And I you." She got out of the taxi, and then, on an impulse, she leaned into the open window before he could get away. "Would you like to come to the country for lunch tomorrow? You could bring your children if you like. There's a lake nearby with ice skating . . ."

"My children are very popular and have dates, but I'd be delighted to come," he said.

"You could take the train to Greenwich. There's one that gets in at twelve thirty. Is that all right? I'll meet you."

"That would be great," he said happily.

"Then I'll see you tomorrow," Daphne said.

She had never done anything like that before in her life.

The next morning she bought good things for lunch from her local gourmet take-out store. She was at the station early, waiting. When Michael got off the train Daphne was relieved to see that he looked just as attractive in daylight as he had the night before. He had brought her a bottle of wine, and a bunch of roses.

"I thought bringing flowers to the country was redundant," he said. "And then I thought: not in February."

"You make me feel guilty," she said. "I should have invited you for the weekend."

Before lunch she took him on the mandatory tour of the grounds. Then they went back indoors to thaw out in front of the fire she had lit in the living-room fireplace. She had not been able to decide where to serve lunch. The dining room was so big, and it seemed so empty with only two people in it. But the kitchen might seem too casual. She would let him choose.

"By the fire," he said immediately. "I'll help you carry everything."

He was shaking up her life already. She liked it.

They sat over lunch for hours and talked and talked about themselves. She found herself able to tell him everything, all the things she had been saving up with no one to tell them to, and all the things she had hidden. She told him about her protected, privileged childhood, and the stigma of her epilepsy when she was dating, and her marriage, and Elizabeth, and Jonathan; how maybe he'd been miserable and couldn't tell them because they all had to pretend to be so damned happy—but she would never know—and she told him about her other boys; especially Teddy, who was her miracle. And he told her about his own life, his hard-working middle-class Jewish parents, medical school, his marriage, his wife's death from cancer, and his children; the unhappy overweight fourteen-year-old girl who ate for comfort no matter how much comfort he tried to give her, and his son, who was twelve and seemed all right. They told each other their feelings and their thoughts, and as they did Daphne realized that although they came from such totally different backgrounds it seemed as if they had known each other all their lives.

They were both the same age and both from New York, but they would never have met the first time they were single, and if they had they would never have thought of going out together. No, not in the Fifties. Their early lives had been set in a pattern made by others. They might as well have grown up on opposite sides of the world.

And yet he seemed to know everything she was thinking, and there was nothing she could not tell him. He obviously felt the same way about her.

It grew dark, and they cleared away the dishes, and she made fresh coffee and they talked some more. It was like an encounter session. They talked all night. He even told her about the first girl he had been in love with, and she told him how she had thought she would never fall in love at all until Richard. Neither of them was hungry or tired. Their midnight confessions were their way of making up for lost time, and also a kind of flirtation. When the sun came up they were still lying on the living room floor by the dying fire, leaning on piled up cushions, finally peaceful and exhausted.

It had snowed during the night. The dogs had gone out through their dog door and were frolicking in the drifts. Daphne and Michael went outside and breathed the crisp, cold air. Plumes of smoke rose from their breath. It was very early and very still. He took her hand, and then they turned and kissed each other. It was as if they had sealed a pact, but she was not sure what it was.

She made scrambled eggs and toast and they ate hungrily. Then she gave him Matthew's unoccupied bedroom to sleep in, and shaving things and a tooth-brush and clean towels, and she went into her own bedroom, and they both slept until early afternoon. Day and night were upside down. They had a glass of wine. The Sunday paper was there, its bulk tied up with string. She looked at him and thought she had never been closer to anyone in her life, and they had never made love . . . but they would. She was sure of that. But now she had to take him to his train.

"Could we have dinner together one night this week in the city?" he asked.

"I'd love that."

"I have to get up so early in the mornings . . . what about Friday? I have a car, so you take the train in and I'll drive you back."

"Perfect."

And then he would stay over.

On Monday Daphne sent Chris flowers, and wrote

on the card: *Thank you for the wonderful dinner and my new friend.*

By Wednesday both Chris and Annabel had called to find out what was happening. Daphne said she thought this probably meant she was dating. She laughed when she said it, because she had always thought dating was so different when you were grown up.

On Friday she met him at his office after work and they went to Woods, a plain, pretty little place with expensive, plain, pretty food. They talked as though the five days they had been apart had been endless and there was an enormous amount to catch up on, although nothing much had really happened to her. It was just that all week whatever she thought of she had saved for him.

After dinner he drove her back to her house in Connecticut. She had expected to be nervous. After all, this was the bed she had shared for so many years with Richard, and she had never done anything with another man but Richard in her life. But she wasn't nervous at all. Michael was the one who seemed nervous, but only for the first moment before he touched her.

Lying beside him afterward, warm and happy, Daphne thought perhaps she was falling in love with him. In her old world that would have meant that he was in love with her too, and had Serious Intentions. She didn't know what it meant in this new one.

They both had children. His weren't away at school, so he had different responsibilities than she did. She lived in the country, so there was the problem of a commuting romance. She couldn't stay overnight at his apartment because of his children, and he started his office hours so early and ended them so late that he couldn't stay at her house during the week. Of course they would have dinner together a few nights a week, but that was all. They only had the weekends. In many ways it was like being back at college again, and that was very strange.

"What are you thinking about?" he asked.

But even though she could tell him anything, she didn't know how to tell him that, because there was nothing either of them could do about it. Getting engaged to someone she'd only had two dates with was more like college than she could bear.

"I'm thinking about you," Daphne said, and burrowed her head into his shoulder. She didn't say anything more.

Chapter Twenty-eight

WAITING FOR THE date of her operation, Emily found herself spending a lot of time looking in the mirror; gently pulling up her cheeks, smoothing out the skin of her neck, trying to imagine how she would look with her new face. She couldn't help remembering those times so many years ago, during her nervous breakdown, when she had peered at her imaginary scar, the product of her anger and confusion, and had felt herself disfigured. Now there would be real scars, but they would be tiny, and most of them hidden inside her hair. Dr. Winthrop had warned her that she wouldn't look twenty again, only like herself but refreshed and better; and she had told him firmly that she had no wish to look or *be* twenty again.

He was doing everything; her forehead, her eyelids, and the lower part of her face including her neck. When he told her he could do all that she was mildly insulted, because she hadn't thought there was that much wrong with her, but then she decided that as long as she was going to suffer she might as well do as much as possible. Although the nurse had given her a three-page typed description of what was to be expected Emily made him tell her everything he was going to do, in detail. He seemed a little surprised, and she decided most people were too squeamish to want to know. But she did; it was *her* face.

"Are you just pulling up the skin or also doing the muscles underneath?"

"I'm doing the muscles too, of course."

Good. Then the improvement would last longer. He asked her if she wanted general or local anesthesia and she said local. He looked pleased, and told her most patients didn't remember anything afterward anyway. She would be in the hospital for three days, and then Peter would take her home. She stocked up on soft foods, because it would be uncomfortable to chew, and imagined herself looking like a chipmunk. Dr. Winthrop said she would be able to go anywhere looking normal by three weeks after the operation. It didn't sound so terrible. She wasn't even scared.

But then, it had happened so fast she hadn't had time to worry. Suddenly she was in the hospital, about to be made new. Nobody had bothered to send her flowers, and her room was bland and impersonal without them. Emily supposed people only sent flowers if you were sick; a facelift didn't count. It was strange to be sitting here all alone, waiting for tomorrow, feeling perfectly well and knowing you'd wake up feeling rotten. She could hardly wait.

Early the next morning a nurse gave her a shot and told her not to get out of bed again. Then they came and took her down the hall and in the elevator on a rolling stretcher, and then she was in the operating room. Her doctor had to introduce himself because he was all in his operating costume, swathed in pale green so she couldn't see anything but his eyes. He asked her if she would mind putting her hands down for a minute. She said sure, and even lay on them, feeling happy, wanting to be more than cooperative. Behind and above her the doctors and nurses were talking about what they'd done that weekend, joking around, acting like people in an office. They acted as if she wasn't even there. It seemed so casual to them, but she was going to be cut up, and that made her a little nervous. There was a large clock on the wall, but she couldn't see the numbers because things were blurry. Closer, she could see her Before Pictures taped up. . . .

She heard instruments clicking and people talking, but now they were talking about what they were doing to her. She was suspended on the cloud of her drugs and couldn't feel a thing.

"Turn her on her side, please . . ."

It was boring and she dozed. She awoke and listened to some more of it.

"Now I'm going to do her eyes."

I certainly want to miss that, she thought, imagining seeing the blood, and drifted away again.

"Beautiful," the doctor said. "Beautiful."

That's me, Emily thought, and went contentedly to sleep.

When she woke up in her room her private nurse was putting ice cubes on her eyes. There was so much bandaging around her face she felt as if she were wearing a gauze football helmet. She insisted she had to go to the bathroom, but when she got there, the nurse holding her arm because she was still so groggy, she went first to the mirror. She looked like the Easter bunny because of the bandages, and she could see so little of her face that she didn't know what *it* looked like, except that it was various strange colors and her eyes were swollen slits.

"Beautiful," she said.

"Don't look," the nurse said.

She was uncomfortable but not miserable. The pressure bandages felt scratchy. Her nurses gave her painkillers and acted thrilled when she asked for more ice cream, and she watched television all night. It was like being a child again, sick and allowed to stay home from school and have anything she wanted.

On the morning of the third day the bandages came off, some of the stitches came out, and Peter came to get her. He was polite enough not to look horrified. By now she was so swollen that her face looked like a round flat dish with an oriental face painted on it. It was still several colors, none of them attractive. Her ears were swollen and gigantic. There were metal staples in her scalp and crisscrossed black stitches all around her ears and knotted in various places in her head, and her hair was lank and greasy, coated with antibiotic ointment. She felt very vulnerable.

Dr. Winthrop came to look at her. "Very good," he said, pleased. "Stay at home and rest, and come to my office Monday and I'll start to take out more stitches."

"I have only one question," Emily said. "Did you take off my ears and sew them back?"

He laughed. "No, why?"

"Because I thought you replaced them with Lyndon Johnson's."

And to think she'd thought she would only look like a chipmunk.

For a week she had to sleep on her back, propped up on three pillows, the stitches hurting. Even after that, she wondered when she would ever be able to sleep comfortably on her ears again. But it was worth it. In ten days she looked almost normal, and in two weeks she was beginning to see what she was really going to look like. All the stitches and staples were out, and she no longer felt like something Dr. Winthrop had stitched together like Frankenstein's monster. In three weeks she was admiring herself. She looked sixteen. She knew that was because she was still so swollen that her normal expression lines hadn't come back yet, but still there would be a great difference from before the operation.

Her rosy, innocent, almost poreless face smiled back at her in the mirror. Her eyes seemed enormous. She hardly even needed all those cosmetics Karen had gone with her to buy and showed her how to use; but she would want them for television, and newspaper photos. The glamorous new wardrobe that Annabel had helped her choose from the boutique was waiting for her in her closet. These clothes were certainly different from the ones that Ken had ripped up in his night of rage. And at long last she had finally been able to get out the last of the grease they'd put in her hair in the hospital. And then, since she had been feeling well enough to go anywhere she wanted to now, a month after the operation she went to the hairdresser to have her hair completely restyled, and as a final act of transformation, lightened a little; because the colorist said dark hair photographed like a lump.

The expanded Emily's Cookies in Westwood was doing beautifully. She suddenly seemed to be surrounded by accountants, lawyers, advisors. Jared's father was putting up more money, and everyone was talking about opening a new Emily's Cookies in Beverly Hills. Imagine—Beverly Hills! Once it had seemed like a dream, the mark of final success. Now it seemed like a natural step.

And the next step was back to the press agent. The two months she had asked for were up.

She couldn't wait to see his face when he saw hers.

"You did good, kiddo," Freddie Glick said nodding, looking her over when she opened the door to her apartment. "A real good job." She wondered if now that she was in her new incarnation she was henceforth to be addressed as Kiddo. "Now I've got some-thing to work with," he said.

"Well, then," Emily said, "when do we begin?"

He started her with interviews on small local pa-pers. It wasn't hard for her to do these first ones; she remembered what Chris had told her and gave basi-cally the same interview she'd done for *Fashion and Entertainment West,* leaving out anything she didn't want to see in print. The women who interviewed her were younger than she, and seemed to find every-thing she said an interesting view of history. She sup-posed the beliefs of the times that had molded—and ruined—her life were indeed a part of modern his-tory, and began to see her past in a more important light. Freddie made press kits containing photo off-sets of these newspaper clippings, plus the one from *F.E.W.,* included a biography he'd written and a new, very glamorous photograph, and sent the kits around. She got the Q&A column on the front page of the *Herald-Examiner,* which was a very big break, and then she started to do local radio.

She'd had no idea there was so much radio. She did interviews where she spoke into a tape recorder in a tiny room, and then she sat in other tiny rooms and spoke into a microphone. The first time she had to do live radio she was terrified. She didn't tell any of her friends to listen, because somehow knowing nobody she actually knew was listening made it easier to pre-tend no one was listening at all. The interviewer was a man her age, and she was afraid he would be of-fended when she started to talk about how ludicrous the rules of the Fifties were for women, but to her surprise he agreed with her and said they were just as unfair for men. Soon they were having a conversation and she was actually having a good time, even though her palms were wet and at the back of her mind was the ever-present thought that if she said something outrageous and horrible and disgusting everybody would hear it.

Peter showed her the sales reports and told her the publicity was having an effect. They had started renovation on what was to be their Beverly Hills store, and it was important that when it opened they do well because the rent was so expensive.

"I want to do television too," Emily told Freddie Glick. "You insisted I make myself over—well, I didn't do it for radio where they can't see me."

"I'm trying," he said. A week later he called her up triumphantly to tell her he had booked her on a local TV interview show. She watched it beforehand to see what was expected of her. Like most of those shows they had nonstop guests, each for about five to ten minutes, and none of them looked nervous. Why weren't they nervous? She was.

As always, she went to the interview with Pat, the young girl from Freddie's office. Freddie never came along in person unless it was a major show. The producers always made Pat sit outside anyway, because there wasn't enough room, so it was just like being all alone and deserted except for having someone to drive her there and back and tell her she hadn't been terrible.

Emily and Pat sat on chairs in the hall outside the studio and watched the show on a television set next to the ever-present coffee machine. Emily never drank anything before a show because she was afraid she would have to go to the ladies' room right in the middle of it, and what would she do? The guest who was on right before her was a man who hypnotized himself and then thrust a long skewer through one cheek and out the other without losing a drop of blood or feeling any pain. His performance seemed endless, and Emily started to feel queasy. How could she talk about cookies after this? She wanted to run away.

"And you wanted to be in show business?" Pat said.

It was her turn. As she entered the studio she passed the skewer man, recovered from his trance, who was wiping a small drop of blood off his face. She looked away. She sat down primly next to the host, who looked pale under his television makeup, and they smiled at each other.

"That was *disgusting,*" Emily said.

"How would you have liked to be sitting right next to him? I don't know if I can do this next segment—I feel too sick."

"Oh, don't be sick!" Emily said, suddenly so concerned for the poor man that she forgot how frightened she was. "We'll just talk . . . I'll tell you about necking at college . . . I won't even mention Emily's Cookies."

"Ah, yes, necking," he said. "I went to college in the late Sixties; we didn't do that anymore."

Emily laughed, and somewhere in the darkness in front of her she heard the staff laughing too. "When do I go on?" she asked.

"You *are* on. See that little red light?" He pointed to the camera, which of course she couldn't see there in the dark with all those bright lights shining down on her, and there was its heartlessly recording little red eye.

"Oh, my . . . gosh." She had almost said Oh My God, but she caught herself in time. You probably weren't allowed to on television; you might offend somebody. She pulled herself together, feeling like the world's biggest fool. She couldn't even remember this man's name—it had gone right out of her head. But he was looking at her with such friendly ease that she thought if she just kept looking back at him that she might be able to survive. "This is my first television appearance," she said.

"Yes, all this success has happened very fast for you," he said kindly. "Tell us about it."

That, at least, she knew how to do. She had done it before. She did it again. When the red light went out and the commercial went on she wiped her perspiring hands on her skirt, because they had taken her handbag with her handkerchief in it away before she went on the set, for some reason she couldn't understand, and then she shook the host's hand. "Thank you," she said. "I'm sorry I was so bad."

"You were charming," he said. "And I thank *you*."

She went back to Pat, who was holding her vanished handbag, and they left. "I stunk," Emily said, mortified. "Freddie Glick is going to kill me."

"I thought you were cute," Pat said. "They liked you. You were a real person."

"That's just what Freddie doesn't want, a real person."

"Well, fuck Freddie," Pat said.

Apparently she hadn't disgraced herself too much after all, because the next week Freddie booked her on two cable shows which were syndicated nationally, and the week after that he put her on *A.M. Los Angeles*. That one really frightened her, because she knew how important it was, but she had planned what she was going to say and everyone was very kind. Five minutes wasn't long, but when you were on the air it seemed endless. And she still had the same feeling that she was going to do something unforgivable, and that it would be irrevocable. She wondered whether that had something to do with her upbringing, all the guilt for things she hadn't even done, or whether everyone who went on TV felt that way.

Freddie came to this one, because it was a big show. He spent all the time he was there trying to sell another one of his clients for a future show and didn't pay any attention to her. Still, after her segment was over, Emily waited for him to tell her if she had been all right. When he didn't say anything she asked him.

"Sure," he said, looking surprised that she had doubted it. "You were fine. Terry held up the cookie tin twice, that's the main thing."

"And how did I look?"

"You looked beautiful. You're very photogenic."

"Thanks," she said. "I guess." She wondered when she would ever be able to know if she had been good or not without having to ask people. Or maybe it didn't matter, as long as they held up the cookie tin twice. But she couldn't really believe that, no matter what he said.

She was so busy with her life and her new career that the divorce from Ken, when it became final, seemed only another event and not the trauma she had thought it might be. Their marriage had ended long ago; this was only a formality. When he saw her in court he looked surprised at her changed appearance.

"You're looking very well," he said mildly. "I guess getting away from me has done you good."

"I guess so," she answered lightly, and smiled. He hadn't even realized she'd had anything done, and he was a *doctor!* But maybe he was too upset about the financial settlement to pay attention.

She had a lot of money now. Ken wanted to keep the house, so he had to give her half of what it was worth, plus half of whatever he'd saved since they'd lived in California. He didn't have to support Kate and Peter, because they were both over eighteen, but neither of them really needed help anymore. Kate was working regularly, and Peter had a good salary from the business. Now that she could move, and live anywhere, suddenly Emily didn't know what she wanted. She did know that she didn't want another house; she wanted to be free.

She rented a two-bedroom apartment near the one where she had been living, this one unfurnished; had it painted, and bought a few things—just the essentials, but nice things that she would want to keep. She thought of it gleefully as a selfish apartment, meant for an adult living alone, everything clean and white and neatly in its place. She had not taken any objects from their marriage, and it delighted her that Ken was stuck with those hideous gold-painted dishes his mother had forced on them when they were first married. They hadn't used them, and now he wouldn't. But she really didn't bear him any ill will anymore: he was the past. They had both been victims of The Rules.

Freddie Glick called her up triumphantly. "Okay, kiddo," he said, "I've got a big one for you. I've got you booked on *The Merv Griffin Show*."

"Oh my God," Emily gasped. "Why me?"

"They're doing a segment on the cookie craze, and they're having some people who started their own cookie business and made it."

"But I'm not famous . . . I mean, Merv Griffin, oh my God." She was both excited and totally terrified.

"Yeah, but you do a good interview. I haven't been having any trouble getting things for you lately."

"Who else is on? What am I supposed to talk about?"

"Stop babbling," he said. "Somebody from the show will call you before for a pre-interview."

"I'm going to faint," Emily said.

"You don't want to do it?"

"Of course I want to do it," she said.

So here she was, a week later, sitting in the Green Room backstage at the studio, waiting to go on a nationally syndicated television show she had been watching for years; Freddie Glick beside her, actually wearing a suit for the occasion. Somebody had told her it was called the Green Room because the performers who waited there turned green with anxiety, and Emily knew just what they meant. She watched the show on the monitor.

"And here is Wally Amos, whose company, Famous Amos, makes nearly five tons of chocolate chip cookies a day . . ."

Five tons . . . I hope nobody asks me how many I make. Look how happy and self-possessed and perky that man looks. . . . I would too if I made five tons of cookies a day.

"And here's Debbi Fields, who is only twenty-seven years old and has a hundred and fifty Mrs. Fields cookie outlets, and a new baby. That's three children now, right?"

At twenty-seven I was having a nervous breakdown, Emily thought. *God, she's gorgeous; she looks like a model. . . .*

"David Leiderman of David's Cookies nationwide, who just opened a new outlet in *Tokyo!*"

And Emily, who hopes to open her new outlet in Beverly Hills . . .

Emily peered at the monitor to see if the audience

looked friendly. Maybe they would like her because she had started so late, sort of a role model or something for the women who had never done anything. She didn't like the idea of real people sitting there looking at her, expecting her to be interesting. She had never done a show in front of a live audience before . . . she had never done *anything* in front of an audience. She had been too petrified even to try out for the school play. Peter had wanted to come to the taping but she wouldn't let him. It was the same dynamic that made her afraid to have her friends watch her when she was performing. And that was what it was, really, a performance. If she just kept telling herself that, and remembering her lines, she would be all right.

But she couldn't remember a thing she had ever said.

Her mind was a total blank, and now someone was leading her out onto the stage, where the hot, bright lights hit her, and she was on the set that looked like a living room, or perhaps an office, with Merv Griffin at his desk, and all those cameras, and *the audience sitting there looking at her.* She sat down and crossed her legs and smiled, wondering if the microphone would pick up the sound of her thumping heart.

"This is Emily Buchman of Emily's Cookies," Merv Griffin said. "A newcomer on the cookie scene. She opened her first factory last summer, in Westwood Village in California, and it was an overnight success. Now she's going to open another one in Beverly Hills, with plans for several more this year. Prior to this she was a homemaker with no business experience at all. When you were back at Radcliffe, Emily, did you ever think that this would happen?"

"No," Emily said. "I wanted to be a doctor. But my career advisor told me that if I wanted so badly to be a doctor I should marry one instead, so I married the first doctor who asked me."

There were some chuckles from the audience; the laughter of recognition, and a few gasps of disbelief. "Well, actually," she said, "he was in premed." More chuckles. They were liking her! She allowed herself to look back at the audience for the first time, and fastened on an attractive woman of about her own age, sitting in the first row, who was smiling at her and nodding encouragement. "In those days," Emily said, "back in the Fifties, we married what we wanted to be. I guess it was supposed to rub off or something."

More laughter—she had apparently said something mildly risqué. The woman in the front row gave her an ironic grin. "Then I guess it wouldn't have helped if you'd married a baker," Merv Griffin said, smiling.

"Well, he might have let me work in his store." She smiled so they wouldn't think she was too much of a feminist . . . just kidding, folks. "Incidentally, *my* cookies are butterscotch chip, not chocolate chip, and I also make butterscotch marshmallow chip." That was for Freddie, the plug so he wouldn't yell at her afterward. Her mind was beginning to work again and she felt as if the whole thing was happening in slow motion. She thought of telling how Adeline wouldn't let her into her own kitchen and she had to bake cookies on Adeline's day off, and then decided it wouldn't go over well. Better to stick to what she did best. Merv was asking her how she got started, and she was telling him, making her success story sound like *Rocky*. Now she told how her son and his friend from college had helped her; making it sound like a nice family story. She said she'd thought of her slogan "Cookies Are Love" because she always felt that way when she made her cookies for her children at home. Merv mentioned how nice it was that she still sent her cookies over to the children at the hospital. Then he asked if anyone in the audience had any questions for any of his guests.

A woman who seemed in her early fifties stood up. "I have a question for Emily," she said; almost timidly, even respectfully. "I always wanted a career of some kind. I had talent in various directions. But like you, I was told to forget about it. Tell me, do you think it's too late to do something different with my life?"

"It's never too late," Emily said firmly.

"Do you mind if I ask how old you are?"

Some rustling from the audience; apparently some of them thought it was a forbidden question. "I'm forty-six," Emily said, taking off a year to conform with the lie Freddie had insisted on putting in the press release. Now there were some gasps, since she obviously looked a lot younger, and some approving murmurs and nods for her honesty.

"Thank you," the woman said, and sat down.

Another woman stood up. "My question is for Emily too," she said. "Was your husband supportive when you started your own business?"

"He didn't have to be," Emily said. "We were already separated." Some laughter. "The point is, it's wonderful if you have someone who's on your side, but you can do it either way. And why doesn't anybody ever ask a man if his *wife* was supportive when he went into business and started to make money?"

There was more laughter, and then . . . applause! They were actually applauding her; smiling, nodding; the woman in the front row whom she'd taken as her mascot and a lot of others, women just like herself who knew she was just like them. They *liked* her! She felt so high she might have been stoned. She sat there in her wave of euphoria loving them, those nice people, who treated her like somebody special, who asked her opinion, who laughed at her jokes, who understood. When the segment was over and she had to leave she wished it had been longer. She sailed backstage where Freddie Glick was waiting for her.

"You were great," he said.

"Thank you," Emily said. She hadn't asked him, and she hadn't needed to. For the first time, she had known.

"You were terrific," some total stranger said, a man who had something to do with the show.

"Thank you," Emily said, smiling at him.

All her life she had wanted to be someone, all her life she had wanted to be important. Those endless sessions with her analyst, trying to work it out, to deal with the need and either make something positive from it or make it go away . . . Perhaps she had wanted to be important because she felt herself so eminently unimportant and valueless that only the approval of strangers could make her whole. But she hadn't felt herself to be valueless for a very long time now. Yet she loved this; to be in control of that huge mass of people, to win them over. She loved being in the spotlight, she loved doing publicity, she wasn't frightened anymore. All she knew was that she had finally found what she liked to do, and she was really good at it.

Chapter Twenty-nine

CHRIS KNEW IMMEDIATELY when Alexander's affair with James was over. It was not because he had started coming home to her directly after work, and staying home for the evening, because James could simply have been out of town. No, it was because Alexander looked destroyed.

It devastated her to know that the man she loved was so unhappy because of his love for someone else, not her. She had seen him look that way before, long ago, when he thought he would lose her, but now he had lost someone else and having her was not enough. She waited for him to tell her what had happened, wondering if she should bring it up first, and then after several days of this he finally did.

They were having a drink together in the living room before dinner. It was January; dark; supposedly the beginning of the fresh new year, but actually the sad end of the holidays, a time of waiting for spring. She remembered when those long January nights had been a happy time of hibernation for them, together in their domestic tranquility, glad the party season was over. It too seemed so long ago.

Nicholas was studying at a friend's house. Chris and Alexander were alone. He had taken to drinking vodka these last few evenings, not wine, saying wine tasted acidic. She knew better.

"It's finished between James and me," he said.

What did one say—I'm sorry? I'm glad? "I suspected it," she said quietly.

"He dumped me," Alexander said. He was trying to keep his tone ironic, but it was full of pain. "He's in love with someone else. I knew it would happen. I'm too old for him."

"Did he say that?"

"That I'm too old? No. But I know it."

"You're also married," she said. "There's seldom a future with a married man."

He gave a thin smile, looking a little less miserable. "You always say it exactly the way it is. I guess this still *is* a marriage."

"It's *our* marriage. Limits, liabilities, and all."

"It's so unfair for you. Separate rooms, separate lives . . ."

They looked at each other. She knew him so well. "This time I'm not going back to what we were," Chris said.

"I know. I don't mind. I don't even mind being old if I can grow old with you."

She smiled. "Yes you do. You mind being older."

"You always understood me," he said.

"No. I recently understood you."

"Really?"

"Yes. Before that I was just learning to."

They sat there for a while in silence. Chris wondered if Alexander expected her to go without sex for the rest of their lives together, or if he hoped she had a lover. He might well ask, or even tell her he wouldn't mind if she did, but she certainly would never tell him. What she had with Cameron was private, special. It wasn't just a physical convenience; it was love, friendship, warmth, romance. She wondered what Alexander had had with James. It hurt to think about it, and knowing it was over did not make it hurt any less. If James hadn't broken off with him nothing would have changed.

"What are you thinking?" Alexander asked.

"That you always have the power to hurt me."

"But you have that power over me, too."

"How?" Chris asked.

"By being unhappy," Alexander said. "I hate it when you're unhappy, and I always seem to be the one who makes you that way."

"I'm not unhappy very often," she said.

"No, you haven't been for a while." There was a long pause. He was looking at her oddly, as if studying her. "And if you left me I would suffer a great deal," Alexander said, finally. "You're not going to leave me, are you?"

He knows I have someone, she thought. "No," she said.

She had loved him for almost thirty years, most of her life. At eighteen she had loved Alexander the stranger, the elusive tragic figure, and then later the elusive sophisticated one; and finally the kind, affectionate one who became her husband. She remembered how she had followed him to Paris after he had left her, after they graduated from college. He hadn't known he was breaking her heart; all he had thought was that he was escaping a place where he didn't dare live his life the way he needed to. It had taken her six years to have the courage to follow him to Paris, and no matter how unhappy she had been in Paris trying to capture him, and even afterward, nothing had been as bad as those six years in New York alone trying to get over him.

"Remember that trip we took?" he said. "The first one, to the South of France, together, to see if we could get along . . ."

"And if we 'got along' we would get married," Chris said. "We both knew what 'getting along' was a euphemism for."

"It was more than that," he said, sounding hurt.

She smiled. "You live your past, I'll live mine." She held up her empty glass and he refilled it with white wine. "Are you very sad about James?" she asked. She sounded to herself like a character in a Noel Coward play.

"Yes. But I'll get over it. It won't be pleasant seeing him at the office, but I'll survive."

She thought that if she and Cameron ever broke up in a way that was not mutual it would be horrendous to see him at the office. But she couldn't imagine that she and Cameron ever *would* leave each other. They both had what they wanted. And even if she wanted more, he would never give up his wife and children. Perhaps Cameron couldn't give a hundred percent of himself to anybody, but he had arranged it so that he would never have to find out.

"And live to love another day," Chris said.

"I don't know how you can stand me," he said.

"I love you."

"I don't know what I've done to deserve you."

"We've had some lovely times," she said. "Besides the terrible ones."

"Yes . . ."

She thought about all the trips they had taken to exotic faraway places with their son ever since he was just a baby, and the peaceful weekends in the country house, and being together at the end of every day. She and Alexander had never had a fight . . . except for the night she found him with another man in their apartment when she was supposed to be away. And even then it was not a fight; it was simply one of the "terrible times." There would always be those. He had learned to be discreet now, but there would be another James some day. Alexander would not change, no more than Cameron would.

"Dear Chris," Alexander said. "I love you."

It wasn't the memory of the good times that kept her with him; it was her obsessive, overwhelming love for him. She would still love him and stay with him if they had never gone anywhere, if they had been poor, if they were still the way they had been at college. It was not all those years they had been together that trapped her here; because every day it was as if she saw him new and was just as glad to be near him. It was not even that they had become each other's best friend; because she would never stop wanting more.

She had her own independent, interesting life, and her new self-respect, and her exciting, fascinating lover, and she was more than content—she was happy—but none of that changed a thing. If some miracle could happen and Cameron wanted to divorce his wife and marry her, or if Alexander could become straight, and she could have her choice, Chris knew that she would not hesitate for an instant.

There was only one choice.

She would choose Alexander.

And so, no matter how much she had grown and strengthened, and no matter how free she'd become, the core of Chris would always remain what it was: the victim of her dream of him.

Chapter Thirty

IT WAS THE end of February, the dreariest, saddest time of the year, but it seemed to Annabel that everyone was happy but herself. Chris had Alexander back, as a companion at least, and he was behaving himself; and she had Cameron too, for the icing on the cake. Daphne was apparently having a romance with that attractive diet doctor. Emma was totally involved in the movie she was working on, still staying at Annabel's, which was a great comfort, even though they hardly saw each other. Annabel could not get Zack out of her mind.

It was pointless to go on like this, unable to forget him, afraid to confront him again and be rejected. She had to know one way or the other, and then, if he didn't want her, she could let go. She asked Emma to find out from her friend Kit, who was in his movie, if Zack was involved with another woman yet. The next night Emma saluted her at the door like a soldier, but with a big smile.

"Spy reporting in," Emma said.

"That was fast." Her heart sank. Everyone must know about his new involvement but she.

"Kit says there is no woman in his life."

"Is she sure?"

"As a matter of fact, she had to go to his house last Saturday to work on a difficult scene with him, and Kit always snoops, she just loves to look in bureau drawers and medicine cabinets and things. So she did. And there was not a sign of a live-in female."

"What about a visiting female?"

"He has only two toothbrushes. Most people do. If she visits, she brings her own."

"You are a *super* spy," Annabel said happily, and hugged her.

That night, when she knew it was nine o'clock in California, she called him; and this time, finally, he answered the phone. The shock of hearing his voice at last sent a jolt of electricity through her. She almost couldn't speak. His voice was so familiar, so close, that she melted, and her eyes filled with tears. "Zack," she said, "it's Annabel."

"Happy New Year," he said.

"I called to explain why I disappeared our last night in New York."

"It's all right," he said, but his voice was tight and she knew it wasn't all right at all.

"No, it's not. You thought I was out with someone else, but I wasn't. I was at my best friend Christine's house, hiding from you because I couldn't face having you go away."

There was a pause while he digested this bizarre bit of information. "But I was going to give you that plane ticket," he said.

"I got it. And then I kept calling you, but you had vanished, and you never returned any of my calls, even when I left a message for you, so I knew how angry you were."

"I don't understand," he said.

"You don't understand what?"

"Why you would pull a thing like that. I thought we were getting along so well."

"We were . . . that's why . . . Zack, it's pretty damn difficult for me to explain this. You know, you get to a point in life where you can't stand to be hurt again. I didn't want to be so involved and have you . . . I mean, you never even said anything about seeing me again. How could I know you were going to invite me to come visit you for Christmas? You never said anything. I didn't want to be just a fling."

"So you made me feel like I was one."

"I'm sorry," Annabel said. "It's been years since I've been this honest with any man. I usually make a smart remark. This isn't easy."

"I thought it would be a nice surprise to hand you the ticket," he said mildly. "Sort of romantic."

Suddenly she was angry at him again. He didn't seem to comprehend at all. "But what was I supposed to do? Be prepared to say good-bye forever and then be grateful that I was saved?"

"What are you talking about, Annabel?"

"*You* know movies," she said. "Remember *Love in the Afternoon,* when at the end Gary Cooper is going away and then he just pulls Audrey Hepburn up on the train with him? That was fine for the Fifties, always being rescued by the unattainable man, and maybe it's all right when you're twenty, but it isn't all right for me."

"Did you call me in the middle of the night, when I'm trying to work on my movie, to yell at me?" he said. Now he sounded angry too. "I have notes to do for tomorrow morning. I have to get up at five o'clock. I can't discuss this on the phone."

"I just wanted to explain," she said.

"And you have," he said. "I'm sorry I insulted you in some way. I didn't intend to. Goodnight."

"You didn't . . ." she started to say, but he had hung up.

Annabel sat staring at the phone for a long time, so depressed she could hardly move. They hadn't discussed anything at all; she'd only made things worse. But she loved him. He didn't even know that—maybe he never had. That plane ticket might have been his way of trying to find out. She still had it, and he didn't want to talk on the phone. All right then, she would talk to him in person.

She made a reservation for the first flight to Los Angeles on Saturday morning. She left the return open. If he threw her out she could go right home; if not, she could stay for a week. She told Maria and Pamela to mind the store, and arranged for Pamela to take Sweet Pea home with her while she was away. She told Chris and Emma, who wished her luck. She did not tell Zack, who thought surprises were romantic, that she was coming.

When Annabel stepped out of the terminal in Los Angeles she was struck by the heat, the sunshine, the palm trees—this when New York was so cold and gray! It was noon. She took a cab to Zack's house. All she had with her was a small suitcase and a large bunch of roses.

She had tried to imagine what his house would look like, and now here it was; set up in the hills in one of those Canyons; a rustic, eastern looking house, an anachronism, almost as if it belonged by a lake in Maine. It had a lot of wood on it, and trees around it. It wasn't even very big. It seemed a perfect house for two people to live in together. Everything was very quiet. There was a black BMW in the driveway, with a normal license plate, nothing cute written on it. She knew it must be Zack's car, and that he was home. She rang the bell.

Her heart was pounding. In the silence she heard a bird squawk, and then the flutter of wings. After what seemed like a very long time Zack opened the door.

He was exactly as she had remembered, but better. But here, in his own world, he also seemed somewhat of a stranger. He was wearing jeans and a sweatshirt, and she had never seen him that way. There were so many things she still had to learn about him. But right now all she wanted to do was to throw her arms around him and hug and kiss him. Instead they just stood there looking at each other, and then she held out the bouquet of roses.

"Peace," she said.

"My God, you are still so absolutely knockout gorgeous," he said, shaking his head, and then he took the roses in one hand and her suitcase in the other and led her into his house. Then he put the suitcase on the floor and the flowers on top of it and gave her a hug that almost dissolved her bones.

" 'Still'?" she said. "It hasn't been *that* long."

"It has to me."

"Me too," she said.

The inside of his house was like the outside; homey-looking wood furniture, some paintings, quilts and things. A lot of old movie posters. A fireplace, a piano. Books and magazines and scripts everywhere. "How long can you stay?" he asked.

"A week."

"Good. I'm going to be working though, you know."

"I know."

"You can come watch if you don't find it too boring."

She had come nearly three thousand miles to discuss their lives and their relationship and he was acting as if she had merely come for a week's vacation. But maybe she was being too impatient. He was being civilized, and she'd had a tiring trip. Zack put her suitcase in his bedroom and showed her the closets and the bathroom, said he would put some things together for lunch, and went downstairs. While she was freshening up she thought twice about unpacking. Maybe their discussion, whenever they had it, would end in another fight. Well, she would worry about that when it happened. She compromised by pulling out a few things that would wrinkle and went downstairs.

He had put the roses in a vase of water and arranged cheeses, fruit, salad, a loaf of bread, and a bottle of chilled wine in a cooler on the dining-room table. He seemed to be able to take care of himself very well. "How about a glass of wine and a tour of the house and grounds and then lunch?" he said. "The grounds takes three minutes."

"That would be lovely."

The rest of the house consisted of his home office and a large kitchen and another bathroom. The grounds consisted of an oval swimming pool, the bottom of which had been painted black so it really did look like a lake in Maine; more trees, some with little green fruit on them that seemed like possible lemons; lush landscaping, and a stupendous view softened by smog.

"It's beautiful," she said.

"You see what you gave up?" he said lightly.

"I gave up more than that."

He smiled at her. When she saw that smile she wanted to go right to bed with him and forget about lunch. But that was how it had been with Dean, and this was Zack. Zack had meals first and sex afterward. Zack did everything step by step, and did not lie about love as Dean had. Zack did not mention love at all.

He took her hand and they went to the bedroom and forgot about lunch until it was four o'clock and they were both starving. So he still surprised her, even in the things she thought she knew. Maybe she really *didn't* know him as well as she thought. "I missed you so much," he said.

"Not as much as I missed you," Annabel said. *Oh, I love you,* she thought. *Why can't you be in love with me?* She pulled her bathrobe out of her still-packed suitcase and they went downstairs to devour everything on the table.

"I want to explain to you why I ran away," she said. "Will you listen?"

"Yes."

"It's not very attractive, when one is having a romance with a man, to tell him about all the other men who broke her heart before she ever met him. It is, in fact, guaranteed to chase him off."

"That depends on the man," Zack said.

"Well . . . let me finish."

"All right."

"Up until my marriage, to the wrong man I might add, it seems as if every man I ever fell in love with left me, and I kept trying to figure out what I did, and finally I decided that the most prudent thing would be simply not to fall in love with anyone at all. That lasted for years, and then I realized it was just not my nature to live without feeling anything, so I let myself fall in love again, even though I *knew* he was eminently the wrong man . . . and despite great dramatic protestations of love, he decided one day he had changed his mind."

"Who's his analyst?" Zack said.

She tried not to laugh. "Please," she said. "This is serious." She felt so relaxed and happy after making love with him that it was hard to feel tragic about what she was remembering. And then she realized that the reason it was easier to tell him now was that he really cared about her. She could see it in his eyes. "And when you and I were together in New York," she went on, "I thought it was just . . . a week together in New York, and I began to feel too much for you for it to be only that, so I ran away and hid the last night because I couldn't stand to say good-bye. I didn't want any more good-byes in my life."

"But how was I to know that?" Zack said.

"You couldn't."

"Do you want to hear my side of it?"

"Of course," Annabel said.

He took her hand. "Look," he said, "I meet this independent, beautiful, intelligent, successful woman, who obviously has her own life, who had an entire life before she ever met me, and I think: maybe I'm making a mistake to fall in love with her. Okay, so then I think: maybe I'll invite her to spend Christmas in California with me. We'll play it by ear, see how it goes. We both have busy lives, careers, our own needs. She's *not* some little girl waiting for me to rescue her, to give her an identity, charge cards, parties to go to. She has all those things. I wouldn't be saving her; I'd be asking her to give things up. And I couldn't do that to you. And, to tell you the truth, I was busy with meetings, and by the time I made up my mind to get the ticket it was nearly time for me to leave, so I thought I'd give it to you as a Christmas surprise. So it was a bad idea. Now I know."

" 'In love with her'?" Annabel said. "You fell in love with me?"

"Yes," he said.

"But why didn't you say so?"

"I don't know," he said. "Maybe you aren't the only person who's afraid to get hurt."

"I wouldn't hurt you," Annabel said. "Never."

"You already did, and you couldn't help it."

"What a stupid thing," she said sadly.

"You know what you remind me of?" Zack said. "A story I read when I was a kid about a little boy named Epaminondas. He went to visit his aunt and she gave him a cake to bring home to his mother. He held it tightly in his fist, and when he got home the cake was nothing but crumbs. So his mother said that was dumb, and the way you carry a cake is you wrap it in leaves and put it on top of your head. So, the next time he goes to his aunt, she gives him some butter; and he puts it on top of his head, and of course by the time he gets home it's all melted. And his mother says, no, no, that's not how you carry butter; butter you wrap in leaves and put it into the brook to cool it. So, the next time he goes to see his aunt she gives him a puppy dog . . ."

"Oh, no!" Annabel said.

"No, the dog doesn't drown. But almost. And on and on, everything he does is what he was supposed to do to the thing before, and of course it's the wrong thing to do. What I'm trying to say, Annabel, is I am not any of the men you knew before. I am the one you know now. So forget about all the others."

"I love you Zack," Annabel said. How wonderful to be able to say it to him at last.

"I love you, too," Zack said. "And that's only the easy part."

They spent all of Sunday together at home, but a great deal of the time he had to work on his notes for the following week. Annabel understood, and was happy just to be with him. In the late afternoon they swam in his pool—he was an excellent swimmer and she was just so-so—and then they made love. He took her out to dinner, to a dark, noisy little Italian restaurant, but they were home at nine and in bed by ten. She still had jet lag so she didn't mind.

"This is my life when I'm working," he said. "But usually I don't even go out to dinner."

"This is most people's lives when they're working," Annabel said.

"Glamorous Hollywood."

He got up at five in the morning, but he let her sleep and arranged for one of the drivers to pick her up and bring her to the set at ten. They were shooting indoors; it was a bedroom, and everything was interesting to her because she had never seen it before. Most of all she liked the way Zack behaved with everyone, constantly moving around with that crackling intensity of his, and yet warm and almost paternal too. He took the actors aside and talked to them gently, in a low voice, and sent them back to do the scene again, and again. They had to do everything again and again, for different camera angles, and in between there were boring waits for setups. But Zack never stopped watching, moving, thinking.

The star, Sarah Very, was smaller than Annabel had thought from seeing her on the screen, but she supposed most of them were. Emily's daughter, Kit, was beautiful. Annabel tried to remember the way Emily had looked back at Radcliffe, and decided Kit looked a lot like she had, but better because the hair and makeup in those days had been so unflattering. Kit seemed very quiet and serious. During all those long waits she withdrew into her dressing room and shut the door, and when she was out on the set again she never joked around or even spoke to anyone unless she had to to be pleasant, as she did when Zack introduced her to Annabel. No small talk about Emma, nothing. A polite smile, a firm handshake, and nice to meet you, good-bye. She clutched her script the way a child clutches a security blanket, even though she knew all her lines perfectly, and at the end of the day she disappeared.

"Want to see dailies?" Zack said to Annabel.

"Sure."

They watched what had been filmed the day before, with some other people, in a small screening room with red velvet seats. Annabel had seen Sarah

Very in several movies and knew how good she was, but she had never seen Kit. Kit was amazing. She was complex, vulnerable, and luminous.

"I was right about the kid," Zack said to one of the men. "She's wonderful."

"And she's been behaving herself," the man said. "You know she's pretty much of a nut in real life."

"This *is* real life," Zack said calmly. "And if she acts like a nut I'll kill her."

"I'm beginning to think those rumors were exaggerated anyway," the man said.

They didn't get home until eight o'clock. Annabel helped Zack put together a light supper and they ate it in the kitchen. Someone had come in during the day and cleaned his house immaculately. After dinner he buried himself in his notes. They were in bed at ten. "I shouldn't do this," he said, beginning to kiss her. "I should be sleeping."

"I'm only going to be here a week."

"I know. That's why I'm breaking my rule."

The next morning she insisted on getting up with him at five, to see everything he did, to be as excited and tired as he was, to live his entire day so she could understand it. But she already did. His creative work was the central fire of his life. That energy and enthusiasm was what she respected about him. She remembered Rusty, her ex-husband, who had been only a playboy, pretending to work, drinking at the country club instead, playing golf, having endless boozy lunches. The worst thing about their marriage had been that she had absolutely no respect for him at all. That, and the fact that he was a bore. Zack would never be a bore. And he didn't want her to become one, just another of those wives who lunched and shopped, killing time. She had sold clothes to enough of them to know what their lives were like; Revenge Shoppers she called them; and she had no intention of becoming one.

This would be fun for a week, living in Zack's shadow, sitting in her chair at the edge of the set, moving quickly to get out of everyone's way, but she couldn't follow him around every day for the rest of her life. She needed to have things of her own, and they both knew it. When she got back to New York she had to go to Europe again for the collections. For the first time she was taking Maria with her, to teach her more about the business, leaving Pamela to manage the boutique on her own. Maria and Pamela were excited about their new responsibilities, and they were ready for them. There had to be some kind of compromise, Annabel thought, some way she could be with a man who lived on the opposite coast and whose work even took him to Europe for months at a time, without giving up her own life.

Zack had fallen in love with *her*, and he liked her the way she was. He didn't want to change her, nor have her change herself for him. And she loved him because he was exactly the person he already was. But she was so happy with him right now that she couldn't think about the future anymore.

The week went by so fast Annabel couldn't bear it. She called Emily just to say hello, and to explain that she was passing through town very quickly. And then she had one more weekend alone with Zack, until she had to go to New York Sunday night on the Red Eye. On the plane she almost cried.

When she was back in New York Zack called her every night, and when she went to Milan and Paris and London he called her there. In April Annabel went back to California to see him again, for another week.

"When I finish shooting and start editing," he said, "you're really going to see a devoted lunatic."

"Devoted to me?" she said.

"No, devoted to my little machine."

"Can I watch?"

"Sure."

"Emma will be so jealous," Annabel said. "She'd give her eye teeth to be hovering over your shoulder in the cutting room."

"She'd probably enjoy it more than you will too."

"We shall see," Annabel said.

"In our own funny way, though," Zack said, "it's still working out for us, isn't it?"

"It is."

"Are you beginning to understand what I meant when I said that loving each other was only the easy part?"

"Yes."

"But you're still willing to give it time to see if it's going to work?"

"Of course I am," Annabel said.

"I'm glad." They looked at each other. "And then," he said, "we'll have to figure out how."

Chapter Thirty-one

By the end of March Daphne and Michael knew they wanted to marry each other. For both of them it was very simple: they were in love, they made each other's lives complete, they were happy now when before they had been simply marking time. Even though he knew all her flaws and scars he still thought she was perfect, his princess. Not in the way Richard had, denying that she had a right to be like other people, but in his own way because she was *his* princess. Perhaps Daphne was one of those women who was always destined to be someone's Golden Girl. She preferred to think of herself as someone who had come through trouble and had survived. Michael thought of her as that too, and admired her and wanted to take care of her.

And she wanted to take care of him. She wanted to meet his children, to win them over, to make them happy. She wanted her sons to like him and his children, to become a family again, or even the family they had never really been. She looked around her house and grounds, the places she had once loved before all the things had happened to ruin them for her, and now all she thought was that they were an obstacle that kept her away from Michael, and that she wished she lived in New York. She began to hate commuting, and the too-brief dinners with Michael that had to end with each of them going home separately, and Sunday nights after their weekends together, when he had to leave. She knew he hated it too.

"This is silly," he said one night. "Spending all our time in cars and trains when we could be together."

"I know," she said.

"We ought to get married."

"I thought you'd never ask," Daphne said.

They decided that he would take her out to dinner with his children, and later, when her boys came home for their Easter holiday, they would all go out together. Daphne knew her sons would not be a problem. Whatever they thought (and how could they not like this kind, charming, sweet man?) they would behave properly. And they still had their time with Richard. She wondered, however, how Michael's children would feel about her being brought into their lives as some kind of replacement.

She met him at his apartment for a drink. It was the first time she had been there, and as soon as she walked in Daphne felt the emptiness. It was like her house; the heart was gone, and everything was too still. The furniture was modern, quite different from hers, but it set off his collection of paintings very well. She liked them all. He had put out some little Japanese crackers in a crystal bowl on the coffee table, and gave her a glass of wine. Then his children came in, all dressed up. Cathy, fourteen, very pretty but very overweight, too fat really to look right in anything stylish, wearing a kind of smock thing. She had Michael's blue eyes and aristocratic features hiding under the pudginess of her face. And Jeremy, twelve, a skinny, active-looking little kid with big dark eyes. He hadn't started his real growth spurt yet, and when he did he would probably be even thinner, which would be worse for his sister.

Michael introduced them to Daphne, they helped themselves to diet sodas—of course—and sat there looking at her. They knew she was important, Michael had told them, and they knew why she was there. She smiled. They smiled; Jeremy warily, Cathy merely politely and barely even that. Cathy looked longingly at the crackers, and then looked away. Daphne wished she had a cigarette. The children remained silent and she wished they were just shy. There was nothing to do but talk around them, so she and Michael did. He told her about his day, and she told him about hers. Then, because he'd just come home from his office, he asked the children about school. Then they went out to dinner.

They went back to Woods, which was one of Michael's favorite places because it was possible to get plain food, attractively presented. Cathy ordered the most fattening thing on the menu. Michael raised his eyebrows at her.

"If you didn't do that," she said to him quietly, with hurt and anger in her voice, "then *I* wouldn't do it."

"Yes you would," he said lightly.

"Cathy's Dad's only unsuccessful patient," Jeremy said.

"I'm not his patient," Cathy said.

"Bigfoot," Jeremy said. "Ouch!" He rubbed his arm where his sister had pinched him and glared at her.

"Daphne's going to think you're savages," Michael said.

"*I'm* not," Cathy said. "*He* is."

"The kids at school call her Bigfoot," Jeremy said to Daphne, by way of explanation.

"I think that's cruel," Daphne said.

"*Children* love to be cruel," Cathy said. "They think it's funny."

Daphne smiled. "Then I guess nothing has changed since I was a kid."

"*You* were never fat," Cathy said. It wasn't a question, it was a statement.

"No," Daphne said.

"Then you didn't have my problem."

"No. I had others, though."

"Really?" Cathy said. She looked rather pleased and interested. "Like what?"

Daphne glanced at Michael. She could read his mind: he was saying go ahead, tell them, who cares? "Epilepsy," Daphne said.

The two kids were staring at her. Here was an adult they had just met, a woman who was here to make a good impression on them, and she was telling them outright, in the calmest way imaginable, that she'd had a rotten childhood too, that she had no secrets, that she could understand.

"Were the kids mean to you?" Cathy asked.

"I wouldn't let them be," Daphne said. "If they were, I ignored it."

"Did they make you feel terrible?"

"Very."

"When you're a fat person," Cathy said, "everybody acts like that's the most important thing about you. They don't even bother to see what you're really like."

"I know," Daphne said.

"No you don't," Cathy said suddenly. "How could you know?" She looked away, dismissing this intruder, and devoted herself to the food on her plate. For dessert she ordered strawberries, and then she loaded them with whipped cream and sugar and gobbled them up almost vindictively. The rest of them pretended not to notice. Daphne asked Jeremy which movies he had seen lately that he liked, and which ones he wanted to see. She felt like a good dinner guest, giving equal time to the person on her left and then the one on her right, but she felt as if she were at the wrong dinner.

At the end of the evening they all walked Daphne to the garage where she had left her car. Even though she knew it wouldn't be for much longer, she felt like the outsider, going home by herself, and Cathy didn't even like her. She leaned down and kissed Jeremy on the cheek. His skin was still soft and childlike. Then she tried to kiss Cathy, but the girl stiffened, and very subtly but firmly pulled away. When, finally, she kissed Michael goodnight, Daphne could almost feel his daughter's eyes boring into her back.

The next day Michael reported to Daphne that his children had loved her, that they thought she was beautiful and nice.

"You *wish,*" she said lightly. "Only Jeremy does."

"No . . ."

"Bring them to the country for the weekend," she said. "I'll try harder."

"Just be yourself," he said.

She prepared her house for their visit. Michael would stay in Matthew's room again, for appearance's sake; he could sneak across the hall to hers when everyone was asleep, not that it would fool anybody. Jeremy would like Teddy's room, she thought, so she would put him there. And Cathy . . . There was a feminine, pretty, girl's room waiting empty. It seemed natural to give it to Cathy, so she did, and tried to ignore the brief stab of pain for the child who would never live there anymore and what could never be . . .

"Whose room is this?" Cathy asked.

"My daughter Elizabeth's."

"Where is she?"

"She lives in a special home. She's retarded. I visit her."

There was a long pause. "My mother would never have given her daughter away," Cathy said.

Only a child, but what power they had to hurt you when they wanted to! "I know," Daphne said calmly. "I didn't know your mother, but I'm sure she wouldn't have."

"My shrink says that I'm angry at my mother for dying, but that's ridiculous of course because I know she couldn't help it. Nobody wants to die."

Daphne thought of Jonathan and her eyes filled with tears. She turned her head away, but not before Cathy saw, and knew she'd drawn blood, more than she'd meant to, and didn't know why. Daphne didn't say anything.

"I guess I'll unpack," Cathy said.

Michael's children did not come every weekend, because sometimes they had things to do in the city with their friends, but now it was April, and her boys were back for their Easter vacation from prep school, and the plan was for all of them to be in the house together. Matthew would need his room again. Jeremy could double up with Teddy, as there were two beds. But Michael? The last door had to be opened, both literally and figuratively. She could not keep Jonathan's bedroom a shrine forever. Ina cleaned and aired it. Daphne helped her move the furniture around to make it look a little different, and bought a new bedspread. But Daphne knew nothing would really change that room, even the presence of Michael who was so alive and filled her life, and besides, no one was actually going to sleep there.

"Who used to live *here?*" Cathy asked. It still didn't look like a guest room, it looked like the room of someone who had grown up and moved away.

Daphne took a deep breath. "I had a son who died. He . . . killed himself." There was a pause while they looked at each other. "I guess there are some people who *do* want to die," Daphne said.

Cathy was at a loss for words. For the first time, at last, she looked at Daphne with some human sympathy, even concern, as if she were more than the interloper who was trying to take her mother's place. "A lot of terrible things happened to you too, didn't they," she said finally.

Daphne nodded. "Maybe now only good things will," she said.

The children got along. It occurred to Daphne that hers weren't all children anymore: Matthew had been accepted at Harvard and would be going there in the fall. He was graduating from St. Martin's at the end of May. She and Michael were planning a June wedding. They had started looking for a large apartment in New York with space for all of them, and she had put her house up for sale. Michael was going to sell his co-op, and he had suggested they also buy a house at the beach for summer weekends. He worried a little that a Manhattan co-op board would not let them in with so many children and two big dogs, but Daphne wasn't worried. She had never been rejected by any place in her life.

During the school holiday she took Cathy shopping for clothes. Cathy hated everything. "I look disgusting," she said. "I wish I was thin like you."

"As a matter of fact," Daphne lied, "I was going to try to lose a few pounds for the wedding. Why don't you and I go on a diet together?"

"You mean for moral support?"

"Why not?"

"But I have to lose at least *twenty!*"

"You have two months, and at your age it's easier than it is for me. You're still growing, and your metabolism's faster. What do you say, want to try it together? You could call me up every night and report how it's going, and tell me what you ate, and how you overcame temptation . . . ?"

"I don't overcome temptation very often," Cathy said.

"I'm going to wear a sort of pale pinkish dress to the wedding," Daphne said. "I see you in apricot. What do you think?" Cathy shrugged. "You're going to be in the wedding pictures . . ."

"I'll hide behind three people."

"No you won't. Come on. It'll be summer. You'll be thin by then. We'll get you a bikini too, for East Hampton. And designer jeans, from wherever you want."

"You sure you won't mind if I call you up every night?"

"I'd be flattered," Daphne said.

"I guess I could try," Cathy said. She looked down at her hands. "I just want to tell you," she said shyly, "that I think you're a wonderful person, and that I think of you as a friend, and I'm glad I'm in your life, and . . . I really like you."

"I love you too," Daphne said.

So the weeks went by quickly. Daphne found an enormous apartment on Park Avenue, and the board accepted them, children, dogs, and all. Between them she and Michael had plenty of furniture, and the painters promised to be finished in time for them to move in before the wedding. They planned to be married in their new apartment by a judge, in the living room; one of the few rooms in this monolith they had purchased that faced the wide and sunny street. There would be flowers everywhere, a wedding cake, and just the family. And then she and Michael would go to Venice, Rome, and Florence, for two weeks.

They didn't care that the apartment was dark; all they cared about was that they would be together. She had always been good at fixing up places, and she knew she could do a lot with the space. She wouldn't miss the country. New York would be her place to roam now. For an instant she remembered those years long ago in New York, when she and Richard were first living together before they were married, in their tiny apartment in Greenwich Village. Everything had been so new and wonderful and romantic; she was confident that they had such happy lives ahead of them; if only she could keep the secret of her illness, if only he would divorce The Waitress and marry her, if only they could have children . . . All those "if onlys." The memories dropped away without regret.

It was all as new and exciting as it had been the first time. No, it was even more so; because this time she had never expected any of it.

Chapter Thirty-two

I am a New Yorker, and since yesterday afternoon I have a stepfather and a stepsister and a step-brother. Life is amazing. The wedding was really nice. I didn't know how I would feel about it, even though I like Michael, and I was nervous, but after the wedding I didn't feel any different than I did before. The only change is going to be getting used to living together, but since this is the first time I ever lived in New York and the first time in years that I won't be away at boarding school, I can get used to everything at once.

Trinity accepted me for this fall. Jeremy, my stepbrother, goes there, and so does the son of my mother's friend Chris, who is named Nicholas, so I already know two people. Sam wants to stay at St.

Martin's and then go to Harvard where Matthew is going, so in between their school vacations I'm going to be here all alone with this new family, except for my same old mother of course. (The "old" is a joke.) My mother said she was really happy that she decided to stay with her instead of going back to St. Martin's, but that she didn't want to pressure me either way. I feel that if I'm going to be a writer it would be good experience for me to live in New York where so many things are happening, and Trinity is supposed to be a very good school. It will also be good experience for me to have a normal family, not that I'm any judge of what that is. (I see that I said "good" three times in the last two sentences, which is something I wouldn't do if I were writing my novel instead of this secret journal. Louis L'Amour was interviewed on the radio and he said using the same word over and over is the thing he changes when he revises his books, so I guess that's a problem writers have. I'm going to have to watch it.)

Michael talks to me like I'm a real person with opinions of value, and he also *listens.* He and my mother are obviously very happy together and in love. There is no tension around here anymore. Cathy is my age, and since she lost twenty pounds for the wedding she's slinky and pretty. It will be excellent to have her for a friend because I don't know what to say to girls, and when I'm ready to start going out with them I'll have to talk. She and I like the same music and the same movies, and even most of the same books, and we both hate math. She admitted that she doesn't know what to say to boys either, because when she was fat none of them would ever look at her except to say cruddy things. I have decided that between childhood and sex there's this great big gap, and we're in it.

My father came to see me today. The apartment was still full of flowers from the wedding. My mother and Michael are in Europe on their honeymoon trip and Matthew and Sam left this morning for The Wilderness Adventure, which is something Nicholas recommended very highly, so here I was alone with him.

"So your mother got married again," he said. It was a comment, not a question, so I didn't say anything. "Do you like him?" he asked.

"Yes," I said.

"Your mother is a person who should be married," he said. He walked around looking at the apartment, which he had never seen before. "Dark, isn't it," he said. I didn't say anything. The truth is I never really noticed. "But big," he said. I nodded. "Some people really need to be married," he said. "Some don't."

"I guess that means you're not going to marry your girl friend," I said.

"Which one?" he said.

"The lawyer."

"Oh, well, we don't see each other anymore," he said. "She wanted to get married and have a baby.

She's young; that would be nice for her. I already have children."

Yes, I thought. You have the Senator, whom you pretend you don't know, and you have Elizabeth, who is supposed to be a secret, and you have Jonathan, whom you never mention, and you have the three of us.

"When do you start camp?" he asked. I told him and then he took me out to lunch and to see *Ghostbusters.* I loved it, he hated it. I think he wishes we were all back in the country playing touch football. I don't. I'm perfectly happy the way we are now. I'm not the one who made our family fall apart, and I'm not the one who put it together again, but that's the way it is when you're a kid— you just get swept along. The strange thing is, I think my father feels that's the way it was with *his* life as an adult. I don't think he realizes he had anything to do with it. I think he honestly believes that everything that happened to us was just some kind of ironic destiny.

Chapter Thirty-three

BY THE END of May they were almost finished shooting the picture. Kit was half relieved and half sorry. The relief part was because all through the filming her whole life had been directed toward the work; there was nothing else, no one else, only the total concentration to put herself into her character's skin, to open herself, to be emotionally truthful, even to bring up things that hurt and use them. At night she fell into bed exhausted at half past nine, turned off her phone and let the answering machine take the calls—and then all night she dreamed about her part and the other people. She had to get up at five in the morning, but she didn't mind, she was ready, her mind already active with the new day's challenges.

On weekends, with her head still full of the part, she had to drag her stuff to the laundry and the cleaners, take a double yoga class both days to keep in shape, buy groceries, and then, finally, study the script. Her father made her let Adeline come once a week to clean her house while she was on the picture, since Kit didn't have time. Kit agreed only because she wasn't there anyway and it was convenient. Ordinarily she didn't want Adeline, or anyone else, hanging around when she wasn't working; especially Adeline, since she could carry stories back to her parents, and was always full of gross free advice. But now that her parents were divorced and her father had Adeline full time, Kit figured he wanted to get rid of her once in a while for the same reason. She could just imagine the kinds of parties he must be having in his house.

Or maybe he was just being a solicitous father. She didn't know anymore. Figuring out a part made her understand more about human nature, that people could be both good and bad in the same instant, so her work made her know more about life instead of the other way around.

But the main reason Kit knew she would be relieved when the filming was over was not because of the single-minded discipline, but because of the fear. All through the picture a part of her was always afraid she hadn't been good enough, because this was the most important role of her life. But then, at the end of every day, Zack told her she had been wonderful, and she felt fantastic. The day was over, she had survived, and he was pleased. He was the authority; she was not. Even when *she* thought she had been wonderful she wasn't quite sure. But after Zack reassured her, she would sail home on a cloud of utter rapture. She had survived. She had not failed. She had accomplished something important. She was talented, special. She didn't have to worry again about not being good enough until the next morning.

But those few evening hours of totally relaxed and relieved rapture were exactly why she would be sorry when the filming was over.

That feeling was better than even . . . sex; which was the best thing she knew. After sex she felt relaxed and satisfied, but never so totally happy and flying. Even when the sexual encounter was a conquest, it was never as triumphant a feeling as the one she had when she knew she had done acting she should be proud of. Her acting was her identity.

One day Zack asked her if she wanted to come see the dailies.

"I don't know," Kit said, scared.

"You never ask," he said, "so I thought I'd ask you."

"Maybe I'll hate myself," she said.

"If I thought you would I wouldn't invite you."

"Okay. Thank you."

He seemed to have totally forgotten about the hideous incident in the pool at that brunch party, and she had even managed to put it away in her file of things that didn't matter. He was apparently having an affair with Emma's mother, who had told *her* mother, who told her, that she was very good in the dailies, but what did they know anyway, civilians? Zack was the only one Kit believed.

Kit sat in the screening room watching herself.

Then, suddenly, it wasn't herself at all, but someone else; and she had total objectivity. That person was fascinating, beautiful. She would want to know that person. You would really care what happened to her.

Then the lights came on again and she just sat there thinking: *I am fantastic; I did exactly what I set out to do.*

"Nice work," Zack said.

"I could never have done one bit of that without you," Kit said.

"An attitude I like," he said laughing, and patted her on the shoulder.

But then, too quickly, it was all over, and he was in the editing room and she was back in reality. He summoned her again to dub a couple of things, which was nice, but the picture was finished, or at least her contribution to it was, and all the free time in the world couldn't make up for what was gone.

It was summer, and she knew she had to start looking for something new, but she felt too drained. She found a boyfriend, a comedy writer. He made her laugh and he had funny friends. He wanted to write something for her. Let him dream on, she didn't do comedy. She called her agent to see what was around.

"Wait," her agent said. "I hear good things about the picture you just did. Let's hold out for something big."

In September the rough cut was ready for the studio to see. After they saw it the executives got all excited, and the studio publicists started to work on the advance publicity right away. As soon as Zack would finish the final cut the studio was going to rush to put out a token early showing so they could get nominated for this year's Academy Awards. They were talking about how she was definitely going to get a nomination for Best Supporting Actress.

Best . . . Supporting . . . Actress! When she thought about it Kit felt so precious and miraculous that she had to move very carefully so nothing bad would happen to her. She wanted it so much that she didn't even dare pray, because how could you pray for something so selfish? But people did pray for love, and for happiness, and for success, so why not she? Being nominated would be all of those things. Zack had said this picture would make her a star, and she had always believed it would, but here was the closeness of the reality, and it was far better than she could ever have imagined. She told them she would be glad to do any publicity she could to help.

The next thing she knew she got a phone call that she was going to be interviewed for *People* magazine, for a piece they were doing on the hot new talent for the winter movie season, including possible Oscar contenders. There was a good possibility it would be the cover story, although of course nobody could say positively yes so soon, and if *it* was on the cover there was an equally good chance that *she* would be the one whose picture was on the cover. It was all happening for her; she felt it now, she was sure; here was that momentum.

"They want to interview you and your mother," the press agent said.

"My what?"

"It's a cute idea—the two of you. Of course the piece will be mainly about you. But they want to show something about where you come from; and your mother's interesting with her new store opening in New York soon, and the other ones . . . what is it, Chicago and . . . ?"

"Dallas," Kit said. She couldn't believe it. Her *mother.* She knew how well Emily's Cookies was doing, and how fast it was expanding, and she'd even seen her mother being interviewed on television, looking very attractive and chic and talking like a confident person instead of that whiny groveling creature Kit was used to, but . . . her mother in *her* interview? How ironic. "What about my brother?" Kit asked.

"Oh, sure, they'll probably take a picture of the three of you. I'll call Emily as soon as you tell me what day is good for you next week."

"Whichever day is good for her," Kit said. She'd never thought she'd be saying *that.* But her mother had been traveling around so much lately that between Kit's movie and then those new stores they'd stopped having their weekly dinners and they hardly even talked to each other on the phone for more than two minutes.

The studio publicist called back to say Thursday at two o'clock at her house. "I had to fight with that Glick person," he said indignantly. "He wanted to do it at your mother's. He seems to think she's the star."

"Well," Kit said calmly, "he works for her, not for me, you know."

Her mother didn't even call until that night. Kit was about to go out to meet David, the comedy writer, and was wondering if she should ditch him before the interview so that they wouldn't describe him as her "live-in boyfriend" when he was really just temporary. He had his own house, after all, but there was already too much of his stuff around hers. "Isn't it wonderful?" her mother said.

"Yes," Kit said.

"Is it really true what I heard, that you might be nominated for an Academy Award, for Best Supporting Actress?"

"Spread it around," Kit said.

"I have my fingers crossed. And what perfect timing this piece will be for my New York store!"

"Yes," Kit said.

"I'll see you Thursday. It'll be fun."

Fun? Kit thought. *Who is this person who used to be my mother?*

"Right," Kit said.

And then we can both sit there in that interview and lie.

And they did. They had both been covering things up for a long time now, and they were very good at it. Emily did not tell about Ken's cocaine or his violence, and Kit did not talk about her own promiscuity. Neither mentioned Emily's nervous breakdown, nor that she had almost let her children die. Kit said she was much too involved in her career right now to think about any special man or about marriage. The reporter didn't even ask Emily about her love life, which Kit thought was rather unkind since her mother looked like she could certainly have one if she wanted it.

They talked on, skirting the cruel realities and touching lightly on the truths that would not hurt each other or themselves. Emily said she had always expected Kit to go to Radcliffe as she had, but she was glad her daughter had done what she preferred and was succeeding at it, and wished she, too, had been given career options at a young age.

It would have been a more interesting publicity story, Kit thought, if she and her mother had told all the shocking parts. But something in her would never allow her to tell those millions of strangers who would read the magazine, and something in her mother apparently felt the same way. Her father didn't deserve to be protected, but he would be. Even her mother, although other people might understand and sympathize, could not be betrayed for what she had done out of desperation so long ago. They were protecting themselves, but they were also protecting each other, and even . . . their family. All these years they had been having their weekly dinners, going through the motions of being a family and not having the faintest idea of what one was. Maybe what it was, was being loyal to people who didn't deserve it, but doing it anyway; out of stubborn pride, and even a kind of wacky, primal, inexplicable love.

Peter arrived in time for the family portrait. The three of them put their arms around one another and smiled and posed for the camera. They pretended to be a perfectly normal, if talented and gutsy, American family. For all Kit knew, maybe they were.

Chapter Thirty-four

THAT SUMMER ANNABEL began commuting back and forth to California to see Zack, and in no time at all she became very adept at it. She knew the airline schedules by heart, had her favorite seat, and kept toilet articles, makeup, and clothes at his house, so all she had to do was get on the plane, bringing perhaps something new she wanted to wear; and a book to read, because how many times could you see the same movie when it wasn't one you'd wanted to see in the first place? It didn't take long for her to accumulate mileage credits, and then she was upgraded to First Class, which she always adored.

Somehow it seemed a much shorter trip when she was on her way to see him than when she had to go home. Traveling to be with the man she missed so much she couldn't stand it was romantic, an adventure. She enjoyed the anticipation. Leaving him because she had begun to feel restless, an appendage, was sad, and yet, for her, unavoidable. She took the Red Eye to give her the most time possible with him, and also because the three-hour time change brought her into New York at dawn so she didn't have to walk into a lonely, empty apartment at night. She would shower and change and go right to work, even though she was tired. And then, at the end of the day, she would bring Sweet Pea home with her, and slip peacefully between her smooth sheets in her own bed, missing Zack but feeling a little guilty because she already was caught up in the hectic pace of her independent life in New York and she liked it.

Poor Sweet Pea did not want to be a bicoastal cat. Annabel had taken Sweet Pea with her to California once, in her cat carrier, but Sweet Pea had hated the plane trip, yowling and crying even when Annabel took her out and put her on her lap. And even more, Sweet Pea hated being locked in Zack's house all day alone while Annabel was on the set with him. Sweet Pea was a creature of habit, and liked the boutique, in her basket or her own place on the window sill, where she could watch all the people; and she liked living with Annabel or visiting Maria or Pamela—and she was a city cat who could never be allowed outdoors. In California she would try to escape, and then she would get killed, by a car or an animal.

"You don't have to go out there anymore," Annabel told her. "But just remember you're *my* cat for ever and ever, even if you do insist on living in New York and won't commute."

Zack was editing his picture now. Annabel watched him cutting with the film editor at the Moviola; and she spent hours with him in the room where he mixed the sound; watching the men at the huge computerized console that reminded her of the organ at Radio City Music Hall, as Zack painstakingly went over and over every little bit of film. She began to realize that movies were made once on the set and again in the editing. At first she found it fascinating, but finally very, very tedious. When lunch in the cafeteria at the sound studio became the main event of her day she realized just how tedious the rest of it was to her. Yet she knew how important it was to Zack, and to the picture, to have every detail perfect. He would probably find her career equally boring, unless he were using it for research for a film.

They knew each other so well now, and respected each other's needs and differences. Their time alone together was precious. But when she left he never resented it; and when she came back he was always overjoyed, as if she were doing him a favor—when in fact she felt the favor was for herself.

Over Labor Day Zack took a long weekend off and came to New York to see her. Emma had gone to India on another picture, full of excitement and shots for every known disease, and this time Zack stayed in Annabel's apartment. Being in it with him was like a holiday. They went to restaurants, and the theater, made love every night, had breakfast together every morning.

"If I do a picture in New York we can live here in your apartment," Zack said.

"That would be so wonderful!" Annabel said.

"And if I go to Europe, will you come with me?"

"Of course."

"You can leave when you get bored."

"I might leave Europe, but I'll never leave *you*," Annabel said.

"I just want you to be happy," he said. "I want to add to your life, not make you give anything up."

"You're always so worried about that."

"I'm committed to you, so I have to worry about that."

He had begun to say words like those to her now: *committed*. He said she would have to be the one who left him, not the other way around, and Annabel felt safe because she had no intention of leaving him no matter how often she went away. This time she could believe in happiness without fear or reservation. *I am not any of the men you knew before. I am the one you know now.*

"Naturally I'd like it even better if your work was right here," she said. "But it isn't at the moment."

"I'll try to find a movie I can make in New York."

"And if you make one in some exotic, far off place it won't be so bad either."

He had brought some of his clothes to keep in her apartment, and a set of his toilet articles were in her bathroom. When he had to go away again it still seemed as if he lived there. He told her he liked to look at her things when he was alone in California, and pretend she was just in the next room, not in New York.

"I'm the one who was so afraid of good-byes," she said.

"But ours are only temporary."

It was strange, Annabel thought, how she had always been at the forefront of changes, even ahead of them. At Radcliffe she had been the dorm pariah because of her honest sex life, which as she looked back at it hadn't been so wild at all. She had been the first woman in what passed for her social group in Atlanta to leave her husband. She had been a career woman and a single mother. Of course, there had been Max to help her bring up Emma, but still . . . And now she was in a commuting relationship.

It might or might not become a marriage, but if it did it would be a commuting marriage. That would not change. Maybe one day in the future, somewhere on their travels, overwhelmed by the romance of a beautiful place, they might decide to rush off and do it. Or maybe not . . .

She did want something else though—more freedom to be with him whenever she wanted to. She had been thinking about it for a while. She had decided to sell forty-nine percent of Annabel's to Maria and Pamela, keeping fifty-one percent for herself. They would be delighted to have more responsibility, she would still have the power, and she knew they would work harder and be completely loyal because it was *their* business too now. When she told them her offer they were overjoyed.

Now she could spend a week, with the weekends around it, every month in California with Zack when he was working there, and she could go to Europe or anywhere else he happened to be. He would of course come in to spend time with her when he was between movies, although that was never very long; but now they would be able to travel together and take vacations. She would certainly continue to go to the collections, with one or the other of her new partners, because she was still the heart and spirit of the business. She would want to go to the collections even if Zack were working in New York. And she would always have her own money. That was something, just as much as personal freedom, that she could never give up.

He had said they would have to find a way to work everything out. She had found it. It might not suit someone else, but it was perfect for her—the best of both worlds.

After their Labor Day weekend Zack went back to California to show the rough cut of his picture to the studio, and he called to tell her they thought it was wonderful. The studio powers were talking about an early release and Academy Award nominations. Annabel fantasized about what she would wear to the ceremonies.

He was working on the final cut, calling her every night very late. "When I finish this," he said, "I wish you would come out here to celebrate with me. If you can get away . . ."

"I can."

She came to California for a long weekend. Zack bought Dom Perignon and beluga malassol caviar, her favorites. Annabel made him come to Tiffany's in Beverly Hills to choose a watch because she wanted him to have it for a celebration present. She saw the perfect one: it had two faces, one for each of their time zones, so he would always know what time it was where she was when she wasn't with him, and would think of her.

"I think I should get one for you, too," he said, and did. They had their presents gift-wrapped. Then they went back to his house, where he had had a special dinner sent in for later for the two of them, from Chasen's, and they both got very dressed up. There was a big moon and thousands of stars, and he had put lighted candles in glass candle holders out by the pool. Against the dark blue sky were the black silhouettes of palm trees and foliage. Below his house there were all the lights of Los Angeles, strung out like a gigantic glittering board game.

Zack looked down at it. "It's not much, but it's mine," he said.

Then they went into the house and gave each other the watches they had bought.

"This is for you," she said. "For all the minutes and hours and days and years of our lives together."

"And this," he said, "is so you'll know that wherever we are you'll still be with me, and I'll be with you, so we'll never be apart."

They kissed and he opened the champagne. She thought this celebration was certainly a lot better than her first wedding, and she knew their intentions would definitely last a great deal longer.

When Annabel got back to New York, she, Maria, and Pamela signed the papers transferring part ownership of the stock in the boutique. It seemed significant for this to be happening in autumn, which had always seemed to her to be the time of a new beginning; perhaps because of all those years she had been starting school again in the fall. You could breathe the air again, the leaves were turning color, and in the streets people walked with a new determination. So many lives had been changed, it seemed, for the better. Chris called, excited, to say she had been promoted to Executive Editor at *Fashion and Entertainment*, of both magazines, *East* and *West*. Emily's newest cookie outlet was opening in New York, she had become somewhat of a media celebrity, and she had bought an apartment on Fifth Avenue, with a terrace overlooking Central Park; to be her real home, even though she would be commuting everywhere too. And Daphne was flourishing in her happy marriage to Michael.

On the spur of the moment Annabel decided to give a little party; just for the four old school friends, as she now thought of them; at her apartment, to celebrate everything. It would be a cocktail party after work, the night before she had to leave for Europe for the collections with Maria. There would be champagne, of course, and caviar, and the thin sandwiches she sometimes served at the boutique; anything she didn't have to make herself.

"This is a 'You've Come a Long Way Baby' party," she told Chris, "but nobody is allowed to smoke."

Her living room was filled with white flowers, and she had brought home some of the tapes she played as background at Annabel's. Modern music, no nostalgia. None of her collection of music from the Twenties to remind her they had been Max's favorites and make her sad, no songs from the Fifties to remind anyone of those innocent, idiotic days at college that had ruined such a portion of their lives. She wanted only songs that had come out this month. Emma would have loved it. But Emma was in India with her Walkman.

They came at six. Daphne and Emily had never seen Annabel's apartment, and said it was marvelous. Except for painting, she hadn't redecorated since she'd moved in, but flowers covered a lot of faults. "This is great," Emily said. "When I get my new apartment finished, which will be some day in the next millennium, *I* will give a party."

"Then I guess I have to have the next one," Daphne said, "since our apartment is as finished as it's ever going to be."

Annabel opened the champagne. "A toast," she said. "To each of us and all our new, wonderful lives."

They cheered and clicked glasses and drank. Emily told them about her new apartment, which had been totally torn apart by the decorator she'd hired and was under construction while she was living in it. "I told him to leave me just one bedroom and a bathroom to use," she said. "Not even the kitchen. I don't care. There are two toilets standing in the middle of my kitchen floor, and no appliances at all. The kitchen looks enormous. All these men come charging in at the crack of dawn to rip down walls. My *interior designer*, who by the way is called that and not a decorator, says when he dies he doesn't want to be remembered as just somebody who re-covered a chair. He didn't want me to live in the apartment while they were doing all this stuff because he said most people who do have screaming nervous breakdowns. But I don't mind the chaos because I know it'll be worth it later."

"What happened to your California apartment?" Chris asked.

"My son Peter is living in it. It has two bedrooms, so I stay in it too when I'm in L.A. Life's so funny—all he ever wanted was a glamorous beach house, an expensive sports car, a beautiful live-in girl friend, and a killer dog to protect it all. Well, he's got a glamorous apartment anyway, and my former car, which is a vintage Mercedes convertible, and a rather terrifying male Doberman named Chip after our cookies, and the last I heard, a lot of girl friends. And he's only twenty-one."

"And an old man already," Chris said. "No more dreams." They all laughed.

"Isn't it amazing how we've ended up," Daphne said.

"We haven't 'ended up' at all," Annabel said.

"Yes," Daphne said, "I guess you're right." She looked at the three of them with affection. "I still sometimes think how strange and lovely it is that we're all here together, good friends, after all the things that happened to us in our lives, and not even seeing each other for so long. The first time we met, at Radcliffe, we liked or didn't like each other for such silly reasons. I remember Richard's father used to say that you went to college to 'meet the right people.' Richard believed that. In his case it was to meet men he would know later in the business world. For us it was to find the right boy to marry. I think I wouldn't have known the right person to have for a friend if I fell over her, I was so scared, and busy thinking about putting up a good front for everybody else."

"*You* . . . scared?" Emily said, amazed.

"Of course."

"But I thought I was the most frightened girl in the dorm," Emily said.

"You seemed to know just what you wanted," Chris said to Emily. "Annabel and I thought you would have grown up to be smug, which shows what *we* knew. I was so taken aback when I did that interview with you and found out what really happened."

Emily smiled. "Yes, I wanted just what they told me to, and I got it. The biggest mistake of my life."

"But we survived our mistakes," Daphne said.

Annabel refilled their glasses. "We certainly did."

"Emily and I had a conversation in Vail once," Daphne said, "about being able to go back and do things differently, sort of a second chance, to do it all

[419]

over again better, and we both said it was impossible. But that's not how I've been feeling lately—I feel I've gotten that second chance."

"I do too," Annabel said. "And that's why I had this party, to celebrate." She raised her glass. "We survived not only our mistakes, but our misguided little teen-aged dreams, and the shattering of those dreams, and went on to become happier and more interesting than we ever imagined. You remember in *Peter Pan*, when Tinker Bell is dying, and Peter turns to the audience and tells them to clap their hands if they believe in fairies; and everybody claps their hands, and Tinker Bell's life is saved. Well, clap your hands if you believe in surprises, and the life you save will be your own."

Chapter Thirty-five

EMILY APPLEBAUM BUCHMAN, forty-eight years old,
beautiful and successful, stood on the terrace of her
new Fifth Avenue apartment on a glorious October
evening and looked out at the world. She had just
come from a small party at Annabel's house, and now
she was dressed up to go to a big one at the Plaza
Hotel. Behind her, in what would eventually be her
new living room, was the mere skeleton of her future
home, where she, too, would entertain, or perhaps
just pause in her busy life for some quiet time alone.
Every day the workmen carted away the rubble they
had created, as if they were getting rid of her old life.
She rejoiced in it.

Below her in the darkness was Central Park, and all
the lighted buildings and streets of her adventure.
She remembered that other terrace, off her former
bedroom in California, where one frightening night

she had stood watching Ken swimming frantically down below; that tiny, ominous figure to whom her destiny had been tied. It was not even three years ago, and yet it was a lifetime away.

Now that she looked back at the woman she had been, that person seemed a sad little friend from her past, but not herself. The self-deprecating, apologizing Emily who had thought herself worthless and unlovable was gone.

She knew there were people who would never love her: Ken, for instance, and even Kate and Peter. She didn't care about Ken; and as for her children, she knew they liked her as well as they were capable of. She had done her best after the worst had been done, and now they were all adults, she and her children, and at least they got along. Some people didn't even have as much. She was too happy lately to let any of this depress her. She was only sorry she hadn't left Ken sooner, but even that was a mistake not worth brooding about. Each thing in its own time.

Her dress was silk with silver threads. Tonight she would dance, and maybe she would meet ten interesting men, or maybe one. She felt as if she were a freshman at Radcliffe again, going to her first Freshman Mixer, with everything ahead of her. This time she had her career, and her success, and her friends, and if she had to she could get along with only these and no man at all; but that was no reason why she couldn't have one. She remembered when she was eighteen, going to the first dance, when Annabel had said they were "the new crop." Out there had been what seemed a whole world of men, hoping to find her, hoping to be found, waiting to fall in love.

She had looked forward to the future then, totally unprepared for what it would really be. Now she was looking forward to it all over again; so much wiser, but still excited, still romantic, her life still unresolved, unfinished . . .

When it came, she planned to be ready.

You're invited to a reunion well worth attending

College classmates Emily, Chris, Daphne, and Annabel will be there. Friends from their days at Radcliffe in the 50s, they found glamorous careers, married "perfect" men, and expected to have "perfect" children. They played by the rules —sort of—but the rules changed midway through their lives.

You'll meet them first in Rona Jaffe's wonderful **Class Reunion.** And catch up with these remarkable women 25 years after graduation in **After the Reunion.**

R o n a   J a f f e

_____ CLASS REUNION	11288-5-43	$4.50
_____ AFTER THE REUNION	10047-X-13	4.50